Ray,

Now that you're into retirement you've got the time to read this. Hopefully you like murder mysteries! It was good working with you when you were here. Now we all miss you.

Hope you are enjoying yourself and not driving that vette too fast!

W9-BGM-508

The Oakland Hills Vodou Murders

by Glen C. Carrington

authorHOUSE™

1663 LIBERTY DRIVE, SUITE 200
BLOOMINGTON, INDIANA 47403
(800) 839-8640
WWW.AUTHORHOUSE.COM

© 2005 Glen C. Carrington. All Rights Reserved.

No part of this book may be reproduced, stored in a retrieval system, or transmitted by any means without the written permission of the author.

First published by AuthorHouse 12/19/05

ISBN: 1-4208-8961-3 (sc)

Printed in the United States of America
Bloomington, Indiana

This book is printed on acid-free paper.

This book is dedicated to my parents Leonard & Gleanor M. Carrington whose love, sincerity, and dedication to family, friends, and neighbors are unpretentious. It is also dedicated to their parents, my grandparents, Waverly and Sally Carrington, Seldon and Oppie Jones, who are now all deceased but whose lineage carries forward. Steadfastness... honor of family... hard work... and nobility of purpose are attributes that served them well. As Norman Thomas (1884-1968) so eloquently stated... 'The secret of a good life is to have the right loyalties and hold them in the right scale of values.'

I want to sincerely thank Jewell Grigsby Martin for all the editing work you provided in the early stages. It was very helpful and necessary And also very special thanks to a college buddy, Charles Marshall Tucker and his 'Jewish mom', Bertha Berman, for their tireless east coast editing hours which seemed never to end. Your hard and creative work is this book's pedigree. As Kathe Kollwitz said... "I do not want to die...until I have faithfully made the most of my talent and cultivated the seed that was placed in me until the last small twig has grown." Writing is only half the task of putting a book together. For your editing help... Thank you... thank you... and thank you.

Then the Lord said unto me, the prophets prophesy lies in my name: I sent them not, neither have I commanded them, neither spake unto them: they prophesy unto you a false vision and divination, and a thing of nought, and the deceit of their heart.

Jeremiah 14:14

Prologue

She exhaled softly now, barely feeling the viscous onslaught of her attacker. No longer could she sense the warmth of her tears as they involuntarily rolled down her cheeks. She had begun her ascent. Still she could hear the increasingly fading sound of her assailant's methodical attack. And now, hovering above her nearly lifeless body, she saw her assailant, an ominous figure wearing a wolf's head! She watched from her new vantage point, the disgorging of feathers by this 'wolf' over that which was once her. A strange bloody object was caressed ever so reverently in the wolf being's hand. It mattered little now…there was a welcoming peace washing over her, a surrendering as her life force flowed ever so gracefully from her limp and battered body...

…On a warm summer morning three months ago, the lifeless body of Hillary Chatham Dillard, was discovered against a tapestry of huge oak trees and stoic weeping willows at a prestigious college located in the affluent hills of Oakland, California. A security guard had stumbled upon her body at precisely 3:27 A.M. while patrolling the North Campus. A twenty-year old junior English and French major, Hillary, was the youngest child of a distinguished attorney who had quietly become an institution. She had been brutally raped, hacked repeatedly with a large sharp instrument and covered with feathers. The severed head of a majestic drake protruded from her mouth, presenting the illusion of a grotesque B-rated horror movie mannequin.

The head campus patrol guard immediately notified the Oakland Police Department. The guard, Edward Ramirez, was interrogated. Preliminary results virtually eliminated Ramirez as the perpetrator. All incriminating evidence pointed elsewhere. Still, Edward Ramirez remained a suspect simply because he had found the body.

Campus resident Woodrow Taft, the University's Sports Director, confirmed the victim's identification. School security knew Taft well, a twenty-five year popular faculty member deeply involved in campus life.

Campus security barricaded the crime scene and waited for police instructions. Media scrutiny would be intense. The victim's philanthropic family held formidable political clout. Franklin Sr., the family scion, headed the Dillard dynasty, an influential legal machine. The investigation therefore required thoroughness, a complete clinical scrubbing.

Hillary, the youngest of four children, two boys and two girls, had been the delight of Franklin Sr. and Heather, her interracial parents. Possessing her father's academic inclinations and her mother's grace and regal statue, Hillary had captured the hearts of all who knew her.

Chapter 1

Mayor Jim Efferton, a man in his mid-fifties and profoundly politically astute, had always made shrewd decisions. He lusted after even higher elective office.

Retired Oakland Police Detective William Monroe Lincoln became involved after a late night call from Mayor Efferton. Lincoln had previously freelanced for Mayor Efferton who chose him because of his tendency to bypass standard police procedures. Although Lincoln had served for twenty years, no one knew his political or social inclinations. The Detective was known as a 'straight shooter', issue focused and a non-meddler.

The following Monday at 6:30 P.M, Bill arrived at the Mayor's office and was immediately ushered inside by his Honor's secretary. The Mayor and the Chief of Police sat in comfortable tufted leather chairs surrounding an exquisite teak hardwood table. Only the Mayor stood to greet him.

"Bill, let me bring you up to speed. It's been three months and no arrests. The political heat is up. We're hemorrhaging...we need another perspective."

Detective Lincoln nodded. When the Mayor wanted anyone to speak, he would simply ask.

"You know our priority. Dillard Sr. is updated weekly. For the last month there's been nothing new. I'll be frank...the Chief originally opposed your involvement. Are you interested?"

Detective Lincoln faced the Mayor. Any law enforcement official worth his salt would beg to work this case.

"Yes, Mayor, I'm interested. Let me hear what evidence you do have."

"Chief, please inform Bill of our current status."

The Chief pulled out several sheets of typed paper and black and white photographs.

"Oakland PD received a telephone call from campus security at Oakland Hills Sky View University on June 1st at approximately 3:35 A.M. A security guard discovered the mutilated remains of a female just a few steps off a North Campus walkway. A visual examination indicated numerous stab wounds, an enormous amount of blood, feathers plastered to the corpse and a severed duck's head stuffed into the victim's mouth. There were partial footprints found at the scene, but no fingerprints, notes or any other type of readily identifiable evidence."

The Chief glanced at these two intense men. Feeling their focus on him he cleared his throat and continued…

"The victim had been sexually violated; seminal fluid was collected. Fifteen stab wounds were identified, each one alone was fatal, and no signs of struggle. No evidence of blood or a foreign substance under the victim's fingernails. Campus background checks have revealed nothing helpful in terms of identifying a possible suspect. Ms. Dillard was not dating anyone, but was good friends with a Caucasian male. The relationship appeared platonic."

The Chief flipped the page.

"Said Caucasian male was, at first, very cooperative, although eventually his family provided legal counsel. Now, everything comes filtered through his lawyers.

"The victim was an honor student and reportedly drug free. She attended numerous campus activities, all positive in nature. Her classmates liked her.

"Edward Ramirez discovered the body. He's been a campus security guard for three years and is not considered a suspect at present. His timeline that evening is well documented and his background check came back clean. He's considered one of their better guards. Ramirez attends law school during the day. He works third shift."

"The feathers and the duck stuffed in her mouth are puzzling. Voodoo may be involved. The religion class includes outside workshops requiring attendance at various local religious institutions. Voodoo is one of the religions discussed, but Ms. Dillard never took that class, nor had her friends. Several students are from places where voodoo is practiced. However, nothing links anyone to the crime. Everyone appears to have an iron clad alibi. Any questions, Bill?"

"Do you think the duck was a prop to divert attention?"

"Don't know."

"What are other law enforcement people saying? Any opinion on the voodoo angle?"

"They are like me... Puzzled."

"What do her friends say? What are their suspicions?"

The Chief looked at his notes again...a reflex action for him.

"They're all over the place. One thinks the male friend is a possibility but offers no proof or reason. Some think it must be a drifter because our victim was such a well-liked individual."

"Any strangers seen on the campus that evening?"

"Yes, due to 'Homecoming'. Still, practically everyone was invited. The victim attended before going to an after-party. Ms. Dillard was last seen alive shortly after leaving the after-party around 2:30 A.M. She had left with two girlfriends, but eventually walked unaccompanied to her dormitory, as she was the furthest away. She parted from her two friends at the front door of their building at approximately 2:45 A.M. This was the last known contact. She was in a jovial mood that night displaying no discernable worries and with no other plans for that evening."

"Was she dating anyone?" Detective Lincoln asked.

"No, not anyone in particular. On occasion, she'd go out with her male platonic friend to do things like shopping or sports."

"What was the relationship between the young lady and her parents?"

"A solid one. Nobody has reported anything to the contrary. Her parents have acted like you'd expect in this situation."

"What about her siblings?" Lincoln asked.

"They all appear very upset over their sister's death. Each one leads a very different lifestyle from the others. We can speculate on the youngest brother's friends, however. His name is Radcliffe, but they call him 'Rad'. He indulges in luxury but without any obvious source of income, at least none that the IRS can track. Still, from every indication, Rad loved his sister and would've done anything for her. So far, nothing implicates him."

"What does your gut tell you, Chief?"

The Chief looked reflectively at the Detective while briefly flipping the pages in the manila folder back and forth.

"I really don't know. I want to say it must be a transient, but what would explain the duck head and feathers?"

The Chief, staring at him, asked point blank, "What do you think, Bill?"

Lincoln sat back in his chair and weighed the evidence.

"No opinion. When can I see the color photographs of the crime scene?"

The Chief responded, "Anytime. I'll tell Kasolkasky. It's still his case." The Chief turned to his boss.

"Mayor, why don't you briefly discuss Detective Lincoln's role."

"Bill, you will have full access to all pertinent information. Right now, the only people who will know you're on the case, besides us, are Kasolkasky and his two lead officers. I don't want the press involved yet. Bill, report any and all findings to the Chief. And Ron, you will keep me informed. Are we clear?" the Mayor asked.

"Chief, when will you be informing Brick?" Lincoln asked.

"As soon as this meeting is over."

"Good. I need to get up to speed on this. Is there anything else?"

Both men shook their head's no. The meeting was adjourned.

Chapter 2

The following morning, Detective Lincoln finished his coffee and checked his watch. He began to dress for his police station appointment. He suspected, now as a police outsider, he would receive limited information. Of course the reverse would be true too. Bill had no desire to put his feathers into their hat.

When Detective Lincoln arrived, he was escorted to Kasolkasky's office. Lincoln had known Brick for several years and considered him to be 'one of the guys.' He was reading a magazine when the door opened and in walked Detective Kasolkasky. Kasolkasky was in his early fifties and looked strikingly athletic. His nickname 'Brick' stuck to him after using one to defend himself in a down-and-dirty, back-alley fight!

"Good afternoon, Bill," Brick greeted him. "The Chief told me you'd be working with us." Kasolkasky extended his hand.

"Hello, Brick. It's been awhile since I've smelled the inside of a police building. It still reeks," Bill muttered. The stench reminded him of his high school days in the locker room after a scorching hot summer afternoon basketball game.

"Yeah, some things never change. And they won't until we start dealing with a better class of criminals."

Kasolkasky stepped to his filing cabinets where he kept his most confidential information, withdrawing several huge manila file folders.

"You're welcome to read these here."

Two hours and four cups of coffee later, Lincoln had completed reading the bulk of the file. Twice, he read the medical report summary, skipping the gory details. He didn't want to get bogged down in medical minutiae.

He sat back and contemplated everything he now knew, concluding there really wasn't much. The victim had no known enemies. She was not the political type, but a normal high-achieving student with few real problems. She was from wealth, loved by her siblings, possessed a healthy warm personality and lacked anything shady in her life.

The crime was obviously planned because of the feathers and duck head, but the question remained: "Was the victim chosen randomly or was she the intended target?" Her brother, Rad, had the most questionable lifestyle, but there was nothing linking him to the murder. Besides, Rad adored his little sister. Of course, if he owed favors or great deals of money to some mysterious person or clandestine organization, that might be a factor.

Detective Lincoln's inquiry would start with the victim's immediate administration's contact. He called the college and made an appointment for six o'clock the following evening with school administrator Woodrow Taft. Taft had identified the body.

There are two modes of acquiring knowledge, namely by reasoning and experience. Reasoning draws a conclusion and makes us grant the conclusion, but does not make the conclusion certain, nor does it remove doubt so that the mind may rest on the intuition of truth, unless the mind discovers it by the path of experience.

Roger Bacon: Opus Majur trans. By R.B. Burke, 1928

Chapter 3

Lincoln arrived at Woodrow Taft's residence promptly at six. Taft lived in a campus apartment adorned with classic Mid-western landscape pictures, a collection of sports paraphernalia that cluttered much of the shelf space and two feline boarders who acted as if they paid the rent.

"Mr. Taft, please tell me about Hillary, and especially what you remember about that dreadful night."

Woodrow always reflected reverently on his thoughts before speaking. He glanced out the window observing the college's peaceful serenity and pondered the irony of them sitting there discussing nothing less than a cold-blooded murder.

"Detective Lincoln, with all sincerity…Hillary was a good person. I can't imagine anyone who'd hurt her. Hillary liked school and had the usual 'normal' friends. She wasn't intimately involved with anyone. I've asked, but none of her girlfriends knows of anyone. There is another student, Benjamin Bently, who was her platonic companion. He was interested in dating her but, according to her friends, she wanted their relationship to remain as it had been.

"The police have talked to him and his family has retained a lawyer. In my opinion he's not our killer. He's a decent young man from an affluent family who treats people well and has no ax to grind. Excuse the poor idiom, please. Most of the students here are from fairly affluent families and are certainly not candidates for socio-political radicals."

"Woodrow, just how well did you know Hillary? What was she really like?"

"We had only a general acquaintance, like my other students. I'd met her family at several social functions so, when I discovered their youngest daughter would be attending our school, naturally I re-introduced myself. I encourage staff members to be aware of certain influential families' offspring. Notably, the Dillard's are just such a family and, historically, they have been financially generous."

"I understand."

"She was a French major and spoke the language fluently. Her mother is of French descent. Hillary was elegant and always dressed fashionably. She was well-educated, well-traveled and very opinionated...had her mother's social flair and her father's academics. She was an optimist. She believed anyone could achieve anything."

"Okay, but, can you think of any, let's say, negatives?"

"No, nothing I can recall."

"Sex, drugs, or rock-n-roll?"

"No, she wasn't the type."

"Woodrow, what was her social temperament?   Was she naive?"

Taft took a few moments to reflect before answering.

"No more than your average student."

"What about her friends? Any flakes?"

"I've made a list for you, but I don't think you'll find any 'flakes' among them. They're all fine upstanding young ladies. Some of them party a bit too much, but I'd dare say we're talking about a different type of socializing than you're obviously interested in. I doubt the killer is a member of this academic community. That's my honest opinion, Detective."

"Now, tell me about that night," Lincoln requested. He wanted some direction from this conversation but, so far, it was like he was driving on sand with slick treads.

"It was a Saturday evening with the big 'Homecoming' dance, which as always was well attended. It's a time when alumni return. Many former students have done quite well.

"I noticed Hillary, but I didn't speak with her because the auditorium was packed. I saw her visiting with former student, Christine DeVeaux, who has become a rather decent-selling author. Hillary was immediately noticeable from her stylish outfits. That's the only time I remember seeing her that evening; it was during the height of the evening's festivities."

Taft slowly shifted in his seat, briefly looking up at the ceiling.

"I went home at ten o'clock to feed my cats. You must remember, I've attended these affairs for more years than I care to admit. I went to bed around midnight and was awakened by the doorbell at three-thirty. It was our campus police; you know the rest."

"Thanks, Woodrow. Do you know anything about the Dillard family that I should know?" Bill had asked a delicate question and he was now more interested in Woodrow's body language than in his verbal response.

"No, nothing out of the ordinary, nothing which would be considered significant. I've only met them at social affairs. Sorry."

Bill noticed nothing unusual about Taft's overall physical response.

"Tell me, are there any rumors floating around campus?" Bill asked. "What are people saying?"

Taft rubbed his chin as though the gesture would somehow increase the thought-flow to his memory bank.

"So far, there has been no logical explanation offered. You'd naturally think that it had something to do with voodoo, but this is America. What do we know about voodoo? I just don't see Hillary involved in any avant-garde religious cult. To tell you the truth, Bill, I don't have any rational conclusions."

"Woodrow, thanks for your time."

Lincoln got up to leave. They exchanged pleasantries before Bill headed to his car. He was a hundred yards from the murder scene and somewhat curious, but still had one more stop to make. He was soon scheduled to visit the crime scene with the campus security officer who had first discovered the body.

Chapter 4

Lincoln left home the following day to meet two of Hillary's girlfriends on Taft's list, Alfreda Henry and Mona Goldstein. Mona was Hillary's roommate when Hillary died. Even though the police had already interviewed both girls, Lincoln wanted to hear their stories for himself.

He knocked on the door at precisely five o'clock. A young lady of medium height with a 'pleasing to the eye' body, dressed in designer jeans and a light blue silk blouse, opened the door. A sparkling smile and bold beautiful eyes greeted him.

"Hello, I'm Bill Lincoln with the Oakland Police Department."

"Hi. I'm Alfreda. Mona is inside. By all means, please, come in."

"Tell me, ladies, do either of you have any idea about who would want to hurt your friend?"

The two young ladies suddenly got quiet, both shaking their heads.

Mona spoke first… "Hillary was the best. She was friendly, beautiful, fun to be around and always very respectful. She came from a good family, one with values."

A tear rolled down Mona's cheek as she sat there; the room became quiet again. Mona looked down and grabbed both knees, hiding her face in her lap.

"I've known Hillary since junior high school," Alfreda said quietly. "She was fun to be with."

"I understand a young man named Benjamin was Hillary's friend," he said to no one in particular.

"Benjamin is a good friend who could no more do something like that than you could!" Mona responded emphatically.

"I heard his family retained a lawyer for him," Lincoln replied in his most authoritative voice.

"Hell, rich people retain lawyers for everything. If my father knew you were coming here today, he'd have sent the family attorney over. I mean… that's just how it is with the well-heeled. The family's attorney is like, well, like family!"

"So, Benjamin is not a very likely suspect I gather?" he asked.

"If you have any doubts you should go meet him," Mona replied. "Don't take our word for it."

Bill observed the two comely young ladies closely. He believed they were sincere.

"What about the feathers and the severed duck head? What do you make of it?"

"It shocked us!" Alfreda asserted. "It sounds like voodoo stuff. I really don't know what to make of it!"

"I wouldn't have believed it before the police showed me those awful pictures," Mona interjected. "It was ghastly, I almost fainted. There's a damn psycho out there! She stared at Bill, her eyes never blinking, while she waited for a response.

"When was the last time that either of you saw or talked with Hillary that evening?"

They were both eager to respond; talking about their friend was proving to be therapeutic.

"We all left the Homecoming Ball together," Alfreda answered. "Terri and I were the last ones to see Hillary alive before she left for her room. Mona and Hillary were roommates, but Mona had left for her room about a half-hour earlier than everyone else. Logistically, we get to my room before Hillary's and the three of us, Terri, Hillary, and I talked for a few minutes in front of Grant Hall. When Terri and I went inside, Hillary started walking towards her dorm room. It was very late and the walkways were empty."

"I went home and straight to bed," stated Mona. "I was exhausted! The campus police woke me when they came to tell me about Hill.

That was our little nickname for her...Hill," Mona said, tearing up again.

"Now, think about this carefully... take your time. Can either of you think of anyone who could do anything such as this?"

Both students shook their heads. Bill eyed each girl intensely. He groped for more questions to ask. "What about any members of her family?"

"No. Hill has a great family", Mona offered. "They're classy. They have impressive jobs and they each seem to know all the right people, that is except for maybe Rad."

"And, what about Rad?" Lincoln asked, his eyebrows rose.

"Oh, Rad absolutely couldn't have done this. He adored his baby sister. However, Rad's lifestyle is what you would call, well... somewhat suspect. Why, I don't even think Hill knew what Rad is really into."

"What do you mean?"

"Well, Rad drives the best cars and dresses 'to kill', but nobody knows exactly what he does. When you ask, you never get a straight answer. You quickly learn to just go with the flow with Rad. He's just so cool; everyone knows him, everybody likes him."

"Yeah, Rad has always been the life of the party," Alfreda chimed. "I understand that since childhood, Rad has craved the spotlight. It's just part of his nature; he's a born extrovert. He enjoys the finer things in life. I'm not sure, though, if 'hard work' is in his vocabulary."

"So," Lincoln said, "Hillary didn't know how Rad made his living?"

"That's right," Alfreda responded, "She just referred to him as 'a successful businessman' if anyone ever asked her."

"What about his friends and associates?"

"Like Mona said, he knows everyone," Alfreda replied. "Rad would usually show up with a lady friend, but there were so many you eventually got the impression they couldn't be very close friends, simply arm ornaments."

Lincoln was getting a much better picture. "Tell me, ladies, was Hillary religious?"

"No, not really. She'd go to church with her parents from time to time if they asked, but she didn't go of her own accord," Mona replied.

"What was her religion?"

"She was raised a Catholic."

"But she wasn't faithful to the Catholic doctrines, I take it?"

"No, Hillary was progressive. It was only for conversational value."

"Was she into some other religion or metaphysics?" he inquired.

"No."

Lincoln had what he needed. Bill knew Rad was not the killer, yet he was interested in Rad's associates and his lifestyle. How could he afford expensive cars and wear fancy clothes? He suspected the father, Franklin Dillard Sr., was not the type to support an offspring's frivolous lifestyle. Franklin Dillard Sr. was known for hard work and fortitude, so supporting a lifestyle based on easy money would be considered out of character. He thanked Hillary's friends and left his business card.

Be not curious in unnecessary matters: for more things are shewed unto thee than men understand.

THE APOCRYPHA - ECCLESIASTICUS 3:23

Chapter 5

On Tuesday, Bill Lincoln met with the local man-about-town and gossip extraordinaire, Jacko. Jacko couldn't be trusted as far as one could spit, but he was an interesting information source. A junkie ex-con, Jacko had amassed quite a record for small time offenses. Because this was the 'three strikes, you're out' era, Jacko was challenged to go straight; he had no intention of going back to the slammer! In fact, he'd often thought about moving to a state without a 'three strikes' law but, so far, just didn't have the energy to move away from his many friends.

Jacko was the consummate hustler who knew all the true Oakland players. Detective Lincoln was two favors up on Jacko. Detective Lincoln had arrested Jacko for drug purchasing. That would have marked Jacko's third strike, but Lincoln let him go. Although a jive hustler and petty thief, Jacko possessed a strong sense of honor.

Lincoln met Jacko at one of the hustler's favorite bars at three P.M.

"Jacko, tell me about the Dillard children. What do you know that might help me?"

The hustler toyed with his drink while considering the detective's request. His hand moved back and forth across his day-old stubble. Patches of gray now covered his slightly lined face.

"Well, these folks are known. Exactly what do you want to know?"

"What the general public doesn't know. Tell me about Junior for instance? What exactly is his game?"

"Junior is trying to play Mr. Conservative. He's got the rhetoric and the dance music going, yet he's as phony as a three-dollar bill. Yeah, sure, he's got the wife, but I hear she's screwing around. I know she's not screwing him! He's just not interested."

"Is anyone playing him?" Lincoln inquired. "How far does this news go?"

"It's vest tight. Right now there's no serious inquiry into Junior's private life. Besides, his political competition consists mainly of novices and except for the incumbent–few care. For now anyway, all the candidates are keeping their campaigns above-board. No one has employed any political henchmen...yet. The people who know Junior's dirt are his buddies so he's safe. Besides, if he wins, they win."

"How about the parents? Do they know 'number one son' is not the 'man' they perceive him to be?"

"Nah, I don't think they do. Of course, Dad isn't anyone's fool. I met him once. I don't know how intuitive the mom is or if her hubby shares his insights with the missus."

"They say mothers always know."

Jacko looked up sharply with disgust: "Yeah, right! I don't believe that crap for a second! My mom was as dense as this table. She lived in an alcoholic fog. Maybe that's why I'm an alcoholic!"

"So, what's he like?"

"Huh! Who?"

"Junior, of course."

"Oh, yeah, well like I said, he's playin' the part of being the man's man. He'll slap you on the back and say all the right things. But you get the feeling deep down in your gut—something's wrong. It's a complex game for him. In one sense it's all bull crap, but on another level, he desires to be the apple of his father's eye by becoming successful in his own right. Still, Junior is 'holding it down' so far."

"What about Junior's wife, Crystal? What's her claim to fame?"

"She attended the same law school. And man, is she a looker! She's got political ambitions of her own, too, but is willing to bide her time. The lady's at all the right political and social functions and she's well connected. Her daddy's an East Coast 'Fat Cat.'"

"So, I've heard. But now, what is she like behind the scenes?"

"I'm sure she's more like Junior than she wants to admit. And check this out, she does a little nose candy now and then, but only around certain people. You know, the ones she can trust. Yeah."

"Have you ever seen her do drugs yourself?"

"Nah. I mean I'm connected, but I ain't that connected. Still, I have my sources...reliable sources too."

"That's exactly why we're here, Jacko."

The Detective reached for his drink and waited. Jacko was a veritable water pipe of information and Bill Lincoln was there to turn on this spigot.

"Well, here's a kick, I understand that when she's doing lines, she becomes quite approachable by either sex! Now, ain't that something?"

"That's certainly interesting," Lincoln remarked. "Any possibility either could be connected to the murder of Franklin's baby sister?"

"I haven't heard anything. Man, that murder was weird. And the strange thing is...there's been nothing on the street. Absolutely nothing! It's like an alien did it!"

"So, you see no connections?"

"Nah. The young Dillards hang-out with all those political types and, while some of those dudes are seedy, they're not murder merchants."

"What about Junior's finances? Anything going down there?"

"Again, man, nothing on the street. Seems he lives within his means. Of course, there's family money on both sides."

"How about the second oldest child, Monique?"

Jacko started rubbing his ear. He then turned his head to watch a couple sit down before swinging back to look once again at Lincoln.

"Monique is fairly conservative. She doesn't really like politics, but she plays her role. She makes speeches if they ask, but she's not about to volunteer. She's definitely not into the drug scene as far as I can tell. Once in awhile she'll go out on the town with her little 'Ken doll,' Macario. He's a Cuban bodybuilder, ya know. You can bet he's got a freaky streak in him too! He's definitely under control when he's with her, but she does travel a lot. And when she's gone, he's floating! Yeah!"

"Does she know this?!"

"She's getting a whiff of it. He got a little tipsy last summer with her and started pulling his macho routine. Ever since, he's been very careful not to drink too much around her."

Lincoln reflected on this tasty tidbit of information. He wanted to meet Macario for sure. "How about her finances?"

"She seems financially responsible. She's really not a party animal. If there's any connection to that murder through her, it could only be through Macario. There, that's my opinion!"

"What's this Macario into?"

Jacko leaned back in his chair, truly in his comfort zone. He could have been Napoleon about to address his troops.

"He's simply a freak! He likes a little coke and the ladies. He keeps his stuff fairly low-key, especially since he's started hanging out with Monique. She's not going to put up with a bunch of news reporters following her around because her 'boy toy' made some public spectacle. She'd cut him loose before it ever came to that. Oh yeah!"

"How does Macario pay his bills? Does he live within his means?"

"Macar is a personal trainer with a fair amount of clients. He's the Latin hunk women go crazy for. He has a professional reputation and a somewhat impressive client list. He drives a late model BMW that looks really good. A real babe magnet."

"Any of these folks into religion or cults?"

"Nah, not that I know of. Just the same old addictions we're all inclined to…sex, drugs and dead presidents!"

"Would Macar try to hit on Monique's sister, Hillary?"

"Nah, no way. Macar's no dummy! A move on Monique's sister would be downright stupid. And besides, there're enough sex freaks here in Oakland to keep Macar satisfied for a long, long time! Yeah."

"So, what's the link between Monique and Macar? Why are they together? What's up with that?"

Jacko again leaned back in his chair contemplating these new questions. "I bet you she's a little nympho freak and that Macar knows how to pull all the right strings! Yeah!"

"What makes you say that?"

"Well, I don't know. I'm just talking."

"Radcliffe Dillard. Tell me, what's his claim to fame?"

"Rad is the ultimate playboy. If there's a party somewhere, well, Rad will find it. He's a man who likes to have a good time all the time. What else do you need to know?"

"How can he afford the fancy cars and all the best restaurants? I understand he escorts quite a few women, too."

"Hey, he's a ladies' man. He supports himself as a businessman."

"And just what type of 'business' is he in, pray tell?"

"Why, all types of things. He's a wheeler-dealer! He can find anything for a price. Just call him Trader Rad! Yeah!"

"So, does he gamble?" Bill inquired.

"Yeah. Rad's into a little gambling."

"How about the drug scene?"

"Look, if money is involved, Rad's into it. Sure, he's got drug connections. He doesn't play around with the little stuff either. If he's going to take a risk, it's at the high end. You can't make any real money playing with nickels and dimes!"

"Do mom and pop know?" the Detective asked.

"That's a good question. I don't know. Let me just say if his father wants to know he certainly has the capacity to find out. As I said before, Papa Dillard is a man who knows a lot of people and therefore, a lot of stuff."

"So, why doesn't Rad work for a living?"

"He does!" responded Jacko.

"I mean, why doesn't he hold a conventional job like his father and his other family?"

"Look, he was brought up rich. He's spoiled. Rad likes to get stuff the quick way, immediate gratification, y'know. And frankly, he's been like that since he was a little kid."

"Has he ever had trouble paying his bills?"

"Who hasn't? I've even loaned Rad money, but that was three years ago."

"And I take it that he likes the hustler's life?"

"Yeah, he's a natural!"

"Has he been in any big trouble recently? Anything that could affect his sister Hillary?"

"Maybe. Possibly. Who knows? After all, Rad does run with the big dogs! Of course I don't engage at that level, so I haven't heard anything!"

"What about Rad and Macar? Do they get along?"

"Look, Rad knows everybody. That's one reason why Macar keeps his stuff so under wraps. I think Macar keeps mum on Rad and Rad reciprocates. Of course Monique is Rad's sister and Macar is not about to behave foolishly. That would be disrespectful to Monique and Macar wants 'in-crowd' access. Image is everything to Macar. Oh yeah!"

"Do you know Edward Ramirez, the security guard who discovered Hillary's body?"

"Yeah, I know Ed. He's a good guy, a straight shooter. Occasionally, he'll hang with the fellas, but he's not a 'player'."

"Any chance he's involved?"

"Look, I seriously doubt it, but you never really know about people."

Bill couldn't think of anything else. Lincoln stood and shook Jacko's hand. He decided to head to the police station to see Detective Kasolkasky. Kasolkasky was out in the field but Detective White, one of Brick's direct reports assigned to the Dillard case, was in. The only new item Bill picked up was that Rad had a relationship with a Big Eddy, a known mobster. Big Eddy was a man who liked to intimidate. Word was something might be up, but they didn't know what. While Detective White was answering Bill's questions, they got a call to head to the lounge to watch the Mayor's press conference. On television they saw a room filled with microphones and television cameras. A spokesperson from the Mayor's office announced that his boss would be out in just a few minutes.

Detective Lincoln inquired into how the press conferences had been going. Dick indicated they were getting tougher. The early ones had been exciting but for the last two conferences, information was thin. The press smelled blood, and as such, the intensity of the questions increased. Even the Mayor's skills of damage control were being taxed. There was no one to whom the Mayor could turn to deflect the questions as he could during a campaign, and now the media was challenging him. Not having good answers was politically deadly.

Suddenly, the Mayor strode to the podium. Lights flashed everywhere as the cameras began to roll. The first question came from a major newspaper across the Bay.

"Mr. Mayor, has the list of potential suspects changed at all from the last press conference, and can you tell us now how many names are on that list which you failed to mention at our last two meetings?"

The Mayor, without hesitating, stated, "Sir, the suspect list has not changed since the last meeting. As you know, it is police policy in the City of Oakland not to disclose material information about an ongoing murder investigation. Constantly asking the same question will only demand I repeat the same answer."

The reporter quickly shouted a response; "Mr. Mayor, I'm not asking you for any names of the suspects which would be considered material information, but only the number of suspects! I do not see how you could consider that material, sir!"

The Mayor listened intently before stating, "I'm sorry but we view the number of suspects as being extremely relevant to our ongoing investigation for managing resources. Thank you for your question. Next question, please."

"Mr. Mayor, are there any significant new leads?" another reporter asked.

The Mayor's ears perked ever so slightly when he heard the word 'significant' emphasized. These reporters were razor sharp! The Mayor had been taking questions on whether or not there were any new leads, running all over the field with them, but simply not scoring. He had only progressed in terms of running down the clock.

"There is new information, but we will all have to wait to determine its significance. As we all know, the facts may or may not be relevant now, but additional material may prove that assertion false. The police are doing everything in their power to assemble the facts at hand and put this complex puzzle together. Next question, please."

"Mayor Efferton, how does the Dillard family feel about the results of the investigation so far?"

The Mayor never liked the Dillard name to be used in these press conferences, but he displayed no discomfort. He merely turned, looking as always, alert, responsive, completely in control of the situation, and waited for the reporter to finish.

"The Dillard family is being constantly updated. Of course, any family who is enduring such traumatic times wants the police to ascertain what happened and why. The police are in the process of doing just that."

"Mr. Mayor, is it true that all leads on inmates who've been released over the last ten years with any type of similar M.O. have gone nowhere?" yet another reporter queried.

This reporter obviously had somebody feeding her inside information; the design of the question was much too good. It struck right to the heart of the matter and the Mayor felt the bite of the dagger. Detective Lincoln had just learned part of this information himself only a few minutes before from Detective White, and he could already see Dick beginning to tighten up when that question was asked.

"It looks like we have a little rat in our midst," quipped Dick, still staring at the monitor. "The boys downtown won't like this. Somebody has been playing 'deep throat.'"

The retired detective glanced at Detective White again and Dick returned a worried look. "Do you know who it is?" Bill asked.

"Not yet, but the leak has to be somewhere downtown. You're the only person here to whom I've mentioned the information and that's because you're on the team. I haven't disclosed it to anyone else."

Though Detective Lincoln was on the team, he didn't know at what level or even what position he was playing; he didn't believe he was one of the starters.

The Mayor was still taking direct hits from the artillery. Then, finally, the Mayor stood at the podium, grasping it firmly, and declared, "I do have some updated news I can report. We've hired an independent investigator. We will leave no stone unturned in uncovering the perpetrator of this ghastly crime. I'll be expecting a detailed report of his findings in the very near future. Thank you for attending this conference. Good day ladies and gentlemen!"

As Bill looked, Dick responded, "It appears I should say 'Welcome aboard.' I guess it's official now, unless there's some other independent investigator I don't know anything about!"

All of a sudden, the press was 'foaming at the mouth', trying to find out who the new outside investigator was. The Mayor had bought himself more time by saying Lincoln would be giving him a detailed report soon.

As soon as they stood up, Detective White was alerted to a meeting in the Mayor's office right away and they were part of the 'festivities'. After that press conference, Lincoln was going to the meeting, invited or not. Twenty minutes later Lincoln sat waiting for the meeting to start.

Suddenly, the Mayor entered and the door closed behind him. Everyone found a seat.

"For those who weren't watching, we just finished my press conference and I was not pleased with the nature of the questions, especially one in particular. I don't fault anyone for not having solved this case. But how do you expect me to keep the public calm when our own police are leaking information? How did that reporter know that all of our leads relating to inmates released over the last ten years led nowhere? Chief Ness, could you please address the question?!"

Everyone turned to face a resolute Chief. "Mr. Mayor, I agree the information appears leaked. I don't know by whom, but I intend to find out. I'll have my secretary schedule a meeting with you as soon as we find out anything."

"Chief," the Mayor responded, "set up that meeting, but I want it held within the next twenty-four hours! And let me say to everyone else attending this meeting that if I discover anyone leaking sensitive information to the press, I'll personally do everything in my power to have that individual removed from the city's payroll. And anyone who tries to cover-up for any such individual will receive, without question, the same fate. We're dealing with a high-profile case here that's attracting the media like flies to a bucket of crap!"

"Now, I want to know if there are any areas we've missed concerning this investigation. Does anyone have any ideas not shared before?"

Detective White asked, "Should we request a more extensive computer DNA matching sort be run in order to go deeper into the criminal files data base?"

"That's an excellent suggestion, Detective White!" the Mayor said. At this point, the Mayor was willing to spend the money even if the effort had little chance of success. The important thing now was to show action; it didn't matter a hoot what the results would be!

Detective Lincoln raised his hand and the Mayor recognized him.

"Mr. Mayor, during the press conference I heard that an independent investigator was hired to work with the police. Am I that investigator?"

"Yes Bill, you are."

"Then I respectfully request my assigned duties. I want it clearly stated what type of reports you are requesting from me and when they are due. But, I want this in writing and if not, I'm out of here!"

"We'll get you the information in writing, Bill," the Mayor had responded with what the Investigator interpreted as some reluctance. Bill had limited the Mayor's ability to side-step issues. This retired investigator was not going to be the fall guy for anyone!

"Are there any more responses or requests?" the Mayor asked. Not hearing any, the Mayor then declared the meeting adjourned.

I am not thinking of those shining precepts which are the registered property of every school; that is to say-learn as much by writing as by reading; be not content with the best book; seek sidelights from the others; have no favourites; keep men and things apart; guard against the prestige of great manes; see that your judgments are your own; and do not shrink from disagreement; no trusting without testing; be more severe to ideas than to actions; do not overlook the strength of the bad cause or the weakness of the good; never be surprised by the crumbling of an idol or the disclosure of a skeleton; judge talent at its best and character at its worst; suspect power more than vice, and study problems in preference to periods.

Lord Action: Inaugural lecture on The Study Of History, Cambridge, June 11, 1895.

Chapter 6

Detective Lincoln sat at his home office desk and stared at the blank page in front of him. He had been sitting for twenty minutes, but was still unsure how to begin this journal entry. He usually started with a simple description of the case. Finally, he picked up his pen and slowly started to write his thoughts.

"It's been three months since the bizarre death of Hillary Dillard and despite the investigation this case still remains a mystery."

Bill looked at the sentence and put his pen down. That one sentence encapsulated his total thoughts on the case. Tired and frustrated he stood to turn the light off. He was finished writing for the evening.

Chapter 7

Detective Lincoln's first meeting with a member of the Dillard family was scheduled for five o'clock. This meeting was with the eldest son, Franklin Jr., who was running for a congressional seat.

Lincoln pulled into the Dillard driveway at four fifty-five and surveyed the Oakland Hills house with its beautiful bay view. He rang the doorbell and the maid appeared. After Lincoln identified himself, the maid led him to Franklin Jr..

"Detective Lincoln, what questions can I answer for you today?"

Franklin Jr., fair skinned, tall and well groomed, had a refined voice and a relaxed manner. He oozed class. He wore his hair closely cut, was clean-shaven except for a slight moustache, and wore a beautifully tailored suit.

"Please, call me Bill. I'm retired and only acting as a consultant. I hope to be of some service to you and your family."

Junior looked at him briefly, as if sizing him up. Bill was as tall as Franklin Jr. and at least fifteen muscular pounds heavier. He could not read the Detective. Bill stood there, bland as a white painted ceiling.

"Alright, Bill, what questions do you have for me?"

Franklin Jr. was not in control of this situation. One bad article indicating he was more interested in winning political office than in solving this crime would surely color his ambitions. "Mr. Dillard, please tell me about your sister Hillary. Knowing more about her can help us tremendously."

"First, call me Franklin. Hillie was a darling, a beautiful human being. She was an incredible girl who probably represented the best of all the Dillard children. She was completely loveable without an enemy in the world. My sister had the unique ability, to see the good in everyone. Hillie was not naïve though. She wasn't going to look poverty in the face and say it's a wonderful thing. Hillie had nice friends, an excellent future and a strong family. She simply cared for people. That's probably the best way to describe her. My baby sister was a genuinely caring person."

"I've heard this description several times so I believe this community has suffered a terrible loss. I'm truly sorry for what happened to your sister."

"Thank you."

The maid who served the wine briefly interrupted them.

"Who might have done this?"

Franklin was silent, reflective. He uncrossed his legs, stood and started pacing the room, his left hand in his suit pocket; his other hand rubbed his neck.

"Bill, I've thought about this constantly but it just doesn't make sense. I can think of outlandish plots and conspiracy theories that would seem viable in a television movie, but after three months of thinking, talking and asking questions, I still can't come up with any logical explanation." He turned and stared at the Detective. "I want to believe it was random, but… the feathers and that dreadful duck's head!"

"Franklin, where were you that night?"

"I was in New York City with my wife on business. We got the call and immediately flew back."

"Is there anything in your background or your wife's that might've contributed to your sister's death?"

Franklin shook his head. "No, not if we're talking about such obviously abnormal behavior. This act against my sister was definitely not 'civilized'. I assure you I know no one who could do such a thing!"

"You're a lawyer by profession, so what about your past clients?"

Franklin sat back down and crossed his legs. "No, not really. I worked exclusively in the corporate world. Our clients were for the most part big corporations and members of the social elite. We didn't handle criminal law, we farmed it out to others."

"Can you think of anyone else in your family whose activities could've contributed to this murder?"

This was the only question Detective Lincoln really was interested in. He didn't know for sure, but he felt Franklin dealt with an entirely different class of people than those who he was looking for.

Franklin sat quietly pondering his answer. "I take what we say is confidential. Is that right?"

"Yes."

"Bill, this information goes no further than you and me. It's not evidence or anything like that. It's only my suspicions."

Detective Lincoln nodded and remained silent; the next words would be from Franklin. Suddenly, Franklin's wife, Crystal, entered the room. She was a strikingly beautiful woman with long hair attracting any man's eye! She introduced herself then held out her hand. Detective Lincoln stood to shake it. She was elegant! She commanded attention and knew it. She motioned for Bill to sit back down.

"Crystal, I've told Detective Lincoln that what I'm about to say is strictly confidential." Franklin looked directly at her.

Crystal returned his gaze and simply said, "I understand." Crystal, also a lawyer, had been a classmate of Franklin's at Harvard Law School.

"Bill, I have no facts to give you but my younger brother Radcliff, who we affectionately call Rad, maintains an affluent lifestyle but doesn't appear to have any identifiable source of income. At least none that institutions such as the IRS can track. But, I'm sure you already know this."

"Yes, your brother's occupation, or lack thereof, has come up before."

"We grew up in a world of affluence. Rad was always the life of the party. He always felt endowed to live the 'good life'. Rad never worked hard, but rather always expected everything to be given to him. At some point you believe people will grow out of this type of thinking… Rad never did. He never finished college. College was just one huge party for him. So, my parents finally cut off his support in an effort to bring him back to reality. Turning off that spigot forced Rad to find other creative ways to make a living and frankly, Bill, I'm not sure what my brother really does for a living."

"Have you asked him?" the Detective said.

"Asking Rad a question he doesn't want to address is like asking a skilled politician a question he needs to evade. After a while you get tired of hearing the rhetoric and just stop asking."

"What do you imagine he does for a living, Franklin?"

"I really don't know. It could be gambling, prostitution, drugs…."

Franklin was starting to talk like a lawyer again, but Bill could not blame him. After all, he was talking about his brother. Franklin stopped speaking. Bill had turned to face the lady of the house!

"Crystal, do you know anything about Radcliff's lifestyle funding?"

"I can only repeat what Franklin has said. Rad is a lot of fun, but nobody knows exactly how he affords such luxury. He drives nice cars and lives in a fabulous place. It's a mystery. We're afraid that soon this will be a question Franklin will have to answer politically."

"What do you think he does?" Bill asked Crystal.

"Being a lawyer I'd rather not speculate."

Bill thought, ironically, he was expecting too much. The confidential information he had heard was what he already knew.

"Crystal, who do you suspect?"

"As Franklin and I have said, we don't know people capable of such violence. You read about them, but you think they can't possibly invade your life. It's been a nightmare. There's no excuse for hurting somebody like Hillie."

"Crystal, is there anything in your past or anything going on now, like a lawsuit, that could in any way be associated with this crime?"

"No. Absolutely not!"

"Do either one of you know any of Rad's friends, past or present, with questionable lifestyles?"

Both shook their heads while Franklin added, "Most of the time when we see Rad it's at one of our homes, usually with a lady friend. Rad usually comes here or to Mom and Dad's. He's been showing up at campaign headquarters on a regular basis, but he's always by himself or again, with a lady friend. I don't really know any of his male friends or business associates. I sometimes hear about them through the rumor mill, but Rad is not part of our regular social group."

"I see."

Detective Lincoln didn't have any more questions and thanked both of them for the interview.

It was now six-thirty; the Detective had made contact with Monique and started toward San Francisco. The two communities were quite different. San Francisco had the classic metropolitan history with the ambiance of world-class recognition and affluence. Oakland was its poor cousin.

It was seven-fifteen when Bill pulled into Monique's driveway. He briefly reviewed his notes before heading for her door. Monique must have seen or heard him drive up because she was holding the door open as he approached.

Bill noted that Monique was one fine female specimen! The effects of her workouts with Macario were quite evident. She was roughly five-feet-five with short wavy hair. They talked extensively about the case for an hour. After he concluded his formal questioning they started talking personally. Monique had a lovely personality, had traveled extensively and told fascinating stories. She was refreshingly adventuresome. Monique was also very frank, talking openly about her relationship with Macario. She respected Macario's dedication to his body but knew he didn't have the mental depth to intellectually stimulate her.

"I guess he's your 'boy toy,'" Bill remarked remembering Jacko's phrasing.

"Yeah, that's about it. What do you think of that arrangement, Bill?" she asked smiling coyly.

"Well, I guess men have been doing it for thousands of years, if not longer, so I guess what's good for the goose might be good for the gander," Bill extolled.

"But do you think it's natural?"

"I don't know what's natural anymore. Tell me, Monique, why haven't you married?"

"I haven't met that special person yet. I must admit I didn't think I'd be single this long. I've met nice men, but there just hasn't been anyone that special yet, you know, my 'soul mate'."

"Have you gotten close?"

Monique paused for a few moments. She had reflected on this question quite often.

"I guess so. I mean I've taken a second, even third look, but there is always something that stops me."

Because of her physical attractiveness he was surprised men were not knocking her door down. This woman was a looker!

"So, what's it going to take, Monique, a knight on a white horse? Are your expectations set too high?"

"They're high, but not quite as high as they were ten years ago. It's hard to determine if they're more interested in becoming part of the Dillard family mystique or genuinely interested in me."

"What do you mean?"

"Look, I know I'm considered attractive because I've been told it enough times. However, the Dillard name is very seductive. I too often get the feeling that people are more interested in my name. They care about me, sure, but the Dillard package is even more alluring."

"Do you wish you weren't a Dillard?"

As far as she could remember that was the first time anyone had asked her that question. She had contemplated it herself, but to no avail. "No, of course not. But when I do meet someone, I'm just not sure if they're looking at me as a person or as a member of this family. I'd like to be considered a trophy on my own merits."

They bantered, talked, and dined for almost two hours before Bill finally said good night. Monique Dillard was an intriguing woman.

A labouring man that is given to drunkenness shall not be rich: and he that contemneth small things shall fall by little and little.

THE APOCRYPHA - ECCLESIASTICUS 19:1

Chapter 8

Inside the Oakland Police Department a meeting had just started. It concerned the status of the Dillard case. Even Chief Ronald Ness was there. Normally the Chief didn't attend his subordinate's meetings, but in this instance he made an exception. He had to be ready to answer questions from the Mayor and the press, both of which would keep the fire to his feet.

"Okay… have we made any progress since last week?" Kasolkasky inquired.

Detective Dick White was acknowledged by Kasolkasky.

"We may have an angle on how to crack Big Eddy. The Mayor's people called last night saying one of Eddy's boys was just picked up for dealing drugs. He's looking at big time. So, if we throw this rat a little cheese, he just may finger Big Eddy for us."

"Good. I want in on this one. Let me know when you schedule that talk! Any other progress?"

Detective Clarence Jones raised his hand.

"What do you have, Clarence?"

"Two things. We've taken blood samples of all male employees at the college, except for three individuals. One is a sixty-five year-old history professor who was in New York giving a speech the night of the crime. We have a tape of him at the podium provided by the sponsors of the event. The second is the Chancellor of the University. He just hasn't had the time. The third is a twenty-year-old student-employee, a political science major, planning to attend law school. He feels his civil rights are being violated and simply refuses to take the blood test."

"And does 'Mr. Don't Tread on Me' have an alibi?" Kasolkasky asked.

"Yep. He was bartending the night of the event. Lot's of people saw him there. Afterward, he and three others drove to San Francisco to attend a private party. He's in several of the pictures taken at that party.

"The second issue is the voodoo angle. There are five employees who are from cultures associated with the voodoo culture. Three of the five are women. The two males originally used each other as an alibi. We've questioned each a second time with each man's story changing only slightly. They were together that evening but their respective time lines have small discrepancies. We haven't made much of it yet, but it's something!"

"What's the guy saying now, Clarence?" Kasolkasky inquired.

"'I thought I got to the place earlier, but I guess I didn't' was his exact quote. The first guy's story is that he stayed and helped clean up after the event before going home to take a nap. He went to an after-hours joint later that evening to meet up with his friend, the second employee. The first guy said he arrived at the original time he gave us and made his way to the bar. His friend was seated at a table closer to the band and some distance from the bar. The first guy said that he waited for about an hour at the bar, listening to the music and talking. The bartender remembers him, but not the specific times."

"Good. Keep digging. Anything else?"

The room was silent. The Chief thanked everyone and left.

"Okay," Brick said, "what's Bill Lincoln up to?"

Dick White grabbed his briefcase and updated everyone.

Detective Jones asked, "How's the Mayor holding up?"

"He's still fried and wants this case solved like 'pronto'. He's caught in the crosshairs and doesn't like it much. Besides, Dillard Sr. is no joke either. Dillard hasn't yanked his Honor's chain too hard yet, however, he's definitely keeping the Mayor on a short leash. The Mayor knows how to play hardball too, so don't mess up and play him cheap. Look, I've seen enough ex-cops trying to live off of a poor retirement check simply because they thoughtlessly challenged the Mayor."

Detective Kasolkasky, although trying to give up smoking, had lit a cigarette–a sure sign that he was feeling the pressure. Turning to Detective White he asked, "What do you have on this guy? What would cause him to betray Big Eddy for us, Dick?"

"As I mentioned earlier, sir, he's facing serious time; he'll sing like a parrot. The perp's name is William 'Willie' Lee Taylor Sr., born and raised right here in Oakland. He's a local high school dropout who's been on the streets selling drugs since his adolescence. A gang banger in his youth, now as an adult, he's got a full rap sheet. He's been busted twice for possession with the intent to sell."

"How did he get hooked up with Big Eddy? And just when did the Italians start enlisting the services of black drug dealers?"

"Today, why it's an equal opportunity crime syndicate!" explained Detective White. "Times are certainly changing; you literally don't know who's working for whom nowadays!"

"So, will Willie squeal?" Kasolkasky inquired.

"Well, suppose you were looking at life without the possibility of parole. What would you do? Finger somebody? Now, of course, afterwards your life won't be worth a plug nickel, but at least you'd still be free, sort of."

"Set up that meeting with Mr. Taylor. Let's see if he knows anything. If not, it's a moot point!"

The interview with Willie Taylor was scheduled for three that afternoon. Bill entered the two-way mirrored interrogation room and observed the prisoner, Willie Lee Taylor, entering the room. Taylor was slight of build and average height. He had a scraggly beard, bad teeth and wore an earring in his left ear. Handcuffed, he wore standard prison issued oversized bright orange overalls and black work boots. Led to a chair, Willie asked for a cigarette. His request was denied; there would be no unearned favors yet. Detectives White and Jones, a white and a black detective respectively, now entered the room. Detective Jones sat next to Willie and Detective White seated himself across the table. Today Detective White would play the bad cop and Detective Jones, the good one.

"Hello, Willie," White announced authoritatively.

"What's up, brother man?" asked Detective Jones using animated gestures playing the good-natured happy-go-lucky policeman role. Willie wore the look of fear and resignation in his eyes; he desperately wanted a cigarette and stared at the detectives across the table.

"Willie, you don't have to talk to us," Detective White interjected. "In fact, if you want to have a lawyer present, that's fine because that's your right. Let's face it, we all know that you're in a tough spot. You'll more than likely be taking up residence at the 'Hilton del San Quentin' and you won't be coming back anytime soon."

Detective White pulled out a cigarette and lit it. He offered one to Willie who readily accepted it.

"Willie, we want to ask you some questions. Your answers might reduce your charge from a felony to a misdemeanor. Get my drift? In fact, when we finish talking with you, we'll be talking with another guy who has information on some fairly high level undesirables! Don't be a fool and think you're in any special situation here, pal."

Willie knew he was in a tight spot. He took a long drag on his cigarette.

"Yeah, okay. What do you want to know?"

"Well, first, who's your employer?"

"I work for myself!"

"Alright, let's do it this way. Who supplies your drugs?"

Willie was trapped. He was being squeezed and there wasn't a damn thing he could do about it.

"I have several sources," he mumbled.

"I want names. If the name I'm looking for is not on your list, I'm out of here. The ball's in your court, Willie! Start dribbling!"

Willie had no choice. "Okay. I get them from three sources."

"Names, Willie; I want their names!"

"Charlie Stone, Rudolf Haynes and Nicky Bruno."

"And who do they work for Willie?"

'Oh God! Help me', Willie thought to himself. 'Damn! What am I doing?' Then, as though in a trance, Willie softly offered, "Charlie works for Mr. 'G' and Haynes and Bruno both work for Big Eddy." He had served them up, the big boys. Willie's mind was reeling now for sure.

"That's good, Willie, we're interested in getting both Mr. 'G' and Big Eddy off the street. They sell drugs to kids– they're scumbags! You can understand that, can't you Willie?"

"Yeah, I guess." Willie sighed, shaking his hanging head.

"We're going to need information on their crimes. That's why we're here, my friend!"

Willie sighed again. His goose was cooked. His drug associates would rip him to shreds if they found out he ratted. These drug guys play for keeps. Willie was screwed!

Tears welled up in Willie's bloodshot weary eyes. "They'll kill me if they ever find out I talked."

"And just how would they find out? Definitely not from us. We want the big boys, the ones at the top, not you small guys."

Willie sat silently while the seconds crept by. Finally, Detective White stood and said, "Well, thanks for your time, Willie. We'll go talk to our other prisoner now."

As if on cue, Detective Jones jumped up from his chair, "Hold on! Hey, wait a minute. Willie hasn't given his answer yet! Now, isn't that right, my friend?"

Detective White looked at a silently whimpering Willie as he raised his still trembling shackled hands in a palms up gesture.

"Which one do you want to know about first?" Willie mumbled.

"Tell us about Big Eddy. How long have you been doing business with the Italian?"

Willie wiped his eyes on his sleeve. He was weighing how much to tell but didn't have much bargaining room. He couldn't see spending the rest of his life in prison. He'd been in that hellhole before.

"For a little over a year now," Willie grunted.

"And what type of merchandise do you purchase from Big Eddy?" Detective White inquired.

"I get a little coke and weed from Big Eddy. He's got some of the best product and count in town."

The detective cracked a slight smile. "Good, Willie, that confirms our beliefs. We don't have any hard evidence yet. You're our key."

Willie didn't say anything.

"We want to bust Big Eddy. If you help us, we can help you. With you we'll have the evidence. And besides, you know how people feel about drugs. You sell drugs, Willie, ergo you're scum. You won't get any sympathy at trial unless we support you."

Willie was chain smoking!

"We'll need a statement from you but a statement coming from a three-time loser is about as weak as courtroom evidence gets. I'm sure you can understand our position, Willie."

Willie's head slumped with a newfound expression of terror glued on his face. The detectives became quite curious. 'Nice cop' Detective Jones got the signal to go into his 'home boy' act. He gently put his right hand on Willie's shoulder while softly whispering into his ear. "Willie, brother, what's happening here? You're looking very distraught my man. You're definitely not looking your best! What's up player? What gives?"

Willie's eyes retained a vacant stare. With his hand on Willie's shoulder, Detective Jones continued gently talking. Detective White left the room to allow Detective Jones to work Willie alone. Detective Jones huddled next to Willie and listened patiently.

After twenty minutes Willie put his head down again and Jones glanced at the one-way mirror motioning for his partner to come back.

"Willie wants to consult a lawyer first before he talks to us."

"Okay, I understand. Let me call the Public Defender's office right now."

"Wait! Willie has dealt with the PD's office before and feels this is much too important for that. He wants to make a call to people who have previously helped him."

"Okay, who does he want to reach out and touch?"

Willie remained silent and listless. He acted like a zombie, just staring at the floor.

"Willie wants to call 'Berkland Law'. He wants to talk to Bennie Pews or Matthew Silverstein, you know, the original 'Zebra boys'."

Detective White remained outwardly expressionless but inside he was reeling; this latest revelation was a potential nightmare. Berkland Law was the name given the firm started by Pews and Silverstein in Oakland during the turbulent civil rights movement of the 1960's. Pews, a black man, and Silverstein, a Jew, were two smart street lawyers who enjoyed nothing more than agitating the establishment by creating confrontational situations. The Black Panthers had often used their help and it was rumored that several Panther meetings had been held in the conference rooms of the now prestigious firm.

"Let me get their number. I'll be right back."

Behind the two-way mirror, Brick Kasolkasky spoke first, "Gentlemen, let's not panic. Dick, get the phone and the number for Berkland Law. Just play it by the book. Willie is just a small time two-bit hustler. They'll more than likely assign one of their junior lawyers to represent him. Don't mention I'm involved or Bill Lincoln for that matter. It's just you and Jones, got it. Just play it cool, like it was an everyday case. Understand?"

Detective White nodded. He retrieved the telephone.

"What do you think, Bill?" Brick asked.

"I agree with you. Pews and Silverstein aren't coming down here just for Willie. He's small potatoes. As long as they think there aren't any big guns involved we'll be okay."

Bill had been shaken too, at first. Detective White entered the interrogation room with a telephone and a directory. Willie dialed the number and asked to speak to Pews or Silverstein. Both were unavailable. Willie described his situation and was told they would assign him counsel. Willie was then escorted back to his cell. The officers talked briefly, agreeing to get back together after the lawyer arrived.

Chapter 9

Detective Lincoln had scheduled a meeting that afternoon with Edward Ramirez, the security guard who had discovered Hillary Dillard's body. The police files showed he had an unblemished record.

Bill arrived on campus a few minutes early and noticed two security officers patrolling the area. He identified himself and was led to a small conference room. Ramirez appeared shortly thereafter.

"Mr. Ramirez, I hope you don't mind, but I need you to tell me exactly what occurred that evening. I've read your report, but sometimes there are little details that we may remember only later."

"Please, call me Ed. And, no, I don't mind telling my story again. Let's walk the security route."

Ed showed Detective Lincoln the checkpoints where he clocked in and the whole routine. Ed conducted himself with confidence, sans bravado.

Lincoln's initial impression about Ed caused him to agree with the police report, namely, the security officer wasn't a likely suspect. They followed the route exactly as patrolled the night of the murder. Ed recalled being on schedule that evening, noting that there had been few distractions because most people were either sleeping or partying. The main activities of that night had been held in the large auditorium– away from the dormitories, both of which were on his security route.

Ramirez stopped at the murder site and described, once again, his actions on that evening; everything agreed with his report.

"Ed, did you know her?"

"Not personally. I've said 'hello', but she was just another student to me. Of course, I was aware she was Franklin Dillard's daughter. There are several kids here with pedigree names. To date, our safety record has been impeccable. We just don't have such 'incidents' up here. This was a first ever."

"Ed, who do you think did this…an insider or an outsider?"

"We know the players on campus. I say it has to be an outsider!"

"How firm are you on that position?"

"Oh, maybe eighty percent or more."

Ed's eyes clearly showed his intensely troubled soul. It didn't matter who had done it. Not only had security allowed a murder to take place, but one of the city's most influential families had died horribly.

"So, what's the word on the street, Ed?" Detective Lincoln asked nonchalantly. This was a delicate question since this was the security officer who had arrived on the scene first and was, theoretically at least, a prime suspect.

Ed's guard went up instantly as he glanced sternly at Detective Lincoln, trying to determine what the Detective was getting at.

"The word on the street is that probably one of those 'rich drugged-out college boys' went berserk and with so much 'money' up here we'll never find the killer. That's the word on the street, Detective."

Lincoln observed Officer Ramirez carefully.

"So, Ed, what's your opinion?"

"It's all just talk. Talk from people who don't know how to do anything else."

"Tell me, did any students take off after the murder?"

"Yes, as a matter of fact, seven…five females and two males. We checked out everyone. They all had rock solid alibis. Their families understandably have concerns over campus security and quite frankly, who wouldn't? I can understand that!"

"Are there any other rumors circulating, Ed?"

Ed looked at Bill again with a piercing glare. He displayed a grim, sour expression, with eyes clear and intense.

"Yeah, there's another rumor that says the security guard probably did it. Is that the one you mean?" Ed asked dryly.

"And what do you say to that rumor?"

"It's just more bull. I've donated a blood sample and didn't hesitate to do it. I did my job that evening. I'm sorry that young lady died, but it wasn't me."

"I know it wasn't you–and believe me, I'm sorry she died on your watch. Well, let's get out of here. Unless you can recall something else, there's nothing more I need from you."

--

Detective Lincoln called police headquarters to ask if Willie's lawyer had arrived yet. He hadn't, so Bill got the address of the gym where Monique Dillard's male friend, Macario, worked. He wanted to check the place out. Sometimes even the workplace could yield important information.

The gym, called the Polo Grounds, was located in an exclusive section of downtown Oakland. The membership fee structure was designed to keep low-income people out and, if Bill's visit was any indication, the policy was working; the gym reeked of affluence.

Lincoln requested a membership application and was presented a beautifully designed brochure. He asked about Macario and was told that the instructor was presently giving a private training lesson. The receptionist offered the well-dressed detective a private tour. The receptionist assured him that Macario would be notified that he had a visitor and would join him once his training session was over.

Bill saw Macario for the first time on a promotional tape providing a brief biography of all of the trainers. The tape mentioned that Macario was born in Cuba but had managed to escape the oppressive Castro regime. He had been into bodybuilding for some fifteen years, including being on this health club staff for five of those years. He'd been giving private training sessions for the last eight years.

After his tour Bill was escorted to the 'juice bar' where he waited for Macario's arrival. The trainer had light olive skin and wore a thin moustache, his hair cut short except for a small ponytail. He was well groomed and even his gym clothes appeared custom made. Macario looked like a Greek god, it was easy to understand Macario's large following of female clients.

"Macario, I understand that you're an acquaintance of Monique Dillard. My name is Bill Lincoln. I'm a retired detective hired by the Oakland Police Department to investigate the death of Monique's sister, Hillary. I wonder if you'd mind taking a few minutes with me?"

Macario listened patiently, displaying no emotion. He focused on the Detective's eyes as Bill talked.

"What do you want to know? I don't mind talking to you. I have nothing to hide."

"Good; this shouldn't take long. Tell me, Macario, did you know Hillary?"

"I'd met her, but I didn't know her well or see her that often. I know her sister, Monique. Monique is one of my private weight-training students and occasionally we go out together."

"Are you friendly with any of Monique's other brothers and sisters?"

"I've only met Franklin Jr. once or twice, but I know her younger brother Radcliffe much better. I get the feeling I'm not really in Franklin's class, but Rad is totally different. He socializes with all types of people. Some people call him 'Money.' I've partied with him many times."

"Macario, Franklin Jr. is a lawyer running for a congressional seat; but, what exactly does Rad do for a living?"

Macario reached for his juice. He sat back, put his glass down and reflected for a few seconds.

"I don't really know and I've never asked him. That must seem kind of funny, but it's never come up. Rad is just a guy who's the life of the party. He always has money in his pocket but I can't tell you where he gets it. I really can't!"

"Have the police talked to you about the case, Macario?"

"Yes. We spent about a half-hour talking."

"Do you have any opinion on who might be responsible for Hillary's death?"

"No. I can't think of anyone who'd want to harm her!"

"Do you think Rad might earn his money illegally?"

"I really don't know. What makes you say that?"

"I'm trying to determine his occupation but nobody seems to know. Maybe that's the connection to this murder."

"Oh, I see."

"Macario, does Rad use drugs?" This was the time to 'put it' to the trainer. His answer would definitely determine the remaining tone of the conversation.

"Man, I don't like this. Why don't you ask Rad? That's his personal business. He should be answering that question, not me!"

Macario, displaying discomfort, had raised his voice slightly.

"Macario, I'm sure you know there haven't been many leads. If I file a report on our conversation as if I think you're holding something back, you realize what's going to happen. It's going to get hot and heavy for you. People will be examining your records wanting to know when and under what circumstances you entered this country...should you really be here. The police can make trouble for your employer too. I don't think your employer is going to jeopardize his business for you. Do you?"

Macario shrugged. Detective Lincoln could make his life very uncomfortable and, ironically, his link to Monique was his problem.

"Macario, this talk is off the record, be assured of that. But don't let me walk away from here with unanswered questions. Believe me, you don't want attention directed at you. No one is saying you're involved, but don't fool yourself. This is not 'Let's Make a Deal' here. So I'll ask you again, as far as you know, does Rad use drugs?"

Macario sat back, his facial muscles tightening. He had every legal right to get up and leave, but if he gave Lincoln reason to write an unfavorable report, the authorities would give him no rest.

"I've seen Rad use drugs."

"Have you used drugs with Rad?"

Macario looked right at Bill.

"This is off the record?"

"Yes. Absolutely."

"Yeah, alright then, I've done drugs with Rad."

43

"What type and how often?"

"I've done a little coke with him from time to time. I don't do much; just enough to give me a little buzz at a party."

"Who provides it, you or Rad?"

Macario got silent again. His choices were limited.

"Most of the time Rad has stuff. He's always provided more to me than me to him. Even though Rad always has a wad of cash, I've never seen Rad sell drugs. He's nobody's fool. He's not about to sell stuff right out in the open to people he barely knows."

"How do you think he makes his money, Macario?"

"I really don't know. I've been to one of the homes that he sold and he can make good money by selling them. If he bought them cheap, why, he could make a killing."

"How often does he do drugs?"

"I don't know. I'm not around him that often but the times I've been with him, he's doing it. Of course, we're at parties so most of the people there are getting high on drugs or booze."

The next question the Detective had no business asking, but he had the power and the opportunity.

"Does Monique use drugs?"

"No. Monique doesn't tolerate drug use and she doesn't associate with people who do. She has a great reputation."

"So, you use it from time to time but it doesn't control you. Is that what you're saying?"

"Exactly. And when I'm around Monique I behave as she does. Hey, everything's a game."

"How would you describe your relationship with Rad?"

Lincoln's expression remained stern. Bill vividly remembered one of his mentor's favorite sayings, a quote by Alexander Solzhinitsyn; 'You only have power over people so long as you don't take everything away from them. But when you've robbed a man of everything he's no longer in your power–he's free again.'

"We're buddies when we see one another. I might party with him one night and not see him again for several months. Or, I could see him three weekends in a row. It depends on our schedules."

"Do you have Rad's telephone number?"

"Yeah. I have it. I've only used it a few times though."

"For what?"

"Well, this is a little embarrassing, but once I was going to Los Angeles to visit a friend so I asked Rad if I could buy a small amount of coke. I wanted some just for the weekend. I was going to help a young lady client work out and I thought if she was a little high, it might help her 'relax' if you know what I mean. She has a boyfriend, but he was out of town that weekend, you understand."

"Did you reach Rad?"

"Yeah. He gave me what I needed but he wouldn't sell me anything. He just said to come on over and pick up a little something, saying he'd feel insulted if I paid."

"Does Monique know her brother Rad uses coke?"

"She suspects he does because he's such a party animal. However, as far as I know, she's never seen him do it."

"New topic. What's your relationship with Monique?"

"Monique is one of my weight-training clients. She's been working out with me for about two years. She's a good student. At times, she'll invite me to escort her to various functions. She's a nice lady. I enjoy being with her. We've been seen out together a few times."

"Next topic. Do you know Big Eddy?"

"I know him. Sometimes he works out here too. He's like Rad. He's a member, but there are long lapses when I don't see him."

"What does Big Eddy do for a living?"

Macario glared at the Detective. This was more forbidden territory. There were some paths you just didn't want to travel. Macario remained silent, but Bill having asked the question, expected an answer.

"I don't know what Big Eddy does for a living," Macario responded in a low tone.

"Macario, what do you think Big Eddy does for a living?" Lincoln asked glaring back directly into his eyes. "Remember, this is off the record."

Macario sat back again grabbing his glass of juice and grasping it tightly. Obviously very uncomfortable now, he took a deep breath, and then scanned the bar.

"I've heard he might be moving drugs and running numbers. I've only heard that; I don't know anything for sure. I've seen the big guy down here pumping iron and I've seen him at parties."

"Have you ever done drugs with him?"

"A few times, but at these gigs everyone is doing drugs with everyone else. It's not like you're there with your best buddies hanging out. Everyone is having a good time and the person standing next to you is your best friend for the moment."

"Tell me, in your opinion is Big Eddy a violent person?"

"Well, I've heard you don't want to get on the wrong side of the guy."

"Does Rad know Big Eddy?"

"Rad knows everybody and everybody knows Rad."

"Do they hang out together?"

"I've seen them together a few times. I don't know what they talked about because I wasn't a part of the conversation."

"Do they do any business together?"

"I don't know."

"In your opinion, do you believe Big Eddie is involved in illegal activities?"

"Sure, I mean, he's Italian, right? You know, the Mafia and that organization thing. Big Eddy's always got a bunch of other Italians hanging around him and they don't look like the type that go door to door selling bibles...get my drift?"

"In your opinion, if they were working together, which one would be calling the shots?"

Macario thought about that question before responding but he really wasn't quite sure how to answer it. Lincoln wasn't giving him any breaks.

"Listen, in my opinion, Big Eddy doesn't take orders from anyone. Not unless he's truly in the mob and then he would take orders from the Don. Rad is a free-wheeler, something like an independent contractor. He's not the type to take orders either. I'd say that if they were doing business together, it would be like a partnership or something like that. Rad might be a big customer for Big Eddy."

"Do you know Rad's brother, Franklin Jr?"

"I know who he is but we travel in different circles."

"Have you ever seen him at these parties?"

"No, that's not his kind of scene!"

"I see."

"However, I did see something interesting one time," Macario disclosed with a slight smirk.

"Oh?" Lincoln exclaimed with interest.

"I did see the Missus at one of these gatherings."

"Are you saying you saw Crystal, Franklin's wife, at one of these parties?" Detective Lincoln asked.

"That's what I'm saying!"

"And what was she doing?"

"Like everyone else, sitting around, talking and having a good time."

"Was she doing drugs?"

"I didn't see her do anything, but she appeared to be feeling no pain!"

"Just what are you saying, Macario?"

"All I'm saying is, at this particular party there was a back bedroom where a few people would go. The door was kept closed. It seemed you had to have a special invitation to go back there. If everything you want is right out in the open there is no reason for someone like me to open a closed door. That would be rude. But, occasionally Crystal would get up and disappear. One could only guess where she was going. However, I didn't actually see her go into that room."

Bill sat back to reflect on this information. He wasn't sure what to do with it, but it was interesting.

Thus saith the Lord; Behold, I will raise up against Babylon, and against them that dwell in the midst of them that rise up against me, a destroying wind.

THE OLD TESTAMENT - JEREMIAH 51:1

Chapter 10

Back at police headquarters that Friday evening, Chief Ron Ness had called an important meeting. The Chief had met with Mayor Efferton about the Dillard case and felt compelled to share with his detectives. A political volcano was churning. The Mayor was calling for more action immediately placing the Chief in a tight squeeze.

The news outlets seemed once again fixated on this murder. It had been a media circus during the case's first four weeks. Then the news establishment granted a brief reprieve…allowing the authorities a bit of breathing space. That window was closing and closing fast!

Now, amazingly, one Jezebel Balboa, some wannabe soothsayer who claimed she could help the police 'solve that horrible voodoo-like murder in Oakland', contacted the Southern California news media. She had been credited with helping the LA police in a limited capacity once before. Naturally the local authorities had an extensive file on Ms Balboa. However, like most clerics or seers, more failures than successes graced her portfolio. It was she who was calling the police to be of assistance as opposed to the police calling on her.

Balboa claimed Haitian ancestry. She claimed to be a formally trained disciple of a powerful 'voodooianne'. Oakland's Mayor saw her as a way to buy time.

Mayor Efferton requested Chief Ness's opinion. The Chief had objected. He had no intentions of being made a national joke. Even if this woman had anything remotely resembling a successful track record he might consider it, but his research had shown otherwise. He'd let the Mayor fly solo on this one.

"Men, please sit down." The Chief proceeded to explain the situation. "Ms. Jezebel Balboa insists she can help us and is asking to be flown to Oakland to the murder site. She also wants to see photographs of the victim to 'read' the pictures. The Mayor sees this as an opportunity to buy some time. Well, what do you say?"

The detectives were surprised, hesitant and trying to collect their thoughts. They had never been under this type of scrutiny before, nor forced into a position quite like this.

"What does the Mayor plan to do?" Detective White asked the Chief.

"He's calling a press conference tomorrow. The Mayor won't allow any missed opportunity or obstacle to block resolving this case. If this psychic can contribute something, then so be it. If she can't, then at most we've only lost a little time."

"Okay, suppose she identifies the killer as John Doe who lives somewhere in New York? Are we committed to going on a wild goose chase?" quipped Detective Jones, "Because, if so, I've got a couple of relatives in Oklahoma that I haven't visited in a while, and I'd just love to chase our killer there!"

The detectives all started chuckling, but the levity soon gave way to a general sense of uneasiness. Using a psychic could buy extra time, but she could chew up valuable resources by sending them down another fruitless path. Chief Ness was the only officer in the room who had worked on a task force using the services of a psychic.

"Who is this woman, Chief?" asked Kasolkasky. "What's her story?"

Chief Ness reached for a folder on his desk retrieving two sheets of paper.

"Ms. Balboa is in her mid-fifties and has made her home in Los Angeles for the last twenty years. She's a local psychic/card reader/healer/whatever. She's fairly well known in her community and has somehow managed to be the subject of local media interest every few years or so. She did play a minor role helping the police apprehend a serial rapist in LA once, thirteen years ago, but has not been associated with any major case since then."

"How did she help in that case, Chief?"

"It says here she saw a vision revealing the culprit to be a young Hispanic. She described the assailant as clean-shaven, with a tattoo on his left arm, about five foot six inches tall. That describes a whole lot of Hispanic males. She didn't have much else."

"So, who was eventually arrested for the crimes?"

"A Hispanic– mid-forties with a beard."

"Well, she was dead-on concerning his ethnicity!" Detective White mused.

The other detectives again started laughing. Something like that would play 'big time' in the media, leaving the detective division looking like the Keystone Cops!

Detective Jones asked "Chief, the Mayor is definitely for it. So, how's this thing going to go down?"

"The Mayor will mention it at his next press conference. He's going to tell the reporters he'll make three photographs available to this woman and that ultimately he'll let us, the department, decide whether anything she offers is helpful. I think it's a very sound approach."

As bizarre as this all seemed, the detectives supported the Mayor's decision. The Chief still had a bad taste in his mouth from his one previous psychic encounter.

The Chief would follow the Mayor's lead and allow the pressure to be placed squarely on Ms. Balboa's shoulders. He fully realized that Ms. Balboa had the potential of leading them down a winding, twisting path with cameras churning at every turn.

"So, Chief, what three photographs have we decided on?" Detective Kasolkasky asked.

"You decide, but I want to see them first before they go out. And, I don't want any photo that could help the real murderer cover his tracks. Understand?"

"Okay, sure. By the way, Chief, do we have the option of sending her fake photos?" Kasolkasky asked, flashing a sly smile.

"As much as I'd like to, no. Let's make sure they're all legitimate. Let's give her every benefit of the doubt. Play it strictly by the book, Brick!"

Detective Jones was assigned to select photographs for Detective Kasolkasky to review and choose from.

"Where do we stand regarding our Mr. Willie Lee Taylor?" the Chief asked.

"We meet with Willie and his attorney tomorrow."

"Remember, I want to be there."

"That's not a good idea, Chief," Brick responded.

"And why not?"

"Well, Chief, you see, Willie contacted the firm of Berkland Law. For now, they're only sending a staff attorney, not one of the big guns like Pews or Silverstein. Those two will most likely be off somewhere looking for bigger fish to fry. You, better than anyone, know what ball busters they can be. They would cause major headaches for us if they, for one moment, believed Willie was really important to us. So, I'd rather avoid having any highly visible persons–like yourself–being associated with Willie's case."

"Okay, good thinking–but keep me informed. I want to be constantly updated as things materialize. Understood?"

"Sure, no problem, Chief."

"Anything more, gentlemen?"

"The research guys want to know if we want to widen the search parameters to go back say five or ten additional years?"

"Go ten more," the Chief responded.

"What about the cost?"

"Let the Mayor worry about that. Now, is there anything else?"

There were no more questions. The Chief picked up his briefcase and walked out. Kasolkasky asked the detectives to stay to briefly discuss the next day's plan.

Chapter 11

Brick arrived early the next morning to take care of paperwork. By this time, Willie Taylor had met with Connie Chow, a skilled reputable attorney from Berkland Law.

The morning meeting was set for ten o'clock. Detectives White and Jones were instructed to show little interest in Willie while maintaining they still had access to another prisoner with relevant information.

The problem was that Berkland Law also represented Big Eddy. The police wanted to work a quick deal. They believed Ms. Chow might soon inform her partners, resulting in a conflict of interest complicating their plan.

At 9:57 A.M. Ms. Chow strolled confidently into the room. A disheveled and handcuffed Willie Taylor arrived by armed escort at 10:10 A.M. The 'grapevine' indicated Willie would do hard time during his local lockup stay. Willie was relieved of his handcuffs, given a pack of smokes, and seated at the table next to Ms. Chow.

Detective White spoke first, "Ms. Chow, this meeting will help both Willie and the authorities. Potentially, we have an attractive deal for your client. Willie has two strikes and the public's intolerance for people who commit felonies is very high these days. We are about to serve his last strike. Your client hasn't a snowball's chance in Hell to win. However, we might be able to assist Willie."

She had analyzed the evidence. The officer's assessment was on point.

"Detective White, we're willing to listen."

"Ms. Chow, you've reviewed the evidence against Willie. You know we're not exaggerating. Now we're willing to help Willie if he is willing to share important information with us."

"What type of information?"

"We want Big Eddy. Willie is bad news, but he's small potatoes. If Willie can provide us with solid, significant damaging information against Big Eddy, then we'll settle for a misdemeanor charge."

"Detective, you've said Big Eddy is a menace to society. If my client agrees to such a deal, what assurance do we have that he'll receive adequate protection?"

"Ms. Chow, if your client can deliver we'll set him up in our witness protection program."

"Detective, do you expect my client to testify against Big Eddy?"

"Possibly, but first, we require your client's complete statement on tape and second, we require your client agree to testify if necessary."

"Who decides whether my client's information is relevant?"

"We do, right here…right now."

"Detective Jones, if Mr. Taylor's story can't help you, then my client is exposed!"

"Ms. Chow, you don't have to take the deal. As we told Mr. Taylor earlier, he's not the only chicken in our pot."

"I'll need a few minutes alone with my client."

After a few minutes of furious writing she lays out Willie's bleak legal position. Willie had few options. Twenty minutes later the detectives were invited back in.

"I've advised Mr. Taylor to provide a 'fictional' account, a 'testing the waters' for now. It just so happens that William has endeavored to become a masterful storyteller; you are invited to listen closely.

The detectives exchanged glances, then nodded their approval. Willie nervously took another drag. He was noticeably withdrawn as he turned to face the detectives.

"Once there was a small time drug dealer named 'Willie'. Not me mind you, but another guy with the same name. He grew up in Oakland and had many opportunities but, for whatever reason, he got caught up in drugs you see. He had a good mother and brothers and sisters, but I guess he just didn't care to do right. Anyhow, he's doing his thing one day and there's this Italian guy, see, who asks if he wants to make some quick dough. Well, who doesn't? Now, this Italian guy has a serious 'rep' you understand, and he's known to pack some heat. You really don't want to mess with this guy. Now, you got to know, there's legit 'reps' and there's bogus 'reps'. This guy's was legit. Ya know what I'm sayin'?"

The detectives nodded.

"Well, this heavy dude pulls Willie's coattail and asks if he's willing to take a walk with him to a bar located down in the seedier part of town. He has to meet a 'Brother' down there on some business, ya know what I'm sayin'?; so, it's a good idea to walk into the place with a 'Brother' himself. Walking in alone or with his usual Italian 'associates' might make folks a little jumpy. Ya know? So Willie asks, 'What's in it for me?' and he's told that he can make a fast fifty bucks just for tagging along. That's it. 'Nutin' else. Just tag along. Needless to say, this sounds really good to my man Willie! Where else can you make that type of money just for walking into a barroom? Ya know what I'm sayin'?"

Both detectives nodded in agreement again.

"So anyway, I told the man that I was down for it see!"

"William!" Ms. Chow cautioned even as she touched his hand.

Willie looked up at her with eyebrows raised.

"Yeah. What?"

"You just said, 'I told the man.' Don't you mean that Willie told the man?"

"Oh yeah, that's right. Sorry." Willie crouched down in his seat like a scolded child.

"So, Willie was in. A quick fifty smack-a-roos sounded 'sweet'! So, they hopped in the Italian dude's Jag and slid. They arrive at that bar and bounced on in. They got there maybe twenty or so minutes early. You see, the Italian dude being careful and wants to avoid any unfortunate surprises. Naturally, he's got to be real careful in his line of work."

"And what exactly is his line of work, Willie?" Detective White questioned.

"Why, he's a businessman of course. He makes things happen. Ya know what I'm sayin'?"

"Well, twenty minutes pass and in comes the 'Brothers' that he's doing business with and everything is looking pretty cool. There's two of them, ya see, and right away they spot Willie. They move over to his and the Italian dudes' table."

"I'm familiar with both of them and I tell the Italian guy that these are the fellas he's looking for. The Italian has heard of them but has never laid eyes on them before that night. He wants to be sure that the people who showed up are exactly who they say they are; you understand–right? The Italian then thanks me and asks me to sit a couple of tables over but not to leave. So, I do what I'm told. Simple as that."

"William!" Ms. Chow cautions again.

"I mean, um… Willie did what he was told. The Italian and the 'Brothers' talk for about fifteen minutes or so. Then everyone gets up. The Italian comes over to me to ask if I want to make another quick fifty and I say "sure"!"

Ms. Chow was about to say something again but instead, just shook her head and sighed deeply to herself.

"So, he slides me, I mean Willie, the first fifty. Now all I have to do, I mean, Willie has to do, is take the ride with him to the exchange spot. We hops back into the Jag and head-off to the place, a ten to fifteen-minute drive away. We got there first, parked and waited. The two 'Brothers' pulled up a couple of minutes later. It's like out in a field of trees and a few abandoned cars, ya know, 'hoopties'. Now the Italian asks me to stand next to him. That's all! The Italian brings out this suitcase see. The other two guys open their trunk and bring out a suitcase too!"

Willie grabbed another cigarette and lit it from the one he had just finished.

"The Italian takes off his suit jacket and turns around to show them that he's not packin'. I do the same. The two 'Brothers' follow suit while standing next to their ride. Then the Italian pops opens his suitcase showing packages of white powdery stuff! The fellas open up their suitcase filled with cash. When we all start walking towards each other with our 'stuff' all hell breaks loose! This other car busts into the clearing and these dudes start firing at us! We jump back behind the Jag and the Italian grabs some serious heavy-duty firepower! I saw shots coming from the hoopties too! Damn! It was crazy mad! Ya know what I'm saying?"

Willie was wide-eyed with obvious excitement as he continued his story.

"You see, the Italian's associates were in those hoopties, man, packing some heavy heat too! Pretty soon the whole thing is over. The two 'Brothers' are hit and their partners' ride is loaded with holes! And the dudes in that other car are dead as doorknobs. Now, these two 'Brothers' get up with their hands waving all crazy. Man were they scared. They're immediately surrounded! The Italian's boys grab the loot, which as it turns out ain't nothin' but stacks of ones tied together with a 'C' note on top of each one. The Italians grab shovels out of their ride and hand them to the two 'Brothers', ordering them to 'Start diggin', fellas". Man was I scared!"

Willie looked as though he was reliving the scene! He definitely had everyone's undivided attention.

"The big guy pulls another fifty out of his pocket, flashing it in front of me. I reach to take it, but he wouldn't let go. He says very slowly while holding onto that fifty, 'Willie, never, ever, mention this night to anyone. Not your sister, not your brother, not even your mother. Nobody! If I ever hear so much as a peep about this, I'll kill you with my own two hands! The only reason I don't kill you right now, is because you did your job like I asked you to and besides that, there are plenty of witnesses who saw you with me tonight. You know I'm a man of my word, Willie. So, believe me, don't ever cross me! You got that?'"

"I say 'I understand.' He keeps holding the fifty while looking me straight in the eyes. Finally, when he's satisfied that I ain't gonna to say 'nutin' to nobody he hands me the fifty. Then he rubs my head, as if to say 'good boy' or something!"

The detectives contemplated Willie's story. Jones and White silently stared at each other. They waited to see if Willie was going to continue. But, Willie remained silent too; he just lit up another smoke.

Detective Jones leaned over, put his elbows on the table and asked Willie what happened to the two guys who were handed the shovels. Willie took a long drag on his cigarette, and then slumped down a little farther in his chair.

"They dug a big hole and dragged their buddies' bodies from the car and dumped them into it. Man, them boys were scared and so was I, to tell you the truth. Then, they were ordered to get into the hole with the other bodies! God, they started crying and pleading and begging.... it was too much! They insisted that they had just been following orders... but it was already too late. The Italian shot them both himself. He screwed on a silencer and ... pop...pop! It was done! The Italian had some of his boys start to cover up the hole and then told me that I should pitch in too. So, I grabbed a shovel and got to work."

"His other boys towed that shot-up car away. I don't know where they took it. Later on that evening, the Italian told me that he could use my services again, from time to time, if I needed some more scratch. I said 'Sure, I could use the dough.' And shortly after that, I was making some fairly decent paper."

"Willie, who were those guys that got killed?" Detective White asked.

"Detectives," Ms. Chow interrupted, "if you recall, my client has just told you a 'fictional story'. Tell us, how did you like it? Do you think my client has any talent for storytelling?"

"He does indeed, Ms. Chow! If we had some evidence that a story of such magnitude was actually true, I'd say your Mr. Taylor could be drinking a cold one at some nice quiet bar in some small town very far away from here by this time next year."

Detective Jones asked, "Willie, do you have any way of substantiating your story?"

"Yeah. Sure. I know where the bodies are!"

"Gentlemen, my client is finished talking for today. I'll need to meet with your superiors soon. But for now, I'd like to finish speaking with my client alone."

Both detectives exited the room. The adrenaline was surging through their veins. This could hopefully give them some long awaited leverage in the Dillard case.

Ms. Chow stood by the window.

"William, what do you want out of life?"

"Ms. Chow, I don't want to spend the rest of my life in prison. That's one thing I know for sure."

"I can understand that, William."

"What else can I say?"

"Let me tell you something, William. Your only chance to avoid prison is for your story to pan out by providing supporting evidence. However, I can't see anyone corroborating your story. You will be standing alone and your history with the law is not sterling. Any prosecutor will have a field day picking your reputation apart. You have a chance in the witness protection program. But, if your information is, for whatever reason, found to be inadequate, your life in the witness protection program would be on very shaky ground."

"What do you mean, Ms. Chow?"

"You'd still be in grave danger—especially after having brought accusations of murder against Big Eddy. The police run this program and I can only wonder how sincere they really are about living up to their end of the bargain. All I'm saying is your life, I believe, will still be in constant and grave danger."

"I know, Ms. Chow, believe me, I know. I've seen that Italian up front and personal. But I still can't see spending the rest of my life in prison, not if I have a choice, that is."

—-

Jones and White were instructed to meet their boss back in his office in fifteen minutes.

"We might have something big if Willie's story checks out!" Jones reported.

"What did he say?"

Clarence spelled out the details to his boss.

Brick whistled. "If Willie is telling the truth, he can just about write his own ticket. We don't want Ms. Chow to know that right now. I do see a huge potential problem we're facing!" Brick suggested.

"What's that?"

"Ms. Chow is a member of Berkland Law and she now knows we're interested in Big Eddy. And, because the Italian is also a client of their firm, there's every reason to believe that she'll tell Pews and Silverstein. She'll tend to protect her client first; so, I think she might remain quiet for right now. She's a pro. If she informs the firm, they'll alert Big Eddy. He'll in turn put out a hit on Willie or flee the city. I don't really see Big Eddy skipping town, but it's a possibility, if things get too hot!"

"Okay. Let's start discussing how we're going to put more pressure on Big Eddy to talk about his relationship with Radcliffe Dillard. Because, that's what this is all about, isn't it? We need to have a plan."

"Hey, don't forget those three photographs to the witch lady in LA. Have you guys picked your five yet?"

"Yeah, Brick. I'll go get them," Jones replied.

Ms. Chow recognized that Big Eddy was the ultimate target of the police's investigation and that he was a Berkland Law client. He was normally represented by one of the principals.

Connie reviewed the facts of the case and came to one viable conclusion. She would remain silent. Her primary duty is to legally defend her charge, Willie Taylor, to the best of her ability. The more secrecy and time she could procure for him the better.

Jones returned to Kasolkasky's office with the pictures. One was a picture of just the victim's face with the severed head of the duck protruding from her mouth, giving the picture a surreal appearance. In the remaining photos, duck feathers covered her entire body making every scene a gruesome one.

The pictures selected were only of the body and not of the surrounding area. The police wanted as little information included in those photographs as possible. They didn't know what 'reading a photograph' meant, but they were sure of one thing, they weren't going to give the psychic lady anything extra.

Kasolkasky approved three of the five photographs to be sent to Chief Ness.

Chapter 12

At four o'clock, Detective Lincoln was to meet with, Jacque Vestable, one of two campus employees known to be from voodoo-friendly cultures. Born in Haiti, Jacque was raised in the States from the age of twelve. He had lived with his aunt and uncle in South Florida. The other co-worker with a similar background was Pierre Reston. Pierre worked as a cook and both men had been employed at the school for over eight years. The police had noticed a slight inconsistency in the stories regarding their whereabouts on that evening.

The two men were unlikely suspects because it was believed the killer was left-handed. Both of them were right-handed. One problem was they were each other's alibi. While both Pierre and Jacque had been reported seen at the club that night, Pierre was seen much earlier in the evening.

Lincoln headed to police headquarters to meet Kasolkasky.

"Let me tell you what's been happening, Bill," Kasolkasky said.

Bill nodded and took a seat.

"A psychic named Jezebel Balboa has offered her services to us. We sent her three photographs yesterday. So, she'll 'read' them today. Do you know anything about this woman, Bill?"

"No."

"We think she's a total flake. Anyway, the Los Angeles department is supervising this 'reading' session with Ms. Balboa. You got any questions, Bill?"

"What photos were sent to her?"

Detective White handed photocopies to Detective Lincoln.

"We met with Willie Taylor and his attorney yesterday. And guess what? Finally, it looks like we just might be able to put some real pressure on Big Eddy!"

"Oh?" the Detective answered. "What's going on?"

"Well, Willie told his story to White and Jones and it's a whopper! He witnessed Big Eddy wack a couple of dealers. He and Big Eddy's boys filled in the gravesite. They buried four dead bodies!"

"Whoa! I'd say that's pretty significant," Bill remarked. "Any corroborating evidence or witnesses?"

"Not yet."

"So, who is Willie's attorney?"

"Connie Chow."

Bill knew Connie did quality work. He was also beginning to believe in Willie.

"When will you meet with Ms. Chow?"

"Hopefully, some time today. The boys and I held a briefing last night."

"And...?"

"First, ...verify the incident actually occurred! If not, we're back to square one. If the story is true, we'll meet with the Chief and the Mayor. If we're gonna bring Big Eddy in it will mean applying some kinda pressure, but what kind? If somebody hauls me into a police station and accuses me of murder, you can bet I'm going to put up a fight!"

"I agree. This is a delicate situation."

"The only way for this to work is to come down on Big Eddy with 'all four feet'. If the evidence exists, we'll nail the guy! We'll 'forget' the most serious charges, provided he's got information about Radcliffe's activities that could break open the Dillard murder case. What do you think, Bill?"

Detective Lincoln rubbed his chin. This was one ugly situation. There was no clear way to go.

"Let me get this straight, you're saying, charge Big Eddy with first-degree murder and then offer to reduce the charges if he tells you something significant about Radcliffe Dillard. So, kill a few folks and get away with it if you have some useful information in another case. That is what you're saying, right?"

"We're open to suggestions, Bill. Any ideas?"

"No, not off the top of my head. Let me give it some thought."

Lincoln despised this facet of police work. The public thought everything was black and white, when it wasn't—not even close.

The telephone rang. Kasolkasky was being summoned. Their meeting was over.

––-

Detective Lincoln arrived at the after-hours joint where Jacque Vestable claimed to have been when the murder occurred. It was four P.M. "Good afternoon, Mr. Vestable, I'm Detective Lincoln."

"What can I do for you?"

"Well Mr. Vestable, what did you tell the police regarding your whereabouts the evening of Hillary Dillard's death?"

"I got off work at ten o'clock, my normal quitting time. Pierre and I were scheduled to meet at the club around 3A.M. Well, I went home to get a nap first; I'm not as young as I used to be. I set my alarm for 2 A.M., took a shower and then came here. I think I got here around three-fifteen. By that time this place was packed. I looked for Pierre at the bar but didn't see him. I was socializing with a few other friends. I didn't run into Pierre 'till around three forty-five. Turns out he was up front by the band. I was going to check the band area but I started talking. We've been coming down here for years so this was no special night."

"According to the police report, Pierre claimed he didn't see you until around four-fifteen. The other people who talked with you don't remember the specific time, but it seems some of them thought it might've been a little later than you've suggested."

"True, I didn't check my watch, but according to my recollections, it had to be around that time. That's all I know."

"I'm told the bartender doesn't remember seeing you 'till around four."

"That could be. I was talking with several different people. I don't think I bought a drink for myself until around four. Other people were buying me beers."

"Mr. Vestable, what do you know about voodoo?"

"I know it's a religion. They say some people still practice it in countries like Haiti."

"Do you practice it yourself?"

"No, I'm a Catholic." Detective Lincoln wondered what that meant. Was he a practicing Catholic?

"Do you know anyone who practices voodoo?"

"No, at least not in this country. Is that what you mean?"

"You're saying you don't know anyone who practices voodoo in this country?"

"Yes, that's what I'm saying."

"Who do you know that practices voodoo?" Detective Lincoln was interested and listened very carefully to him.

"I know some elders back in Haiti who I believe still practice the religion. I haven't seen them in over twenty years though. I don't get back much; it's too expensive."

"Have you ever been in trouble with the law, Mr. Vestable?"

"No, sir. I haven't."

"When was the last time you visited Haiti, Mr. Vestable?"

"I believe it was five years ago."

"I thought you just said you haven't seen your relatives in twenty years."

"I did."

"But you just said you were in Haiti five years ago."

"Yes, but I didn't see those people who may still practice voodoo. They live in the extreme rural areas. I don't get back there much."

He found Jacque's answer believable because he himself had traveled to various islands; depending on your time and energy level, you might not ever make it past the beach areas.

"Have you ever heard of any voodoo ceremonies being held around here in California?"

"I'm sorry, but I haven't."

"How well do you know Pierre Reston? Do you go out together much?"

"He's a good friend. Maybe twice a month we'll get together for a drink."

"Where did you first meet Pierre?"

"I met him on the campus. When I got the job I heard a guy from Haiti worked there as a cook. I went over to meet him and we've been friends ever since."

Lincoln was recording his answers but not quite sure where to go next.

"Are you married, Mr. Vestable?"

"No. I'm divorced."

"How long have you been divorced?"

"Almost five years now."

"Are you still on friendly terms with your ex-wife?"

"Yeah, sort of. We talk occasionally. We have two kids, a boy and a girl. They're grown now, but they're still our kids. There are still things that you do as a family."

"I understand; I'm there myself. Tell me, Mr. Vestable, did you know Hillary Dillard?"

"No, sir."

"I'd like to get the telephone number of your ex-wife, if you don't mind."

"Sure. No problem."

"Who initiated the invitation that night? Did you call Pierre to go out for a drink or did he call you?"

"I really don't know. It goes back and forth. I don't remember now."

"Well, that's it. I don't need to ask you anything else. Thank you for your time."

Lincoln walked back to his car. The interview confirmed the police report; he hadn't noticed any obvious discrepancies. He was scheduled to meet with Pierre Reston tomorrow. As he was getting into his car his pager went off. It was from police headquarters. He dialed the number and was rerouted to Brick Kasolkasky's car phone. He heard Kasolkasky's voice.

"Bill, where are you?"

"I'm in downtown Oakland. I just finished my interview with Jacque Vestable at the after-hours club."

"Come over here. We're in the field that Willie Taylor told us about. We just dug up four bodies right where Willie said they'd be!"

"I'll be there in ten minutes."

He drove to the location where police cars, with blinking lights, had completely cordoned off the entire area. Kasolkasky had left word to let Detective Lincoln through. Bill noticed Brick standing next to Willie Taylor's attorney, Connie Chow. There was someone in Brick's car with an identity mask on. Kasolkasky confirmed it was Willie Taylor.

Willie was brought along to direct them to the field. After he identified the area, he was placed in the police car and given a protective identity mask. The coroner's team was placing decomposed remains into body bags. The incident had taken place a year earlier. Lincoln noticed the media's absence. Only Kasolkasky's department and the Coroner's office were there.

Ms. Chow had insisted that 'William' be placed into protective custody immediately. Willie now had a whole new set of circumstances. Willie was trading in one form of prison for another.

"Let's get Willie out of here," Kasolkasky instructed.

Two officers drove Willie away as the investigation started a new direction. Bill wasn't sure where this lead was headed, but his gut told him they were barking up the wrong tree. There was no doubt that Rad Dillard was involved in some shady dealings, but Rad loved his sister. Of course, he might have owed a great deal of money to someone and her death could have been a form of payback. But, so far, nothing was in the rumor mill.

About three hours later, Lincoln received another call from Kasolkasky. A judge had just issued a warrant allowing the police to search Big Eddy's residence for a particular type of gun. The initial ballistic report indicated that the bullets recovered from the crime scene were from the same type of Italian gun that Big Eddy was known to carry. Kasolkasky asked if Bill was interested in participating in the search but Lincoln declined.

At eleven twenty-two that evening, officers and detectives knocked on the door of Eddy Tevelle's house. They were there to conduct the search for one Italian Luger. To prevent their ripping the house apart Big Eddy showed them where the weapon was kept. The police confiscated the gun. Big Eddy was taken into custody charged with possessing a weapon allegedly used in the commission of a crime. It was late, so Big Eddy was forced to spend the night in jail. He would not get a chance to talk to his lawyers until morning.

And they will deceive every one his neighbor, and will not speak the truth:
they have taught their tongue to speak lies, and weary themselves to
commit iniquity.

THE OLD TESTAMENT - JEREMIAH   9:5

Chapter 13

The Chief and Detective Kasolkasky were already sitting in the
Mayor's office when his honor arrived at 5:59 A.M. Kasolkasky
spoke first.

"Gentlemen, I must emphasize the necessity of deciding our next
plan. We don't have the luxury of waiting!"

The Mayor raised his hand and interrupted.

"Let me see, Detective Kasolkasky, if I understand the situation.
Your men, on a tip from a man who is now in our witness protection
program, dug up the bodies of four suspected drug dealers yesterday.
Each body is currently registered under John Doe toe tags. Their
murders happened approximately one year ago. The person who
masterminded this massacre is a resident of our city; and, the police
also believe that this same individual sold drugs to, or with, Radcliffe
Dillard. This alleged drug dealer, alias 'Big Eddy', might serve as
the catalyst that results in our eventual connection between himself
and Mr. Dillard. This person, a Mafia type, will not cooperate unless
extreme pressure is brought to bear."

Everyone continued listening as the Mayor continued…

"Right now everything hinges on whether the bullets dug out of
the victims match the ballistics tests performed on the gun found

in the possession of this Big Eddy. If there's a match we've got our pressure. If we offer him a deal like…he gives us certain information concerning Radcliffe Dillard, we'll help him by claiming there may not be enough evidence to charge him with the murders. The political fallout, if the media gets wind of the idea– that we're willing to leverage the gangland killing of four men in the community for information in the Hillary Dillard murder case, would be tremendous! Do I understand the situation?" the Mayor asked.

"Precisely," answered Chief Ness.

The Mayor leaned back in his chair, folding his arms. It wasn't playing with fire–it was like juggling nuclear bombs. He could see the advantages, but he couldn't ignore the magnitude of the disadvantages.

"Who's Big Eddy's lawyer?" the Mayor asked.

"The seniors at 'Berkland Law'. You know Pews and Silverstein, they're publicity hounds. The media loves those guys!"

"And that's the last thing they'll want!" the Mayor insisted.

"What do you mean?" Kasolkasky asked.

"Would you want to be defending an Italian accused of killing four blacks in Oakland? Their lawyers will be in our corner, regarding publicity."

Silence blanketed the room. The Chief and Brick agreed with the Mayor on that point.

"And gentlemen, before we go any farther, this meeting never happened."

"We understand. "

"Mayor, what about the ramifications, of letting the killer of four men make a deal?"

The Mayor thought hard. There was little room for error.

"If there is sufficient evidence he must be charged. If not he can't be charged. I don't care who it is. We treat all citizens the same."

Brick was catching on. This bull session with the Chief and the Mayor was to weigh the tough questions.

"Mayor, four black men were murdered in cold blood and all the evidence points to one white man, whose gun may have been the one used in this mob style killing. Are we not to have some semblance of justice?" the Chief asked.

"Yes, sir, if that's the gun. Was the gun in the possession of the accused at the time of the killing?!" queried the Mayor.

The Mayor's question rang hollow signaling a political death rattle. If he used this tactic, he might as well pack his bags now and leave Oakland.

"Damn. This one is tight. I don't like it," the Mayor grumbled. He stood up and started pacing the floor. "Any ideas, gentlemen?"

"The gun may have been removed briefly from his possession, without his knowledge, in order to frame him?" Kasolkasky offered.

The Mayor glanced at Brick. That answer didn't feel right either.

"Have they done the ballistics test yet?" the Mayor asked.

"Not yet," the Chief answered.

"Ron, we need Bob Mackey here. There are questions here that only the District Attorney can answer."

The Mayor nodded. "I know. I called Bob last night. He'll be here at 6:30 AM. I wanted to spend a half-hour with the two of you first."

"Jim, just where are you going with this?" the Chief asked. This is the second time he used the Mayor's first name–further confirmation that this meeting 'never happened'.

"I want significant progress in this Dillard case and so far we're getting nowhere."

"What about this new situation? We've got four men in a grave. We also have a guy in the witness protection program that witnessed how they got there. This case looks pretty good so far."

"You're absolutely right; it's a good case. But I really don't care a rat's ass about solving the murder of four drug dealers, especially when compared to solving the Dillard case. I say good riddance! If we can get valuable mileage out of this multiple murder thing, great. But, we're going to take our time and evaluate it very carefully."

"Jim, obviously we need to keep this thing tight. I will not put the police in the position of appearing to cover up something as heinous as a multiple killing."

There was a knock and the Mayor answered it. Bob Mackey, the District Attorney, walked in and shook everyone's hand.

"First, Bob, I want you to know this meeting is strictly off the record. Feel free to leave if you're uncomfortable. I hope you'll decide to stay and help," the Mayor said. "I'd feel much better if we all called each other by our first names."

Everyone agreed to that suggestion. Bob surveyed the room. He was comfortable.

The Mayor turned to face Kasolkasky. "Brick, this was your bust. Update Bob."

Brick filled Bob in.

Bob knew the Mayor was looking for political shelter and, if necessary, the Mayor would sacrifice everyone there.

"When will the ballistics test be done?"

"Probably within the week. You know we can't change the schedule unless a President dies."

"Have there been any inquiries from the families of the victims?"

"No. There have been no official reports filed."

"Who else knows about the recovery of those bodies yesterday?"

"Only my men."

"Where's Big Eddy?"

"In jail. We picked him up last night."

"Then, what is your legal question?"

"Okay, now suppose there is a chance to get vital information on Radcliffe Dillard's business dealings through Big Eddy. Let's assume that we have Eddy in a tight enough spot to force him to talk. We'll still need to throw him a bone to get him to talk. Remember, this guy has 'Mafia' written all over him. He won't be easily intimidated."

"What do you suggest we offer him?"

"His freedom?"

Bob was an elected official himself, so he realized any exposure from this would be impossible to fight. Bob could be a risk taker, but it had to be carefully calculated risk.

"Gentlemen, you're dealing strictly in a hypothetical world. My advice for now is to simply follow the letter of the law!"

"What does that mean? The law can get very vague at times." Kasolkasky stated.

"That's exactly my point. Follow the law. Do not circumvent established protocol. When there is room to maneuver–do it, but don't cut any corners. Play the cards you are dealt, but, don't try to stack the deck."

"Thanks, Bob," declared the Mayor. "That's sound advice."

The Mayor began pacing again. His instincts told him to play this thing close to the edge, to take the risk, but Bob's assessment put everything in better focus.

"Gentlemen, I thank you for coming. Our mission is clear. We follow procedure. We've got four murders to solve; and, we have a suspect and a witness. Now, there's no legal mandate to disclose our information to the press. Let's go about our normal business and try to solve this case."

"Mayor, there's another issue," the Chief stated.

"Ron, is it an issue that's appropriate for everyone in this room to hear?"

"Yes," the Chief replied.

"Okay. Let's hear it then."

"Well, last night, right after I called you, I received a phone call from Marshall Tucker, the commander of the Los Angeles district where Ms. Jezebel Balboa resides. He informed me of receiving a phone call from his detective, the one who had just talked with Ms. Balboa. She had reviewed the photographs we sent and she was disturbed. She studied them alone for roughly fifteen minutes before asking to be taken home. Later that night she had a vision so upsetting that it woke her. She called Tucker's officer."

There was a slight pause. The Mayor asked, "And what did Ms. Balboa say, Ron?"

"Ms. Balboa insisted she saw the mark of Damballa on the victim's back, in her vision."

There was uneasy silence. The DA found the conversation absolutely fascinating after he had finally figured out who Ms. Balboa was.

The Mayor spoke first, "And who or what is Damballa, Chief?"

"That's the voodoo god."

"And what is the god's mark?"

"Supposedly it's the first letter of his name accented when written by a dot in the middle."

There was a pause from the Mayor; he waited before asking the next question, one that was painfully obvious.

"Ron, is the voodoo god's mark on her back?" the Mayor finally asked.

All eyes were glued on the Chief.

"Yes."

There was silence. Their whole focus had shifted in seconds. Would they start chasing ghosts and demons now? The Chief's greatest worry was now before them. The Mayor was trying to figure out how to spin it. This latest turn of events would make the whole organization a farce; and he, a man who had built his reputation on seriousness, had no intention of letting that happen.

Ms. Balboa had already contacted the media in Los Angeles. So, it wouldn't be long before this story clawed its way north.

For now, the Mayor had his political cover. The Mayor had already stated publicly that he'd go down any avenue, within reason, to solve this case. However, he never in his wildest dreams believed they'd be facing this!

The Mayor immediately planned to review Ms. Balboa's file. He didn't know what Ms. Balboa's game was, but, he was a patient man. His patience and intellect had always served him well. He would play the game, but he'd keep a close eye on her. He had an image to maintain and being associated with some 'black magic' woman in such a high-profile case was not the image he wanted to project. He had squashed others before her and now he was making his plans to make sure that demons and dreams would have no foothold. Not in his town.

Chapter-14

After Detective Lincoln's meeting with Jacque Vestable, he drove to Jacque's ex-wife's apartment to ask her questions before Jacque might decide to call her. If Jacque were telling the truth, he probably wouldn't feel the need to call, but if not....

Mrs. Vestable confirmed almost everything her ex-husband had told him. As he was about to leave, he thought of one more question, "By the way, what religion is Jacque?"

She hesitated for a second before finally answering, "I guess I'd call him a non-believing Catholic. I always had to drag him and the kids to church but is that so unusual?"

Bill checked his watch; in forty-five minutes the press conference would begin. He hustled back to headquarters. The LA reporters, having uncovered the psychic's story, were anxious to hear whatever Ms. Balboa might have to say. The Mayor had hoped for more time to evaluate the situation; but he also couldn't afford to have Oakland get wind of this story through the Los Angeles news media first. He had to attempt to maintain his control.

"Hello, Clarence, what's the story on Ms. Balboa? Do you think she's for real?"

"I don't know, Bill. If you look through her file, you certainly won't come away convinced of that."

"What's the status of the Big Eddy case?"

"He's already contacted his lawyers, so you can expect him to be back out on the streets any time now. And, I'm sure we'll be talking with his attorneys soon enough."

"And how's Willie Taylor doing these days?"

"I'm not sure. You do know he's been placed in the witness protection program and that contact with him is impossible, especially at my level?"

"Right. Hey, does Willie have any family here?" the Detective asked curiously.

"He's got a daughter and a son. I'm fairly sure they both live here in Oakland. From what I understand, he hasn't had much contact with his son, but he does spend time with his daughter. The son, unfortunately, has followed in the father's footsteps. 'The sins of the father...'"

Clarence and Bill entered the conference room. Ten people were already there with more coming through the door. A few moments later the Mayor came striding onto the platform. Every item of clothing he was wearing was perfectly coordinated. He made a short statement before opening the press conference to questions.

"Mr. Mayor, what is the next step? Will you bring Ms. Balboa here to view the crime scene?"

"Good question. At this time the next step is for the Oakland Police to determine. Only they have the authority to properly decide the merits of Ms. Balboa's information. I'll await the Chief of Police's decision."

"Mr. Mayor, do you believe in psychics?"

"I don't know. I've never had occasion to study the matter. I do know that sometimes I don't truly understand this world as well as I'd like to believe I do," the Mayor smiled. "Frankly, I've never met a real psychic. So, I have no basis to give an informed opinion. Are there any other questions? Yes..."

"Mr. Mayor, what would you say is the current status of the Dillard case and do you feel you've made any significant progress to date?"

"We're making progress but sometimes it's difficult to measure. There really haven't been any 'breaks' in this case. But rest assured we will bring the perpetrator of this ghastly deed to justice. Our task force is in place and we are pursuing several promising leads. Unfortunately, I am not at liberty to disclose to you what they are at this time. I can say this…as evidenced by the subject matter of this press conference, we will leave no stone unturned. Yes, right over here."

"Mr. Mayor, when do you expect the police chief to give you an answer concerning Ms. Balboa?"

The Mayor didn't like the tone of his question. He made a mental note not to call on this guy again for a while.

"Actually, I suspect the police chief will make his recommendations soon. I would expect an answer probably within the next few days. Next question, please. Yes…"

"Thank you, Mr. Mayor. Mayor, it's been over three months since the murder. How long do you expect to keep the case open?"

"We'll keep working until every possible lead has been exhausted. As new information comes in, we will aggressively investigate it. Thank you. That has to be the last question for today. I'm scheduled for another meeting in five minutes. Thank you all for coming out."

When Detective Lincoln arrived home, he found a call from Monique Dillard, which he returned immediately. After the second ring he heard her voice.

"Bill, the reason I called was to ask if you'd consider escorting me to my brother's upcoming campaign cocktail party next Saturday. It's a fundraiser and should be a lot of fun. What do you think?; are you available?"

He decided that this was potential casework because he could obtain useful background information just by being there.

"I'm available. What's the dress code?"

"Most of the men will be in a suit and tie."

"I can do that."

"Well, let me go. I'll plan to pick you up next Saturday at five since the affair is on your side of the Bay. Is that okay?"

"That's fine. I'll see you then."

"Goodbye, Bill."

Back at police headquarters, Brick Kasolkasky was meeting with Chief Ness. The Chief was against cooperating with Ms. Balboa and he intended his position to be leaked to the press.

"Chief, I'm not saying she isn't a fake, but she did know classified information. And, when the press finds out, they'll be on her side. It's been three months and we still haven't had many decent leads. Yes, we've got an opening with Big Eddy, but that won't be anybody's cake-walk."

"Brick, you're right. But remember there's the other side of this equation. I'm taking a conservative stand; I want the Mayor to overrule me. I'm going to stay on the right side of police procedure. I want more information from Ms. Balboa before I agree to fly her here. Most people will say she made an educated guess. She's familiar with the voodoo culture so how difficult was it to say that the voodoo god's mark would be found on the victim's back?"

"I'm just saying, the press is going to go against you on this one, Chief."

"You're right about that. However, the Mayor will be the one on the hook, not me. This lady is a fraud. I can sense it."

"So you're going to tell the Mayor it's the police's position to refuse to bring her to Oakland on the grounds that she has not demonstrated sufficient evidence of her psychic ability?"

"You got it. The Mayor will then have two options; he can side with the police or he can overrule–he'll overrule. If I were in his position, I'd overrule the police. We'll deal with this witch lady alright, but I want to deal with her on my terms. I want to be able to say later on that it was the Mayor who invited her here to view the crime scene."

—-

Matthew Silverstein arrived at police headquarters at nine that morning to see his client Eddy Tevelle, a.k.a. 'Big Eddy'. Two uniformed policemen escorted a handcuffed Edward 'Big Eddy' Tevelle into the room. Eddy sat silent until the officers left.

"Hello, Eddy."

"Matt."

"Why are you being held? What's the charge?"

"Apparently a couple of drug dealers got careless last year and ended up dead and then dumped in an open field. The cops just got a tip from an informant and dug the bodies up. They're now saying, I'm the shooter. Why they even got a search warrant and searched my house. They confiscated my gun. They hauled me in last night."

"Who tipped them off?" Matt asked.

"I don't know. No one's talking."

"Eddy, where were you the night of the murders?"

"Anywhere but there. Hell, I don't even know who was murdered. I don't know anything. They came banging on my door last night. Look, I actually went and got the gun for them. I didn't want them 'messin' up my house looking for it."

"Eddy, do you know anything about these murders?"

"Hell no! Absolutely, positively nothing!"

"Let's get you out of here."

"Matt."

"Yes?"

"I put the word out last night to find out who's trying to set me up! An hour before you got here, I got a message. I'm not telling you what that message was right now, but I want you to get a message to the cops when you get a chance. Tell them I want to talk to Willie Taylor."

"Who's Willie Taylor?"

"Don't worry about that; just be sure to relay my message when you get a chance."

Thy dead men shall live, together with my dead body shall they arise.
Awake and sing, ye that dwell in dust: for thy dew is as the dew of herbs,
and the earth shall cast out the dead.

THE OLD TESTAMENT - ISAIAH 26:19

Chapter 15

Later that afternoon Lincoln was scheduled to meet with Pierre
Reston, the other Haitian college employee and friend of Jacque
Vestable. On the night of Hillary Dillard's murder, Pierre and Jacque
had rendezvoused at an after-hours joint in downtown Oakland.
Evidently, Pierre's whereabouts had been accounted for on that
evening. Pierre, having that Saturday off, had agreed to work with
an off-campus caterer, preparing food for the annual 'Homecoming'
event. He had been cleaning up until almost three that morning
with the rest of the catering crew. Pierre was also seen later at the
bar around three-fifteen. He had gone directly to the bar to deliver
drink mixes to the bartender from catering that evening. The caterer
himself verified Pierre had left him at just a few minutes before three.
Obviously, Pierre was not a suspect.

Mr. Reston agreed to be interviewed at home. Upon arrival, the
Detective knocked twice, and was greeted by Pierre's wife. The
heady aroma of Caribbean cuisine saturated the house.

Pierre's story was the same as Jacque's, with one exception.
The one slight discrepancy was that his friend Jacque had reported
seeing him, Pierre, at the bar around three that morning; but, no one
had confirmed this. Pierre stated that he had not seen Jacque until

later that evening because he, Pierre, was up front listening to the band. He was under the impression Jacque would meet him up there. He remembered meeting Jacque around four that morning. He also remembered it was very crowded– mainly because the band was so good!

Detective Lincoln asked Pierre when it was that he had first met Jacque. Pierre recalled that it was on the college campus around the time Jacque first began working there. Once again, everything agreed with the reports the police had originally filed. Now the next question was about Jacque's religion. Pierre confessed that he wasn't sure but that he really didn't think Jacque was into religion. The Detective, satisfied, prepared to leave. As he was walking out he asked one last question. "Where would one go to witness a voodoo ceremony in the Bay Area?" Neither Pierre nor his wife had any idea.

—

Lincoln found his old informant Jacko sitting at the bar having a drink, watching a ball game. They took a table a few seats from the bar.

"What's this about?" Jacko asked.

"Just a few minor details, nothing earth-shaking. Tell me, where does one go to witness a voodoo ceremony in Oakland?"

Jacko smiled. "Changing your religion?"

"No. I'm still working the Dillard case. I just visited with a couple of Haitian-Americans and neither could help me locate a voodoo ceremony. Can you help me out here?"

"If there's such a place, I can find out!"

"By the way, I'm sure you've heard by now that the police have picked up Big Eddy. What's the word on the street, Jacko?"

"Well, duh, the word is–the police have picked up Big Eddy. Yeah."

The Detective waited a moment. He wasn't in the mood to play games. "Anything else?"

"Well yeah, now that you mention it. There's a rumor going around that somebody ratted him out, so naturally soon there'll probably be one less rat in this world, if ya know what I mean."

"Have you heard if the police have anything solid on Big Eddy?"

"Well, it's been suggested that Big Eddy will probably be back out on the streets throwing a party by this weekend. Matter of fact, I think the invites already went out. Why, I was told I'd be getting mine soon. Yeah."

"I understand the police have Big Eddy's gun."

"Indeed, that's right."

"It was taken from Big Eddy's house. Ballistics tests are due soon. They're fairly certain this weapon was used in the murders last year."

"Yeah, so I hear. I sure hope the police get their man."

"Just what are you suggesting?"

"Let me put it this way, sometimes what you see on the outside is not what you find on the inside. Ya get my drift?"

"What are you saying, Jacko?"

"The word is Big Eddy has in his favor a peculiar little habit."

Jacko smiled at the Detective. He enjoyed his drink while waiting for the lawman to ask the question.

"Okay, what's this habit?"

"Well, and you didn't hear this from me, but–those in the know say Big Eddy has a habit of changing the gun barrel whenever he uses his gun on a particular nasty piece of business. It's his 'anti-ballistics test' syndrome. Big Eddy likes this particular gun, so he just changes the barrel. Yeah."

Lincoln could see the police were going nowhere again. If this latest revelation is actually true, Big Eddy would be home soon–relaxing.

"Have you heard anything regarding the Dillard case, Jacko?"

"Not a thing. All's quiet on the western front my man!"

"Thanks, Jacko."

As Lincoln headed home, he began thinking that they would not be able to put any pressure on Big Eddy because this guy was always one step ahead. Bill pulled into the driveway and as he was getting out he felt his beeper vibrate. It was Brick.

Brick informed Bill he was calling from the scene of a crime. It appeared to be another voodoo murder. The victim, a black male, was covered in chicken feathers and had the head of a chicken protruding from his mouth! Bill quickly wrote down the address and was on his way in a flash.

Detective Lincoln was driving his car for a full fifteen seconds before realizing he hadn't turned on the lights! It was late; the street was deserted as he sped along running red lights. He parked behind the flashing lights of a police car and walked over to the taped-off crime scene. He saw Kasolkasky from a distance and waved.

A young male's body lay on its back. The head of a chicken, still dripping blood, jutted horribly from his mouth while chicken feathers clung to the body like the matted hair on a towel after washing a furry dog. The scene looked surreal.

As the coroner's van was pulling up flashbulbs were going off documenting the grotesque scene. A dog walker had discovered the body. The dog had pulled his master in the direction of two dilapidated buildings and as they got closer, the man noticed something lying on the ground. The dog owner immediately called the police.

Lincoln observed the body plastered with chicken feathers. There was blood everywhere, especially in his groin area where a dirty cloth, something akin to a mid-sized towel, lay soaked. He looked at Kasolkasky. Kasolkasky stared dead into Bill's eyes and then made a gesture with his hand, taking it from one side of his neck to the other, as if cutting his own throat. Observing the very graphic motion, Lincoln understood immediately. The victim had been castrated. And, as if it couldn't get any worst, his eyes had also been gouged out! The deceased had died a very violent death!

The crime scene officers were everywhere now gathering their samples. So far, the evidence was scarce. There was no murder weapon and the bloody footsteps of the murderer had quickly vanished. There must've been a car close by allowing the killer to escape unnoticed. The buildings were abandoned. This was not a part of town that invited foot traffic, especially at this late hour. The body also lacked identification. The police had their work cut out for them. The media would gladly put a picture of the deceased on television.

Kasolkasky assigned four policemen to check with all the open establishments in the area and to search every nearby street. The media waited anxiously. They had had their second 'voodoo' murder in four months. The headlines would be screaming tomorrow!

The Mayor expected a report within the hour. Two sensational murders in his city in a relatively short space of time was no feather in his cap. He had run on a law and order platform but now the chickens may have started 'coming home to roost'!

The corpse was carefully placed in the coroner's truck. All potential evidence was placed in evidence bags. There wasn't much. Lincoln had just returned from walking the area when he saw Kasolkasky sitting in his car. Lincoln opened the other door and sat with him.

"What's going on here, Bill?"

Kasolkasky was in a dour mood and his voice was flat. "I don't know," Bill mused, "could be the beginning of a spree of serial murders with heavy ritualistic overtones. I've never seen this before. It damn sure ain't good."

"The media will go ballistic," Kasolkasky responded. "We'll have every two-bit reporter in the country here by tomorrow! We've got to do a thorough investigation. No screw-ups!"

The events outside reminded Bill of ants scurrying around trying to get ready for the winter. The pressure had just been wrenched up a notch and people's careers would be on the line. Bill looked up at the sky and thought, how appropriate, there was a full moon tonight!

Chapter 16

The press conference was scheduled for eight that morning. People were packed like sardines and the mob of television cameras appeared like a plague of locusts outside the building.

The whole room became quiet as Mayor Efferton walked purposefully across the stage. His face held a solemn expression; his body language was all business.

"Ladies and gentlemen, thank you for coming. I'm going to read a short statement and then open the floor to questions."

He took five minutes to deliver his speech.

"Mr. Mayor, do you think this could be the work of a serial killer?" a well-known reporter asked.

"At this point we definitely have to consider that possibility. However, let's remain cautious; we have nothing conclusive yet. It's far too early in the investigation to conclude that it's the same perpetrator. The 'M.O.' is so unique we feel justified in saying that there appears to be a connection. Next question, please."

"Mr. Mayor, do you personally believe in voodoo?"

The Mayor glared at the reporter, hesitating briefly before answering, "No, I do not. Next question, please."

"Mr. Mayor, have the authorities established any kind of connection between the two victims? Was there possibly a personal or business relationship or anything else the police have been able to uncover?"

"Thus far we have been unable to positively identify the second body; barring that, there is presently no reason to establish a relationship between our two victims. Next question, please."

"Mr. Mayor, should we expect more 'voodoo murders'? And if so, what are the police doing about that?"

"No, of course not. However, we hope the results of our investigation will allow us greater insights that will provide us with some logical answers. To date we have followed-up on several promising leads but none have provided anything substantial yet regarding the first murder. We have a talented team of investigators in whom I have the utmost confidence. Next question, please."

"Mr. Mayor, are you going to bring that lady, the one claiming special 'psychic' abilities, into this murder investigation? Tell us, what is her status? And, do you intend to use her?"

The Mayor was caught in a Catch-22. He needed information, but this inquiry would put him in a bind.

"I will let Chief Ness respond to that question. Will the police be using Ms. Balboa on this case, Chief?"

The Chief stepped up to the podium as the Mayor moved aside. He too was all business.

"Our current recommendation to the Mayor and the City Council is not to use Ms. Balboa. Ms. Balboa has contacted this department once. Although the information she provided was correct, it was so general in nature that it wasn't compelling enough to seriously consider using her now. We're asking her to provide us with other more specific information and we do intend to keep the lines of communication open."

"Chief Ness, exactly what information did she provide to your department that was correct?" a reporter from the East Coast asked quickly.

"Obviously, that information is confidential, sir."

"Chief Ness, does the Mayor agree with your decision?"

"That I can't answer. You'll need to ask the Mayor yourself."

"Chief Ness, in your opinion, is there a ritualistic serial killer loose in this city?"

"We don't have a definitive answer for you at this time. If it is determined that the two cases are related, we could certainly draw that conclusion, but if the second murder is a copycat, then we have an entirely different problem on our hands."

"When will you expect you'll know whether the two killings are related?"

"It depends on what comes back from the lab tests and what our detectives, who are analyzing the evidence, are able to uncover. Please, allow us time to do a thorough job!"

"How much time do you need, Chief? You've been working on the Dillard case for almost four months! What's the status of that case?"

The Chief felt like horsewhipping this guy! His comments, although true, did not do justice to the amount of effort both in hours and in resources expended. Then again, maybe the comment was a fair one simply because they were no farther along than they were four months ago!

"This press conference is about the murder that occurred last night and if possible, I'd like to confine our questions and answers to that singular event."

"But now really Chief, don't you think the two cases just might be related?" another reporter asked, his tone dripping with sarcasm.

"As I stated earlier, at present, we're not sure if it's the same killer or if it's a copycat. Our lab people have not filed a final report yet. It will be several days before the lab report is completed."

"Chief Ness, did you specifically say you would not be using Ms. Balboa?"

"I said the police made a recommendation to the Mayor and the City Council not to use her at this time. We work for the Mayor and the Council, and we have not officially heard anything to the contrary. So, I can only assume we will not be utilizing Ms. Balboa's services 'at this time!'"

The press sensed blood...if they felt there was an opening they would drive a Mack Truck through it.

"Mr. Mayor...Mr. Mayor, are you going to use Ms. Balboa's services on this case? Do you agree or disagree with the Chief's position?"

The Mayor stepped back to the podium. This was a volatile situation and it would be too easy for comments to be taken out of context.

"I'm recommending we do the same thing with Ms. Balboa regarding this latest murder victim. I'd like to send three photographs of this crime scene to her. She did say something correct about the Dillard crime scene. However, as the Chief suggested, it could be just a lucky guess."

The press conference continued for another forty minutes. It had all the elements the media loved and, if the Mayor wasn't feeling the pressure before, he was certainly feeling it now. Everyone was.

The initial coroner's report was issued at 5 P.M. to a very small group of people. Nothing new was learned. The cause of death was the loss of blood suffered as a result of the numerous stab wounds. There was one interesting finding though. The killer appeared to be right-handed! The police might indeed be dealing with a copycat. The Mayor ordered three photographs of the most recent homicide sent to Ms. Balboa in Los Angeles by 10AM the following morning. He wanted her to make some type of statement early in this case, before rumors started flying.

Once more Lincoln felt his buzzer tickling his side. He checked the number; it was Jacko. He left Bill the name of a woman who conducts voodoo rituals, a Madame Marie 'Mama' Francois. Jacko also suggested that guests should expect to donate at least fifty dollars to be invited to attend such a ceremony. Madame Francois lived somewhere in Oakland and had proved to be a difficult person to locate. Jacko did not have her address nor did he know how to find her. He was only given her name.

By the end of the day three photographs had been sent to Ms. Balboa by overnight courier. The identity of the victim had not been determined yet and the media was still trying to obtain a picture. No pictures had been offered to the news organizations; no missing persons reports had been filed and no phone calls had been received concerning a missing father, son or brother.

Chapter 17

A t 10:30 A.M., Kasolkasky called. "Bill, we've heard from Ms. Balboa this morning."

"Already? What did she have to say?"

"Well, our man down there handed the photographs to her. She held her hand about three or four inches away as if sensing for some kind of energy emissions. Then Ms. Balboa remarked on how awful this killing was. She said there is a wicked man out there.

"Our guy then asked, 'Do you know who did this?' and she shook her head and said, "No, I don't know who did it, but it's not voodoo! The mark of the voodoo god is not on this man. Somebody is trying to make believe this is voodoo!' He asked how she knew and she just said, 'I know!'"

There was silence again as both Lincoln and Kasolkasky were thinking.

"Brick, is the voodoo god's mark on this one?"

"No."

Lincoln's mind was racing. Was this lady for real? Did she really know or was she guessing?!

"So, Brick, what are the police going to do?"

"I don't know. I'm meeting with the Chief in an hour and I want you there, Bill."

"I'll be there."

Lincoln believed Kasolkasky was willing to talk to Ms. Balboa. It seemed she had one foot in the real world and the other in a place most Westerners couldn't fathom.

Bill arrived at police headquarters shortly before the scheduled meeting. The same small core group of individuals comprised the task force...the Chief, Kasolkasky, Detectives Jones and White, the Mayor and Bill Lincoln.

"Gentlemen," the Mayor addressed everyone, "please be seated. Chief Ness will bring us up to speed on Ms. Balboa."

The Chief recited the story while the Mayor listened intently.

When the Chief finished, the Mayor questioned whether any information should be released now. He didn't see much political mileage either way.

"Anybody care to make a suggestion?"

The Chief spoke first. "I recommend we don't do anything. Very little can be verified. She's correct regarding the voodoo god's mark and, I grant you, Ms. Balboa cannot be dismissed. What I'm saying is, we're far from having enough information to make a decision regarding Ms. Balboa."

"Thank you, Chief. Anyone else?"

Detective Lincoln decided to comment. "The fact that she made two correct calls does not mean she's for real, nor does it mean she's a fake. We can bring her here and still deal with her from a respectful distance. I don't think anyone is going to believe she's part of the team, just a tool to be used."

"Thank you, Bill."

"Gentlemen," the Mayor stated, "This is not an easy call. I must say usually I have an instinct about these things, but this one is baffling. I find this particular incident and the individual, Ms. Balboa, very difficult to read. However, my instincts tell me we have little choice.

"For if the media discovers Ms. Balboa has given two correct answers and we didn't use her, we'll be deemed incompetent. Right now she has provided one correct answer and the other is undetermined. We don't know for sure if the second murder is a copycat. We don't know who the victim is and we haven't given a photo of the deceased to the press."

"Mayor, the police are officially giving the press a picture of the victim in a few minutes and they'll be running the picture on the five o'clock news."

"Thank you.... I'm going to direct the Chief to bring Ms. Balboa to Oakland. I don't want this in the news, but I'm a realist. I know that's going to be difficult. Ms. Balboa is not media shy. Alright... this meeting is over and thanks for coming everyone."

Detective Lincoln started his search to find the infamous Marie 'Mama' Francois. Detectives Jones and White didn't know her so he figured the best thing to do was to find Jacko.

Later that evening, Lincoln left police headquarters and headed towards Jacko's three favorite watering holes. Jacko was not to be found this time, nor had anyone seen him. Bill sat at a bar contemplating his next move. He ordered a scotch on the rocks while watching the baseball game on the television in the bar room.

After the seventh inning, an idea came to him so he asked the bartender if anyone there had a foreign accent.

"What type of accent? Hell, this is Oakland, there are lots of foreigners here!"

"I'd prefer a good Haitian accent."

"I don't know. There's a Russian, an Italian and a Jew over there and I think those guys are African," he said pointing a finger.

Lincoln approached the Africans in the corner. They were students. He informed them he was a policeman and showed his badge, which aroused their curiosity. He explained his situation. Bill wanted one of the students to call a number and ask the person who picked up the phone if they knew Marie Francois. The students said they would help him.

They would pretend to be an uneducated person interested in attending a voodoo ceremony. They'd say a friend had told them about 'Mama' Francois, the one who could talk to the spirits. They wanted to meet her and attend her next ceremony. They got the picture. Bill retrieved the phone numbers of the two Haitian men who worked at the college that he had interviewed before and dialed Pierre Reston's number. He handed the phone to the student. It started ringing.

"Hello?"

"Hello, this is the Reston residence," a female voice answered.

"Yes, me trying to reach 'Mama' Francois," the student said in a very slow masked accent.

"Who?," the voice inquired.

"'Mama' Francois, the voodoo lady."

"I'm sorry, but you must have the wrong number."

"So sorry. Bye."

Lincoln looked at him but the student shook his head. There had been no name recognition.

Bill dialed the second number, the home of Jacque Vestable. The phone continued to ring. He then dialed the number for Jacque Vestable's ex-wife and while it was ringing he handed the phone back to the student. After the second ring, a female voice answered.

"Hello?"

"Hello, me trying to reach 'Mama' Francois."

"I'm sorry, who?"

"'Mama' Francois."

"I'm sorry, but you have the wrong number. Nobody by that name lives here."

The student handed the phone back to the Detective. Bill decided to call it a night. He couldn't locate Jacko and the phone calls were unfruitful. He thanked the two students and bought them a round of beers.

He went over to the bar to finish watching the game. Voodoo didn't seem to have much of a following in this town.

As he sat watching the baseball game, the show was interrupted for a news release. The police had released a picture of the victim of the second 'voodoo' murder and the photograph had been recognized and the victim identified. Bill was glued to the screen along with everyone else. The reporter announced the victim was a twenty-four year old African-American male named William Taylor, Jr. He looked at the picture of the young man and sure enough, like watching a police sketch artist add or remove years from a photograph, the picture was the young version of their own Willie Taylor who was in the police protection program. Bill got an eerie sensation. He was thinking about what was going on when his beeper went off. It was

Kasolkasky. He returned the call. Kasolkasky needed him down at police headquarters.

Lincoln arrived fifteen minutes later and walked briskly into Kasolkasky's office. Detectives White and Jones were already there engaged in an extended conversation.

"Bill, have a seat, we've been discussing the situation. We just got started a few minutes ago so you haven't missed anything."

"Is the victim our Willie Taylor's son?" the Investigator asked.

"Yes."

"So, do we have a serial killer, a copycat or something else?"

"That's the big question. I think we have something else."

"So do I. I don't believe in coincidences. Where was Big Eddy that evening?"

"Big Eddy was in a crowded sports bar. He even paid the owner some extra bucks that evening to make sure the surveillance camera was running during the whole time. He was definitely not at the crime scene."

"You mean this guy just happened to pay the owner to make sure his security cameras were working that evening? For what purpose would anyone do that except they would need an alibi?"

"Regardless of what you think, he has his alibi."

"Well, Brick, what do we tell the media? Are we going to tell them we don't think this is the 'real' voodoo killer or a copycat?"

Kasolkasky contemplated an answer. At first he was going to respond quickly, but then he thought about the question again and realized the answer was not that simple.

"If we tell the media we think it's a copycat, namely Big Eddy's people, they'll want to know why Big Eddy would do such a thing which brings into play another set of problems. The media would wonder why the police department would even consider cutting a deal with a person who might be connected to a brutal murder. It would be unthinkable. Any pressure could not be offset with the possibility of a deal." They were in a bind.

"We're up the proverbial creek without a paddle," Kasolkasky responded.

"So, the question remains, just what do we tell the media?" the Detective asked again.

"I'll leave that to the Chief. That's his problem. My job is to get information and to keep a lid on this thing."

Kasolkasky's secretary, who had a phone call from attorney Connie Chow, interrupted them. Brick said he would take it. Ms. Chow was Willie Taylor's attorney. Willie had dug a hole for himself and now that hole was collapsing around him. Kasolkasky talked with Ms. Chow for a good ten minutes before they finished.

Ms. Chow needed to see her client. Kasolkasky would set up the meeting. Kasolkasky also indicated he was sure that if Willie did not elect to testify he would probably be released from the program and would also have to face the original drug charges.

"Sounds like Willie is playing in the big leagues now and he doesn't have a glove, bat, or uniform," the Detective said bluntly.

"What do you think he'll do?" Detective Jones asked.

"He won't testify against Big Eddy," Bill responded. "I don't know what else he might do, but he won't testify."

"If you're right, we're nowhere again," Kasolkasky stated.

"I'd say that's accurate but it depends on your perspective. We may still have the ultimate weapon in the form of our voodoo witch lady. Why, she could lead us to the 'Promised Land', Brick," Lincoln said this with just enough lift in his voice. He didn't know if anyone thought he was being serious.

"So, you think that's the key to unlock this thing?"

"Well remember, she mentioned before anyone else, that the second murder was not connected to the voodoo god."

In our age there is no such thing as "keeping out of politics." All issues are political issues, and politics itself is a mass of lies, evasions, folly, hatred, and schizophrenia.

George Orwell: Orwell
Reader, edited by
Richard H. Revere, pp. 363-4.
Politics and the English Language.

Chapter 18

On the following day, Saturday afternoon, Detective Lincoln escorted Monique Dillard to a fundraiser at her brother Franklin's house.

After parking, the doorman escorted them inside and onto the terrace. The guests were a veritable 'Who's Who' representing the Bay Area's society elite.

Monique and Bill walked over to a small gathering of people who were conversing with the gracious hosts, Franklin and Crystal Dillard, Monique's brother and sister-in-law. As they approached, Franklin smiled at his sister.

"Welcome to the fundraiser," Franklin said.

"Thank you. You have quite a group assembled here. I hope the donations are generous."

"Let's hope so. If I remember correctly, it's Bill, right?" Franklin asked.

"Yes, that's correct."

"Well, it's not everyday I get a visit from the Oakland Police Department you know. Actually, I think you're my first."

"Well, I'm retired, so technically you're still in the clear."

A few minutes later Franklin excused himself to go visit with more people, specifically those with the money. Monique saw a friend and went over to talk while Crystal remained talking with Bill. Crystal was wearing a most appealing dress while being the perfect hostess.

"So Bill, thanks for coming and bringing Monique."

"I'm just the escort. She would have been here without my services."

"Perhaps, but Monique looks better with such a good man by her side. Are you a good man, Bill?" Crystal asked with a devilish smile.

"I would certainly hope so. I'm not sure if I'm the one who should be answering that question though. Some may say I'm biased."

"Are you married, Bill?"

"No. Once upon a time I was, but that ended over seven years ago. Still, we're good friends and we have two beautiful almost grown daughters."

"Well, do you have a girlfriend? I can't believe a good looking man like yourself is sitting home alone at night."

That was an interesting question considering he'd escorted Monique to this event. He wasn't quite sure where Crystal was heading. He also wasn't sure of his answer. She'd caught him off-guard but rule number one was, when in doubt, always tell the truth.

"There's a lady who I see from time to time who's a very nice person."

"Tell us, how's the case going?"

"Not as well as we'd like. Every time we get an opening the door quickly closes on us. Actually, if a case is not solved within the first forty-eight hours it may never be resolved."

"Yes, I know. After all, I'm a lawyer...remember?"

"True, I forgot. You attended the same law school as your husband if I'm not mistaken."

"Yes, that's correct. My, but you do have a good memory."

"I guess that's one sign of a good detective," he mused.

"Yes, I'm sure it is. Well, let me circulate now and be a good hostess. I'm very glad you came, Bill. If there's anything I can do for you, just give me a call." She smiled and touched him on the shoulder.

If he didn't know better, he'd say that was an invitation. It wasn't so much what she said, but how. She certainly didn't have to touch him, but when a woman did, it usually meant she liked you.

"Are you enjoying yourself, Detective Lincoln?"

Lincoln turned in the direction of the voice that was so easily recognizable.

"Yes, Mayor. How are you?"

"Fine. There are many interesting people here who I've not seen in a long time. I must say, Detective, you do get around. One never knows who one might run into these days."

"Well, sir, I'm trying to upgrade my social contacts."

"Yes, aren't we all," he chuckled.

Moments later, Monique joined them.

"Why, Mayor, don't you look simply smashing. I just love that suit on you!"

"Ms. Dillard, you do put a gleam in these old crusty eyes as I gaze at you in that fabulous dress! You do have the capacity to put a momentous strain on this slow pumping heart!" the Mayor beamed.

"Now, Mayor, I do believe you're trying to get my vote. If you weren't a politician you wouldn't even notice what I was wearing."

The Mayor gazed into her eyes and smiled broadly. He was obviously enjoying bantering with Monique.

"If I were a younger man you'd have trouble on your doorstep young lady! And with that comment, I'm going to move on before I have trouble on my own doorstep with my wife. I better see where she is. The Mayor should not be seen spending too much time with beautiful single ladies. I have an image to keep you understand. And of course, my dear, I want that vote in the next election!" The Mayor, still grinning, turned and walked away.

"He's a charmer," Monique acclaimed

"Yes, I guess he is at that. The Mayor could charm the rattle off a rattlesnake," Bill replied smiling.

95

"I do like Mayor Efferton. He's just so… personable."

Minutes later Bill noticed a new visitor; Radcliffe Dillard had walked onto the veranda. By his side was a lovely lady Bill didn't recognize. She had blond hair and appeared of Nordic stock. She was very pretty and seemed to know several people.

They walked over to Franklin and Crystal to greet them. Everyone was talking, laughing and generally having a good time. Radcliffe was clearly a likeable fellow who enjoyed social contact. As they continued to talk Lincoln noticed Radcliffe looking in his direction. Suddenly, he started walking toward Bill. As Rad was moving toward him, Bill realized it was Monique who had Rad's attention. After all, Monique was standing immediately next to Bill. Radcliffe grabbed his sister in a bear hug while she hugged him back.

"Hi, Neeky."

"Hello, Rad. Give me a kiss."

"You know you don't have to ask!"

"You're looking good, kiddo. You must be living well."

"Good genes, Sis. But look at you, you're looking great! You're going to break a lot of hearts looking like that. I might have to hire bodyguards for you to keep the men back."

"Why, Brother, you're too much," Monique smiled. "Rad, let me introduce you to Bill. Bill is my escort this evening. He's a retired policeman so I'd say I'm fairly well protected, at least for this evening. Bill Lincoln, this is my baby brother Radcliffe, who you should call Rad because that's what everyone else calls him."

"Hello, Bill, nice to meet you."

"Good evening, Rad. I've heard a lot about you. I understand you're the life force of the Dillard clan."

"That's correct. My brother and sister inherited that god-awful conservative blood. When I discovered I had a little of it in me, I went to the nearest hospital and had a complete blood transfusion. My dear sister and brother are conservative enough for the three of us. I've been trying to breathe a little life into them for years but they fight me on every front. However, I do believe I'm getting through to Neeky here. I think she's starting to loosen up some."

"Now, Rad, I'm loose enough. I'm just not as loose as you."

Everyone was laughing and Bill saw why Rad was the life of the party. He had carefree ways and a relaxed persona. He obviously enjoyed the good life, especially beautiful women. Bill didn't see this guy as a person who could murder his sister or have anything to do with it. However, he might be indirectly involved. Right now there was no evidence of anything other than a suggestion by a street hustler named Jacko that Rad was a sometime business associate of Big Eddy. That type of hearsay evidence was not going to legally convict anyone of anything.

Rad and Helga mingled with the other guests. Monique and Bill drifted into numerous conversations while soft music streamed onto the veranda. One hour later, Crystal announced that Franklin would be saying a few words of thanks and making some remarks.

He walked out with his wife to a platform constructed the day before. Franklin delivered the standard cliches and jokes as a typical politician would. He was a polished speaker; although not as well groomed as the Mayor, he was much younger and this was his first foray into political waters.

About ten minutes into his talk, the razor sharp incisors of Franklin Jr. were displayed showing he was not just another 'pretty face'.

"There is too much crime on our streets. My good friends, none of us is safe. None of us. My sister was discovered brutally murdered over four months ago and there is not the slightest indication of who murdered her. We've had a second ritualistic murder in the heart of our city a few days ago and where are they in determining who did it? The only response I've heard is that we're going to bring in a voodoo woman to help us. Did you hear what I said ladies and gentlemen? Did you hear me? I said our city officials have invited in a lady witch doctor. Are these the officials we elected to city government? Are these the people you want making decisions concerning your hard earned dollars?"

Franklin Jr. went on for another twelve minutes of hard-hitting 'take no prisoners' rhetoric. Bill noticed a reporter from the local media. He believed this reporter had been called by Franklin Jr.'s spin machine. This speech would receive tremendous press coverage tomorrow. Tough talk was expected from the local candidates who always threw their hat into the ring but who had virtually no chance of winning. However, tough talk from the political in-crowd was rare.

The Mayor had a perturbed look. He had gone the full emotional route from being in a relaxed jocular mood to one of reserved rage. The Mayor's wife was holding his arm and rubbing it as if to say it was no big deal, but the Mayor was not paying any attention to her. He was listening intently and anyone who knew him could see in his glare he was chalking up points, one by one, against Franklin Jr. The Mayor understood politics better than most and deplored what he was observing. Franklin Jr. was not running for Mayor and had no need to be dumping on him like this.

The Mayor contemplated whether Franklin Sr. could be behind this move, but didn't see the old man's imprint. Franklin Jr. was trying to show people that he makes his own decisions. This didn't have the old man's shrewdness and was downright tawdry. Invite the elite to your house and then throw mud. The Mayor would not play his game tonight. He'd keep his distance and mark his time.

The speech ended with polite applause. The Mayor, although livid, took a deep breath and resumed talking to his wife as though nothing had happened. At first, most people steered clear of the Mayor, but then gradually drifted over, engaging him once again in friendly conversation. From all outward appearances the Mayor looked and acted the same. However, when Mayor Efferton and his wife left an hour later they did not say goodbye to the host and hostess.

Monique and Bill left the affair an hour after the Mayor. Bill had engaged in conversations about Franklin's speech with many different people, but he had not discussed it with Monique. In the car he waited for her to bring the subject matter up, but she didn't.

Monique thanked Bill for being a very entertaining escort and then she lightly kissed him on the lips before saying goodbye. It was a very soft kiss which he would remember along with her perfume for a long time.

Fifteen minutes later his phone rang.

"Hello,...Bill?"

"Yes, Mayor."

"Please be in my office at 7:30 A.M. tomorrow morning."

"Yes, Mayor."

The Mayor didn't show anger emotionally, but he'd get even. Franklin Dillard Jr.'s speech had put fire in the Mayor's eyes and, like the changing of the seasons, it was only a matter of time before someone would get burned!

Chapter 19

Detective Lincoln walked into the Mayor's office at 7:27 A.M. to observe the chief executive reading the front-page article. From the Mayor's perspective the piece was very bad indeed.

"Hello, Mayor," Lincoln said as he walked into the room.

"Good morning, Bill, please sit down. Coffee?"

"Yes, thank you."

The Mayor got up and poured a cup. Bill was in a somber mood and Jim's body language was…quiet.

"Detective, let me get to the point. Do you remember that little incident that would have prevented you from receiving your pension?"

He stared at the Mayor, wondering what the heck was going on. He thought this meeting was about the Dillard case and the speech of last night.

"What did you say, Mayor?!" he asked, bewildered.

"You do remember the investigation against you that would have prevented you from receiving your pension, yes?" the Mayor repeated in an irritated voice. He expected people to listen to him the first time.

Lincoln slowly counted to five before speaking. "Yes; I mean, how could I forget it?"

"Well, we have movement there again. I've heard Internal Affairs might review the charges."

"Why?"

"I don't know anything more other than that. And if I did, I'm certainly not at liberty to disclose it."

Lincoln was silent. The Mayor was talking about a charge that alleged Detective Lincoln had killed an ex-con who was about to be captured by the police. The allegation was that he had used the infamous second gun—the one that all police officers are assumed to carry. His official weapon had not been discharged.

Two cops, on a tip from an anonymous source, had entered a deserted warehouse looking for a perpetrator. They had both entered by the same door and then separated. Detective Lincoln had gone upstairs, leaving his partner to search the ground level. While upstairs, a gun discharged killing the suspect. Bill's partner swore that he hadn't seen anyone else. Detective Lincoln testified that when he heard the gunfire he went to the room from where the shots had originated and cautiously opened the door. Inside it was dark. He turned on the light and discovered a body lying in a pool of blood. He heard footsteps moving down the back stairwell. He took another careful look around to make certain the room was empty, before checking the stairwell.

His partner arrived as he was peering down the dark stairwell and, seconds later, Bill ran to the bottom floor to hopefully catch the 'perp'. His partner followed but by the time they got outside there was nobody around. A heavily wooded area was only seconds away and a person could easily have been waiting there in ambush.

After an Internal Affairs investigation Lincoln was considered a potential suspect. The deceased was a person that Detective Lincoln had put behind bars for several years. This same individual had threatened Detective Lincoln's life in court after being found guilty. The original internal police investigation had reached an impasse due to lack of evidence and had been labeled inactive and inconclusive. The Mayor had become involved and had even defended the Detective. Now the Mayor was telling him individuals unknown were revisiting the case.

"Bill, don't worry, I'll look into it. However, I need you to devote your full attention to this Dillard case. I'm not happy about my situation while this Dillard case remains open. We need to create our own breaks. I want everyone operating at maximum capacity!"

"I understand, Mayor," he responded in a monotone voice, his eyes riveted on the chief bureaucrat. Bill didn't like the Mayor's implied message that he could essentially control this past investigation. Lincoln felt like a puppet on a string with the man standing only a few feet from him acting as his puppeteer.

"You're doing a decent job, Detective, but I need your total effort. We have to solve this thing."

The Mayor stared straight at him. He was being unscrupulously scrutinized. He didn't like it.

Detective Lincoln, with unpleasant thoughts running through his head, was becoming perturbed.

"Bill, how did you come to be invited to the Dillard function last night?"

This was really none of the Mayor's business. However, he didn't want to get on Jim's wrong side right now.

"I interviewed Monique after first talking with her brother Franklin Jr. and his wife Crystal. Afterward, we talked. Later, she called and invited me to escort her to the function. That's the first time I'd seen her since that first interview."

"Did you and Ms. Dillard discuss the speech her brother made last evening?"

"No. I was ready to. I waited for her to bring the subject up, but... We talked about everything else. Frankly, it's rather curious that we didn't talk about it. I'm calling her sometime this week to ask about her brother's remarks. I know Ms. Dillard likes you very much as Mayor. I'd speculate that she was just as surprised by her brother as were most of the other people there."

"Bill, we need to make serious progress. I don't know what prompted Dillard but those remarks made the front page. We need responsible people in positions of authority! Which means Dillard has certainly lost my vote! But more importantly, he's lost my respect! We're going to put that fag back in his closet where he belongs! Detective, I do expect your full attention! Now, I've got another meeting. Thanks for coming in."

The Mayor stood but they did not shake hands. Lincoln turned and left the room; he was not in a good mood. The city's chief politician was saying to him, in a not so subtle way, that he was to totally dedicate himself to this case. This case was to become his life until it was solved. The Mayor was getting heat and was passing it downstream. Detective Lincoln was back in the pressure cooker and the temperature was rising.

As Lincoln walked back to the police station, he reached into his pocket and pulled out a package of cigarettes. His nerves were on edge.

"Hey, Clarence, Dick, what's happening with you guys?" Detective Lincoln asked as he walked through the door and took a seat.

"We're bringing in the witch doctor lady. The Chief is against it but everyone else figures we have nothing to lose. Kasolkasky has been talking with Ms. Chow. She wants to talk to her client. We agree with you, Detective; Willie Taylor is probably not going to testify."

"Does anyone think differently?" Bill asked.

"The Chief believes we can still put pressure on Willie. Willie's now forced to stay in the witness protection program. His life is not worth two cents if he attempts to walk away. Besides, if he doesn't cooperate we can just bring the original charges against him."

"What about Willie's daughter?" Bill inquired. "He's already lost a son. Have we protected his daughter?"

"We're protecting Willie, not his daughter. His contract doesn't cover anyone else. We've notified the daughter and have sent an officer to speak with her. Ms. Chow has talked to her twice. The daughter is out of the city right now."

"Why does the Chief bother to pursue Willie?"

"Remember our original premise, Bill? If there is anyone in the family that might be tied to the murders, it has to be Radcliffe. He's got the most 'unusual' lifestyle. Now, the Chief knows that Big Eddy is probably behind the second voodoo murder. That's a no-brainer, but why can't the two still be connected? It's like you have a secret weapon at your disposal and only you know the code. Suppose Radcliffe reneged on a large payment to Big Eddy and Big Eddy felt compelled to send a very clear message. He uses this voodoo gimmick! Now, a punk named Willie Taylor is about to snitch on him. What do you do? The two murders could very easily be related, each for a different reason."

Bill thought about it. So, this was the Chief's theory. He had to admit there was some logic.

"But what about the mark of the voodoo god? How come it's found on one victim and not on the other?" Lincoln asked.

"That can be explained two ways. Maybe the alleged mark was not really a signature mark at all. Sometimes we read things that aren't really there. When you take those psychology tests and the therapists ask what that ink spot represents, how many people give different answers? That's the Chief's point. Possibly the same person committed the second murder but wanted to make it look like a copycat! Under that scenario, the omission of the alleged mark is intentional."

"Why do you say alleged mark?"

"Because we're not sure. I've read four books on voodoo and only one says anything about any particular mark. Voodoo rituals are different depending on who is conducting the ceremony. That picture of an alleged mark may have only been a smudge. It may not be anything. Is it a sign because some psychic in Los Angeles, of all places, says it's one? We don't have confirmation from any voodoo experts. Take the witch lady out of the equation and we've got a fit for these two crimes."

"I still think we've got some work to do. What's the motive?"

"Radcliffe owes Big Eddy big-time. He's having serious trouble paying the Italian back. Radcliffe blows him off too many times and Big Eddy takes things into his own hands and sends that clear message. Look at the one he sent Willie Taylor."

Bill thought about it some more, admitting to himself that the story had legs. Still not fully convinced of the motive, he was at least willing to entertain the idea.

"So the Chief expects Willie to testify?" Bill asked again in an incredulous tone.

"Not at this point in time, but Willie has no choice!"

"Willie does have a choice. He can do nothing. What do soldiers do when the opposing army completely surrounds them with no hope of escape? Some fight to the end, some surrender and some blow their own brains out. Willie has several options. We don't know which one he'll ultimately choose."

Everyone agreed. Willie was not the type to stand on principle. To expect Willie to suddenly develop character and take responsibility was ludicrous.

"Also," Bill remarked, "I don't think the District Attorney will touch this case, not with the flimsy material evidence being presented by Willie. Would you?"

Both detectives shook their heads.

Brick Kasolkasky strolled into the room, his head down, focussed on the floor. He and the Chief had just put together a schedule of things to do. The days were all filled with assignments and Bill noticed that this Friday night he was assigned to stake out Big Eddy's house from 8 P.M. to midnight. He was expected to be back on the stakeout the next morning from 10 A.M. until 6 P.M. Lincoln had a date with Susan that evening but decided he'd cancel it.

"Any questions?" Kasolkasky asked.

Everyone looked up but no one said anything. Detective Lincoln felt like he was back on the force and at the mercy of the whims of his superiors.

"Okay. We have two basic objectives. One is to maintain around the clock surveillance on Big Eddy and the second is to get that psychic up here. The Chief thinks we're wasting time with her but the Mayor will make the final decision there. Our city's leader is not in a good mood, so be careful. I suggest you tread lightly. If you need the Mayor, go through me first."

"Why are we watching Big Eddy's house, Brick?" Lincoln asked.

"Because we are. That's the way it's been planned."

"But why?"

"Just do as you're told, Bill, and cut the crap! Any other questions?!"

There weren't and with that Kasolkasky left the room.

Twelve hours later, Bill headed home for the evening. Once there he found a message from Susan to call her. During the conversation he cancelled their date and Susan felt that something was wrong. The conversation became strained and they ended it. Bill felt someone had put a 'bug' in Susan's ear and now she was making inquires. He didn't know who was behind this, but it didn't make much difference because he hadn't done anything wrong.

It was almost eleven o'clock but not too late for him to make another call. He picked up the phone and dialed Monique's number.

"Hello?"

"Monique, this is Bill Lincoln."

"Bill, how are you? It's nice to hear your voice."

"Monique, I have a question for you."

"Sure, I like your questions. Let's have it."

"Last Saturday, at your brother's house, we both heard his speech. It was intentionally unfavorable toward the Mayor. After the speech we had several conversations and opportunities to discuss it, but never did. Don't you find that unusual?"

"No, not really. I think we both felt somewhat uncomfortable especially since we had just been enjoying ourselves with the Mayor. Besides, it's only politics. My brother is running for office and we all know how candidates will say or do almost anything to get noticed. I don't think my brother is any different."

"What about the fact the Mayor is not his opponent? Don't you find Franklin's remarks made in such a public forum somewhat curious?"

There was a moment of silence before she spoke. "Yes, of course you're right. I was totally surprised by his remarks. But obviously my brother doesn't consult with me."

"I wouldn't think so. Is there any reason you know of that would make him do that?"

Another awkward moment quickly passed. "I could speculate, but I'd rather not. I wouldn't want to start any rumors."

"Well, if you change your mind and decide you want to talk about it, I'd be more than willing to listen. Something is going on that coincidentally started immediately following his speech and I'm trying to understand it. I will respect your decision and not press you anymore."

"You can press, Bill, but I don't think you'll get the answer you're looking for from me."

"Well, since I can't get you to reveal any deep dark secrets tonight, I'll let you get your rest. I've got to get up early tomorrow and I definitely need my beauty sleep."

"Well, Bill, I hope things settle down for you and I definitely hope you solve our case soon."

"Good night, Monique."

"Bye, Bill...and call me again...soon."

"Sure."

So Monique had a theory and Lincoln was curious about what it was. He'd call her again in a few days. He needed to know what she suspected had caused her brother to make those inflammatory remarks. The fact that Mayor Efferton referred to her big brother as a 'fag' was also interesting. The Mayor did indeed have sources, but the use of that term said something about the Mayor too. Bill's man on the street, Jacko, seemed on top of things. He was the first person who mentioned that Franklin Jr. might be gay.

Chapter 20

Lincoln, up early, headed to police headquarters. The team's morning assignment was to review the records of all ex-cons released during the last ten years who had committed ritualistic-type murders. If they found nothing they'd go back an additional ten years in their search. That evening, they would start watching Big Eddy's house.

Late morning, Kasolkasky requested Detective Lincoln drive Ms. Chow to the safe house where her client Willie Taylor was being detained. Bill gladly accepted the assignment...anything to escape the paperwork paralysis.

Detective Lincoln picked up Ms. Chow in an unmarked police vehicle. He had known Connie Chow professionally for several years and occasionally had spotted her at noteworthy social events.

"Ms. Chow, I'd appreciate it if you'd keep your eyes open for anyone following us."

"Please, call me Connie. And that's a good idea, Detective Lincoln."

"It's Bill. When was the last time you talked to your client?"

"Three days ago. He's nervous and very worried about his daughter."

"I understand. Do you know what he's likely to do?"

"No. His temperament is constantly changing. He's okay one day, jittery as heck the next. He's in a terrible situation."

"He's crossed the line, Connie."

Bill continued to drive while Connie played look-out. He wasn't sure if she was really checking to see if they were being followed.... she seemed preoccupied. After two miles of driving in silence, Ms. Chow started talking again.

"Bill, I'd like your opinion."

"Sure, on what?"

"I don't know if it's my imagination or not, but for the last several days, I think I'm being watched."

He glanced at her, then re-focused on the road. She seemed normal.

"By whom?"

"These guys look like thugs."

"Have you told anyone?"

"No, just you."

"Sounds like you need to be sure first."

He drove along for another mile before Ms. Chow spoke again.

"Bill, I know for sure."

"You know what for sure?"

"Two guys stopped me on the street a few days ago when I was returning from lunch."

She stopped talking and peered over at the Detective.

"And then what?"

"They asked how Willie was doing. I said, "Willie who?" They smiled, then said, 'Tell Willie hello. And Ms. Chow, as a lawyer, you should be advising your client to do those things that are in his own best interest...and yours. We just want Willie to do the right thing. We just want you to do the right thing too!' After that, they walked off without a care in the world. I felt nauseated. I felt scared. I'm still scared."

"Why are you telling me this, Connie?"

"You have a reputation for being a straight-shooter. I suspect that's the reason you only got as far as you did in the detective ranks. And since you're not a policeman anymore, you won't give me the standard line. I want your opinion."

"Connie, you have a well earned reputation for being a fighter. People know how you protected your parents from those Asian street thugs. You, lady, have backbone."

"This is a different breed of thug, Bill."

"That I know. Do you own a gun?"

"No. I don't believe in guns as a solution...to anything."

"Get a gun, learn how to use it, and put your beliefs on the shelf with Santa Claus and the Easter Bunny!"

"Is this any way for us to live?"

"Ask Willie Taylor's son."

"There has to be another way, a better way."

"I'm not in the illusions business. You saw what happened to Willie Jr.; you've been warned! You can ignore the warning, that's your call. Many are noble in death!"

The car was quiet. Ms. Chow had turned away from him and Bill could sense her sadness. Her short jet-black hair was still. She stared out the window without seeing.

"Do you have any children, Connie?"

"Yes. I have a daughter in college."

"Where's your husband?"

"We divorced years ago; I never remarried."

"They sent a message to Willie Taylor by way of his son."

Connie continued to look away from him. It seemed even as the images outside the window were moving by, that their car was stuck somewhere in time.

"Do you love your daughter, Connie?"

"Yes, of course. Very much."

"If you're going to pursue your noble act of helping all people, then at least call your daughter. Warn her; advise her to go somewhere and not to tell anyone where she has gone. Not even you!"

"Is this what my life has come to?"

"Yes. There is a dangerous criminal element out there. Parts of our once noble society are breaking down... we are witnessing that reality. A reality which if not acknowledged could cause one extreme displeasure."

"There aren't many alternatives are there?"

"Get off the case. Resign. Let somebody else handle it."

"Would you do that?"

"That's irrelevant. I'm not you and you're not me."

"But would you do that?"

"Connie, again, that's a useless question. We live by different codes, have had different experiences. I own a gun and will use it. I'm a man...you're not. We grew up in different families, have different values. Don't make a decision based on my actions!"

"I know I'm reaching for the moon but I want somebody to tell me what to do. I usually make good decisions but I've never been in this position before. I'm not so much afraid for myself as I am for those around me. No, that's only partly true. I am afraid for myself. I'm also angry. I want to represent Willie Taylor. He has a legal right to be represented."

"Connie, these thugs believe they have a 'natural' right to impose their will on whomever they choose, unless we take a stand against them. No one said it's going to be easy. Freedom is not always something that is given...sometimes you have to earn it"

"But, I'll feel defeated if I resign from the case."

"I know."

"But what would I do if I invited harm to my family?"

Bill pulled over to the side of the road, stopping the car, but left the motor running. He could see she was under great emotional turmoil. There was no easy answer.

"Connie, resign from the case. Think of your family. Do you want to put them in harm's way?"

"Of course not. I love my family. But I also feel I have a solemn duty. I'm a good lawyer. Do I abdicate my responsibility to someone else because I can't take the pressure? I wouldn't respect myself if I did that."

"I understand. And how will you feel if you get a call informing you that your daughter was found raped, gutted and smothered in feathers?"

Connie looked out the window again. Once again she was deep in thought but the answers were not there to be plucked like an orange tree laden with fruit.

"I don't have an answer for you yet. I feel like I'm heading down a dark tunnel. I just don't have an answer."

"Oh, but you've already given me your answer. You're going to do your job until you tell me different."

With that last comment Bill shifted the car into gear and drove toward the safe house. The guard let them in…the place reeked of cigarette smoke.

Connie and Willie went into a third room and talked. An hour passed before the door opened and Ms. Chow motioned for Detective Lincoln to come in. Willie was sitting, legs crossed, smoking.

Connie spoke first. "Mr. Taylor has requested protection for his daughter."

Bill thought Willie must be soul-searching. "I'll bring that request to Kasolkasky. I believe he'll support it."

"Mr. Taylor would also like some idea of when the case can be expected to go to trial."

"I'll get the best estimate we have."

"Mr. Taylor also has a hypothetical question."

"Hypothetical?"

"Yes. For instance, what will happen if he decides not to testify?"

"I believe the police will simply file their original charges. He's currently used up his second strike in a three-strike state. I don't think there's much else to say. Naturally, they'll release him from the witness protection program. Then he'll be out on his own if he can make bail. If not, he'll remain in the county jail until his trial."

Ms. Chow asked, "Mr. Taylor, is there anything else?"

Willie shook his head no. That was it. Bill stepped back outside and a few minutes later Ms. Chow indicated she was ready to go. They said nothing until they reached the car.

"How did it go?" Bill asked Connie.

"As expected. There are many sensitive issues before us."

"Does Willie know about your situation…about the thugs who approached you on the street?"

"No. That's not his concern. That has to do only with me."

"Connie, these people don't evaluate situations like you do. Don't make the mistake of thinking they're ordinary folks making ordinary decisions. They will destroy anyone that threatens them."

"Bill, I want to tell you another reason why I wanted your opinion."

He looked at her but he didn't say anything. He sat back to listen, maintaining a blank expression.

"I was one of the fifteen people on the commission that reviewed your case back when that individual was shot in the warehouse. You have a good reputation for police work. I understand why the Mayor is using you. Now, suddenly, for no apparent reason, your case has somehow been 'reactivated'. I don't know why. I'm sure you're just as mystified."

The look in Bill's eyes revealed his answer. He listened closely to Connie's every word.

"We've met once recently to discuss whether or not to re-open the case. The commission is still contemplating that possibility."

"So, what are your feelings about the case, Connie?"

"Bill, there's not enough evidence for me to judge. As a legal problem solver I make decisions based on the evidence presented."

"Connie, what does your non-legal personality say? I'm curious."

His head was slightly bent with eyes wide open and raised eyebrows. He watched her, carefully studying her body language. He had interrogated and interviewed many in his life. His military and police experience had sharpened his skills considerably. He now had an almost innate sense about when someone was telling the truth. Body language was the key element.

"Allow me to say this, I once heard you use a phrase that I agree with."

"And what was that?"

"You said you don't believe in coincidences. Sure, they might happen once in awhile, but any more often than that and you've got a problem."

"Yes, I remember that comment."

"So, that's it. The man who died had once threatened you. He goes to prison and comes out. There is a police call that someone may be breaking into a warehouse and you and your partner were first to arrive. A man winds up dead. Indeed that was quite a coincidence. But again, I still don't believe there's enough evidence to go forward."

"That still sounds like a lawyer's answer, Connie."

113

"I guess it is."

There was a brief silence before Bill said jokingly, "Get out of here, I'm getting back to work." Bill was scheduled to work from eight until midnight that night watching Big Eddy's house. He headed home to get some much-needed rest.

At eight that evening Bill relieved the officer on duty. There had been no unusual activity. This was Bill's first day on watch and the second day of police team surveillance of Big Eddy's house.

At nine, two couples dressed in evening attire rang Big Eddy's doorbell. A few minutes later more people arrived. Detective Lincoln had counted twenty-five people at one point. He didn't recognize most of the people, but recorded the names he knew and took pictures of everyone.

As he was watching, a car drove up and Bennie Pews, one of the founding partners of Berkland Law representing Big Eddy, got out along with his wife. Fifteen minutes later Bennie's partner and co-founder, Matthew Silverstein, pulled up. Bill reported to headquarters. His instructions were to get good pictures, if possible.

At ten-thirty Radcliffe Dillard appeared escorting a beautiful Asian woman. Bill took more pictures.

Bill's watch showed eleven o'clock, one more hour before he would be relieved. Suddenly, a knock on the window startled him. He rolled down his window to talk to Big Eddy's bodyguard. The detective was invited inside.

He dialed Kasolkasky's number. But Kasolkasky had left instructions to not disturb him unless it was important. Bill decided this wasn't that important so he went inside Big Eddy's house.

The party was in full swing. Bill socialized with everyone, getting names and professions.

"Hello, Detective Lincoln, I'm so glad you decided to come join us."

"Thanks, Eddy."

"And I'll get you our guest list. Your pictures may not come out. It will save you much time and effort trying to identify my guests."

"Your generosity knows no bounds."

"Tell me, Detective, how's Willie? Are you guys keeping him warm and comfy?"

"Willie is doing fine."

"Please, tell Willie I said hello and that I send my best."

"I'll be sure to relay the message."

"Do you have any leads yet on that second voodoo murder?"

"We have our suspicions," Bill replied.

"Anybody I know?"

"Unfortunately, I'm not at liberty to say. It's still confidential information. Tell me, Eddy, do you have any theories as to who might be guilty?"

"None whatsoever. I have a theory though. I suspect that Willie Taylor Sr. must've done something real bad if this is directed at him. What do you say about that, Detective?"

"As you said, it's only a theory."

"Well, have a good time, Detective."

All in all, Bill failed to learn anything new. He left around two that morning with the other guests.

Woe to them that devise iniquity, and work evil upon their beds! When the morning is light, they practice it, because it is in the power of their hand.

THE OLD TESTAMENT - THE BOOK OF THE
PROPHETS - MICAH 2:1

Chapter 21

The following morning Kasolkasky informed Bill he had a message yesterday from some guy named Jacko. Lincoln read the note. It said, 'She does her thing the last Sunday of the month. Call for next performance. Got number from Marcy. Say you work with Marcy at the Oakland waterfront. You want a blessing from Mama for your new baby.' That was all. Jacko did good work. The note referred to Marie 'Mama' Francois, the woman who allegedly performed voodoo ceremonies. He dialed the number. The phone rang four times before someone picked it up. Bill summoned his best Jamaican street accent.

"Ello?"

"Ello! Dis Mama Francois' house?"

"Who wants to know?"

"This be Michael Kingly. I from de islands, mon. Me co-worker, Marcy, give me dis number. She tell me I can find Mama Francois here."

"What do you want with Mama?"

"Me want to 'tend her ceremony'. We want ar newborn baby be blessed!"

"Are you a believer?"

"Yeah, mon. And me have contribution for Mama. Marcy say me should bring fifty doolar. That okay?"

"That's the right amount. Bring it with you."

"Where?"

"The last Sunday in the month go to 666 Natas Lane. It's out in the country so look at a map. The ceremony starts at 10 P.M. Mama will bless your baby then."

"Me wife and me baby may be still on the island then."

"No problem. Mama will make a charm for her with special blessing powers."

"Great. I'll be dere. Goodbye."

He hung up the phone, finally feeling some relief. He was getting closer to meeting Marie 'Mama' Francois.

Next Sunday was the last Sunday of the month, which was excellent timing, for once. Kasolkasky informed them Ms. Balboa was flying into town the next morning to visit the site of the first murder. Lincoln resumed his paperwork assignments. Everyone worked a long day.

—

Ms. Jezebel Balboa, the psychic from Los Angeles, arrived at the Oakland Airport. Detectives Jones and White, her escorts, were curious about meeting Ms. Balboa, but feared being labeled as the officers who used 'black magic' police techniques. Ms. Balboa was the only one who had indicated there was an unusual mark on the deceased body of the first victim, Hillary Dillard. She had also correctly indicated there was no similar 'mark' on the second dead body, that of Willie Lee Jr. This single fact led to Ms. Balboa's crime scene invitation.

Forty-five minutes later they knocked on Kasolkasky's door.

"Hello, Ms. Balboa. It's a pleasure to meet you."

"Hello, Detective Kasolkasky, the pleasure is all mine."

"Ms. Balboa, this is Bill Lincoln. He's a retired detective working with us."

Bill stepped forward and shook her hand. He towered over her like everyone else. Her hands were soft and small, in proportion to her size.

"It's a pleasure to meet you, Mr. Lincoln."

A chair was offered to the psychic.

"Ms. Balboa, is there anything more you can tell us now since you've reviewed those pictures?"

"I don't have anything more to tell you. A picture is only that. It can't replace being there. It's important to be at the scene as quickly as possible because psychic vibrations from the event may linger. The spirits must be acknowledged; if not, they will be angry and go away, returning perhaps for their vengeance."

"What do the gods want, Ms. Balboa?" Kasolkasky asked.

"I don't know, Detective. Maybe if I was there I could answer your question."

"Ms. Balboa," Bill asked trying to get involved in this conversation, "what do the gods usually want? I mean, in general, what do the gods do?"

"Mr. Lincoln, don't people pray to their Christian God to ask for favors? And don't people act a certain way because their Christian God expects it?" Ms. Balboa asked with dramatic emphasis, pressing her hands together in front of her, prayerfully. She was making the point that most people pray for something.

"Yes. I understand your point, but my question is, 'Does the 'Voodoo God' want something different than the Christian God?'"

"What makes you think they're different?"

"I don't know. Are they?" he inquired.

"Do you know anything about voodoo, Mr. Lincoln?"

"Not really. I know it's a religion. I don't know many of the details."

"You must learn more. Do you believe in spirits?"

"I can't really say that I do. I don't believe in much I can't see or touch!"

"Then you are a fool, Mr. Lincoln," she stated bluntly. "The spirit world is glorious, simply magnificent. You can't see your Christian God, Mr. Lincoln. Or can you?"

"No. You're right."

"The Voodoo God comes to those who believe. He has chosen few to communicate with. I have been chosen, but I can't tell you why. For some unknown reason, he interacts only with women. We bring life and he is life. There is much not understood regarding the spirit world. Much can only be communicated once the spirit is with you. There is much we don't know."

Bill wasn't getting it. He heard her words but didn't comprehend their message. She continued fulfilling his beliefs.

"Then please tell me something I definitely don't understand. How did you know there was a mark on the victim in the first murder if you weren't there and you only had the picture?"

"A strong feeling came upon me when I viewed the picture. As I said earlier there are many things we can only feel. I have lived in the voodoo culture. I have seen things that you have not. Don't ignore the powers of the spirit world gentlemen. You must first believe in order to understand!"

Kasolkasky asked if she was ready to visit the first crime scene. When she nodded, everyone headed for the door.

--

Twenty minutes later they arrived at the location; campus security had cordoned off the area. Ms. Balboa first surveyed the scene from a slight distance, then walked the perimeter of the designated area and finally asked to see all the photographs from that dreadful evening. Afterwards, she returned to walk the perimeter again. The psychic stopped at the marked murder spot. She knelt and touched the ground, remaining quiet for several minutes.

Soon it appeared Ms. Balboa had entered another world. She began a deep-pitched humming sound while her body gently swayed. She spoke in 'tongue,' a dialect similar to a Buddhist chant. Everyone stared but nobody moved.

Dozens of students now stood behind the ropes watching with crane-like postures. Ms. Balboa's chanting had switched into moaning then back to chanting. A few moments later she was praying. She wanted the spirit to enter her body, an offering to the Voodoo God.

Ten minutes drifted into fifteen. Ms. Balboa remained in her trance-like state. The number of students swelled. Bill noticed Tommie Cheng standing among the students. Tommie was a newspaper reporter who worked for the largest East Bay newspaper organization. Somebody had obviously tipped him off.

Bill talked with the reporter. Tommie Cheng had received an anonymous telephone call from a male with a Caribbean accent suggesting he come to the college today. Bill told him what he could. Both agreed to try to keep the other informed.

Bill walked back to the spot where Ms. Balboa was still on her knees in a trance-like state with about forty onlookers observing the scene. Finally, Ms. Balboa stood, looking a little wobbly but standing. Bill, observing her body language, was unable to read anything special. Minutes later the detectives escorted her to the security building.

"Ms. Balboa, can you tell us anything?"

"There is very little to tell. It's been too long. I needed to be here right after the killing. The spirits will usually linger for awhile... after a sacrifice."

"A sacrifice? What do you mean, Ms. Balboa?"

"Voodoo gods sometime demand blood. We mortals do not understand the spirit world very well. Sometimes the gods make requests we can't understand. Your Christian God sent his son to be killed so that Christians could learn something. The great voodoo god is no different. They are trying to teach us but we don't want to learn!"

"Don't you think that God sent his son to teach people?" Bill inquired.

"Of course. But the Christian God knew what would happen. Could God have protected his son Jesus? Of course. But did he? No. God gave us a lesson. The voodoo god is no different. Sometimes Damballa demands a sacrifice of human blood so that we too can learn. Thus, He is a very loving god!"

Bill experienced mental fatigue. The Oakland Police Department had invested in a round-trip ticket from Los Angeles but it didn't appear it had bought much.

"What can you usually gather from a scene the spirits have recently vacated?"

"I can't tell you that unless I was there. If the gods want to leave a message behind they will. You cannot control a god. The gods control us!"

"Ms. Balboa," Detective White said, "you're saying there is nothing at this crime scene that can help us. Your 'special powers' are of no help to us today. Is this correct?"

"Yes, Detective, unfortunately you are correct."

The detectives sat back in their chairs looking at each other. No wonder Ron Ness was the Chief. He warned everyone, but was ignored.

In order to save time, Detectives White and Jones both stood and thanked Ms. Balboa for coming. They would check on the next flight to LA to make sure she was booked. Ms. Balboa was startled by the comment.

"Detectives, don't you want to hear the remainder of my observations?"

Everyone stared at Ms. Balboa. Detective Lincoln was not sure what else she had to talk about but they certainly had more than enough time to listen.

"Well, Ms. Balboa, go right ahead," Bill said. "What else is on your mind?"

"I need to tell you about the pictures! This is the first time I've seen the complete collection of photographs. You only sent me three. Remember? But, I saw all the pictures today. Yes!"

"Ms. Balboa, what do you see in the pictures?"

"They spoke to me. I felt the presence of the voodoo god. There were several pictures capturing it. It's magnificent, wouldn't you say so, gentlemen?"

They all nodded their head as if they knew what a magnificent voodoo presence felt like. "And the mark tells us that this one was protected by the spirit."

The room went silent. That last comment made no sense.

"Ms. Balboa," Detective Lincoln interjected, "if that was a mark of protection, then why is the girl dead?"

Ms. Balboa looked at him as if he was a dunce. "The girl was protected by the gods but the perpetrator violated that sanctity. The murderer is an infidel!" she cried out, pounding her petite hand on the table. "An infidel, my good men. A filthy infidel!"

Bill didn't get it, her last emotional outbursts were a non sequitur. Bill looked at his associates and saw only blank expressions. He wasn't alone on this.

"Ms. Balboa, what are you saying here?" Detective Jones asked.

She looked almost exasperated. Her features were taut, her eyes energized. She was still holding her hand with her index finger extended. She gave the impression of a fiery preacher who had just finished an emotional sermon and now rested with both hands on the podium looking out over their congregation.

"I'm saying the murderer is not a believer in voodoo. This was no voodoo sacrifice! The gods did not take her. On the contrary, they were protecting this child. The man who committed this dastardly, cowardly deed was a pretender. He's familiar with voodoo, but he is not a follower! He walks among us, but he is not one of us. He is like us, in his appearance and his manners, but he is only acting! This crime was a hoax perpetrated in an effort to cast suspicion on the voodoo world. Mark my words, gentlemen, when you find this butcher, you will be surprised! You will say, 'I don't believe it! It can't be!' Mark my words, gentlemen! Mark my words!"

Chapter 22

The task force met to update Kasolkasky and his boss. Chief Ness was uncomfortable with the situation. The Chief found the story interesting, but totally out in left field. Kasolkasky and the others were not sure. Afterwards, the Chief invited Detective Lincoln to accompany him to the Dillard estate to update the family.

Detective Lincoln had never met Franklin Sr. or Heather Dillard for that matter. It would be an hour before the meeting so Bill started reviewing the Dillard family file.

Dillard was born in New York City to humble parents who had instilled in him a sense of self-worth and personal respect. He was expected to do well in school because after all, he was a Dillard. The lack of money was irrelevant. Poverty was no reason to ignore homework or perform poorly in school. Poverty was an economic condition only; there was no shame in being poor, but it was inexcusable to have impoverished values. Dillard's parents worked hard and expected all three of their children to do likewise.

There were two boys and a girl. Franklin, the eldest, became an attorney. His sister, the next oldest, was a nurse and his youngest brother became a school superintendent in Virginia. Franklin met his wife, Heather, while he was an undergraduate student at Boston College. Heather was from France. She was a language major who spoke five languages fluently and was a political- social activist intensely involved in campus activities.

Heather first met Franklin in class and was captivated by his lack of social and political interest, combined with his complete dedication to his academic studies. Eventually he became her project, culminating in a great friendship. Both were extremely bright but complete opposites. They were intriguing to each other. Franklin and Heather became an 'item' by their third year.

After graduating Franklin entered Harvard Law School and Heather joined the staff of a Massachusetts congressman. They married during Franklin's second year of law school. Franklin had never, in his wildest imagination, dreamed he would ever marry outside his race, but he had found his life partner. Heather never thought in racial terms, which always amazed Franklin.

Franklin finished in the top five percent of his class and immediately secured several job offers. He elected to remain in Boston. After seven years he accepted a partnership with a small law firm in Oakland, CA, that had just landed a large lawsuit. Franklin was hired to litigate the case. …He won. After that success the small law firm began to grow into one of the top legal firms in Northern California. Now, the firm employed two hundred twenty lawyers in offices located in top cities across the nation.

Franklin and Heather raised four children in the Oakland Hills. Heather was very active in many different causes but decidedly took more of a background role once her children were born. When her children were grown, it gave her the time to champion causes, but her energy had abated.

The Chief and Bill drove to the Dillard estate, which occupied one-and-a-half acres. It was a beautiful house with impeccable landscaping. They were informed their meeting would begin upon Mrs. Dillard's arrival. Mrs. Dillard usually didn't attend the meetings but she would this time.

The Mayor worked the agenda, orchestrating everything. He gave an outline of the evidence and the theories the police were pursuing. Words were a politician's lifeblood; they lived or died by them. Franklin Sr., who also made his money using words, responded after the Mayor's commentary.

"Does anyone here disagree with any of the Mayor's comments?" Dillard asked.

No one disagreed.

"Is there anything of material value that needs to be added?"

Everyone shook his head.

"Does anyone have any faith in this psychic?"

The police chief finally spoke. "Franklin, I'm against it and I've gone on record. We don't need this type of 'analysis' to become part of the investigation. We could waste precious time and be misled. There are no controls."

"Chief," Mrs. Dillard said, "my little girl has been dead for four months and it does not appear you're close to solving the case any time soon! If this lady has a chance of helping, shouldn't we give her the benefit of the doubt?"

It was an emotional plea from the victim's mother, which, unfortunately, the Chief had witnessed far too often. He had been involved in enough lawsuits where the police were held to task because they were using some looney-based idea.

"Mrs. Dillard, I sympathize with you. But this woman could cause great harm. Suppose she's a fraud and just wants publicity?"

"It's been too long, Chief Ness. My baby is lying cold in her grave. We need some fresh ideas. Mayor Efferton, what's your opinion about this psychic?"

Bill didn't know if she was just being a mother or if she was going for the jugular. She was putting the chief executive dead on the spot.

"Heather, I don't have the perfect answer for you. We're still evaluating her. I've had a number of people read her file and I've gone through most of it myself. And while I admit I do have mixed feelings here, I can tell you this, I don't want us to miss anything. The Chief makes an excellent point. We have to be careful."

Franklin Dillard, looking at the investigator, said, "Detective Lincoln, what is your opinion of the psychic? I believe you have as much experience with her as anyone else here."

"I agree with the Mayor. We'll need more information. I don't know enough to give you an intelligent answer one way or the other."

Franklin Dillard studied Bill but decided not to ask another question. Instead he turned back towards the other gentlemen.

125

"Chief, what exactly is the status of Mr. Tevelle? If I understand correctly, you were interested in applying considerable pressure on this 'gentleman'. Has that occurred?"

"He's presently out on bail. We have an individual in the witness protection program that is willing to testify against Mr. Tevelle. Mr. Tevelle is currently working with his lawyers to avoid prosecution. We are making very slow progress."

Bill was wondering just how far this line of questioning would go. Would details follow? They were trying to 'squeeze' Big Eddy by pressuring Willie Taylor to squeal like a pig. All of this was being done in an effort to ensnare one of their own, their son Radcliffe. Franklin Sr. was just too bright and too connected not to know. The only remaining question in Bill's mind was whether Mrs. Dillard knew.

Franklin took control once again. "So, presently there are basically two lines of inquiry into this investigation. Is that correct?"

The Mayor responded. "Yes, but we're also looking for anyone convicted of ritualistic types of crimes resulting in murder."

Mrs. Dillard interrupted the Mayor. "I want to know more about this Mr. Tevelle. Why is he under suspicion?"

Her husband answered, "The police believe Mr. Tevelle (alias Big Eddy) is responsible for the second voodoo murder. The person who's in the police's witness protection program is a man named Willie Lee Taylor Sr. Mr. Taylor apparently has information damaging to Mr. Tevelle. The young man who was the victim in the second voodoo murder was Willie Lee Taylor Jr. The police suspect there is no relation between the two murders. They believe Mr. Tevelle ordered the death of Willie Taylor's son and used the voodoo murder concept to disguise his crime while putting pressure on Mr. Taylor to not talk. Mr. Tevelle is considered a Mafia type."

"Why would a Mafia-type person want to murder my baby? Could someone please answer that question?"

"That's the thing that doesn't fit, Heather!" Franklin responded. It's the gap the police have been unable to piece together."

The Mayor, the Chief and Detective Lincoln all remained quiet. This was Franklin Dillard's show. Bill surmised that the parents had not discussed the possibility that Radcliffe could be involved, not by the way she asked that question.

This told him that the legendary Franklin Dillard Sr. indeed had a soft side, at least regarding his family. If the Chief thought dragging Radcliffe into the equation was going to be easy, he was out in left field. The difficulty of putting pressure on Big Eddy, to talk about anything, was evident.

Ten minutes later, the meeting was officially over.

–-

Bill was at home resting when the phone rang. Instinctively, he checked his watch. It was only ten o'clock. It felt later. He picked up the phone on the second ring.

"Hello, Bill, this is Connie Chow."

"Good evening, Connie. To what do I owe this call? Business or pleasure?"

"How about rumor? How do you classify that?" Connie opined.

"Let's have it," he responded getting a slight sinking sensation in his stomach. Connie Chow had never called him at home before. She did not strike him as a person who would pass on a rumor, not unless there was some foundation to it.

"I got a phone call this evening from a commissioner regarding your Internal Affairs case. This unnamed person said a witness has been identified … one who had not given testimony before. Allegedly, this witness is purported to have indicated that Bill Lincoln knew the release date of the prisoner found dead in the warehouse. The witness may also testify that you even knew the address where the alleged victim worked."

There was silence. Connie stopped. Bill was waiting for more.

"How come they can find somebody years after the fact but they couldn't find anyone during the investigation? Someone is conveniently creating evidence here!"

"I just thought you'd like to know."

"Thanks, Connie. Someone's manufacturing this stuff!"

"Bill, are you okay?"

"I was alright until this phone call. I don't exactly care for these kinds of surprises."

"I know. Bill, I'll talk to you later."

"Thanks for the call, Connie. And how are you doing with your little thug friends? Have you heard anything from them?"

"No. And I hope that I don't."

"How's Willie?" Bill was curious about her client. He was in a dangerous position testifying against Big Eddy.

"He seems fine. He was glad when they put his daughter into the witness protection program. That gave him some sense of relief."

"Are you advising him to testify against Big Eddy?"

"I can't discuss that with you, Bill. That's confidential."

"I understand. And, Connie...."

"Yes, Bill."

"If you're thinking of moving forward and having him testify, make sure you take every precaution for your safety too. Oh, and call me anytime. I'll be more than willing to talk about what a person can do to protect themselves."

"Thanks. I just may take you up on that offer."

He hung up the phone. He was livid. Somebody was lurking in the shadows and he didn't like it. The information Connie relayed had tripped a lever inside him. His brain, now in overdrive, started to analyze everything in minute detail. You don't box animals in, not if you can avoid it. A cornered animal was a dangerous animal and Detective Lincoln was beginning to feel cornered.

Chapter 23

The next morning during break, Bill called Crystal Dillard. She easily accepted a 1:00 P.M. lunch invitation.

Kasolkasky dropped by at twelve-fifteen to check on his team.

"Bill, I have a special assignment I want you to look at early this afternoon."

"Oh? What is it?"

"The Chief wants somebody to have those photographs looked at by another voodoo practitioner. Remember the photos of the crime scene provided to Ms. Balboa? I'm assigning that project to you."

"I can certainly do it, Brick. I'll postpone my luncheon meeting today with Crystal Dillard. Maybe she'll find the time next week," he said casually.

"Keep the luncheon engagement. You can take care of the photo project later."

Bill still wanted to know why Crystal's husband had made those off color remarks about the Mayor at the fundraiser. He had asked Monique but she did not care to speculate. Crystal had been very friendly the night of the fundraiser. Her conversation had been lively and she had ever so softly touched him, as she brushed past. Women usually didn't do that unless they are interested. Jacko, the street hustler, implied that Crystal would not be receiving any Girl Scout awards this year. The detective was curious.

Bill walked into the restaurant at twelve fifty-five and waited. She arrived ten minutes later, apologizing for running late. She wore jeans and a light chiffon top.

"I must say I was somewhat surprised by your call. Obviously, one can still be caught off guard."

"I know. Surprises never cease to amaze me."

"So, to what do I owe the pleasure of this lunch?" Crystal coyly asked. She had a lovely smile...like a movie star.

"Crystal, I must admit that I was taken aback by your husband's remarks on the night of the fundraiser. I was not the only one so affected considering the coverage in the papers the next day."

Bill got right to the issue. He could very easily become distracted sitting there admiring her.

"Yes, I can see your point. But, Bill, didn't you ask Monique the same thing that night?"

"No. I thought the topic might naturally come up in our conversation that evening, but it didn't. We talked about everything else. I'll admit I waited to see if she would bring it up."

"Why you're just a curious fellow, Bill. They say curiosity killed the cat you know."

"Thank God I'm no cat," he smiled.

"So, what do you think, Bill? You must have formulated an opinion."

"But that's just it, Crystal, I haven't. To me, it makes no sense. Your husband is running for a congressional seat and yet he's taking shots at the Mayor. The Mayor's not running for Congress."

"Politics is a strange profession. What motivates people is very interesting."

So far Crystal wasn't saying anything. Her beautiful lips were moving, but he was not learning anything. He'd just have to wait.

"How's Monique doing?" Crystal asked.

"I don't know. It's been a while since I've talked to her. I've been too busy with this case."

"I thought you and Monique would have hit it off. It sounds like you two are moving fairly slowly. What's happening, Bill?"

"I need to explain something here. I met with Monique because of my interview with her. It was completely work-related. I gave her my card; also intended to be work-related. Monique called a few weeks later asking me to escort her to your event. Now, we've talked briefly on the phone once, since that initial meeting. I'm not sure we're talking about a relationship here in the same context I think you mean."

"Bill, did you linger at Monique's house after the official interview was over?"

"Okay, yes. For an hour or two."

"Or three. Did you enjoy yourself?"

"Sure."

"Are you physically attracted to Monique?"

"Perhaps."

"Are you intellectually attracted to Monique?"

"Perhaps."

"Did you accept Monique's invitation to be her escort?"

"Look, that's a rhetorical question. Besides, you already know the answer, Ms. Riddler." Crystal lit up at this reference for her. She was smiling broadly with glittering eyes.

"Did you feel good when Monique asked to be escorted by you?"

He looked at Crystal and smiled. "I'll ignore that question on the grounds of its irrelevance."

"So, Bill, you've answered in the affirmative to questions seeming to indicate a particular direction. I guess the court is trying to determine why we have non-movement. What's causing the obstruction, Sir?"

"How about I'm simply too busy?"

"An insufficient answer for a male. A totally appropriate answer by a female, but not a male!"

"I beg to disagree."

"I kind of like the thought of you begging," Crystal asked in a slow, seductive voice, while she reached over and slowly rubbed his arm for an instant. She sent a signal. He was trying to decipher it.

"I think begging is so unrefined," he said cautiously, but he didn't know why he was being cautious.

"It depends on who's doing the begging. Proper begging can be an art form. I do believe men have been practicing it for years. Some have elevated it to a science!" she grinned.

"It would be very difficult to argue with that assessment, Crystal."

"A wise man would not argue the point!"

"I will agree, but only to maintain my status, hopefully, as a wise man."

"You're doing well, my dear. Your status, so far, is secure; but the day is young. Let us not pass judgement too quickly. I hope my dear sister-in-law is not about to let this one get away. I am a little concerned."

"How's Rad doing? The first time I met him was at your fundraiser. He's a lively fellow."

"Rad is enjoying himself like he always does. I like Rad. The Dillards can be so formal at times, but not Rad. He likes the sporting life. Sometimes I think I should have married Rad. Of course, marrying him might be too much. I like a good time, but I'm not sure if I could do it twenty-four seven. Apparently, Rad can."

"I just saw him for only the second time last week. I met him at Big Eddy Tevelle's party."

"Oh, really. And how was he? Was he his normal fun-loving self?"

"Rad was Rad. He had ladies on both arms. He was having a good time."

"That sounds like my brother-in-law."

"I was surprised to run into him at Big Eddy's house." Bill wanted Crystal to pick up the ball here and run with it, but so far she hadn't.

"Why, Rad knows everyone. And if there's a party, Rad's there."

"Apparently so. Tell me, Crystal, does anyone know what Rad does for a living?" he chuckled, trying to take any seriousness out of his inquiry. "I'm really interested in the answer."

"Only Rad knows and everyone else speculates. He's never shared with me. I can't imagine he's shared with anyone else. So, everyone would be subject to the hearsay rule!"

"I keep forgetting you're a lawyer."

"So do a lot of people," she smiled mischievously.

"I suppose it works to your advantage."

"Yes. It usually does."

They finished their lunch and Bill headed back to headquarters. He had tried one more time to get Crystal to offer any suggestions about her husband's comments, but she declined to take the bait. He didn't learn much about Radcliffe either.

Before Bill went back to work he stopped home to pick up his miniature tape recorder, which was small enough to leave no bulges in his clothes. He planned to start using his tape recorder with his bosses. It was illegal to use one without notifying the other party, but that's for those who play by the rules. Rules were being violated behind his back and he preferred an even playing field.

He found Kasolkasky in his office. Kasolkasky had twenty minutes to talk before his next meeting, so Bill quickly brought him up to speed on his luncheon with Crystal, enhancing it in a few places.

"What I need to know, Brick, is if I get an opportunity to bust Radcliffe Dillard should I do it? There are two things going on here and I want clarification on the game plan."

"What do you mean, Bill?"

"I mean the Chief doesn't believe in this voodoo crap and we need to put pressure on Big Eddy. But, the Chief was sitting in Dillard's house talking to the parents like he doesn't want them to know their son may be a suspect. The Mayor and the Chief talk about Big Eddy and Willie Taylor, but never mention Radcliffe. You were there, Brick."

Kasolkasky said nothing but nodded in agreement.

"So, I want to know if I'm in a gray area where I can bust Radcliffe, do I?"

He stared at Kasolkasky while waiting for an answer.

"Let's ask the Chief. I don't have an answer for you, Bill."

Kasolkasky had an appointment on the Chief's calendar two hours later. As Bill was walking back to the office, he reached into his sports jacket pocket tripping the off button on his tape recorder.

The afternoon was uneventful. The paperwork grind continued forward with no real suspects being identified. At five minutes of five Detective Lincoln headed for his meeting. When Bill arrived, Kasolkasky took his boss through the problem of dealing with Rad.

The Chief looked over at Bill. He understood Bill's dilemma. The Chief had been pushing putting pressure on Big Eddy and Bill was now putting the Chief's feet to the fire. Did the Chief have the guts to call Radcliffe's number if the opportunity presented itself?

"Bill, this is a decision that can only be made in the moment. We can't prejudge without knowing the nature of the incident. But, you know we'll support you regardless."

"No, I don't know that, Chief, and that's why I'm here. I'm telling you right now, if I get into a situation where I have to make a judgement call, I'm going to play it safe. Unless I hear something different, I'll play it according to the letter of the law. I'm not going to arrest Radcliffe unless I clearly find him violating that law."

The Chief didn't like Bill's answer. Treating Radcliffe with kid gloves was a doomed plan. Radcliffe was a very elusive character. He always appeared beyond the law. To put pressure on a guy like Radcliffe would require cunning and ingenuity. Detective Lincoln was not about to be creative, unless directed.

The Chief held up his hand then buzzed for his secretary. A few seconds later his secretary rang him back. The Chief announced that the meeting would be moving over to the Mayor's office. Five minutes later they strolled into Jim Efferton's office.

The Chief spoke first. "Mayor, we have a situation which requires your keen insight."

The Mayor didn't say anything, but he was observing the Chief's body language; it concerned him. The Chief explained the situation.

The Mayor, listening closely, was already looking at the bigger picture. He also understood Detective Lincoln's dilemma and now the question was how to address it. Chief Ness had led the trail right to Mayor Efferton. The Mayor was not about to let the Chief off that easy. This was politics. If you're going to play you have to be willing to get down into the pit with the big boys. That meant getting one's hands dirty.

"Chief Ness, how have you instructed Bill? After all this is still a police matter."

"I haven't instructed Bill," the Chief replied.

"Please do, Chief. After you advise him, I'll give my opinion. But you instruct him first." The Mayor was a master strategist. Chief Ness was going on record one way or another.

"Before I do," Chief Ness remarked, "I'll follow the honorable Mayor's lead. Brick, how did you instruct Bill?" The hot seat had just shifted to Kasolkasky!

"I haven't, but I will. Bill is to stay within the law at all times. If he's going to be aggressive he must be cautious. We're police officers and at all times we must be conscious of the law. Let's do this by the book. If there is any doubt, remember, follow the letter and intent of the law."

Detective Lincoln sat there playing the game. He would let all three of his superiors in this case ditto each other and, after their speeches, he'd let them know what he had heard.

"Okay. I got it. I'm going to play it safe. If there is any doubt, err on the side of the law. I will assume Radcliffe Dillard is an innocent man unless I determine differently. Thank you gentlemen."

With that last comment, Bill Lincoln stood and left the room. The police department was now right back where it was before hiring him. They had nothing. The Mayor had been willing to pursue a voodoo angle, but not the Chief. The police chief was in a spot because he believed Radcliffe could play an important part in this thing. But now Bill Lincoln had let it be known that he would not play the fall guy. The Chief was pissed and the Mayor was not pleased.

"So," the Mayor asked, "how do we put pressure on Radcliffe Dillard to talk? From what I see, Bill Lincoln has taken us farther down the road than anyone else. He's made two contacts inside the Dillard family. The opportunity for Big Eddy to talk about his relationship with Radcliffe is fading and I have little faith in Willie Taylor. I don't think he'll testify. Even if he does, who's going to believe him? So, can somebody answer any of my questions?"

The only other people in the room were Brick Kasolkasky and Ron Ness. They both looked at one another and remained silent.

"Chief Ness, you have no faith in the voodoo angle. Therefore your only path is breaking Big Eddy or getting Radcliffe to talk. Can you tell me if your plan is to do either?"

"We're working this case as hard as we can. We've got Willie Taylor in the witness protection program..."

"Spare me the details, Chief," the Mayor said, cutting off the Chief in mid-sentence. "I know the status of the investigation. My question is what are your next steps? What are your plans to break Big Eddy?" The Mayor was looking directly into the Chief's eyes, holding the Chief's gaze.

"We're doing our best," the Chief responded.

"Ron, is your current objective of using Willie Taylor's testimony your primary plan to break Big Eddy?" the Mayor asked in his best no-nonsense voice.

"Yes."

"As a professional law enforcement officer, what is the likelihood of this strategy working?"

The Chief was in a box. If he said it was high, he was a fool. If he said it was low, without having an alternative plan, he would be playing right into the Mayor's hand.

"At this point I'd say it's probably less than fifty percent."

"How much below fifty percent?" the Mayor asked bluntly.

"I'd have to think about that," the Chief responded gingerly.

The Mayor turned and faced Kasolkasky. "Brick, in your professional opinion, what is the percentage of success?"

"I'd say about two percent."

"That's about twice the number I had in mind," the Mayor retorted. "So, Chief Ness, Brick and I agree with you that the percentage is less than fifty percent. I think you need another plan."

The Chief didn't say a thing. He just looked at the Mayor.

"If you believe Radcliffe is involved, you need to go after him. I'm aware of the politics. Franklin Dillard Sr. will be a major factor, but he'd be a factor, regardless. If we don't find his daughter's killer he'll be a major problem too. I believe we can trust Detective Lincoln because he's not rash. He's a thinker. If he gets an opportunity he'll make the best of it."

The Chief spoke up. "Suppose we arrest Radcliffe. Then what?"

"We simply don't know what will happen," the Mayor responded. "But, at least we'd have something to eventually begin applying pressure on the guy! Right now, we're nowhere. Brick, what do you think?"

"We're still analyzing the voodoo angle. Bill's working on some leads. Putting pressure on Big Eddy is going to be difficult. I don't see Willie Taylor holding up; he can't take the pressure. Also, I'm not sure we can take the political pressure that Franklin Dillard Sr. can put on us should it come to that."

"Suppose Radcliffe is involved?" the Mayor asked.

"If that's the case, then I believe the old man will not come down hard on us. But we'll be heavily exposed until then."

"Gentlemen, I believe we have little choice. I believe we need to give Bill the green light. Agreed?"

After a brief discussion all reluctantly agreed with the Mayor. The Mayor's secretary reached Bill by pager. Bill got the page and called the office. He was in conference with Detectives Jones and White but told the secretary he'd be over in five minutes. Bill knew the individuals in the Mayor's office had changed their minds. It was the only sensible thing they could do.

Detective Lincoln returned to the meeting once again and sat down. The Mayor spoke first. "Bill, we've been discussing the situation and have come to the conclusion that the only way to get Radcliffe to talk is to put some serious pressure on him."

He immediately interrupted the chief politician. "Excuse me, Mayor, but when you say we've been discussing the situation, who is this we?"

"Detective Kasolkasky, the Chief and myself."

"Okay," Bill nodded. His tape was on.

"I want to make sure we're all very clear on what's being discussed," he continued.

"We want you to know we have absolute confidence in you. You've got our consensus to go after Radcliffe," the Mayor responded.

"Thanks, but I need more than your consensus. We need clarity. I'll need your support afterward if, indeed, I'm able to get anything on him. I want everyone to agree that I'm being given a green light to be aggressive in my pursuit of Radcliffe and that I've got your continued support if we take Radcliffe down. I can't take the potential media firestorm alone. I know that. It must be unanimous. I don't want to hear a different story at some news conference later on."

"We understand your concerns, Bill," the Mayor commented.

They talked for another fifteen or twenty minutes with Bill questioning them intently on every aspect and nuance he could think of. The tape captured it all. If he got the opportunity to arrest Radcliffe Dillard, he'd have ammunition to protect himself, particularly if one of the three people that he reported to started singing a different tune.

Men never do evil so completely and cheerfully as when they do if from religious conviction.

Blaise Pascal: Pensees.

Chapter 24

It was the last week of the month and Detective Lincoln had made arrangements to attend Marie 'Mama' Francois's voodoo ceremony on Sunday, the 30th. He also had to decide whether or not to bring Detective Jones along. Detective Dick White also wanted to come, but Lincoln quickly ruled that out, since White was white. Bill had never attended a voodoo ceremony but he knew enough not to expect many white strangers. Whether he brought Detective Jones or not depended on how well Clarence could portray the role of a West Indian, complete with accent.

Minutes later, Clarence entered the room dressed in jeans and black soft leather shoes, a dangling left earring, a shirt with cut off sleeves and his open collar displaying a shiny gold necklace. A blue and white polka dot bandana was wrapped around his head hanging down his back. Dark shades concealed his eyes and a fake tattoo on his right biceps read 'Caribbean King.' He strutted into the room with a big grin.

"Hey, mon, what it be? Long time no see!"

Clarence walked up to Bill and grabbed his hand like a gang member greeting another, pumping it hard and grinning in Bill's face. "You like some jerk chicken, my mon? I just cook some…it be smokin', mon! I like it wit me special sauce. It hot, mon. Can you take the heat?"

"Alright, Clarence, you're coming with me on Sunday, but let's not go overboard with the role. How about playing the character of a quiet reserved Jamaican businessman?"

Clarence stepped back and cocked his head. He started rubbing his right palm against his chest. "I don't know, mon, me got big talent just oozing to get out. Big talent!"

"Something is definitely oozing, Clarence. By the way, did you read those books on voodoo I recommended?"

"Yeah, mon. That's some interesting stuff. I didn't know they had ceremonies around here."

"I didn't either, until now."

They spent the next hour together concocting a story for their voodoo excursion.

--

Sunday evening, Bill and Clarence rolled along on a rural road in a thirty year old Pontiac Bonneville kicking up dust clouds the size of Mt. Rushmore. The car needed a serious paint job and a good tune-up, but otherwise it ran. They found 666 Natas Lane, a huge, dilapidated two-story house with chipped paint, old rusted ornaments hanging from ill-conceived locations and a curved, unpaved driveway. The paint was a dull brown giving the house a somber look.

Weeping willows were scattered around the property with twelve huge sycamore trees guarding the house in the foreground. A porch surrounded the front and side. Bill envisioned an old southern gentleman sitting out on the veranda enjoying a mint julep.

The two men got out and examined themselves for anything that could bring attention. Everything was fine other than a price tag dangling from Clarence's new phony eyeglasses. After removing the tag they started walking towards the entrance.

Detective Lincoln knocked. A large man, in need of a sunny disposition, opened the door. The man was wearing a sports jacket and Bill could tell by the bulge beneath his coat the man was carrying a 'piece.' Detective Lincoln spoke first. "Hey, mon, dis be Mama's place?"

"Who wants to know?" the large man asked. His beady eyes focused squarely on the two new men. Obviously, he was leery of strangers.

"Me name's Michael Kingly. Spoke with Mama's person a week ago. She say to come on out and she will make a charm for me unborn child. Som'ting to keep away da evil spirits, ya know. She say to bring fifty doolar and me did."

"And who's that?" the large man said looking at Clarence.

"Oh, him. Why tat's me cousin. Him named Frankie. Him got de car."

The man looked at Clarence again and when he turned his entire body moved like a robot with his neck fused together.

"Give me the money. I'll let you in one at a time. But first, I'm going to search you."

Lincoln pulled out two twenties and a ten, which the large man counted, then he motioned Bill through the door first. As he entered the man carefully observed Clarence before closing the door in his face. Bill was checked for a weapon and after finding none the large man re-opened the door and the frisking procedure was repeated on Clarence.

"You can go back now," the man said, pointing his finger. Bill and Clarence started walking.

There was activity everywhere; people were standing around, talking and drinking. The atmosphere was similar to that of a concert with people patiently waiting for the main event. The two lawmen were inside sampling punch in the kitchen when a lady approached them, introducing herself as a close associate of Mama's.

"Welcome. I don't think I've met you gentlemen before. My name is Francisca."

"Me name's Michael Kingly and this here's me cousin, Frankie. Mama is making a charm for me baby to keep the evil spirits away." Bill used his hands in expressive gestures as he talked.

"Oh yes, you spoke with me. Did you give your money to the gentleman at the door?" Francisca asked.

"Oh yes. De big mon," Bill replied.

"He's part of our security team," Francisca responded.

"Mama make me charm?" he asked to keep the conversation going.

"Yes. And it should work well. Mama took her time with it. She's very good."

"Dat's what me hear."

"Does your cousin need anything?" Francisca asked while looking at Clarence.

"Hey, Frankie," Bill boldly inquired, "ya need som'ting?"

Clarence finally talked for the first time since he had been inside. "Nah. Me just the driver tonight, mon. Me cousin, Michael, can't drive worth crap. Em no have a car and me not letting him drive mine. No way mon. Me drive 'im 'ere and save me car."

"I see," said Francisca. "Here, let me get you boys some fine Jamaican rum to go with that punch."

Outside, an unmarked police car with an African-American and a Hispanic-American undercover cop, each dressed in casual clothes, pulled into the parking lot. They eventually found a parking spot and just sat in the car for a half-hour or so watching the house. The parking lot was cemetery quiet when they finally got out; opening the trunk, they retrieved a special night vision video camera. They methodically walked around the area filming the license plates of all the vehicles. They finished and quietly left the area without anyone from the house having noticed them.

The people inside the house began moving to the backyard where a platform was set up. The light illuminating the stage came from huge fire lanterns, which gave the setting an eerie feeling. There was also an unusual fragrance, like someone had put incense in the lanterns. Three drummers played conga drums; many in the crowd started dancing to the music. It was a driving, methodical rhythm. The primal beat gradually entered your mind as it must've done thousands of years ago, when early mankind first swayed to the driving rhythm of the drum.

The percussive pulse kept coming, like an endless country road, while getting ever louder. A dozen minutes later, a large dark-skinned man dressed in black walked on stage. He proceeded to move rhythmically...back and forth...side to side, slowly scanning the crowd. Sternness gripped his person. Suddenly, he began to engage the crowd. Many of the people who crowded the stage were reaching up in an effort to touch the man, but he stayed just beyond their eagerly outstretched fingers.

Seconds later, a woman garbed in a long flowing white dress appeared on stage. She sat in the lone empty seat, a large throne-like chair. The crowd, upon seeing her, immediately started to chant... Mama...Mama Francois ...Mama... Mama Francois... Some cried out for Mama to bless them, others to remove some curse. Obviously, they believed Marie Francois possessed awesome power!

Another man walked on stage and placed an empty bowl at her feet. The dark-skinned man in black was still moving on the platform. Bill didn't know where it came from but now the man held a live chicken by its neck. He began to strut up and down the stage talking and shaking his fingers at the people, working them into a frenzy!

Next, as if by magic, there appeared a gleaming knife in the man's right hand. A hush came over the crowd when they saw the knife, which he held high above his head. Everyone watched spellbound. The man in black began crying out a chant of offering to their great voodoo god. The crowd was transfixed. The man then turned and faced Marie Francois, while she stared back. He raised the chicken along with the knife above his head; his arms were trembling as he continued calling out his praises. He walked toward Mama Francois, standing at her feet; he towered over her. Then, suddenly, he took the knife and sliced the chicken's head off! Blood flew everywhere. His black clothes obscured the blood on him, but she was wearing an exquisite white gown and now there were crimson red blotches splattered across the front of it.

The man went down to one knee; he directed the blood flowing from the chicken into the bowl sitting at Marie Francois' feet. When the draining of the blood was completed,he unceremoniously tossed the chicken's carcass aside. He then held the knife, lifted the bowl and said something, while looking directly into Marie Francois's eyes. He drank from the bowl, still looking at her. The man then handed Madam Francois the bowl as the drums started beating again. Everyone felt the methodical rhythm. The crowd swayed as the beat grew louder and stronger. The man in black stood in front of Marie Francois and began showering her with great praises.

"You, the chosen one, the one he will ride should he come this night! Summon The Magnificent One; announce that we stand ready to receive him. Tell him to come so that we may praise him. The exalted one will protect us if only we ask. You are his messenger. It is you who he has chosen to receive his Holy Spirit. Drink the living blood. Demonstrate your worthiness… prepare for his great spirit; for then he will know that you are his willing vessel. Drink the blood and call him now, so that we may bear witness!"

The crowd observed the proceedings completely transfixed as a predator would watch potential prey enter its strike zone. It was so quiet it was surreal. Twentieth-century western culture was deactivated; they were now spiraling back several centuries in the past, into a different cultural time zone. Marie Francois brought the blood bowl to her lips, drinking deeply, and allowing the warm red fluid to drench her dress. She then fell to her knees and remained there. The man in black started speaking in tongue, encouraging the crowd to join in with him. They called for the great voodoo god to appear!

Ninety seconds later, Mama Francois slowly lifted her head; she turned and focused on the man in black. Her whole demeanor was now serpentine-like. The man in black cried out, "Damballa, are you Damballa? Are you among us O' Great One?"

The crowd silently watched as the man in black threw something on one of the lanterns, extinguishing the fire. He moved to another lantern repeating his actions. It became darker and Bill was thinking that the voodoo god must like it dark. There was only one fire lantern going now, the one furthest from the stage.

"Damballa...Damballa," the man in black cried out again, while looking at Marie Francois on her knees before him. Suddenly, she moved toward him in snake-like fashion, slithering across stage, as if possessed.

"Look," the man in black cried out to the crowd, "The Great One is with us! Damballa lives! Damballa lives!" he shouted while walking up and down the stage exciting the crowd. He was pointing at Marie Francois slithering around the stage before he turned back to the crowd and roared at them, "Do you want the great voodoo god to bless you?! Who wants his blessing?!"

The crowd cried out in response, pleading to be blessed. Slowly now the man in black started walking into the crowd until it had completely engulfed him. He was taking their money and giving them something in return, but Bill couldn't see what it was. Marie Francois remained in the center of the stage in a coiled-like position with her eyes fixated on the man in black. Her tongue slid in and out like a serpent's.

"What do you think, Clarence?" Bill asked.

"Don't even ask."

The man in black was still working the crowd when every so often Mama Francois slithered from place to place before stopping and coiling. Her tongue still mimicked a snake's.

It was almost forty-five minutes later before the man in black climbed back on stage and walked over to the snake-like Mama Francois, once more towering over her. He mouthed several strange phrases causing her to go limp; immediately two people waiting in the wings came out to pick her up. They loaded her on a stretcher signaling the end of the ceremony. People soon began drifting back into the house. Francisca, the woman who Bill and Clarence had met inside that night, came over. She had something in her hand.

"Mr. Kingly, here's your charm! It'll keep evil spirits from your baby."

He graciously accepted the small package while wondering what was in it. "Thank you. Mama tis truly a powerful voodooiane! Can me stay and meet her?"

"Let me check."

Bill and Clarence mingled with the crowd for another hour before Marie Francois graced the room. She was wearing a long dress beautifully imprinted with colorful patterns, a turban and sandals. She had a rustic look but an urbane presence about her. It was difficult to get near her because of all the people who wanted to talk with and touch her. It was much later before the two lawmen actually spoke with Ms. Francois.

"Michael and Frankie, I'd like to introduce you to our great voodooiane, Madam Francois," Francisca announced. Michael and

Frankie each took a little bow toward Mama to show their respect. Mama bowed her head in return.

"Tis a pleasure to meet you, Mama," Bill said. "Me have 'eard great things about you. Great things."

Clarence added, "The ceremony was very very good. Me tell me cousin, Michael, she de best I ever see."

"Thank you, gentlemen," responded Ms. Francois. "It's good to have you here. Did you get the charm I made for you, Michael?"

"Yes. It is right over dere," Michael said, while pointing his hand at his possessions lying on a table in a corner. "How do it work, Mama?" he inquired.

"You must rub the baby with it before it goes to sleep. Do this for two weeks. Newborns are most fragile then."

"Michael will listen to Mama. Me do exactly as you say because me want me baby to be strong and healthy. Me don't want no evil spirits touching her."

"Good. Then rest assured, your child will be safe."

"Mama. Me have one question."

Marie Francois looked at him and smiled. "What's your question, Michael?"

"Me visited LA a few years ago. And there me went to another voodoo ceremony to receive a blessing so I could get me a good job. Couldn't find no job. Paid thirty doolars to this voodoo lady named Jezebel Balboa and me still couldn't find no job! That's de other reason why me here...couldn't find no work in LA. How come dat voodoo woman couldn't help me find no job?"

"Many pretenders lurk out there, Michael. Or perhaps the great voodoo god was unfriendly. Did you do exactly what you were told?"

"Oh yes, Mama! Oh yes."

"Do you have a pure heart? The Great One knows."

"Guess so. What is this pure heart stuff?"

"Well, Michael, it may be you were trying to buy good blessings instead of truly earning them. I don't know. Then again, the voodoo lady may be a fraud."

Bill was thinking he wasn't getting far using this approach. She sounded like a politician.

"How can me know dis woman fo' real, Mama?" he asked waving his hands to emphasize his concern.

"I'd have to talk to her. I can't tell from your story. The world of voodoo is a special world."

"She took me money. Didn't get no job."

"I don't know, Michael."

"How me know she for real, Mama?"

"You don't."

"Me work hard fo' me money. She just took it!"

"You're sure, Michael?"

"Yes, Mama; me know some dudes who may want to have a special meeting with you. Dey some heavyweights. It could be of great benefit to you. Are you interested, Mama?"

"I'm always interested in meeting interesting people, Michael."

"Good, Mama. Tell me now, how do me get a hold of ya. Do ya have private number?"

"Here's my special card, Michael. This is the best way to reach me."

"Okay, Mama. Me and me cousin ar' outta here."

There wasn't anything more. Marie Francois moved to the next group of people and Bill and Clarence exited the premises.

"So, what did we learn tonight, Clarence?" Bill glanced over at his partner who was contemplating his answer.

"Geez, I don't know, but I'd hate to be a chicken hanging out in this neighborhood!"

Chapter 25

Detective Lincoln arrived at headquarters the next morning early for the 8 o'clock staff meeting. He was informed that Macario, the Cuban bodybuilder, had been arrested the prior night on a minor traffic violation. A small amount of cocaine was found on him. Booked and in jail, he awaited arraignment.

"Were you tailing him?" he asked the Captain.

"Periodically. We watch him twice a week, usually Friday nights and Saturdays throughout the day. Last night we tracked Macario back to Radcliffe Dillard's house. He was there for about an hour. When he left, he committed a minor traffic violation. So naturally, our boys pulled him over. The arresting officer felt he was acting strangely. He searched him and found a few grams of cocaine."

"Did he say where he got it?"

"He's not talking."

"Did he make his one telephone call yet?"

"Yes. He called Radcliffe."

"Do you know who his attorney is?"

"Nah, not yet."

"I think I'm going to try to visit him today," announced the Detective.

"I think that's a good idea," Kasolkasky replied.

"By the way, we have a small problem, Bill." Chief Ness directed his attention at Detective Lincoln. The Chief's body language was sending mixed signals. Bill was curious about the slight change in the top cop's tone of voice.

"What's that, Chief?" Bill asked.

"We were just informed that the conversation between Radcliffe and Macario last night may have been accidentally taped by Internal Affairs. We're set up to tape conversations, by court order, on telephone four. Macario was supposed to make his call on telephone three but another prisoner was using it at the time. As you know, Bill, we can't eavesdrop because we're sworn police officers." The Chief continued looking straight at him as Bill maintained eye contact.

"And I can? Is that what you're saying, Chief?"

"All I said was as sworn police officers we couldn't."

"So why haven't you destroyed it yet, Chief?"

"It's scheduled to be erased at 5:00 P.M. this evening. Standard procedure. Electronic burns are done once a week."

"I know it's been awhile since I've worked down here, but that site was in a restricted area. I'm not authorized."

Kasolkasky immediately started speaking. "Bill, remember that project I wanted started before you told me you had a lunch meeting with Crystal Dillard?"

"Yeah."

"I still need you to do it. Part of the required information just happens to be in that restricted area. I've arranged a security pass for you. You're scheduled to be there at 1P.M. Sergeant Thompson will direct you. Any questions?"

"No. I'll be there."

After the meeting ended, while inside an empty bathroom, Bill reached into his pocket, turning off his tape.

At 11A.M., Bill received a call from Crystal Dillard inviting him for cocktails after work. He agreed to meet her at 6 P.M. at the same hotel where they met for lunch. He was hoping he'd learn something this time.

At five minutes before 1 P.M., Bill began walking to the restricted area. He knocked twice and Sergeant Thompson opened the door.

He followed Sergeant Thompson to the designated area. While talking to Bill the officer motioned towards a tape machine. He asked if Bill wouldn't mind holding down the fort while he went to the head.

Bill studied the anointed tape player. He put the labeled tape in the machine, put the headset on and pushed the 'on' button. After a few seconds of forwarding and rewinding, he heard the ringing of a phone and then...Macario's voice.

"Hello, Rad?"

"Macar?"

"Yeah. I'm in jail."

"What! What happened?!"

"They pulled me over for a traffic violation. They said I was acting funny and searched the car. They found some coke in my pocket."

"Damn!"

"I know."

"The other stuff in the car is okay?"

"Yeah."

"Look, they can only get you for a misdemeanor. Don't say anything. I'm sending a lawyer down first thing in the morning!"

"Okay!"

Bill heard the click of the phone ending the conversation. He rewound the tape and played it back, this time recording the conversation onto his tape. Sergeant Thompson returned twenty minutes later to show Bill where the 'other' information was. When Bill returned upstairs he went to Kasolkasky's office. When he got there Brick was doing paperwork.

"We need to search Macario's car again. There's dope inside."

Kasolkasky picked up the phone to order a more thorough search of Macario's car. When he finished, he turned around, glanced at Bill and pushed back in his chair while folding his arms across his chest. Bill was leaning against the cabinet looking at Kasolkasky. Neither said anything. Both were thinking.

Detective Lincoln headed home at four-thirty to prepare for his 'date' with Crystal. He decided to shower, shave and wear a suit. He wasn't sure why he was doing it. Maybe it was because she was such a beautiful woman. He checked the mirror twice before getting into his car.

Once inside the hotel he scanned the area for Crystal. He was confident she'd be late. He'd never known any beautiful outrageous flirt to be on time and he'd never known a 'real' man, with an abundance of testosterone cruising through his veins, to not wait either.

At 6:15 P.M., a waiter approached, informing him the party he was waiting for was in Suite 324. The man pointed to the appropriate elevator and then left. Bill was intrigued. However, he first went to his car to retrieve his trusty little tape recorder.

Bill arrived at the room and briefly scanned the hallway. He then turned on his tape and knocked twice. Crystal opened the door and invited him into the room. She was poured into a well-tailored black suit and wore black stiletto heels to match. She wore her hair stylishly up and her make-up was perfect.

"I felt this would be much more appropriate considering who my husband is. Wouldn't you agree?" Crystal asked with a devilish smile. Her whole face lit up when she smiled. She was captivating. He felt excited just watching her.

"I'm easy to please. I'm really not one for cliches, but… umm… you do look marvelous. I'm surprised Franklin doesn't tie you up every night and forbid you to leave the house."

"I could certainly go along with at least one part of that scenario, Detective," Crystal smiled again sending more warm vibrations throughout his system.

"What can I get you to drink? I'm drinking a Chardonnay made for the gods. Like a glass?"

"By all means. I'll have whatever you're having."

"Good answer," Crystal said with another bemused smile while she turned seductively and walked to the bar. His eyes followed her every step. She was exquisite!

"Tell me, Crystal, did you have a good day today because you seem rather lively."

"I had a wonderful day. It feels good to be alive and by the way, I like that suit on you. You wear it well."

"Thank you."

"Did you go home and change just for me?"

"Why yes, I did."

"Why?"

"Because I've been programmed by two or three million years of social conditioning? It's the Pavlov's dog syndrome. Man see woman, man start slobbering."

"And after the saliva starts flowing, then what?" Crystal asked, while sitting down directly across from him, crossing her legs. She was smiling again with twinkling eyes.

"The unskilled man is doomed. He's a puppet with no more chance than the Christians had against the lions. He might as well give the woman whatever she wants because he hasn't a snowball's chance in Hell. Another cliche, oh well."

"And a skilled man, Bill? What chance does he have against the 'devious' ways of the skillful and determined huntress?"

She sat there with that same devilish little smile, caressing her glass of chilled wine, never once taking her eyes away from his.

"Limited. Very limited. As E.P.B. White said decades ago, 'Give a woman an inch and she'll park a car on it'." He smiled.

Crystal chuckled. "How's Monique?"

"I haven't spoken with her since last week."

"What's not happening there, Bill? I still think you two would be good for each other. What's not clicking?"

"Well, perhaps it's my involvement in this case and perhaps because I already have a lady friend, but that's merely conjecture."

Crystal smiled again. "Such commitment! Bill, I had no idea you had such high moral standards." With that she then slowly uncrossed and crossed her long sexy legs.

"Quite the contrary. I was simply saying I'm extremely busy."

"Oh. So are you saying you're not a person with high moral integrity?" Her beautiful eyes were still focused on his. She was working him over and he knew it.

"I don't know what moral integrity is anymore. You give me the situation... I'll give you my opinion. It's all relative."

Crystal continued smiling at him. She was extremely attentive with that wicked smile etched on her face. Then as before, she uncrossed her legs but, this time she brought them up underneath her and sat on them.

"Okay. How about a married woman who is bored and looking for a little action on the side? Is that immoral enough for you?"

"That might be more normal and rational than having bored sex within a marriage. I guess it depends on the people. I won't make moral judgements but I can give my honest opinion. For instance, I can't believe in a god with all the pre-packaged hypocrisy and ambiguities. That's all mumbo jumbo to me."

"Why, Bill, you're a credit to your race. You've broken out of that matrix."

"I had too much awareness to stay asleep. I got tired of closing my eyes and my mind."

"What about mommy and daddy? You don't want to hurt them do you?"

"I don't want to hurt myself, first and foremost. And what about you, Ms. Riddler?"

Bill's term of endearment caused Crystal to wiggle around slightly, presumably to get more comfortable. As a consequence she was also showing a lot more leg now.

"When I saw Mommy playing Santa I realized parents have the capacity to lie. And of course, Dad playing post office with the neighbor's wife told me all I needed to know about morality."

"The old post office game. How many times have I seen that one?"

"I just needed to see it once because I was such a precocious little girl and after all talk is cheap."

"Hum...daddy's little girl." He could easily imagine Crystal controlling her father.

"Yes, but not Daddy's little dummy. Mother Dear played that role."

"So, Crystal, am I ever to learn about your husband's remarks that evening? I'm still curious." Bill tasted his wine. It was delicious. Then again, he expected it to be.

"How curious?" Crystal asked seductively. "How much are you willing to pay?"

"What type of currency are we talking about here?"

"Why, you know...the oldest bartering system in the world."

"I'm going to have to read my history books when I get home this evening."

With that, Crystal got up, walked over to the bar and refilled her drink. She walked back toward Bill but stepped past him to the light switch, flicking it off! Two small perfumed candles now lit the room. Crystal pushed another button and soft music was playing. Turning, she walked straight toward the Detective, put her glass on the table and settled down sweetly in his lap. Her hand went to work on the back of his head. Slowly, deliciously, she started to rub his neck while looking deeply into his eyes.

"Just how bad do you want this information?" she purred softly.

"Um...I don't know; this is beyond my field of expertise."

"Is it? Somehow I find that response interesting, but most unlikely. I've noticed you're into cliches. Well, I have one for you."

Crystal definitely had a way of getting a man's attention and by now there was little doubt that she had definitely 'peaked' his interest!

"I'm listening."

"Well...is that a fat roll of quarters I'm feeling, or are you just happy to see me Big Boy?" she cooed in a bewitchingly Mae West voice.

"You have a most active imagination."

"That's what my father always said. Apparently, I also have a very 'stiff' imagination too," she purred.

"Your daddy was very observant."

Crystal was fondling his ear. "What do you want right now, Bill? Share your thoughts with me. Who knows, your every wish could become my every command."

"That's just what I'm afraid of," he said weakly.

"Oh, is the mind strong but the flesh getting a little weak?" she breathed hotly in his ear.

He was thinking, 'Greater words have never been spoken' as he attempted to shift his legs, but to no avail. Crystal enjoyed her position.

"Do you like fruit, Bill?"

He was thinking again, 'Where was she going now?'

"I like most healthy things."

"Well, I like bananas; how about you?"

"A very good source of potassium."

"I actually like the shape of bananas."

"I don't see anything so unusual about it, compared to other fruit."

"Mind you now, I don't like them soft. I like them long, thick and hard, Bill."

"I'm sure the nutritional content is similar, regardless of texture," he sputtered out.

"I like to hold them in this hand, Bill. I like the way they feel; it makes me... how'd you say? Oh yes, 'vibrant' when I squeeze one. They're so incredibly delicious that I find myself 'willfully desiring' one everyday...every...day!"

"Well...umm...let's see...sounds like you might have a serious potassium deficiency."

Crystal had his 'full' attention now! He was thinking that if he had this kind of focus in school, he'd be a nuclear physicist today.

"Oh, I do. But alas, Franklin unfortunately doesn't share my taste!"

"There are many ways to serve up fruit, Crystal."

"Well, you should know that I prefer mine served methodically... very slow and very hard."

Again he tried weakly to change the subject. "Have you thought about apples? You know...'an apple a day' and all that?"

Yes, but, I want a banana. And, I want what I want ...now. Now tell me, what do you want, my good man?"

This was a situation every man dreamed about but would never have come true. Bill was living a fantasy; he thought, unfortunately, sometimes you get just what you wished for.

"I suffer from a dream deficit disorder, my dreams are very boring. They're always 'GP' rated."

"Now that's funny, because mine are always rated triple X!"

"I guess I'm not about to learn any new information tonight, am I?"

"Oh, I can promise you there are new things, wonderful sensuous things for ...the Riddler...to teach you tonight. You can be absolutely sure about that!"

Bill was confident that Crystal was right but he wasn't going to say it. He wasn't about to throw gasoline on this roaring fire.

"I was referring to your husband's speech."

"I sure wasn't."

"Could you give me a hint?"

"Let's just say I enjoy being on top."

"I was still referring to your husband's speech."

"But, as you know, I was not."

She was fast; he knew he was at a distinct disadvantage. "We seem to be having two different conversations."

"It does appear that way. Why don't you tell me your wildest fantasy my hard, I mean, my good man?"

"I was trying to do that."

"I mean your most outrageous sexual fantasy. We must concentrate only on your pleasure, Bill. That other business can be done anytime. Now, think about what you've always wanted to do …with… a…slut!"

His mind was spinning like a pair of dice in a high rollin' crapshooter's hand now. Who would believe this?

"I really need to try to determine the motive behind your husband's remarks."

"Bill, that's so boring and besides, your body is telling me that it's more interested in determining something else."

"The flesh is weak, I'll admit to that."

"Well, what would you like to do right now?"

"Let's just say my mind and my body are at odds."

"What's our problem? It's certainly not underneath me!" Crystal rubbed his neck slowly, still staring entrancingly into his eyes. She slowly opened two buttons of his shirt and gently, yet firmly, stroked his chest. He was on cloud nine.

"I don't date married women."

"Morally offensive?"

"No, too many hassles. There are available single women without the major headaches called husbands."

"What a shame, because you're a great specimen of manhood. I dressed for you, too."

"That's a gorgeous outfit. You wear it well."

"Oh, but that's not what I mean. I guess I'll have to take this little suit off and show you."

This lady was too bold! He had just never met a woman this aggressive!

"Maybe not, I'll take your word for it. I'm just trying to uncover your husband's motive!"

"I'll make you a deal. After you help me undress, we'll check to see if you're still carrying that rather large roll of quarters. Then I'll give you your answer. If you're still carrying that hard roll, I'm going to dedicate myself to buttering it all up! Now, if you aren't, economically speaking 'inflated', you're a free man and the pressure…well, the pressure is off."

Bill was trying to stay cool, but his hormones had strapped on jack-boots and were marching like a mongoose in a tub of marbles… vigorously, through his system.

"What's behind door number two? Contestants are always given choices."

"In this game there is no door number two, not if you want an answer to your question."

Crystal started to rub his neck again while smiling, still looking directly into his eyes.

"Do you always get what you want?"

"Always…"

Her fragrance was driving him crazy! Crystal gently stroked his face. She had a feather touch, soft and sensuous. She then pulled herself slightly up on his lap, kissed her finger and then put her finger against his lips, holding it there. Crystal watched him intently for several silent moments before lightly kissing Bill in a series of short pecks at first, and then each one getting longer. She then slid her tongue into his mouth. The Detective's willpower had deserted him like a gentle autumn breeze blowing a leaf from a tree.

An hour-and-a-half later Bill and Crystal dressed. Crystal had just finished brushing her hair and was preparing to go home. Bill was sitting on the end of the bed watching her. She had finished with her makeup, picked up her purse and walked over and kissed him goodbye. It was a slow, soulful kiss and she snuggled against him so that he could once again feel her body. Moments later, as she was about to reach the door, Bill asked his question one last time.

"So, why did your husband make those remarks about the Mayor?"

Crystal turned around and leaned against the open door. Her hair was now down, cresting on her shoulders as she struck an extremely feminine pose. She stared at him, liking what she saw. She held his gaze, then gave him a sly smile. A deal was a deal. And, Crystal was a woman of her word.

"Because the Mayor was 'seeing' me. Good-bye, Detective."

Chapter 26

"Hello, Macar."

Macario nodded at Detective Lincoln.

"May I sit down?"

"Sure."

"The police informed me that a few grams of cocaine were found on you yesterday."

"I made a small mistake."

"We all do. Hopefully the small ones don't hurt us too much."

Macario was silent. He was in a card game with few cards to play.

"The police were about to let you go but decided to take a closer look inside your car. Is there anything you want to tell me now? If you cooperate it will be easier for you. The more you tell us on your own, the better."

"What do you mean? Did you find something?"

"At least four pounds of high grade powder. You're not going home today, Macar."

Macario remained silent. If life were chess pieces, he was an isolated pawn.

"If you tell us the whole story we might be able to do something for you. If not, you'll certainly face the full force of the law."

"I'm not saying anything, not until I see my lawyer."

"You're sure?"

"Very."

"See you around." Bill got up and left.

Detective Lincoln wanted to talk to Marie Francois again, only this time as a policeman, to have her evaluate Ms. Balboa. He called Ms. Francois's number. Bill went into his 'Michael Kingly' routine and got an appointment to see her at week's end.

At home that evening, Bill had poured a drink and was about to record his notes, when the phone rang.

"Hello?"

"Bill?"

"Hello, Monique, how are you?"

"Fine. I just received a call saying Macar was in jail. Is this true?"

"Yes. I saw him this morning."

"What happened?"

"Who called you?"

"My girlfriend, the one who exercises with me. She had a class tonight and Macar wasn't there. She inquired at the desk but they gave her such a strange answer that she started calling around."

There was a moment of silence. Bill listened carefully before deciding she was telling him the truth. Then he said, "The police, after stopping him on a minor traffic violation, found a few grams of cocaine. They impounded the car. Officers searched the car later and found several pounds of coke. It's obviously for more than personal use."

"I'm so sorry."

"Why?"

"Because I know him. He's not a bad person."

"Will you continue to see him?"

"It's not like we had a conventional relationship."

He noticed she qualified her answer.

"I didn't say anything about a conventional relationship. I asked, 'Will you continue to see him?'"

"No. I don't associate with people who use or sell drugs."

"Bill, I forgot, my brother Rad is having a party next week. I'd like you to escort me."

"I accept. Let me know the details soon."

"Okay. Goodbye."

"Goodnight."

He was feeling good. He reflected on how he had enjoyed Monique's company the last time at the fundraiser at Franklin and Crystal's house. Two hours later, the phone rang again.

"Bill?"

"Yes."

"This is Connie Chow."

He could tell she was upset. "What's wrong?"

"Someone shoved a letter under my door. The words are cut out and glued on to form the body of the letter."

"What does it say, Connie?"

"It's a childish poem. 'Roses are red, Violets are blue, Willie won't make it and neither will you.' And then it says, 'Greetings from LA'."

"LA? What's in Los Angeles?" There was a long pause; he could feel Connie's anxiety.

"My daughter," she said softly.

"Where do you live, Connie? I'm coming over."

Connie lived in a gated community condo in the Oakland Hills. Bill arrived a half-hour later.

"Let me see the letter."

It was exactly as Connie had described. Being found under her door sent another message...a gated community meant little in relation to providing safety.

"Where's the envelope?"

Connie went to the kitchen and returned with a blank, legal size standard envelope.

"Was the letter the only thing?"

"...Yes."

She said it so softly, without real conviction that Bill stared at her.

"Connie, are you sure?"

Her head was faced downward, there was something wrong. She turned, then went back to the kitchen bringing out a second sheet of paper. On that sheet were the words, 'Don't call the police.'" Below it was a snapshot of her daughter cut out of a ten-year old newspaper article.

"What are you going to do?" he asked.

"I'm going to go see my daughter tomorrow and hopefully send her away. I'll secure the locks on my doors and put in a better security system. I must call the police. And Bill, I'd like you to teach me how to use a gun."

"When do you want to start?"

"I'll call you when I get back in town."

"Bill?"

"Yes."

"We're meeting the guy who claims you knew more than you testified."

"Who is it?"

"We don't know. His name has not been released."

"I want to know who it is."

"When I'm able to tell you, I will; but right now, we don't know, not for sure."

Knowledge without integrity is dangerous and dreadful.

IBID., CH. 41

Chapter 27

Three days later Bill helped Connie Chow buy her first pistol. Then they spent nearly two full hours at a nearby firing range.

The following evening, Bill and Clarence rolled up in an unmarked police car to meet Marie Francois. They parked in the driveway of a house located on Forest Lane in a remote area of Oakland. The house was modern and looked normal enough, unlike the site of the voodoo ceremony. Bill straightened his necktie before knocking on the ripped screen door.

"Man," Clarence retorted, "baby eagles could fly through the holes in this thing."

The same large man guarding the other house opened the door. The bulge under his arm was still quite noticeable.

"Hey, mon. Michael Kingly here to see Mama. This here's me cousin, Frankie. You meet him before. She around?"

"Mama's here," the large man said observing them closely. "Come in."

The man escorted them to the living room where Marie Francois and Francisca were sitting.

"Hello, Michael and Frankie, come sit down," Ms. Francois said.

"Good evening, Mama," Bill replied in his normal voice. Before sitting down, he grabbed his wallet and flashed the badge the department had given him. Clarence also displayed his shield.

"Ms. Francois, my real name is Bill Lincoln and I'm a private detective working with the Oakland Police Department. This is Detective Clarence Jones. Mama, we need your help."

Ms. Francois and Francisca were both speechless. The large man was standing there listening, completely bewildered. Ms. Francois finally broke the silence.

"Detectives? This is a surprise," she stated hesitantly, not knowing what to expect.

The dark skinned man on stage the night of the ceremony entered the room suddenly, glaring at Bill and Clarence. His tall, stoic persona projected a menacing look. With aristocratic ambiance, he displayed obvious contempt toward the strangers standing before him in his house.

"Who are you?!" he demanded.

"The police," Clarence replied while flashing his badge.

"Ricardo. Please...sit down," a subdued Marie Francois requested.

Ignoring her, he remained standing. Obviously no woman could tell him what to do.

"I want you out of my house! Now!" Ricardo stood commandingly, feet spread and his hands on his hips. His posture was threatening; arrogance rolled off him like water off a duck.

"I have papers I could serve... right now!" Bill barked back authoritatively, "And whether I do or not is entirely up to you! The violation of the animal rights ordinance, building code violations, alcohol infringements, and unsanitary code violations. Or you can allow me to explain my real reason for being here today. Decide. I can serve you and you'll be standing in front of a judge before you know it. We'll also have squad cars around your house every day, especially the last Sunday of the month. Your choice is simple. It's your call."

Ricardo quickly assessed the situation. He could play the macho man, maybe win this battle, but certainly lose the war.

"What do you want?" he said sternly, trying to save face.

Bill sat down again and continued talking to Ms. Francois.

"We want your opinion on Ms. Jezebel Balboa." He took a few minutes to explain the situation. Ms. Francois nodded along with Ricardo who also agreed to the request. Ricardo concluded it was far better than having the police swarming around in his business affairs.

The following morning there was a staff meeting in Kasolkasky's office. The Macario situation was the main topic.

"We've got the goods on him," Brick told the Chief. "Four pounds of the white lady and his citizenship papers are suspect. We're going to charge him with everything we can. We should expect he'll have an excellent lawyer, but this city and its people are fed up with drug dealing and drug dealers. Should we leak anything?" This question was directed at the Chief.

"Let's wait. Where'd he get the drugs?"

"He's not saying."

"He was at Radcliffe's house just before he got busted?"

"That's right, Chief."

"I want every piece of dirt you got on this guy Macario. Squeeze him like a lemon. By the way, who is his lawyer?"

"One Jorge Mills Santana."

"That Hispanic guy out of Florida?"

"That's the one."

"Damn. These two-bit criminals get these high-profile lawyers. How do they do it?"

The answer was so obvious no one bothered to respond.

"Let's make sure we do this one strictly by the book. Anything else?"

Detective Lincoln raised his hand. "Clarence and I have made contact again with the voodoo lady here in Oakland and she's agreed to see Ms. Balboa to render her opinion. I'd like to fly Ms. Balboa up here to have the two of them meet."

"And just what would you expect from such a meeting, Bill?" the Chief asked.

"I can't say for certain, but I feel they both should meet with us."

"Good idea. Put one con lady with the other and see what happens. Sure. Let's do it!"

The rest of the day was uneventful. Surveillance of Big Eddy's continued. Bill had put in four uneventful hours that afternoon. Later, at home that night, the phone rang around eight.

"Hello."

"Bill, this is Connie."

"Hello, Connie, what's going on?"

"We were to interview that person who claims you knew more than you testified to, but they failed to show up today. No explanation was offered. I thought you'd like to know."

"Interesting. Whose witness is it?"

"The DA's. He said he didn't know what happened to the guy and that he'd get back with us. We adjourned after that."

"Thanks, Connie. Any contact from your 'friends'?"

"No! Thank God."

"By the way, you're doing well with your shooting lessons."

"Thanks. You're an excellent teacher. Are we still on for day after tomorrow at six?"

"Yes."

"I'll be there."

"Good-bye, Connie."

Bill was ready to relax for the evening. He had finished writing in his journal and was about to catch the news when the phone rang.

"Hello, Bill?"

"Yes, Mayor. Wait a moment, let me take a pan out of the oven." Bill grabbed his tape recorder. "Okay, I'm back."

"A close source informed me Franklin Jr. was asking about my personal finances. I'll squash this inquiry before it gets started. Check into his background. Start with his sexual activities. Goodnight, Bill." The line went dead.

He reached to turn off the tape recorder. The Mayor was dragging him into places he didn't wish to go.

Bill snatched the phone off the hook. He began dialing the local bars looking for Jacko. Eight calls and twenty minutes later, he found him. He was at a downtown grill whose bartender reminded him that Jacko didn't like phones. Jacko would wait there for him.

--

Bill and Jacko sat a discreet distance away from the crowd.

"You said once before you thought Franklin Dillard Jr. was gay. Why?"

"It's all over the grapevine. Yeah. It's as good as that."

"How do I get confirmation?"

"You don't. You're not part of that in-crowd."

Jacko lit a cigarette, blowing a smoke ring upward.

"Okay then, who's his boyfriend?"

"Who wants to know?"

He wanted to say the Mayor, just to get Jacko's reaction, but he decided not to.

"I do."

"Oh yeah? And for what reason?"

"Police business."

"I can try to find out but this is gonna cost you. Yeah, big time."

That answer told Bill that Jacko considered his debt paid off. Jacko was now charging for his services.

"How much?"

"Two grand my man…two grand. Yeah."

"Sounds kinda steep."

"Yeah, it is. Take it or leave it. And, if you can find a cheaper source, then by all means, go for it."

Their business was done…Bill headed back home.

--

The following morning, Bill was working at his desk trying to put together the endless pieces of the murder puzzle when the phone rang.

"Bill, it's Monique."

"Hi, to what do I owe this unexpected pleasure?"

"I'm visiting Macar today. Are you still available for lunch?"

"Sure! What time?"

"How about one?"

"Fine. See you then."

Today, Bill's team was preparing for the meeting between the two voodoo ladies. Jezebel Balboa was being flown into town early in the afternoon and Marie Francois would be chauffeured in at four o'clock. Ms. Balboa was told the police wanted her to meet with a psychic from Oakland and she agreed. The fact that the psychic was also a voodoo practitioner was never mentioned. Bill took a break from his paperwork to call Crystal Dillard at campaign headquarters.

"Hello, Bill."

"Hi, Crystal."

"Tell me something wonderful to brighten up my day."

"You've been on my mind," he ventured hesitantly.

"That's nice, but, I'd rather be on something else of yours right about now!"

His hormones signaled red alert. "Please…will you behave?" he asked guardedly.

"Do you really want me to?"

"You didn't answer my question."

"And you didn't answer mine."

"I have a question for you."

"Oh, you have much more than just a question for me," she purred again.

Bill was aroused but he was also learning her style.

"You mentioned bananas the other night."

"A banana a day is my once-a-day vitamin."

"You also mentioned that your husband didn't serve them to your taste."

"You certainly do. Why you did such an excellent job that I probably won't need my daily vitamin today or even tomorrow for that matter. I'm still so…energized!"

"I'd like the answer to a question."

"You know my information is not free."

"We've been down this road before."

"I'd say you've been 'up' this road before. Trust me, I'm very good with my geography. I know which way 'up' is."

This woman was the most outrageous flirt he had ever met.

"Okay, what's your price?"

"First, I can only promise you a personal hearing, not an answer. You'll get to ask your question up close and personal. With your powerful persuasive personality, I'm confident you'll be able to score points with the judge."

"Let me think about your offer."

"Yes, think 'long' and think 'hard'. Bye, Detective."

He had to sit there for a time before returning to the conference room because his hormones had been awakened from their sleepy hibernation and were dancing the Charleston to a full-swing band!

At twelve forty-five, Bill left to meet Monique. Monique was already in the restaurant when he arrived. She wore a short white dress with large blue polka dots that was terribly attractive on her.

"How's Macar?"

"He's okay. He's plenty sorry he's caught up in this mess."

"Did he reveal who was responsible for his being in this situation?" Bill asked.

"No. I didn't ask and after a few minutes, I wondered what I was even doing there. We really have so little in common."

"Did he mention your brother Rad?"

"Rad? No. Why?" she inquired, quite perplexed.

"Why, because he was observed leaving Rad's house just before he was pulled over. So, I was just wondering if Rad's name came up in your conversation. Macar was at his house for more than an hour."

"Do you think Rad's involved?" she asked.

"I don't know. But, there's room for speculation, especially when his own family doesn't know his true occupation."

"I only wish I could disagree with you, Bill."

"What's your older brother like? Do you guys get along?" Bill wanted more information on Franklin Jr.

"Frankie was a typical big brother. He watched out for us and tried to run our lives at the same time," she smiled.

"Was he always so conservative in his views?"

"Oh no. He did his dirty little deeds like the rest of us. He was more discreet though. I guess that's the lawyer in him." She was smiling sweetly at him.

"Was he a ladies' man like Rad?"

"Nobody is like Rad. Frankie had a few girlfriends but I can't remember anyone he went crazy over. He took Victoria Cromwell to his prom. They're still good friends."

"Did he know Crystal before law school?" Bill was also curious about Crystal.

"No, I believe they met there."

"Do you like her?"

"Oh yes, she's a fascinating person."

"In what way?"

"She's a combination of things. She's multi-faceted, like a crystal. Frankly, she's an enigma."

"Interesting." He believed that was a perfect description.

Bill wanted to ask if she thought Franklin was gay, but didn't. There was no real evidence and besides, that question might be viewed as inflammatory. They continued exploring safer topics while enjoying a lovely lunch. An hour later, he reluctantly returned to work. At two o'clock Detective Jones took off for the airport to pick up Jezebel Balboa. The big meeting was scheduled for four o'clock. Bill had no idea what to expect from this meeting between Marie Francois and Ms. Balboa.

The meeting started fifteen minutes late. Ms. Balboa was there, wearing her signature tall flamboyant hat. Ms. Francois was scheduled to arrive in thirty minutes.

"Welcome, Ms. Balboa, nice to meet with you again," Kasolkasky greeted, smiling broadly.

"Detective, hello."

"First, I'd like to thank you for coming. You remember everyone here, Detectives White, Jones and Lincoln. Our Chief is at another meeting."

"It's my pleasure."

"Ms. Balboa, a local psychic, will be arriving shortly. Perhaps she'll be able communicate with you better than we can, but while we're waiting, we'd like to review our notes with you."

For the next thirty minutes or so, they interviewed Ms. Balboa, while a tape machine recorded the conversation. At four forty-five, a knock announced Marie Francois's arrival. She was immediately introduced to the Los Angeles psychic.

Ms. Francois sat down directly across from her downstate spiritual peer. She observed Ms. Balboa like a cat observing a mouse. Did the great voodoo god Damballa select her or was she a fraud like so many others? She would see.

"Our local psychic, Ms. Francois, was updated recently; we informed her of your observations. I'm turning the meeting over to Ms. Francois." Detective Lincoln faced the Oakland voodooaine, "Please, ask your questions."

Mama turned slightly in the chair, shifting into a more comfortable position. There was no noticeable change in her facial expression, which was alert and inquisitive.

"Ms. Balboa, you say you have seen the sign of the voodoo god on the victim's body in the photograph. Is that correct?"

"Yes," she answered, holding eye contact firmly with Mama. Ms. Balboa's back straightened as if she was in the military and a higher-ranking officer had just appeared.

"You are referring to which voodoo god?"

"The almighty one, of course."

"Do you call him by name?"

"Oh yes. Damballa."

Ms. Francois's expression remained unchanged. She was unimpressed, having been here before with countless others.

"Do you...know Him?"

"I know Him."

"And how did you come to know it was Him by looking at the photographs?"

"A true voodoo priestess knows a sign left by the Master."

Ms. Francois, moving slightly in her chair, reached into her bag, removing a small item no more than three inches in height, which fit easily into the palm of her hand. It was jet black with the devilish face of a man carved into it. It felt like cold porcelain. She extended the object to Ms. Balboa who looked at it, but wouldn't touch it.

"Is this the image of the god to whom you bow?"

"This is blasphemy!" Ms. Balboa yelled. "Who are you to present such mocking idols?! Such a hideous depiction of Damballa!"

"It was a gift to me from Him."

"That's a lie! Damballa bestows no such gifts. He is the receiver of gifts! How dare you mock his name!"

This rebuff inflamed Marie Francois.

"Damballa gives to those he has selected. I am she who receives the great snake. He brings me to Legba, to share His knowledge. He need leave no mark to identify His domain...for all is his domain!"

With that, Ms. Balboa immediately stood and stormed from the room, slamming the door. Detective Jones followed her while everyone else remained seated in the room with Ms. Francois. Mama stood, retrieving her coat.

"That woman is a fake!"

"How do you know?" Bill inquired.

"Trust me, gentlemen, I know!" Ms. Francois then walked boldly from the room.

Everyone sat looking at the door through which now Marie Francois had also exited. The room was now devoid of energy.

That evening, Detective Lincoln was scheduled for four boring hours of surveillance at Big Eddy's house. He sat in the van, brooding. Two hours passed before a knock on the door startled him! It was Big Eddy! He was dressed in a suit that must've cost more than two thousand dollars. He walked over to the passenger side of the van and put his hand on the door handle, indicating he wanted to get in. Bill unlocked the door.

"Detective Lincoln, you really get the plush assignments," his sarcasm bit hard on Bill's resolve. "You must be really high up on the ladder down there," he said mockingly.

"We take the assignments given."

"How's Willie doing? Is he prepared to testify?"

"I believe so," Bill lied. "Why do you ask?"

"Oh, you know, I wouldn't want anything bad to happen to him. The Good Book says, bad things can happen to bad people."

"Does the Good Book say that, Eddy?"

"If it doesn't, it should," Eddy remarked off-handedly while staring at Bill. "He's already had a terrible loss. I just want the man to be happy. You understand."

"Maybe if you just confess your sins, everything will be alright."

"Let's not start drifting into fantasy, Detective. That's not a very productive activity in your line of work. How's our Ms. Chow doing?"

Bill tensed slightly at hearing Connie's name.

"She's only doing her job, Eddy," Bill glared. His eyes focused sternly on the Italian. Both knew this was a serious moment. The van was quiet. The two men stared each other down, neither relenting. An eternity seemed to pass before Eddy slowly opened the door to get out. While putting his right foot on the ground he made his final remarks.

"And I'm only doing my job!"

The door closed abruptly as Big Eddy walked toward his house with the Detective's eyes on him all the way. You couldn't toy with this man. Big Eddy was no two-bit hustler.

Chapter 28

It was nine o'clock Saturday evening, the night of Rad's party, and the house was already filled with people. Monique and Bill parked in the ample driveway. Rad loved parties, but liked his own best of all. A band played the latest songs as platters of hot food and cool drinks sat in convenient locations. Tuxedo clad waiters scurried around serving the guests. The doorman was about to take Monique's jacket when Rad's lady friend took the garment herself. She put the jacket upstairs. Fifteen minutes later they spotted Monique's big brother and sister-in-law, Franklin and Crystal.

"Hi, Frankie," Monique said, "and Crystal, wow, I love that dress!"

"Hello, folks," Bill added.

"Bill and Monique, good to see you guys. I guess everyone is here," Franklin said, kissing his sister.

"I want that outfit, Monique. I look like a school girl compared to you," Crystal beamed. "And, Bill, you could be a model," she chuckled. "Franklin, we need to go home and change."

"I'm surprised to see you here tonight big brother; what gives?"

"Remember, Monique, he's looking for votes," Crystal interjected.

The band was playing a popular song. Crystal stepped up and grabbed Bill's hand.

"Monique, I'm stealing him for this dance because, if you let him, Franklin will talk him to death. Come Bill..."

It was a fast tempo dance. They squeezed onto a spot on the dance floor. Crystal was wearing a sleek black dress. It was sinfully short and she wore it wickedly. The noise was too loud for conversation and when the band finished they went right into another number. When they got back, Franklin spotted two other couples he knew so he and Crystal moved across the room.

"Have you seen Rad yet?" Bill asked Monique.

"Not yet. I'm sure he's not far away. Would you buy a lady a glass of wine, sir?"

He smiled while escorting her to the bar.

"And by the way, I want the first slow dance with my date. My sister-in-law certainly doesn't waste any time."

Two hours later, they sat on the balcony. It was a lovely night to engage in meaningless small talk. Ten minutes later, Macario spotted them.

"Hello, Monique."

Monique, surprised, turned toward the familiar voice. "Hello, Macar, I didn't expect to see you here. You look well. I believe you know Detective Lincoln."

Macar observed the lawman. "Yes. How are you, Detective?"

"Fine thanks. How are you?"

"I'm managing; thanks for asking."

Normally Bill would have excused himself, but he didn't. If someone wanted him to go they'd have to ask.

"Are you back at work?" Monique asked.

"Yeah, for now. The owner is none too happy, but my lawyer advised him that firing me would be grounds for a lawsuit."

"I hope you get your life back together, Macar; I really do," Monique said compassionately.

Macario understood that if Monique wanted to talk to him privately she would have asked Bill to leave. She hadn't done that. He made a few more meaningless remarks.

"I'll see you guys later."

"Good-bye, Macar," Monique said softly. Bill didn't respond.

"He looks good but his spirits are low," Monique said.

"He's not in the most enviable position. His employer wants him gone and that's not something one can take lightly. Are you still his student?"

Monique had turned away to look at the full moon. There was a beautiful cloud formation drifting aimlessly in front of it. The scene was so beautiful it reminded her of a postcard setting entitled 'Heaven's Gate'.

"Technically, I'm still his student, but I'm not attending any of his classes."

"Punishment?"

"I don't associate with people who traffic in drugs."

"You didn't suspect anything before this happened?"

"I thought there was a possibility, but there was no proof."

There was a time when he would challenge that response, but he let it go like a piece of driftwood floating down a swiftly moving stream. Bill now selected his battles more carefully.

"So, how are your parents?" He changed the subject.

"Physically, they're doing well. However, the loss of Hillary is slowing grinding everyone down. They need to know something." She didn't have to say anything else.

"How are you holding up?"

"Sometimes I really enjoy life. Then there are days when I can't stop thinking of her."

"That's to be expected."

"Are you saying this type of tragedy is normal?"

"No one is saying that, Monique."

A pregnant moment passed.

"Sometimes I feel dead inside."

He didn't respond. Intuitively he knew that this was a time to listen. He sat back in his chair holding his drink. This was her moment.

"Detective Lincoln, fancy meeting you here."

Bill looked up at a large figure dressed immaculately in a tailored leisure suit.

"Big Eddy."

"It's good to know you don't always spend your nights relaxing in a van outside my house."

"Every once in awhile they let me out."

Eddy turned and faced Monique. "Hello, Monique, you look great."

"Thank you. How are you?"

"Very well. Detective Lincoln is keeping my house well guarded. I feel so very secure." Eddy turned to face Bill again. "I trust you're having a good evening, Detective."

"I am, so far."

"Will I be seeing you tonight?"

"You're seeing me right now."

The Italian stood there grinning for a few moments. Life was good. The police were spinning their wheels and everyone knew it.

"Well, I don't want to wear out my welcome, so I'm going back inside."

"Good-bye, Eddy. Have a nice life," Bill said sarcastically.

"You don't like him," Monique suggested.

"I don't cater much to drug dealers. And I'm certainly not partial to murderers."

Monique looked abruptly at Bill when she heard the word murderer. "What are you talking about?" she asked.

"Just between you and me, the police believe Big Eddy was responsible for the second voodoo murder."

"Big Eddy? How did the police come to that conclusion?"

"I can't disclose that information, but I can say, I believe it too."

"Is there any connection between the first murder and the second?"

"We don't think so."

Monique sat back, having become momentarily anxious; any news concerning her dead sister naturally interested her. "Bill, will you ever find the killer?" she asked in a soft voice with a note of quiet resignation.

Bill looked at her. He wanted to avoid the question but he couldn't. "I don't know, Monique. I certainly hope so. But, the odds are not in our favor."

Monique turned and stared at the stars again. Her mind was completely on her sister now. There was nothing he could do. The mourning process would take its course.

"Hello, Bill. I thought that was you."

He turned and looked up. He didn't recognize the voice.

"Oh, hello, Mrs. Efferton. Where's the Mayor?"

"He was right behind me. I think he's talking. You know how he likes to converse. He's got to start soliciting votes. The elections are not too far off. Oh hi, Monique, I didn't notice you dear."

"Hello, Mrs. Efferton. You look very nice in that outfit."

Mrs. Efferton smiled while nodding her head. She heard footsteps, turning she watched her husband's approach.

"Bill, Monique, hello. How are you? I was wondering where you were, Monique. I didn't see you inside."

"We took a break for some fresh air and solitude."

"How are your parents?"

"They're doing fine, Mayor, thanks for asking."

"Are they here tonight?"

"No. They're out of town. They haven't been attending any social affairs, not since Hillary passed."

The Mayor was about to say something but changed his mind. "We're doing everything in our power to catch this killer. I'm sorry it's taking so long. We're not getting many breaks."

Monique, facing the Mayor, spoke. "Thank you, Mayor. I know you are."

"If you need anything, anything at all Monique, please call."

"You know we're there for you," the Mayor's wife added.

"Mayor, who's this witness the DA is trying to get to testify against me?" Bill asked.

"I don't know. The DA is keeping this one under his hat."

Bill didn't say anything more. But he couldn't believe the Mayor didn't know.

"So, here's where the in-crowd is," Crystal announced.

Crystal and Franklin Jr. had just walked onto the porch joining the growing congregation. Everyone exchanged pleasantries. Bill was curious about how the Mayor and Franklin would react after their last encounter at Franklin's house. So far, both were courteous to each other and the Mayor left minutes later.

"So how's the party going?" Monique asked.

"It's going. There are tons of people" Crystal replied.

"You know Rad," Franklin mused.

"What are you guys doing? How come you're not inside?" Crystal asked.

"Just talking," Monique said, "nothing too heavy."

"I hope you got her on the dance floor, Bill. She needs to be showing off that dress. I'm jealous." Crystal was beaming. She was busy being the consummate social animal in her element. Franklin was standing by her sipping wine.

"No speeches tonight, Franklin?" Bill asked.

"No. This is Rad's thing. However, I'm certainly more than willing," Franklin smiled slightly.

"Let's not spoil the fun," Monique said.

The band began a popular slow song and Monique grabbed her brother Franklin's hand to go dance. Monique wanted to talk to him about Hillary in private and the dance floor seemed like the best place right then. They left Crystal and Bill together on the porch.

"You look absolutely delicious in that suit, Detective Bill Lincoln...a fabulous desert without the calories. All we need now is a little whipped cream."

"I'm not sure if I should say thank you or not."

"Of course you should."

"Alright, thank you."

"You're welcome. Do you like my dress?"

"It's ...whew...breathtaking."

Crystal was sitting a few feet from him, her legs crossed and showing a lot of silk stocking. Asking him that question was like asking a lion if he liked raw meat.

"Can you imagine what I'm wearing underneath this dress?"

'Here we go again,' he thought, again feeling the familiar twinge of his hormones stirring. The first came while staring at her 'Barbie Doll' legs. Now she was on the prowl. She was so flirtatious. He'd derail her by dramatically changing the subject before she got to him.

"With whom does Franklin have sex?" He was fairly confident that this would stop her in her tracks.

"I'm wearing a diamond studded thong and I'm dying to show it to you. It's very very sexy. I'm sure you'll agree," she purred.

Damn! Seconds ago he was worried about first base. She was already rounding second and looking at third. He had to will himself to focus. Ice-cold discipline would save him. He must concentrate on his subject matter, not hers.

"Does he have a boyfriend?" This would stop her.

Crystal didn't even blink. "It's a well known fact that diamonds are a girl's best friend. But in this case, you might argue that they are also a man's best friend. You should see how they sparkle in the moonlight."

She had reached third base and was headed for home. He would try again, but Bill knew he had a Little League arm and with this female he was way behind in the count.

"Who is Franklin's boyfriend?"

She sat there now shamelessly flashing that diamond-studded garment. "I know you, Bill, a woman can always tell. You know I won't stop you. I'll submit to anything you want," she purred once again, in a slow, sensual voice, taking her tongue and slowly sliding it across her lips. "Anything that you want is yours. Anything."

She had walked in from third base and crossed home plate without breaking a sweat! His hormones were on full marching orders wearing dress uniforms. Every one of them stood at full alert, saluting the flag and pounding out the 'Star Spangled Banner.' Suddenly, he heard footsteps and Monique and Franklin were back.

"How was the dance?" Crystal asked.

"Great. The band is very good," Monique replied.

"I got their card. We may use them at one of our events," Franklin said.

"What are you two discussing?" Monique asked.

"Just shooting the breeze," Crystal responded. "Bill was filling me in on police stuff. That's a world I'll leave to him."

"Well, Crystal and I need to get to another event. Are you ready dear?" Franklin asked his wife.

"I'm ready. We'll see you guys later. Bye."

At midnight Bill and Monique decided to leave. It had been a wonderful evening; the party was still going strong. Bill couldn't find Rad's lady friend, so he decided to go upstairs to look for Monique's jacket. Monique waited at the foot of the stairs. He looked in the first two rooms, but there was no coat. He walked to the next room where he found various garments on the bed, but not Monique's fur. As he approached the fourth room, a lady opened the door and walked down the hallway right past him. She appeared headed to the bathroom and never even glanced at him. He opened the door and immediately smelled drugs. There was nobody in the small foyer, but he heard voices in the larger room in back. He could smell the marijuana combined with something else in the air. It was definitely narcotics.

He had to make a decision. He reached behind his back to take out his gun. He also pushed the on-button on his tape machine. He clicked off the gun's safety lever as he locked the door behind him. After all, he didn't want anyone walking in unannounced. He held the gun firmly while entering the next room.

Bill stepped silently up to the small group and yelled, "Freeze! Put your hands up! Lie down on the ground now!" he barked like a Marine drill instructor. "Get down, now!" Three of the four automatically dropped to the floor, but one didn't, Big Eddy. He just looked at Bill and coolly remained sitting smoking a thick Cuban cigar.

Bill walked directly up to him, put his gun square in his ear and started barking orders. "Lay down, now. Drop that thing in your hand, now! Drop it!" He was talking for the tape machine and for the others in the room who were face down. He wanted them to believe Eddy had something in his hands.

"Put it down, now! I said to put the weapon down! Now!" He cocked the gun; the sound of the cold metal click filled the room. Big Eddy slowly moved, putting the cigar in the ashtray before lying on the floor. For the moment, he didn't know what Bill was capable of doing.The three men on the floor were Macario, Big Eddy and Rad. The woman was someone Bill had never met. Bill confiscated the drugs and called the police. The authorities arrived within thirty minutes, ending the party. The four people were arrested and hauled downtown. Detective Lincoln offered transportation to Monique but she declined saying her cousin would drive her back to Bill's home to get her car. She was not sure how she felt about Bill. She had invited him to her brother's party and he had arrested him. Of course, the drug factor added a different twist. She was confused.

Word of the Dillard arrest would travel through the grapevine at supersonic speed. A meeting was called in the Mayor's office at seven in the morning with everyone's attendance mandatory.

Chapter 29

Since everyone was there, the meeting came to order promptly at six forty-five. There were solemn expressions worn by all except for Detective Lincoln. He had done his job. The Mayor, dressed in a smartly tailored brown natty tweed sports jacket, took control.

"Gentlemen, you've all been updated on what has happened. Our first question is 'Do we have a case?' The rumor being circulated is that our Investigator Lincoln planted the evidence."

Bill was incensed by the remark but didn't say anything. He knew the routine. The Mayor turned and faced him.

"Bill, I'm sorry, but I have to ask, did you plant that evidence?"

"No." He wanted to say it strongly, but he just answered the question without any emotion.

"There are allegations you've done that type of thing before. And there's that case from a few years ago. You know, the one that was eventually dropped by Internal Affairs. Now, here we are today and that same case is being revisited."

"You're questioning my integrity? What about the integrity of the people I arrested? Macario was just busted for drugs. Big Eddy is a convicted felon and is currently being investigated for murder. And Radcliffe is a man, living a grand lifestyle, whose own family doesn't know what he does for a living. Why don't we wait for the lab reports because I'm willing to bet that the blood work will come back positive for drugs on all four." He knew his story would hold up.

"Our case is fairly strong. However, Bill, you're our weak link now, especially with that case from your past being investigated again."

Bill reluctantly acknowledged the Mayor's point. However, it was only an allegation and he also felt he could weather the coming storm.

"We need everything nailed down tightly. Where's the evidence?" the Mayor asked.

"The drugs were confiscated at the crime scene and booked at three in the morning by the criminologist," Kasolkasky responded.

"Do the newspapers know?" the Mayor asked.

"Not yet they don't."

Bill thought he could hear the Mayor's mind churning.

"When can we expect them to know?"

"There's no advantage for either side to broadcast this publicly," the Chief pointed out.

The Mayor listened intently, constantly analyzing the situation. He believed the Chief was right, that they had a little time to wheel and deal. Since it was unlikely there would be a press conference in the foreseeable future, the Mayor was noticeably more relaxed. "Chief, look, you've got Rad right where you want him," Bill observed. "You can bet that Macario will sing like a bird and now we've even got direct evidence against Big Eddy. You'll never get him on the Willie Taylor thing but now…now Big Eddy's got a real problem. You can bring serious pressure to bear and open Rad up like a can of worms."

The Mayor noticed that Bill had used 'you' repeatedly and not 'we' in his statements. Bill was discreetly reminding everyone that all of this had been the Chief's idea.

"We're a team here, Bill," Chief Ness barked. "Let's remember that." It was obvious that the Chief noticed Bill's particular choice of words too.

"Right," Bill answered. "Now ultimately I don't feel Rad's really involved and I've mentioned this before. You have more faith in that theory than I do."

"We must examine all possibilities," the Chief responded.

"And we have. I just think we're headed down a dead-end street. That's all I'm sayin'. "

"Well, we'd have a clean bust if your record was clean!" the Chief snapped. His tone had become ugly, his mannerisms threating.

"We have a clean bust and my record is irrelevant. We have the goods on them. This whole case would be further ahead if you'd stop wasting time on irrelevant issues!" Bill snarled back.

"This is a complex case. We've done a good job, all things considered!" The emotional level of the conversation was escalating and the Mayor was letting it 'roll' like a back alley craps game.

"You haven't done squat! This case was going nowhere and that's why I was brought in. Remember? Why I've moved the case farther along than your whole inept department!" Bill hammered. The rules of etiquette had disappeared like a wisp of smoke.

"That's bullshit, Lincoln! Cut the crap! We have to follow procedure. We don't go off and do our own thing. There's the damn law and the Constitution! Have you heard of them?!" the Chief yelled back. Now his face was cherry red and with both hands he gripped the sides of his desk. Kasolkasky had moved to stand between the two men. The Mayor was sitting and listening. This conversation was to his advantage. He'd take information by any means necessary.

"That's the damn problem! You follow the rules so strictly that you can't see anything else. You have no room for creativity. We spend time and resources watching Big Eddy's house in a van all day and all night knowing he knows we're there. Do you think he's going to do anything criminal when he knows we're watching him? And I'm being ordered to sit in that damn van for hours! Does this make any sense to you, Chief?! Is this a good use of my time?!" Now, Bill was yelling.

"We all have to do the tedious dirty work sometime, Lincoln. Your problem is that you think you know everything! This organization is made up of rules and regulations which we're obligated to follow, dammit!"

No one was talking except the Chief and the Detective.

"Well, suppose the orders are just plain damn stupid, Chief! Then what? Just plain ass backward and stupid!" Bill was slowly spitting out his words like he was nailing shut a coffin while taking his time to do it right complete with exaggerated motions.

"We have jobs to do and procedures to follow. Everything is not going to pan out. We have to look at the whole picture, which is what we're paid to do, Lincoln. We don't use crystal balls here. Here, we do our jobs!"

"Is that right? What about your job of collecting blood samples from all male personnel at the college. Have you completed that job, Chief? It's been damn near five months and have all the men at the college been tested? Hell no! And that's my point. That job is not completed but you have the audacity to have me sitting in a goddamn van! Does this make any sense, Chief?!"

The Chief's face had taken on the color of a ripe summer tomato. Both hands still gripped the sides of the desk. The veins in his hands and face were clearly visible.

"All relevant people have been tested at the college. Damn, Bill, do you think the professor who was in New York that night is the suspect? Would a reasonable person think that?!"

"All I said was not all the personnel have been tested. And that's a fact. Were your orders to test only reasonable men under suspicion on campus? No, it was to test all men and that hasn't been done. Or has it?" Bill turned away from the Chief and sat back down. He was still simmering.

The Chief said nothing. He figured that Detective Lincoln had gone off of his rocker. It was the old 'reasonable person concept' with Bill making one point and the Chief another.

The Mayor interjected, "Gentlemen, thanks for the entertainment but we've got business before us. What's our next step?"

"Now's the time to turn up the heat. We start paperwork on every charge we can drum up to see who's going to talk. We keep them squeezed and separated. We need to keep the media out of this if we can." Kasolkasky spoke for his boss since the color in the Chief's face had only intensified. The Chief, still standing behind the desk, had released his grip on it. Detectives Jones and White remained silent.

"Brick, let's get all male personnel at the school tested. That will cover us with the media in case that question ever comes up. It's unlikely we'll uncover any new information, but I believe both the Chief and Bill are right. I'll let your team determine whether or not watching Big Eddy's house should be continued. Discuss it. I'm not a policeman, but I'm not sure if we're utilizing our time wisely right now. Let me know what you decide. Anything else?" the Mayor asked.

No one spoke. The meeting was over. Bill walked out first while the Chief stayed behind to talk to the Mayor. Bill stepped into the bathroom to put cold water on his face and to turn his tape off.

At ten o'clock that morning, Bill took a break to page Monique. He wanted to know how she was doing. It was an hour later when she called.

"Hello, Monique. How are you?"

"I've had better days."

"Are you upset with me?"

There was a brief pause. "I don't know what I feel. I'm upset with Rad and I'm perplexed about you. I should be mad with you I think. I don't know."

"Have you seen Rad?"

"No, visitors aren't allowed yet."

"Some are saying I planted the evidence."

"That's silly."

"That's the rumor. It's not a game, Monique."

"I know. But who would say that?"

"Your brother's defense lawyers and a certain segment of society."

"I'll talk to you later, Bill. Good-bye."

Two days later the pressure on Bill started building. Detective Jones asked him if he was sure the evidence was not planted. It was only he and Clarence in the room. Bill spoke slowly and stated clearly, in case there was a tape, that he hadn't planted any evidence. He didn't even make any jokes because he knew how clever attorneys could use recorded statements.

The following Friday, Internal Affairs sent a request to talk with him about his other case. It was a preliminary talk according to the notice. He had the right to decline, but he didn't.

The paperwork from the lab had been misplaced. Nobody knew where it was! All four people arrested at Rad's party had been arraigned and had pleaded not guilty. The only good thing was that police surveillance of Big Eddy's house had ended. At eleven that evening Bill received a phone call. At that hour news was rarely good.

"Hello."

"It's Connie. I just got a call from our commission. The District Attorney has rescheduled our interview with our mystery person. We'll interview this person on Wednesday."

"What's the name?"

"We weren't told."

"Typical. Well, have fun that day. I'd appreciate any information, if you can spare it."

"Goodnight, Bill."

He put the phone down and got ready for bed. At eleven-thirty the phone rang again. There was no doubt this was bad news coming. He'd bet six months salary on it.

"Hello."

"Bill, this is Betty. Our daughter's getting strange and threatening phone calls. She's scared. I called the police."

"Which one? Amanda?"

"Yes."

"When did this start, Betty?"

He heard her struggling for words. She was obviously distraught.

"Calm down and tell me exactly what happened."

Betty took a few deep breaths and then explained that yesterday, Amanda had started getting crank phone calls from people using Detective Lincoln's name. They said, "Your daddy is fooling with the wrong people. Tell your daddy to stop planting evidence on innocent people."

"What are you doing, Bill?" Betty said. "Look what you're doing to our daughter!"

He was getting upset. "I'm not doing anything. It's the caller who's wrong, Betty!"

"Think about our daughter, Bill." As usual, she wasn't hearing anything he was saying.

"Betty, I'm going to call Amanda right now. I'll talk to you tomorrow."

He finally got his ex off the phone. He needed to have a talk with his daughter. It was after midnight and Bill was mad. Someone was threatening his family; he wasn't going to sit back and take it. Someone had just crossed the line!

At four that morning Bill's phone rang again! This time, instinctively, he reached for his gun as he picked up the receiver. His action was automatic. The gun was in his right hand and he didn't even realize it was there. His senses were instantly at full alert.

"Hello?"

"Bill, this is Kasolkasky."

"What's up?" He was as straight as a statue straining to hear. The phone was tightly wedged between his shoulder and his ear.

"I just got a call from the lab."

"The lab?" Bill was in a fog, his brain was not computing.

"We've got a match."

"A match? What are you talking about?"

"We know who raped Hillary Dillard that night."

"What? You have a match!"

"That's right."

There was a lull in the conversation while he waited for the answer. All he heard was silence. He couldn't wait any longer.

"Who?"

"You won't believe it."

"Who?"

"Staff meeting is at seven this morning. You'll find out then!" A click then…silence.

Only the man who has enough good in him to feel the justice of the penalty can be punished; the others can only be hurt.

WILLIAM ERNEST HOCKING: THE COMING
WORLD CIVILIZATION, HARPER, 1957.

Chapter 30

Early the next morning, Brick Kasolkasky's team was fully assembled. He walked to the center of the room with every eye watching him.

"This information is completely confidential and goes nowhere!" were his first words. "You don't tell anyone; you don't even mention this to your priest at confession! Do you understand?!"

Everyone nodded robotically. Kasolkasky, with surgeon-like precision, pulled a sheet of paper from a folder. He stood straight as a soldier looking as solemn as a verdict rendering judge. The detectives stared at the paper in his hand.

"The preliminary lab report identifies the donor of specimen 'x214', otherwise known as the alleged perpetrator of Ms. Hillary Chatham Dillard's murder, as Dr. Nathaniel Dubois Broussard, Chancellor of the University."

The officers stared at each other squinty eyed with wrinkled brows. The magnitude of the revelation sent their collective cognitive minds spinning.

"What?!" exclaimed Detective Jones. "I don't believe it!"

"Dr. Broussard? Who would have guessed!" added Detective White. "You can't trust anyone!"

"I find this incredible," uttered Detective Lincoln. "Are you sure?"

"It was your astute observation, Bill, that clinched it. You reminded us that we hadn't done our jobs completely. The Chief ordered us to take blood samples from every male attending the affair that evening. But, we never got Dr. Broussard's. He was always too busy! Now it's obvious why," Kasolkasky remarked.

"But why kill her?" Detective Jones asked.

"I don't know. Only Dr. Broussard can answer that one. Who knows what's in the mind of a killer!" Kasolkasky hammered.

Abruptly, the Mayor and the Chief entered the room, drawing all eyes toward them like iron filings to a magnet. They wanted to address the team. The news would break quickly and the Mayor wanted to be out in front.

"Gentlemen, in my extensive experience of serving the public, I have never come across a case that has so completely shocked me. I've known Dr. Broussard for many years and frankly I'm shaken to the core. I still can't believe it! But we have the evidence. I find no joy in this task. A judge is reviewing an arrest warrant now. Chief Ness has assigned Detective Kasolkasky's team to arrest Dr. Broussard. Detective Lincoln, you are to be there too and the Chief concurs."

The Chief spoke next. "I also want to express my thanks to all the men who worked on this project. You did an excellent job! I also want to apologize to Detective Lincoln. At our last meeting, I was unprofessional, and there is no excuse for my behavior. I apologize to the rest of you as well. Thank you, Detective Lincoln, for being the professional that you are."

Bill nodded. The event was moving past him like a freight train. Two hours passed before the arrest warrant was ready.

Dr. Nathaniel Dubois Broussard lived in the Oakland Hills for over twenty-five years raising three children there. The Broussards were highly regarded.

The unmarked car parked in front of the Broussard residence at 10:45 that morning. Detectives Kasolkasky, White, Jones and Bill Lincoln slowly walked up the stairs in a funeral like procession to ring the bell. When the door opened, Mrs. Broussard was standing there wearing a white apron covered with flour.

"Hello, officers, please come in."

"Good morning, Mrs. Broussard," said Detective Kasolkasky. "Is Dr. Broussard home?"

"Yes."

"We need to see Dr. Broussard…right away. It's very important."

Mrs. Broussard directed the officers to the study. She knocked twice…the door opened.

"Dr. Broussard?"

"Why, yes, what can I do for you?"

"May we come in, sir?"

"Of course, gentlemen. Please, come in." Dr. Broussard was of average height, slightly overweight, with long wavy white hair. He wore horn-rimmed glasses and had mannerisms of an absent-minded professor. None-the-less, this long-term Chancellor was noted for his political savvy and academic scholarship.

Dr. Broussard stepped back allowing the men to enter. Everyone seemed so somber on such a beautiful morning. The one who had asked to come in now stood directly in front of him.

"My name is Detective Robert Kasolkasky with the Oakland Police Department. I am here to arrest you for the murder and rape of Hillary Chatham Dillard."

"What? Is this some kind of a joke? Surely, you jest!" Dr. Broussard's face turned stark white. He was a Creole, with a fair complexion normally, but now wore the color of a corpse.

"This is no joke, Dr. Broussard."

He looked deep into the face of each detective, each man standing like battle-weary soldiers, showing only the weight of the situation in their expressions.

"Have you all gone mad?! I'm the Chancellor of the University! I'm an educator!" His emotional plea fell on deaf ears. They just stared at him.

"Gentlemen, please sit down and let's talk about this!"

Out of respect for the man, Detective Kasolkasky agreed. The detectives observed him closely. He never displayed the demeanor of a man hiding anything. Dr. Broussard sat quietly, talked calmly and answered every question put to him in an open and thoughtful manner. Bill studied the man's body language too, deciding this man was either the best liar he had ever encountered or he was framed.

Mrs. Broussard confirmed everything her husband said. She had been isolated before being asked a litany of questions, gladly answering every one, also without calling for a lawyer. Dr. Broussard mentioned that he kept a journal and habitually recorded everything.

Dr. Broussard showed the police his journals which dated back more than twenty years! Bill had seen violent criminals and pathological liars during his many years of service, but these people displayed no signs of aberrant behavior. Dr. Broussard's detailed memory of that evening at first bothered Detective Lincoln. However, Hillary was one of his students and she had died horribly. It was entirely plausible that he wanted to remember everything possible relating to the dreadful incident in an effort to prevent it from ever happening again. Dr. Broussard also wanted answers; after all, wasn't that natural? Of course the killer knew all the details too. Bill's brain told him this man must be the killer, but his gut disagreed. He was confused.

The other detectives listened politely but their decision had been made. He was arrested and booked!

—-

The revelation dominated the news, attracting reporters from all over the country. The journalists flew into Oakland to attend a news conference set for tomorrow morning. The phone rang at the Detective's house around seven that evening.

"Hello, Bill."

"How are you, Monique?"

"I want your honest opinion."

"On what?" He just went through the motions. He knew the subject matter.

"On Dr. Broussard, of course. Do you believe he did it?"

"I don't know." Bill played it safe.

"On a scale of one to a ten, where are you?"

"In the middle. The science says yes but everything about him says no."

"I've known Dr. Broussard most of my life. I'm having difficulty believing it. I'm saying to myself, 'If I can't trust Dr. Broussard, who can I trust?'"

"What do your parents think?"

"They can't believe it. Yet, they feel they can't reach out to the Broussard family either. It's very difficult for them."

He could only imagine the emotional turmoil they faced. They had been close to the Broussards for many years. Their children had grown up together.

"Bill."

"Yes."

"If you had to pick either yes or no, one or the other, do you think he did it?" Monique was desperately searching for answers that he just couldn't provide.

"Unfortunately, I don't have enough information to make an informed decision."

"Please, Bill. If you had to choose, which one?"

Bill didn't like to be cornered. She needed to get her emotions under control.

"Pick up a coin, Monique, and flip it. Heads, he's guilty and tails, he's not. There's your answer."

"I'm sorry. I didn't mean to put you on the spot."

"Apology accepted."

"I want to call Mrs. Broussard."

"Then by all means do it."

"I don't have the energy."

"Then don't."

"You're not much help!"

"I'm not quite sure what you need, but I can't simplify a complex situation. I think better of you than that."

Monique waited a few moments before saying anything. She thought about his comments and realized that she was being unfair to him. After all, it was she who had known Dr. Broussard for so many years.

"Thanks, Bill. I'll say goodnight."

"Goodnight."

He kept thinking about the case. It felt strange, like an illusion. It made absolutely no sense that Dr. Broussard could be the killer. But then again, sometimes the hard cold truth stares you in the face and you had no choice but to accept what is.

--

The press conference started at 9 A.M. The Mayor, as always, was immaculately dressed. After delivering the stunning details, the Mayor was ready to receive questions from the media. A field of hands rose and waved emphatically.

"Has Dr. Broussard confessed? Do you have a motive yet?"

"At present, Dr. Broussard maintains his innocence."

"Where was Dr. Broussard at the time of the murder? Did he attend that evening's event?"

"Yes, Dr. Broussard was there. Three other professors saw him leave the building after midnight. His only alibi is his wife."

"Do the police have a theory about why he did it?"

The Mayor was only taking questions from the national media boys and a few of the special locals first. Everybody else would have to wait.

"No. While the police believe he's their man, we don't have a motive yet."

"Is he a sex freak? Is there anything in his history that indicates he's abnormal?"

"No. His background check, so far, is clean."

The press conference continued for another forty minutes of relentless questioning, but few answers of any real substance were given. Bill still felt a strong desire to talk further with Dr. Broussard. He needed to know the 'why', his faith in civilized society had just been rocked to its very core. If people of Dr. Broussard's stature could not be trusted, could anyone?!

At four o'clock Bill attended an impromptu meeting with the Mayor.

"Bill, we've finally got our man. But, we have Radcliffe Dillard up on drug charges. Although originally we suspected he was involved, now we know he's not. I wish we had not arrested him." The Mayor's comments hung heavily in the air. Detective Lincoln just left them hanging.

"I wish I was on the French Riviera sitting on the beach," Bill responded.

"Life would be easier especially if we didn't have to deal with this bizarre high-profile case too. You'd think the odds of two such cases occurring would be infinitesimally small, but this is Oakland. Anything can happen here."

"People shouldn't sell drugs," Bill snapped. He was getting tired of people making their remorseful comments. The clock couldn't be turned back.

"What have you discovered about Franklin Jr.?" the Mayor asked.

"Nothing, so far. That type of information is difficult to get. I have a source. If he finds out something it'll cost us a couple grand."

The Mayor raised his eyebrows. "Does your contact take cash only?" he mused.

"I believe he'll take a bank check."

Bill was not making it easy. The Mayor would like the option of getting Radcliffe out. He was looking down the road.

"I have faith in you, Bill. We can find the funds if the need arises."

"What's happening with that internal investigation about me?" he asked. "Who is this mystery witness the prosecution has?"

"I don't know. The DA is keeping quiet. Nobody's talking. If I find out anything, I'll let you know."

"Is there anything else, Mayor?"

"No. That's all. Thanks."

Bill closed the door and ducked into the first bathroom he saw to turn off his hidden tape recorder. Back in the office he called several local bars to find Jacko, leaving messages all over town. Detective White had informed him the police had received an interesting piece of news. Investigations had concluded that among the cars at Marie Francois's house on the night of the voodoo ceremony, a Gleanor Bynum owned one. The name didn't match up to anyone they knew, but the car was registered to the same address as Jacque Vestable's ex-wife. Further investigation revealed her to be Jacque's ex-sister-in-law.

"Interesting," Bill exclaimed. It was a small world indeed. Detective Lincoln simply didn't believe in many coincidences. "So, the car was there. But, who was in the car?"

"That's the sixty-four thousand dollar question," Detective White replied. "I think you and Jones should take a ride."

"Definitely. Where's Clarence?"

"Getting coffee."

"What do you think about Dr. Broussard?" Bill asked.

"He did it. The guy is too smooth, plus he knows too many details."

Detective Lincoln reflected on what he had just heard. Everything fit, but what was the motive? "Okay. Let's say he did it. Why did he do it?"

"I don't know and who cares? Guys like him are so disturbed we may never know why."

"But suppose he's telling the truth?"

"Let's get real, Bill. We can speculate about whether Santa Claus exists too. Why don't you do more research to satisfy your demons? Me, I'm satisfied."

Bill dropped the subject. A clerk indicated Bill had a phone call. It was from Jacko. Bill left to meet him.

—

"Hello, Jacko. What's happening?"

"I heard you wanted to talk."

"I want to get a status report."

"If I had something, I'd contact you. You got the money?"

"I'll get the money. There are people in high places who are very interested."

"There's no rush. I've been asking around but I'm running into a brick wall. In fact, I've been advised to find another line of work."

"By who?"

"I'd rather not say."

Jacko turned away, picked up a pool stick and started shooting pool. Leaning against a wall, Bill studied him. Jacko continued playing as if Bill was not there.

"Suppose I could increase your fee?"

"I'll pass. I know how to take good advice when it's offered."

"Can you point me in a direction?" he asked knowing he had probably reached a dead-end.

Jacko took another shot before looking up. "Yeah! I can direct you to that door," he said while using his pool stick to point. Detective Lincoln didn't move for a whole minute before finally walking away.

—

Bill and Clarence went to Jacque Vestable's ex-wife's house to determine who drove the car the evening of the voodoo ceremony. Mrs. Vestable answered the door. She remembered Detective Lincoln from his previous visit.

"Who is Gleanor Bynum?" Bill asked after sitting down.

Mrs. Vestable was wary now. "That's my sister. Why?"

"Last month her car was seen parked at a voodoo ceremony in rural Oakland. We'd like to know why your sister was there."

"Voodoo? My sister doesn't know anything about that. She's Catholic."

"Her car was there. We have it on tape."

Her eyebrows rose in bewilderment.

"Is she here?" Clarence asked.

"Yes. I'll get her."

Moments later, Mrs.Vestable returned, followed by a middle-aged woman wearing a flowery blouse and black slacks. She wore no make-up, but her complexion was flawless so she had no need too.

"This is my sister, Gleanor."

The woman nodded her head, but didn't say anything. She thought surely this must be some mistake.

"My name's Detective Lincoln. The police department videotaped a voodoo ceremony on Natas Lane several weeks ago and your car was there. Were you at that ceremony?" He looked directly into her eyes and she held his gaze.

"No. I don't know what you're talking about. I've never been to any voodoo ceremony! Besides, I'm Catholic!" She didn't flinch or try to avoid eye contact.

"How do you imagine your car got there?"

"I don't know."

"Did anyone borrow your car that night?"

A flicker of enlightenment showed in her demeanor. "Yes. I let Jacque use it a few weeks ago. He had car trouble. It was a Sunday and I needed my car for church to attend our afternoon program. I told him he could use it afterward. My sister works Sunday evenings or else he would have used hers."

"Can you check the date of that program?"

"Oh sure, I can do that now. I'll be right back."

Ms. Bynum returned almost immediately with a church program for a community project to fight teenage drug abuse. The program date was the same day as the voodoo ceremony.

"Is Jacque in trouble?" Mrs. Vestable asked in a concerned tone.

"We just want to know why was he there. He had every right to attend. I'd appreciate it if you wouldn't call him. We'd like to talk to him without giving him the opportunity to make up a story."

The women agreed, but only after ten minutes of discussion and the assurance that this was for intelligence gathering purposes only. Bill and Clarence drove back to headquarters where Clarence arranged to meet with Jacque Vestable while Bill walked over to the jail to see Dr. Broussard. The educator appeared worn out, but healthy.

"Dr. Broussard, is there anything you want to share with me?"

"Yes, I'm innocent. This is all a horrible mistake. The lab obviously erred in some way."

"Have you ever dated Hillary Dillard?"

The question jolted him. "What? Of course not!" Dr. Broussard responded incredulously. He was not a man who dealt with the ridiculous very often, but now he must.

"Do you ever remember being alone with her?"

Dr. Broussard settled down. Intellectually he understood people must ask him these offensive questions, therefore he must answer. He took a deep breath and tried to relax. "I've never been alone with her and I've known her all her life. Her parents are my good friends. I've seen her on campus a few times, but I've hardly ever talked to her since she's been a student there. Regrettably, my schedule is very busy."

"Doctor, are you a faithful husband?"

Dr. Broussard scrutinized Bill. The academic had a resigned expression and obviously wanted to talk, but hesitated. He got up and paced a few steps. Bill waited.

"Detective, I've been married for thirty years. Are you asking me if I've been sexually faithful for all those thirty years?"

"That's what I'm asking and that's what others will surely want to know too."

Dr. Broussard dropped his head for a moment taking a deep breath. He then raised his head again.

"Then the answer is no. You see, between ten and twelve years ago I had several affairs. I was on the road a lot and I got very lonely. I'm not proud of that. But I can say I've been faithful for at least the last ten years. Does that mean anything?"

"I'm a detective, not a priest. I'm looking for the facts. Does your wife know you were unfaithful?"

"Possibly, for although I never exactly told her, I believe she suspected something those many years ago. Still, she never questioned me. She's a very special woman, Detective, and also very wise. I've come to realize that."

"And if she had asked you back then, what would you have said?"

"I would have told her the truth. I know it would have hurt us, but that's what I would have done. Lies only beget more lies."

Bill wanted to discontinue his present line of questioning. He couldn't see how an old love affair could have relevance in this case. Besides, it would only further damage this family, yet he knew he could not stop there.

"Dr. Broussard, who were these women?"

"Detective Lincoln, I'm most reluctant to disclose their names. I fail to see the connection. Naturally, should it become relevant, I would. That is the way it must be, for now anyway."

"I can appreciate your position and I would probably do the same. Tell me, what is your ethnic heritage?"

"I'm Cajun. I was born in a small town some twenty miles outside New Orleans called Clawdance. My family was very poor. I was raised a Catholic. I always did very well in school, the nuns made sure of that. My father wanted me to work with him catching crayfish and lobsters in the bayou, but the nuns wouldn't hear of it. They put the fear of God in my father. I received small academic scholarships during my youth enabling me to get a good education."

"Do you have brothers and sisters?"

"Yes, I have three sisters and two brothers, all of whom still live in the general area of my home town. They all seem to be doing well. They haven't succeeded academically like me, but they're all good people with stable jobs."

"Are your parents alive?"

"My father drank himself to death twenty years ago. My mother is still alive, but in poor health."

Bill appreciated the flow of information. Usually, when lawyers were involved, the channels shut down.

"Do you know Jacque Vestable?"

"No."

"He's an employee at your school."

"That may well be, but I don't know him. What does he do?"

"Do you know Pierre Reston?"

"No. And who might he be?"

"He also works at the school."

"I'm sorry, but I don't know either gentleman."

"One is a cook and the other is a maintenance worker."

"I'm sorry, but I don't know them by name. If you show me pictures I may recognize them."

Detective Lincoln made a mental note to get two pictures of the workers. "Do you have any enemies, Dr. Broussard?"

"There are people who oppose some of my policies, but we are more than civil. I can't think of anyone who'd want to harm me. I do know people who desire my job."

"Can you provide me with a list of people who might strongly dislike you?"

"Yes, but these are public figures and well educated people, not violent criminals. I'll give you those names right now."

He handed the Professor his small notepad and a pen. Bill observed that Dr. Broussard was right-handed. After a few minutes he handed back a list of seven names to the Detective.

"Dr. Broussard, I'd like you to take a two-minute test right now for me. Would you do that?"

He didn't hesitate. "Yes. That sounds reasonable enough."

"I'll be right back."

Bill returned thirty or so minutes later with several items in his hand. The jailer opened the door allowing Detective Lincoln inside the cell. The jailer stood outside holding a stopwatch. Bill put the wastebasket on a chair in the corner. He had a ball of paper mashed into the size of a baseball, two decks of cards, a melon, a pen and chalk. Detective Lincoln drew a chalk line on the floor.

"We're going to videotape the test unless you object."

"No. I have no objections. But, I am curious."

"Dr. Broussard, you only have two minutes to complete these tasks. You must go through both decks of cards and remove the three lowest sets of numbers which are the twos, threes and fours from one set and the three highest, the queens, kings and aces, from the other set. Make sure they're in separate piles. You then have to shoot and make two baskets from behind that line. You shoot, retrieve the ball and go back to the line. If you can do those tasks and there's any time left, I'll yell out the third request. However, I doubt there'll be enough time. Understand?"

He nodded, yes. Bill gave him the two decks of cards and looked at the jailer. The jailer pointed his thumb up. Detective Lincoln looked back at Dr. Broussard. He was anxious.

"Are you ready?"

"Yes."

"Begin!"

Dr. Broussard ripped open the two decks of cards and started separating them into the designated groups. He started to count out loud to measure his time. It seemed the time was racing away. He made two piles of cards, but eighty seconds had expired. He reached for the paper ball, ran behind the line to shoot for the basket, but missed horribly. He hustled to retrieve it and raced back beyond the line. He shot again, made it; he couldn't believe he had scored one. He raced to the basket again, grabbed the paper ball and ran back. He was down to fifteen seconds. He shot again and missed. He retrieved the ball and shot again and missed again. He was flustered. He was trying his best but the clock was down to a few precious seconds. He missed again.

Bill yelled out, "Only five seconds left. Forget the basket. Take the pen and stab the melon in the center ten times. Hurry!"

Dr. Broussard grabbed the pen, raced for the melon on the bed and started stabbing it repeatedly when Bill said, "Okay, time's up. Stop."

Dr. Broussard was still going at it to get his ten stabs in before he stopped, even after the seconds had ticked off. He sat down, slowly, feeling mentally exhausted. Detective Lincoln stepped in the cell, retrieving the items. He said nothing more. The jailer once again secured the door. Seconds later Bill and the jailer walked down the hallway talking softly. Soon, all Dr. Broussard heard were the echoes of their steps moving steadily away.

"So, how did he do, Detective?" the jailer asked.

"What did you observe?" Bill responded.

"He almost finished the tasks."

"True. Now, what's his power hand?"

The jailer thought for a few seconds before saying, "The right one?"

"That's what I was testing for, his power hand."

"Did he pass?"

"There was no pass or fail answer. I simply needed to know which was his power side. I didn't want him telling me, I needed to see for myself."

Detective Lincoln gave all the items back to the jailer before leaving. As he was walking back, he was thinking that unless he was severely mistaken, the expert medical personnel believed that the killer in the first voodoo murder was left-handed!

Chapter 31

Promptly at 8 A.M. the staff meeting started. Brick wanted to review all the evidence against Dr. Broussard. If this case had any holes in it he certainly didn't want the proverbial finger pointed in his direction.

After ten minutes, Detective Lincoln interrupted the rhythm. The Police were only asking each other the easy questions. "His lawyers are offering a polygraph test to be administered by the police. Both he and his wife are willing to take one anytime, anywhere."

"Those things are unreliable, Bill. You know that."

"They're also willing to take the truth serum, sodium pentothal, and to be hypnotized by a police staff doctor too. They'll do that today, tomorrow or anytime we say. Why don't we accept their offer?"

"Don't be naive, Bill. These are two very sophisticated people. It's just a bluff."

"So, why not call their bluff? What do we have to lose?"

"The case. He's clever enough to figure out how to pass those tests. He's very bright and he's very desperate. We know he killed that girl. Therefore, if he fails the test he's no worse off. If he passes he can use that to support his 'not guilty' plea."

"He claims he's innocent. He didn't say not guilty," Bill reminded the group.

"That's only a technicality," Kasolkasky asserted.

"He's right-handed."

"How do you know?"

Bill described his interaction with Dr. Broussard and then showed the tape. Soon afterward, they resumed their conversation.

"So, Broussard is right-handed...big deal!" Kasolkasky replied after viewing the tape.

"Our medical experts believe that our killer is left-handed," the Detective pointed out. The room fell silent as everyone reflected on this point.

"Why are you bringing this up now, Bill?" the Chief asked.

"Well, I thought we should be examining all the facts, not just the convenient ones. The defense will certainly bring this point up. So, why don't we address it proactively?"

"Bill, the defense has its job. We have ours. We need to concentrate on nailing this guy," the Chief insisted.

"And, in doing so I think we also need to focus on all pertinent facts, Chief."

"Okay, let's assume the killer was left-handed. Apparently Broussard is not. Does that mean two people couldn't have been there? Look, Broussard is still our man. Let's not get sidetracked here."

With that, everyone got back down to business. The Chief's suggestion of two perpetrators certainly helped to ease Bill's mind.

"What's the good doctor's religious affiliation?"

"He claims he's Catholic. But he's also Cajun, so he's only one step away from who knows what. Who knows what he learned down there in the bayou."

"Anybody come up with any sex related stuff on him? This guy's a freak and somebody out there knows something."

"I would suggest we confiscate his journals," Bill offered.

"Good idea. Let's get a court order right away."

Later, around two o'clock, Bill and Clarence interviewed the maintenance worker, Jacque Vestable, on campus.

"Mr. Vestable, you told us that you knew nothing about voodoo and that you had no knowledge of where voodoo ceremonies were held. Are these statements still accurate or do you wish to change anything?"

Jacque Vestable had the look of the deer caught in oncoming headlights. He hesitated. The detectives waited patiently.

"So, I ask again, do you know where any voodoo ceremonies are being held locally, Mr. Vestable?" Detective Lincoln asked gruffly.

"Yes, sometimes."

"And do you attend those ceremonies?"

"Sometimes."

"Now, why lie to us?"

"I was scared."

"Scared...scared of what?"

Jacque shrugged his shoulders, clasped his hands together and started twiddling his thumbs. "I don't know. People just don't understand voodoo."

"So, you felt the natural thing was to lie to the police in a murder investigation?"

"I'm sorry. I was wrong."

"What else did you lie about?"

"Nothing."

"What about the time-line of your whereabouts that evening? You gave us one time-line and your friend, Pierre, gave us another. Tell me, just why should we believe you? After all, you are an admitted liar!"

Jacque sat there uncomfortably. Detective Lincoln menacingly slid a sheet of paper in front of Jacque demanding that he write down how often he attended the voodoo ceremonies, the people he was involved with and to what capacity. Jacque just sat there staring at the paper.

"All right, arrest him for obstruction of justice."

"Wait a minute," Clarence interjected, playing the good cop. "Give him a chance. He's got a job he could lose for Christ's sake. Listen...take a break. Let me talk to him."

Bill glared at Jacque then looked over at Clarence who had his hands up in a pleading fashion. Then, glancing back at Vestable, announced angrily, "I'll be back in twenty minutes," pointing straight at Jacque as he left the room.

Clarence sat next to Jacque coaxing him to start writing everything he knew about his contact with the local voodoo world. He mentioned

Marie Francois's name and Ricardo. He coyly let Jacque think that he knew more than he did and kept hinting that Detective Lincoln would surely lock him up for obstruction of justice. In another room Bill had called Ms. Francois. Detective Jones and the interrogation room were both wired.

"How long have you attended Mama's ceremonies, Jacque?" Clarence asked.

"For only a couple of months."

In the next room Bill was pursuing a similar line of questioning with Ms. Francois. She said Jacque had been coming for about two years. This guy was still lying!

"Do you have an active role in the ceremonies?" Clarence asked.

"No. I just go to watch."

"Does he have a role in your ceremony?" Detective Lincoln asked Mama.

"No, not yet anyway. He's working hard to get one though. He's been talking with Ricardo for a year about participating. As you've noticed, Ricardo is not very receptive."

Bill's mind flashed to Ricardo. He believed Ms. Francois. "Why does he want to play a role, Mama?"

"I imagine he believes he has special knowledge or powers and he wishes to cultivate them. But, he hasn't impressed Ricardo yet."

"Did he say how he developed these powers of his?"

"He claims he got them from some voodoo priest somewhere. It's been quite awhile since I've heard his story. I hear so many such stories from so many people that frankly I lose count."

"Where did you first learn about voodoo, Jacque?" Clarence asked.

"From the elders in the Haitian village where I grew up. It was the custom there."

Over the wire Bill told Clarence to ask Jacque about when he first got involved with voodoo here in the states.

"Voodoo is my religion. Once it touches you, it's always with you."

"Who were your teachers here in the States?"

"I'm sorry, but I'd rather not say."

Bill wanted that answer.

"Is Marie Francois the highest priest or priestess you've known?" Clarence asked.

"The second highest. She is very blessed."

Bill scratched his ear. He was very interested in this conversation but he didn't know what to ask next.

"What are your feelings about Ricardo? Is he the highest?" Clarence asked Jacque.

"No. Ricardo is not a priest. He's only a facilitator. The Great God does not visit Ricardo."

Bill talked to Ms. Francois to confirm Jacque's latest statement. Jacque was correct.

"So, you're not going to tell us who the high priest is?"

"That is not my call to make. Someone else may well disagree depending on his or her experiences. I'm only saying I believe there is one with even greater powers than Ms. Francois."

Detective Lincoln fed Clarence his next question to ask.

"Does Mama know this person?"

"No. I don't think so."

Bill switched over to the phone and asked Ms. Francois, "Who's the highest priest or priestess you know?"

Marie Francois didn't hesitate at all. "Why, I am, of course."

"Who's next, Mama? Whose powers are second only to yours?"

"The rest are all frauds. They're all imitators. The Great God himself has told me this. I alone am the chosen one."

Bill had run into a wall. He picked up the mike and instructed Clarence to ask Jacque if his ex-wife knew about his voodoo activities.

"No. Besides, she's a Catholic and would not understand. She was raised here in this country and is not familiar with the old ways."

"Why didn't you try to convert her?"

"She's much too headstrong for that. I knew she'd be a good mother...that was enough for me. She's a good church-going Catholic. Anything else is just foreign to her."

Bill couldn't think of any more questions and the interview was over. But the one thing Bill noted was that Jacque wrote right-handed.

--

At home that evening Bill received his first phone call at seven from Connie.

"How are you doing? Any more visits from our 'friends'?"

"No, Bill. And I'm hoping it's over."

"Where's your gun?"

"It's in my purse. I hate to admit this but I feel safer with it." They chatted for a few more minutes.

Bill finished his domestic chores before calling his daughter, Amanda. A man's voice answered catching Bill off-guard.

"Hello."

"This is Bill Lincoln. I'd like to speak with Amanda."

"Amanda is not here. Who are you, Sir?"

"I'm her father. Who are you?"

"This is security."

A sinking feeling had hit Bill like a blast of cold air. "Why are you there? Where's Amanda?"

"Amanda's been sent home because she's been receiving threatening phone calls. We've been in touch with her mother. I've been assigned to answer the phone here for a couple of hours each night for the next several nights."

"When did she go home?"

"This morning, Sir."

Bill was livid. Why hadn't Betty called him? He'd wait until he calmed down before calling her. While sitting there thinking about his daughter he reached for the phone to call the McDerch family. It had been almost six months since he'd spoken with them. Bill had done military service with their son and, in fact, had even saved his life. The McDerches were a wonderful family.

Their son, Leonard, was nicknamed 'Iron Hands'. He was a huge man who stood six foot-eight inches tall and weighed two hundred seventy-five pounds. He could easily palm a basketball with three fingers! He was powerfully built but possessed the gentleness of a child. He had gone off to Vietnam a healthy warm human being, but returned quite a different person. He looked the same, but due to severe head injuries suffered, he had virtually no short-term memory left.

Lenny had been the troop's point man. With the patience of Job and the eyes of a hawk, he could sit in one position for hours, regardless of weather conditions, stalking animal or man. Because of his innate ability he was the best sniper in the troop. He was also absolutely loyal, a soldier's soldier, following orders blindly. If you asked him to carry a grenade into an enemy's foxhole, he'd only ask which one.

"Hello, Mrs. McDerch. This is Bill Lincoln."

"Hi, Bill. When are we going to see you? Lenny is always asking about his favorite Major."

"I was thinking about seeing him soon. Is he still in the same facility?"

"Yes."

"I'm looking forward to it. I'll probably see him tomorrow."

--

Around nine, he decided to call Monique to see how she was doing. The conversation ended with Monique inviting him to her house the following evening to meet with her father.

Chapter 32

Around 6:55 P.M., Bill arrived at Monique's home and was escorted to the living room where he greeted Franklin Sr.

"Detective Lincoln."

"Good evening, Sir."

"What's your opinion of Dr. Broussard…guilty or innocent?" Dillard peered straight into his eyes. His legs were crossed and he leaned forward slightly, hands clasped on his knee. His gaze remained fixed on the Detective.

"The physical evidence strongly suggests he's guilty. However, he doesn't behave like a guilty man. Plus, I performed a simple experiment and as a result I don't believe he plunged the knife into your daughter. But, what do you think, Mr. Dillard?"

"I've known Nathaniel for twenty-five years. He's been to my home. We've had dinner at his. Our children grew up together. I don't want to believe he killed my daughter. Nate is a kind, decent man and his wife is a beautiful human being. I find it difficult to believe. But, I'm not a fool either. If he's the one, I'll see him burn."

"What are your plans, Mr. Dillard?"

Dillard stood and walked to the window. He remained motionless as he stared outside. His back was ramrod straight. He was a man who stood up to his burdens.

"I want to hire you to investigate Nate. You should know that I'm helping him hire a team of defense attorneys. I want you on that team."

"You're hiring lawyers for him?"

"I'm helping with the financing."

"Why?"

"To know the truth. If you're on that team, you can be my eyes and ears."

Bill agreed it was a workable plan. "But you realize I'm still working for the police."

"Stay there, you'll collect two checks. The police have a lazy streak. Just look at them. They stumble onto the first plausible suspect and they're ready to close the investigation. They only made progress when you came on-board."

"So, in other words, you're asking me to act as a, well… double-agent?"

He stared at the Detective and Bill was unable to look away. His presence was riveting.

"Your job is to investigate the murder. That hasn't changed. You'll have even more incentive to dig deeper now. Tell me, what has the force ever done for you anyway, Detective?"

The last question cut to the core. That insight sealed the deal. Dillard certainly knew how to motivate people.

"Mr. Dillard, I want a letter of employment from you spelling out our deal. The letter should clearly state that I'm not working to hinder the police investigation, but to enhance it. I'm not about to be hung out to dry. Do we have a deal?"

Dillard reached into his inside suit pocket and handed him an employment contract. "Take a few days to read it over. I'm sure you'll find it meets your needs. Now, will there be anything else?"

Bill wanted to ask him about his son Radcliffe, but didn't. If Dillard wanted to say something he would've.

"No, nothing that I can think of right now."

"Good, I'm going home." Dillard walked into the kitchen to say goodbye to Monique. She walked him to his car, returning a few minutes later.

"I'm not on your hit list for what I did to your brother am I?" Bill asked.

"I discussed it with Dad. He said I should be mad with Rad. Of course he's right."

"Is that all he said?"

"He did say he admired your aggressiveness, although he thought you might be a bit impulsive too. Let's just say he has mixed emotions and leave it at that."

"And how do you feel about me?"

"I, too, have mixed emotions. Where you're concerned you had to make a decision. I guess I'd be totally on your side if he were not my brother."

"Tell me, how do you feel about your father helping with Dr. Broussard's legal defense?"

"At first, I thought he'd gone mad. But my father is very astute and very wise and therefore I've learned never to second guess him."

"He certainly appears to have covered all the bases." Bill was thinking about the employment contract now in his pocket. Dillard had anticipated Bill's reaction. "Have you ever known your father to be dead wrong about something?"

Monique reflected thoughtfully on that question.

"On occasion, Dad has backed a few people he wished he hadn't and he's even lost a few court cases, so I guess he's human. But I've never known him to guess wrong on fundamentals. He's helped all of us make better decisions in our lives."

Bill stayed for another half-hour then drove home.

—

The following morning Bill drove up to the Westside Psychiatric Center to visit Leonard 'Iron Hands' McDerch. Detective Lincoln's name was on their permanent visitor's list.

He had been having the same conversation with Lenny for twenty years. After Lenny's operation he had lost all short-term memory. For twenty years now he believed he was leaving the next day. He still thought Bill was a Major stationed in Vietnam. Bill knew he could still give Lenny an order and it would be acted on immediately.

They discovered years ago that you could brief Lenny and he'd learn, but the next day he was back where he originally started. It was frustrating. There was no resolution. Lenny lived in this endless cycle where one day never became the next.

Bill spent little time with Lenny that day because he was anxious to get back. A special grand jury was hearing arguments in his own case.

--

"Mr. Barnes, would you please state your full name for the record, Sir."

"Mr. Thomas Kenneth Barnes."

"Your address."

"459 S. Broadway, Apt. 822H."

"Is that in Berkeley, CA?" the District Attorney asked.

"Yes."

"Please tell the Grand Jury your story relating to the death of one Harvey Gooding, who died by gunfire in a warehouse at 4679 S. Telegraph Avenue in Oakland, CA on the date indicated before you."

"The police received an anonymous call indicating that my friend, Mr. Gooding, was engaged in criminal activity at the warehouse. I understand that call was triggered by a burglar alarm signal from the warehouse. Two detectives, John McCormick and Bill Lincoln, were dispatched to the scene. The officers, once inside the building, heard gunfire just after they separated. Detective Lincoln went upstairs while McCormick searched downstairs. Lincoln discovered the body. His department-issued weapon was tested. The gun had not been discharged. Lincoln testified that although he had seen no one, he had heard footsteps on the back stairs. Lincoln's partner, McCormick, had not seen or heard anything. McCormick even suggested Lincoln could have had a second gun. You should also know that Lincoln had arrested the deceased, Harvey Gooding, twice before. In addition it seems Gooding had actually threatened Detective Lincoln's life in court after the second arrest."

Barnes looked at the Grand Jury before pushing back in his chair to get more comfortable. His heart was pounding so strongly that he believed everyone could hear it.

"I was the one who made the anonymous call."

There was complete silence. Everyone's attention was riveted on Barnes.

"I'm an ex-con. I was afraid to come forward because I'm not supposed to associate with known felons. Harvey Gooding was an ex-con too, but he was also my friend. We met in the joint. Detective Lincoln was the cop who put Harvey away. Harvey threatened Detective Lincoln after the verdict was delivered. I knew Lincoln would keep an eye on him. When Harvey was about to get out of prison, Detective Lincoln approached me. He wanted to know who was going to sponsor Gooding and where he was going to live. The only other time I had seen Detective Lincoln was five years earlier in that courtroom testifying, so when he approached me I knew something was up. Somehow I knew Harvey wouldn't live long once he was released. I could see it in Detective Lincoln's eyes."

The District Attorney slowly turned around so as to let the words linger like a wisp of smoke floating in the air.

"When did you make the anonymous call, Mr. Barnes?"

"At about two o'clock. I remember the time because I had had lunch with Harvey and he told me what he was planning. I knew I had to get him to stop. He was headed down the same dead end path all over again. I had to help my friend."

"And so you called the police?"

"Yes."

The District Attorney whirled back around, now staring with an incredulous expression.

"Mr. Barnes, are you telling this jury that you, an ex-con, called the police on your friend, also an ex-con? Do you honestly expect anyone to believe that?"

"I knew Harvey probably would not get caught. It was just to put a scare into him. Besides, I also called him right after I called the police. I told him I had heard a rumor that the police would be checking out that warehouse that afternoon."

"So you alerted him?"

"Yes."

"And what made you suspicious about Harvey's death?"

Barnes looked at the District Attorney long and hard before leaning forward in his chair. "When I discovered that Detective Lincoln was one of the officers who responded to the call that day there was no doubt in my mind what had happened. He killed my friend. I know it like I know the back of my hand."

"Thank you, Mr. Barnes. Are there any questions from the Grand Jury?"

"Did you know Detective Lincoln had been dispatched to the warehouse?" Juror Number Seven asked.

"No. I just made the call. I didn't know who would respond to the call."

"From what location did you phone?" Connie Chow asked.

"I called from a telephone booth."

"Where?"

"A few blocks from my house in Berkeley."

"Where did you have lunch?" Connie asked again.

"I don't remember. I believe it was at the local restaurant up the street from my house."

"Surely you remember where you had lunch on the last day you saw your friend alive?"

"Yes. It was at that restaurant."

"Does this restaurant have a name?"

"The Ginger House."

"And what did you have for lunch that day?"

Barnes looked at the District Attorney. He didn't know he was going to be asked so many detailed questions. "I'm not sure. It was probably a hamburger."

"Who paid for it?"

"I did. It was my treat."

"How did you pay for it?"

"I paid cash."

"What form of transportation did you use to get there?"

"I walked. It's only a few minutes from my house."

"How did Mr. Gooding get there?"

"I don't know. I assumed he drove."

"Did you see him drive there?"

"No." Barnes was starting to get a little irritated. There he was, being grilled by this woman. She was firing questions like a lawyer.

"When you finished lunch, did you leave together?"

"Yes."

"Did he go get his car?"

"Yes. We shook hands then he went around back to get his car. I started walking home. I never saw him again that day. I don't know what he was driving."

"Did you both have dessert?"

"I don't remember. Maybe. Yes, we probably did."

"What was he wearing that day?"

"I don't remember."

"A suit and tie, perhaps?"

"No. He worked in a warehouse. He had on work clothes. I don't remember the color."

"Bright colors or more subdued?"

"I can't remember."

"The police record says you contacted him. Why did you call him at two P.M.?"

"What do you mean?"

"You just had lunch with him. Soon after you felt the need to alert him."

The witness was silent. Connie Chow waited for a few more moments. "Well?"

"I don't know."

"Thank you, Mr. Barnes. I have no more questions at this time."

Connie had used the list of questions Bill suggested. It was important to ask as many detailed questions as possible. The Devil is always in the details.

--

At the following morning's meeting, retired Detective Bill Lincoln was informed that his services were no longer required. The special police task force investigating the death of Hillary Dillard was officially finished. Both the Chief and Kasolkasky felt they had enough evidence for a conviction and that there was no need to spend additional taxpayer dollars. It was now smart public relations to rid themselves of any potential 'excess baggage'.

Bill's first stop, after leaving police headquarters, was at the lockup to visit with Dr. Broussard. After spending forty minutes with him, Bill drove to the educator's home to research the doctor's journals. He wanted to read the passages surrounding the night of the murder.

Mrs. Broussard allowed Bill to spend several hours reading in Dr. Broussard's study. So far, there was nothing he read that he didn't already know. Afterwards, he spent another half-hour or so talking with Mrs. Broussard. She clung to the story she gave the day her husband was first arrested. Again, he had learned nothing new.

At home that evening, Detective Lincoln was washing dishes when his phone rang.

"Hello, Bill."

"Hi, Connie. How was the Grand Jury meeting?"

"We heard from the guy who claimed he had made the anonymous call to the police."

"What does the Grand Jury think?"

"I think you're probably going to be indicted."

Bill was silent. He had hoped it wouldn't come to this. "Who is it?"

"A man named Thomas Barnes."

"That weasel!" This couldn't be happening. This guy was nothing.

"You know him?"

"Yeah. He's an over-aged punk who has a rap sheet as long as my arm! This guy would sell his mother for ten bucks. Is this all the District Attorney has?"

"Apparently so."

"Well then, now I can get a good night's sleep."

"Bill, I don't think you should take this too lightly. The DA would not go out on a limb, especially if this is all he has."

He reluctantly agreed that Connie was right. Was he being a little too cocky? He'd have to wait. "How's Willie holding out?"

"He's scared. He's talking about bailing from the witness protection program. I can't say that I blame him."

"And you. How are you holding up?"

"So far, so good…and you?"

"I've got the old good news/bad news syndrome. I'm not sure what's what sometimes."

"You need to take a break. This could be the perfect time. Rumor has it you're off the case."

Even though Detective Lincoln knew how fast the word on the grapevine traveled, he was somewhat surprised that Connie already knew. "I'm off the police's payroll, but I'm now working on behalf of our alleged killer, Dr. Broussard."

"Really? My, but you do get around. Who's paying you?"

"I'd rather not say just yet anyway."

"Well, if you're not going to disclose any juicy details, then I'll let you go. Be careful."

"Bye, Connie."

--

The following morning Bill was scheduled to meet with the team assembled to defend Dr. Broussard. The lead attorney was Texas lawyer Hank Buckston. Buckston was a slow talker who always wore his ten-gallon cowboy hat and cowboy boots. He liked to use his heavy southern drawl, which he produced at will. However, just last month, he argued a case before the Supreme Court and if you didn't know any better, you'd have sworn he was from Boston.

"Good day, Mr. Lincoln," he said in his nasal southern drawl.

"Mr. Buckston, you look just like your pictures." They shook hands.

"Oh my, now I'm scared. Next, you'll be telling me you believe everything I say too."

"Hardly. I'm a detective, not a farmer. I can usually smell it well before I see it."

"Good. I like a man who can cross a field without getting his shoes dirty. Allow me to introduce you to my assistants, Buddy Miller and Dana Andrews," he announced with that marvelous 'tortoise-speed' delivery.

Both attorneys stood and shook Bill's hand.

"Now, the first thing I'd like is for us to sit down and chat. I'm the type of lawyer who doesn't ask his client if he's guilty. The client doesn't know. After all, he's not the lawyer."

Bill sat there and smiled inside. The bull was flowing freely already! Lawyers were a funny group of people. Who else would say a person didn't know whether they'd done something wrong?

"Mr. Buckston?"

"Yes, Sir."

"Our client will most assuredly tell us repeatedly that he is innocent. Look, he's the Chancellor of a college, surely he must know if he's committed a crime."

"Thank you, Detective. You have no doubt noticed my tendency to forget the educational level of my clients. So, what's his answer to how his sperm got there?"

"He doesn't know. It's either someone else's sperm, or, someone else put it there. It's not his doing according to him."

Buckston sat there examining those words, mulling them over in his mind. "I understand some three different independent labs have all concluded that it was his sperm?"

"Indeed."

"How good are these here labs?"

"Top of the line. Impeccable credentials."

"And what is our client's mental state?"

"He's as sane as anyone in this room."

"Well, we'll need a professional opinion, Detective."

"I'm just saying Dr. Broussard is an intelligent, rationale human being who is not likely to play the wacko game."

Buckston sat back placing his hands behind his head. He let out a big yawn while observing the Detective. "So, are you saying he did it?"

"No, I'm saying the laboratories have confirmed his DNA and that Dr. Broussard is not a walking incompetent."

"Looky here now, his sperm is found at the scene of the crime. Now just how does he propose that it got there?"

"He simply doesn't know."

Dana Andrews spoke next. "Okay Detective, his sperm is there and he didn't put it there. Therefore, the natural conclusion is someone else would have had to put it there. It's our job to determine who this someone else is."

"Ms. Andrews, how often does your boyfriend leave sperm lying around your house?"

"I think our first question to Dr. Broussard should be has he donated to a sperm bank?" Ms. Andrews replied.

Everyone agreed.

"Let's assume he hasn't," Bill responded. "What then?"

"Let's not go there until necessary," Buddy Miller remarked with his first words.

"Detective, please share your opinion. Ironically, it was your insights that led to Dr. Broussard's arrest. What do you think?" Buckston asked.

He studied each person before he spoke. He reminded himself that these were defense lawyers who would be looking at any opening for their client. "If I were on the jury and the trial was tomorrow, I'd vote guilty. I'm assuming the current evidence is the same that's in our possession. That DNA is conclusive in my mind. However, Dr. Broussard could have convinced me otherwise if it wasn't for the DNA. He exhibits no criminality in his physical presence or his conversation. He talks fluently without contradictions. I'd call him an innocent man, that is, if it wasn't for the scientific evidence."

All three lawyers contemplated Detective Lincoln's observations. But before anyone could respond, there was a knock. The door opened to reveal Dr. Broussard escorted by police. His handcuffs had been removed.

"Dr. Broussard, welcome. We have a number of questions for you. But first, we'd like to hear any statement you'd like to make. I don't give a hoot whether you believe you're innocent or guilty. I'm here to work on your behalf. So, I'd appreciate it if you didn't address that matter," he said with his drawl flowing like barbecue at a Texas cookout.

"Mr. Buckston, I'm innocent. Let me state that for the record. I could never do such a thing. I don't know how my sperm got there. Someone either put it there or some other terribly horrible mistake has been made!"

"Dr. Broussard, have you ever donated sperm?" Buckston asked.

"No. Never."

The mind is the man, and knowledge mind; a man is but what he knoweth.

FRANCIS BACON: THE
PRAISE OF KNOWLEDGE.

Chapter 33

The bold headlines in the morning paper read, "**FRANKLIN DILLARD, JR. REJECTS POLICE MURDER SUSPECT!**" The article detailed an exclusive interview with Franklin Dillard, Jr. concerning his run for political office with that same interview drafting a discussion about the suspect the police arrested. Franklin Jr. made it abundantly clear he had little faith in the city's administration. He blasted the Mayor for having minimal control over fiscal obligations coupled with a limited vision of where he wanted to take the city. For his part, Franklin Jr. would wait for the trial, but he had miniscule faith that the city's police department possessed the intelligence to conduct a thorough investigation. The article was a direct, 'no holds barred' put-down of the Mayor and his cronies.

Bill's phone rang at 6:45 A.M.

"Hello."

"Did you see the headline this morning?"

"No, Mayor. What does it say?"

"I suggest you read it for yourself. Call me back in one hour. I want your full attention focused on getting that information on Franklin Jr." The phone went dead. Bill hung up the receiver and walked outside to retrieve the paper. The Mayor would be hounding for dirt on Franklin, Jr. Bill found himself caught between a 'rock and a hard place'... Franklin, Sr. on the one hand and the Mayor on the other, each with enough power to make life extremely uncomfortable for him. It was also interesting that Dillard Sr. had, so far, not shown any interest in helping his youngest son get out of trouble. Rad appeared to have been left to fend for himself. An hour later Bill returned Jim Efferton's call.

"Hello, Mayor, I read the article."

"What have you dug up on Franklin, Jr.?"

"Nothing. My contact has declined to do any more research. Someone has persuaded him to 'seek other employment' as he put it."

"Who?"

"He wouldn't say." Through the silence Bill thought he could hear the wheels turning in the Mayor's mind.

"I need information, Bill. And I expect you to get it."

"I'm not working for the police anymore. Remember, I've been relieved."

"No problem...you're on my payroll now, just like before. Now, get that information!"

"Mayor, the investigation into my background by the Grand Jury has resulted in Thomas Barnes being called to testify against me."

"Yes, I heard."

"What's your take on this?"

"Well, if he's the DA's only witness, you're reasonably safe. Goodbye." Click. The line went dead.

The Mayor was right. Bill got dressed and drove to Buckston's office. All three lawyers were there. "I left early yesterday right before you finished up with Dr. Broussard. What's your opinion?" the Detective asked Buckston.

"He's our greatest asset. He's educated, speaks well and is not afraid to answer any question. Quite frankly, I want him to testify. This man simply has too much credibility to be the likely killer. He's been a pillar of his community for twenty-five years. I believe in him."

Bill listened, but he was unimpressed. He had never met a lawyer who didn't say that he believed in his client. "And just how do we explain finding his sperm?"

"First and foremost we've got an innocent man in our charge. With that in mind we're checking to see if the labs made a mistake. However, the three independent lab's consensus makes that highly unlikely. So, by default, someone had to have planted that evidence."

"Could that person be the donor of the DNA?"

"No, that's highly unlikely. We assume Dr. Broussard is innocent. Therefore we must find the real perpetrator!"

Bill sat down. Dealing with lawyers was always a challenge. "Okay, so I'm looking for a person who stole Dr. Broussard's sperm when he was not looking, or maybe I'm looking for his identical twin brother."

Buckston stared at the Detective when he heard the term twin brother. Bill returned his stare. He didn't believe this.

"Bill, does Broussard have a twin brother?"

"He has brothers, but he's never mentioned any of them being an identical twin."

"We need to ask."

"What about the lab tests?"

"Check to see if it's statistically possible for the owner of the DNA to be a twin brother."

"I'll check. Suppose he doesn't have a twin brother?"

"We'll worry about that later."

Bill left. During the next two hours Bill visited Dr. Broussard in jail and talked with the lab. Broussard had no identical twin. Besides, the lab report had statistically eliminated that possibility.

When he walked into the police station he was told that Jacko, his street informant, had been admitted to the hospital the previous night. He was found in an alley, badly beaten. If it weren't for the security guards, who heard a disturbance and went to investigate, Jacko would most likely be dead. Detective Lincoln phoned the hospital and was told that Jacko was comatose!

Bill contacted Marie Francois to secure a meeting with Ricardo. They would meet that night at eight. At first, Ricardo was not interested, but the Detective reminded Ricardo of how very interested the authorities would be in his unlawful activities.

Buckston called requesting that the Detective fly to the hometown of Dr. Broussard to look for information. Detective Lincoln agreed. He made reservations to fly to New Orleans in three days.

Bill met his girlfriend Susan for a late lunch at a downtown restaurant. While they were eating, Radcliffe Dillard, wearing a stylishly expensive suede sports coat and an exquisite platinum chain and medallion, just happened to stroll over to their table.

"Why, Detective Lincoln, I didn't know retired policemen could afford the prices here."

"Hello, Radcliffe. Unlike some of us, I do earn a legitimate living and can afford to eat at some of the more upscale restaurants every now and again. I'm not destitute quite yet."

"Well, if I can help with the tip, just let me know." Rad turned to Susan. "Hello. My name's Radcliffe Dillard." Rad extended his immaculately manicured hand.

"Hello. My name is Susan Lambert."

"My dear, you look absolutely stunning! I absolutely love the way you wear your hair. Are you by chance a model?"

Susan blushed, enthralled by Rad's obvious flirting. "Of course not. I'm much too old for that."

"Now you're pulling my leg. You're not Detective Lincoln's daughter?"

"Now, Mr. Dillard, you're teasing me."

"Okay, then he's your older brother. Yes?"

Susan smiled, "Well, that's possible."

Bill was listening but was not smiling. He was wondering what Radcliffe was up to.

"Ah, if only I thought there was even a slim chance of getting to know you better, I'd jump at the opportunity. But alas, I can see the Detective stands in our way. What a shame. Oh, the possibilities."

"Why, Mr. Dillard, you are something else. I bet you know exactly what to say to all the ladies."

Rad leaned over, kissed her hand and replied, "The words come easy when confronted with such beauty."

"Mr. Dillard, can a woman trust you?" Susan beamed.

"But, of course."

"Yeah. Like leaving a wolf guarding the hen house," the lawman remarked.

"Detective Lincoln is just jealous."

"When's your trial, Radcliffe?" Bill asked

"What trial, Detective?"

"Well, if I'm not mistaken, I believe you're facing drug possession charges."

"Very funny. However, I believe those charges will be dropped... by you. I'm sure you haven't realized the mistake you made just yet. But, it's only a matter of time before you see the error in your ways. Goodbye, Detective." Rad turned back to Susan. "And goodbye, Miss Lambert. It was indeed a pleasure meeting you. You have made my day."

He kissed her hand once again and started walking away when suddenly he stopped, turned back around and said, "I certainly missed you the night of my party. I'm not sure why Detective Lincoln didn't bring you instead of my sister. Oh well, just the same, it was nice meeting you."

Susan's smitten look had dissolved like butter in a hot skillet; she now looked sternly at Bill. His appetite went south. Rad had just nailed him!

"What did he just say?" Susan inquired.

"He said I escorted his sister to his party."

"Is that true?"

"Yes. That's the only way I knew how to get there."

The meal never finished...Susan asked to leave. The atmosphere in the car was as cold as a side of beef hanging in a meat-locker. When she got out, Susan slammed the car door!

A minute later, the car phone rang as he sat there; Jacko had come out of his coma. He headed for the hospital. At the visitor's counter he flashed his badge. Bill walked into Jacko's room a few minutes later, barely recognizing the informant. Jacko had received a horrible thrashing. His face was severely swollen and bandages were everywhere; he looked like a mummy.

"Who did this to you, Jacko?"

"You did," Jacko mumbled in a hoarse whisper. "I got to thinking about that money and started asking around again about your boy, Dillard Jr."

"I understand they would have killed you if it wasn't for the security guards hearing the assailants."

"Yeah, you can believe that."

"They'll be back, Jacko. You can count on it. These boys don't like loose ends."

Jacko turned his head away from the Detective. Bill waited a few seconds before preparing to leave. He was sorry that Jacko had been beat up, but he felt no responsibility. Jacko and he had made a deal. It was the con man's responsibility to protect himself. "See you around, Jacko, probably at your funeral. Any messages you want me to convey to anyone?" He waited a few seconds before starting to walk out.

"Detective?"

The Detective heard Jacko's whimper, stopped and turned around. "Yes, Jacko?"

"Can you help me?"

"Help you how?"

"I need to get out of Oakland."

"First, tell me who beat you up?"

"I don't know."

"Then I guess I can't help you, Jacko. See ya."

"Detective."

He stood there waiting with his back to Jacko. He was staring at the floor. "What?"

"It was Big Eddy's henchman."

Bill turned around. "Luka?"

"Yeah, Luka"

"Why?"

"Because, like I said, I was asking around about Frankie Junior. You know Big Eddy and Rad are buddies. And, you know I had been given a warning, which unfortunately, I ignored. You see I was doing okay for money, but then I suffered two gambling loses and my money got a little funny. Anyhow, I made a stupid mistake. Now my life is screwed."

"So…who's Dillard's lover?"

Jacko stared at him with hollow eyes. After all, this was the question that had put him where he was in the first place! "I don't know. I wish I did."

"Alright then, can you point me anywhere?"

"I'm sorry, I have nothing solid to give you. I just don't know."

"You have my word that I'll talk with some people downtown to see what they can do for you. I'm not exactly in favor with the police anymore. But I'll try to do something for you if I can. That's the least I can do."

"Thanks, Detective…yeah." Jacko closed his eyes to go to sleep. He would need lots of rest to recover from Luka's beating. Bill took one last look at Jacko before leaving the room.

Detective Lincoln returned to Buckston's office to report his findings. There was no identical twin brother, but that didn't matter because the DNA tests were conclusive. The DNA was Dr. Broussard's alone. Dana Andrews then announced, "We know the answer then. The sperm was planted." Bill was perplexed. However, he was getting paid as a member of the Broussard team so he'd play the game. Dr. Broussard had insisted he had never donated sperm so the Detective had no idea where to go next.

"Bill," Hank Buckston said, "please, sit down."

Bill sat by the lawyer's desk.

"Why would Dr. Broussard kill Hilliary Dillard?"

"Search me. I have no idea." Bill knew, like the darkness of the night, that the lawyer would have an answer. A lawyer could always see the goal line for his client.

"Exactly. That's my point. There's no motive. There's no legitimate reason why. Therefore, we must conclude he's innocent. He's been a productive member of your community for over twenty-five years. There must be another answer."

"I'm open to any suggestions," Bill responded.

"Have you made reservations for New Orleans yet?"

"Yes."

"Good. I have a list of his relatives, their addresses and their telephone numbers. They've all been notified that you're coming."

He was thinking about the last time he was in New Orleans. He'd spent a weekend in the French Quarter and had had a great time. "Also there's one thing the Los Angeles voodoo lady said that you should know," Bill mentioned.

Buckston lifted his glasses up to rub his right eye. He had never dealt with voodoo before and he was wary. "What's that?"

"Ms. Balboa predicted that the person that we arrested would shock us. She said, 'He walks among us but is not one of us.'"

Buckston didn't know what to make of the statement. He was relatively confidant neither side would venture down the voodoo path, not unless it became absolutely unavoidable.

"And what does that mean?"

"Well, it accurately reflected the reaction of most in this community when Dr. Broussard was arrested."

"Would you put her on the stand?"

"No, not unless I was desperate."

"Well, thank heavens we're not there yet. I saw the tape of the experiment you gave Broussard. That's additional proof of his innocence."

Bill looked up at Buckston. "I wouldn't go quite that far. He still could've been there, albeit, with someone else actually committing the murder."

"Nah. It feels, well, off-base. I mean, it's possible but it just doesn't sit well with me."

The investigator dropped the subject. He had made his point.

"Bill, keep an open mind. We haven't even begun our investigation. We're a long way from concluding anything. You yourself said that your intellect said one thing and your intuition another. Let's get more under our belt before we start drawing conclusions."

"Okay. That's fair enough. What do you need done today?"

"Can you get a sense of where the police are with their investigation? I'd like to know if they've uncovered anything new or unusual. They're supposed to notify us of course, but they'll take their sweet time, not disclosing anything important until they absolutely have to."

"I'll drop by the station. By the way, has Broussard disclosed the names of the women he had affairs with yet?"

"Yes. All the relationships are around ten years old. There are five names on the list; one is deceased. I don't hold out much hope they'll provide any useful information. But, what have we got to loose?"

Bill, reviewing the list, noticed the notes written beside each name. Two of the women were college administrators back East. The third name was accompanied by very little information. The comments about her said she was a student and nothing else. It appeared they had had a one-night affair. The fourth owned her own business and lived in California. He put the list in his pocket, mentally assigning it a low priority. His immediate concern was interviewing the various members of Broussard's family still living in New Orleans. Still, he decided he'd check Dr. Broussard's journals that afternoon to determine if any of these women was mentioned.

Bill burned three hours at the Broussard house pouring over the journals and found mention of all five women. The two college administrators attended seminars with Dr. Broussard. Broussard mentioned them as speakers at the events. The third person listed, the one with so little information, was described as a student attending a one-day seminar. Apparently he had met her while visiting another campus. The fourth woman was a generous donor to the school he had attended as an undergraduate. He had met her at a 'Homecoming' weekend. There was a special dinner for the 'successful' alumni. They were conveniently seated at the same table. The fifth name was a political science instructor who had died five years earlier in a tragic car accident.

All the indiscretions had occurred over a two-year period, some eleven years prior. Dr. Broussard claimed he had become depressed, bored with his life. He had yearned for excitement and found it in the arms of other women. He still loved his wife and always would. The other women knew he was married, so he hadn't deceived them. Bill would contact each of the four to determine if Dr. Broussard was being truthful.

"Mrs. Broussard, has your husband been faithful?"

She didn't want to answer, but she was not going to hide anything. She knew the stakes were too high.

"I don't believe so. I've never actually asked him. However, there was a time and it's been quite a few years ago, that I believe my husband may not have been the best husband a man can be."

"What makes you say that?" he inquired.

"A woman knows, Mr. Lincoln. My husband's actions after several out-of-town meetings years ago were strange enough for me to become suspicious. I can't point to anything specific, but I had a feeling. Call it a woman's intuition."

Later, Bill drove to his scheduled meeting with Marie Francois and Ricardo.

"Where's Ricardo, Mama?"

"He'll be here soon."

"Have you done any research on Ms. Jezabel Balboa?"

"She's a fraud. I called a few acquaintances in Los Angeles. She's nothing more than a small time fortune-teller. She gets in the local news once every three to four years as a local interest story. She's nothing."

"How did she know there was the voodoo god's mark on the body?"

Ms. Francois became quiet. She had to think about that question.

"Damballa has never left signs!"

Now Bill was quiet. He was trying to remember how the identification of the voodoo sign happened. It was Ms. Balboa. Nobody else had suggested anything about voodoo.

"I want to show you the picture of the mark."

"I don't know why. Damballa is not some celebrity leaving autographs for the public."

Detective Lincoln, hearing footsteps, turned around. It was Ricardo. He was standing in the doorway, his presence dominating the room. Bill didn't bother to address him. He'd wait for Ricardo. Both Ms. Francois and the Detective were sitting before Ricardo seated himself.

"Ricardo, tell me about Jacque Vestable."

"What do you want to know?" he asked directly.

"How long has he been attending your voodoo ceremonies?"

"About two years."

Ricardo was not a conversationalist.

"What does he want from you?"

"He wants to be my partner."

"Will he?"

"No."

"Why not?"

"I don't need him."

Detective Lincoln wished Ricardo was a bit more talkative.

"Does he claim to have special powers?"

"He claims to be special."

"Is he?"

"I haven't seen anything special about him."

This was like pulling teeth to Bill. "What type of powers does he suggest he has?"

"That Damballa acknowledges his existence."

"Does he?"

"I told you, I haven't seen anything."

"What type of person is Jacque?"

Ricardo continued staring at Bill. "What do you mean?"

"Does he tell jokes? Is he dependable? Does he lie?"

"He's a man who wants more power and he'll do anything to achieve that."

The Detective thought about that last answer. Ricardo measured men by a different standard.

"Did Jacque ever mention where he might've received his belief that he might have voodoo powers?"

"No."

Bill knew Ricardo was lying.

Chapter 34

At 6:45 A.M., Willie Taylor woke up and automatically reached for a cigarette. Willie was a product of the poor streets of Oakland. Many of his decisions were not in his own best interests. He didn't envision a long future so ruining his health by smoking was a moot point.

Willie rolled out of bed, grabbed his towel and headed to the bathroom across the hallway. The bathroom was outside the main bedroom, that way the officer could see the witness several times a day. If not, witnesses could hole up in their rooms cutting off communication too easily. Most already suffered from isolation and depression.

Willie stumbled into the hallway expecting a greeting from the guard, but heard nothing. Oh well, the officer was probably sitting in the living room.

Willie entered the bathroom. He laid his towel down to grab his toothbrush. As he pulled back the shower curtain to turn the water on, he saw the bloody decapitated head of a chicken lying on the floor of the shower. Willie freaked out, spun backwards, crashed into the wall and then fell to the floor. He scrambled to his feet and rushed back to his bedroom, slamming and locking the door shut. With heaving chest and rocketing blood pressure, Willie's eyes were fixated on the door as he frantically put on his clothes. His ears were geared for sound but so far, he heard nothing.

Willie's eyes never left the door; his heart pounded like someone had strapped him to a jackhammer. He was sweating profusely, knowing he must get out; but he was afraid of opening the door. Instinctively he searched for a weapon, seized a broom lying against the wall and broke off the end. This was his club. He held the wood like a pit bull locking onto an enemy in battle and slowly walked forward, grabbing the door handle and still listening intensely. But, he heard nothing. He stood there for a full ten minutes; beads of sweat formed on his temples. Finally, Willie summoned all his energy and nerve. Slowly he nudged the door open and peeked outside. He saw nothing and began his silent flight to the outside door.

Stepping slowly and carefully, he reached his destination and placed his left hand on the knob. His right hand, with large blue pulsating veins flushed with adrenaline, managed the stick. Willie was now a lethal weapon. He looked through the peephole and seeing empty space, opened the door and stepped into the hallway. Willie walked briskly to the elevator, pushed the button and rushed back to the open apartment door...the elevator whizzed to his floor. The elevator gate opened as the unit sat waiting. Willie didn't see anyone come out; so...he ran...he ran to the elevator. William Lee Taylor Sr. was technically, if not officially, back on the streets.

Two hours later Bill's phone rang.

"Hello."

"Bill, this is Connie. I was just notified by the police. Willie skipped! He's flown the coop!"

"What happened?"

"I don't know and nobody's talking."

"Do you think Big Eddy knows that Willie's on the run?"

"I don't know. I certainly hope not. The police are trying to keep it quiet."

"Where's his daughter?"

"She's still in protective custody. She's much too scared to run. What should I do Bill?"

"Stay by your phone, Connie."

"Okay. I can do that. Thanks, Bill. Goodbye."

Somehow, someone had gotten to Willie. Bill knew Willie couldn't survive long on the run. He was a marked man.

Several days later Bill flew to New Orleans where Dr. Broussard's eldest brother met him at the airport and drove him to his hotel. The eldest brother was Rodrick. He was rough looking, typical of those who were accustomed to long hours of physical labor. Rod was protective of his younger brother and had tremendous respect for his sibling's meteoric rise to such a distinguished station in life.

"What was Nathaniel like as a child?"

"Well, Nate was always smart. And boy did the nuns and the priest love him. Heck, whenever any of us wanted to know anything, we'd just ask Nate. Shoot, I'm five years older, but even I'd ask him questions related to schoolwork. You see he was never too interested in learning how to hunt or track animals. Our Pappy wanted all his boys, including Nate, to know how to feed themselves; he would always get on Nate's case for being such a bookworm. We couldn't protect Nate from Pappy, but the nuns could, and they gave Pappy hell every chance they had."

"Did Nate like girls?"

"Yeah, especially the smart ones. He was no different than the rest of us. Except of course, he placed them on a pedestal. I always thought Nate was somewhat naive when it came to females."

"Could he fight?"

Rod had to think about that one. "Nate never really fought; not like the rest of us. He was more of a mediator. He had the gift of gab and could talk his way out of most anything."

Bill reflected on those words, wondering if this was what he was trying to do now. "Who would you say knows him best?"

"Well, I'd say Mama and the nuns. That's 'cause he spent more time with them than anyone else. We boys liked to hunt and shoot, not Nate, he mostly hung around the women-folk."

Rodrick drove Bill to his sister's house; there the Detective spent several hours meeting with all three sisters and another brother. He heard many good things about Dr. Broussard, but he was more interested in hearing some negatives. He still had learned nothing new. His next interview was with Mother Rebecca. Mother Rebecca was close to ninety years old and still worked a full day on church-related activities. Bill went to her office where statues and pictures of Jesus hung on the walls in a cluttered non-discernable pattern. The religious artifacts were everywhere. Perhaps she was preparing for a yard sale?

"Mother Rebecca, what type of young man was Nathaniel Broussard?"

The nun was busy fiddling with something so he wasn't sure if she heard him. He was about to repeat his question when she began to speak. "He was a good boy and very smart. He always listened to his teachers. Young boys are very different today. Even the young girls are different."

"So, didn't Nathaniel ever do any bad things?"

"Certainly not. Nathaniel was an angel. He always did as he was told."

Bill had never met a child who was an angel. "When's the last time you spoke with Nathaniel?"

"Last year. He was here last year. Nathaniel tries to return home each year. Sometimes business will bring him home too. He's grown into a wonderful man. Yes, simply wonderful."

"Do you happen to know his wife?"

"Why yes, she's a sweetheart."

"I agree. I've enjoyed talking with her. Mother, as you know, sometimes people change over the years. Do you think Nathaniel loves his wife?"

Mother Rebecca looked at him and said strongly, "Of course he does!"

"Could Nathaniel ever cheat on his wife?"

The nun frowned; it was abundantly obvious that she didn't like hearing such things. "Nathaniel is a good Catholic boy who would never do such a thing. The state of marriage is a holy union. Nathaniel would never break his vows!"

"I can assume you believe Nathaniel is innocent?"

"Naturally!"

"Mother, does Nathaniel have any enemies here?"

The nun shook her head. Dr. Broussard was a living saint to this woman and she disapproved of the questions that the Detective was compelled to ask.

"Nathaniel is loved by all here. He has many friends and loving relatives. And we're all very proud of him."

"Do you happen to know anything about voodoo, Mother?"

"Don't you ever speak to me of that horrible abomination...it is pure evil...do you hear me! Pure evil! They say it's a religion, hmm! Why it's nothing but the devil's handiwork! Satan himself is behind it. You mark my words young man. You mark my words..."

He spent another ten minutes with Mother Rebecca, but again learned nothing new. He found Rodrick waiting in another room. Bill was scheduled to finish the evening interviewing four of Dr. Broussard's childhood buddies.

During the next few hours he heard more positive things and only small, insignificant instances of misbehavior by the then young Nathaniel Broussard. He wanted to meet the mother. Dr. Broussard's siblings were not sure if they wanted him to talk with their ailing mother. She was very close to death. So far, they respected the manner in which Bill was gathering his information. The family would decide the following day if he would be allowed to talk with Edwina Broussard, the matriarch.

Detective Lincoln returned to his hotel where he spent the better part of the evening recording his notes and retrieving his phone messages. The first message had come from Susan. She asked that he return her call. The second was from Connie Chow. It seemed her commission would meet yet another witness who was alleged to have pertinent information concerning the case against him. The final call was from Brick Kasolkasky who wanted to meet with him as soon as he got back. He would call Susan later.

He dialed Connie's number. She picked up on the third ring. "Connie, Bill here. I got your message. Who's this witness?!"

"Once again we don't know; no names have been disclosed."

"I find it strange that the names of these people are never given beforehand."

"I have to agree with you."

"Well, if you get wind of who it is and you can tell me, please do."

"I will."

"Anything more on Willie?"

239

"No. Nothing yet."

"I have to go. Keep me posted. Goodnight."

"Goodbye, Detective. And, good luck."

Bill made his last call to Brick Kasolkasky, deciding to leave a message for him at the police station. Brick was probably home, but the Detective didn't have any particular desire to talk to him that night. Had it been that important, Brick would have said so.

The following morning Bill was told he could meet with Edwina Broussard. He hopped into Rod's old beat up pickup truck that looked like it had been in a prolonged battle with Mother Nature. His mother's house was in a rural section of bayou country with only dirt roads and very poor drainage.

Forty-five minutes later they sputtered up to a small wooden structure where the Broussard's had raised their family. Dense trees and shrubs surrounded the home. Inside, the air reeked of death. It was dark and the dank smell of medicine, most likely homemade, lingered.

Detective Lincoln was escorted into Mrs. Broussard's room by two of her daughters. A rail-thin woman lay in bed, a mountain of hand-made quilts covering her. She sat up, supported by several pillows. Her gray hair flowed freely down her shoulders. Life had not been kind to this woman.

"Mother, this is Mr. Lincoln from California. Mr. Lincoln knows our Nathaniel. He's down here on business and he promised Nathaniel that if he got a chance, why he'd stop in and visit our family. Mr. Lincoln, this is our mother, Edwina Broussard."

Bill extended his hand. Mrs. Broussard smiled and shook it feebly. She was happy to meet anyone who knew her sweet Nathaniel.

"Hello, Mrs. Broussard, Nate asked me to tell you he loves you."

"Thank you Mr. Lincoln. How is my Nathaniel?"

"He's doing just fine but is very busy. His wife and family are all healthy."

Edwina Broussard now beamed! The Detective didn't want to lie to her, but he had little choice. Her children didn't want her hearing bad news about her precious Nathaniel, not on her deathbed.

"I hope Nathaniel is taking care of himself. I hope they're not working him too hard."

"I don't know about that, but then again, he's the boss."

"He was always smart, you know. We always knew he would go far."

"Now, Mrs. Broussard, Dr. Broussard warned me that even though he was just a normal kid growing up that you might speak too highly of him."

"Nathaniel's so modest, he was the perfect child. He listened to his mother and the nuns. His daddy wanted him to waste his precious gifts hunting and tracking, but we stood up for him. God had touched Nathaniel. You could just tell it and the nuns knew it too."

Again, he was getting nowhere. After another twenty minutes Bill said his goodbye, then strolled back into the living room. There was a Catholic priest standing by the fireplace conversing with Rodrick and his sister. Bill was introduced to Father John Sebastian who would administer the last rites to Edwina Broussard when it came time. The priest was in his early seventies and had met Dr. Broussard on numerous occasions when visiting the family. He had hardly known him as an adolescent. The well-respected Father John had been servicing the family's spiritual needs for almost thirty years. It was this priest who had recommended the policy of not upsetting Mrs. Broussard with her son's dire situation.

"It's nice to meet you, Detective Lincoln. How's Mrs. Broussard today?"

"She's fine, Father. She's Dr. Broussard's number one fan."

"Yes, Edwina derives great pleasure from talking about her Nathaniel. By the way, how is Nathaniel's case coming?"

"It's early yet and besides, he has a team of excellent lawyers. We're trying to do the necessary background work. That's why I'm here now."

"Are you getting what you need, Detective?"

"I'm getting consistently supportive stories about his good character from his family and friends. One would expect that." He wanted to say something else, that so far it had been one major waste of his time. Did this holy man expect the alleged killer's people to provide him with any kind of evidence to convict?

"Yes, I see your point. What do you need to help you in your investigation?"

"We need the murderer to step forward and confess! Beyond that, we need evidence pointing to someone. Evidence that is credible."

"Are there any leads?"

"Oh yes. But only to Dr. Broussard."

Except for the crackling of the fire the room was quiet. The shadow of death loomed in one room even as Bill stood in another delivering his gloomy forecast.

"What do you know about the practice of voodoo hereabouts, Father?"

The priest was surprised by the question. He then realized it wasn't so much the question but the tone of the request.

"Unfortunately, it is still practiced among a small segment of our population. Typically it's the less informed and the less educated who make up the majority of the believers. We're constantly reaching out in an effort to enlighten everyone."

"Would you happen to know any voodoo priests?"

"Voodoo priest, I'm afraid for me that's an oxymoron. Although, I could direct you to several Biblical references wherein is conveyed the definition of those having the authority and responsibility for prescribing scripture."

More mumbo jumbo…Bill was still left wanting for an answer. He decided to ask another way. "Father John, do you know of anybody who conducts voodoo ceremonies or who is considered a leader in the voodoo culture here?"

"Detective Lincoln, we discourage any participation in voodoo. It's a pagan religion and therefore unholy."

This again was no answer. Obviously he would have to ask someone else. He needed to talk with people that were not family or friends of Dr. Broussard, so he made plans to dump Rodrick.

An hour later, Detective Lincoln arrived at the local police station for a scheduled appointment. Bill was escorted to Captain Bell's office.

"I've been reviewing the files since before you arrived but I'm afraid I have nothing substantive to report on Dr. Nathaniel Broussard. We do have a few files on his brothers and a rather large one on his father. It turns out that daddy was a wild one. He liked to smoke, drink and fight, which usually occurred in that order. This excessive behavior was the root of his demise."

"But nothing on Nathaniel?"

"That's correct."

This did not surprise Bill. Since he was their little saint, the community would do everything possible to protect him.

"How about any negative rumors associated with him?"

"Nothing that I know of and believe me, I've asked around."

"Tell me, have you ever met Dr. Broussard?"

"Yes, several times at official ceremonies but I don't know him personally. I've only engaged in small talk with him."

"What's your opinion?"

"Really, I don't have any. He seems to be a likable guy based on my limited contact."

"In your opinion, is he capable of having an affair?"

The Captain pondered the question. He cocked his head then placed his hand under his chin. "What man isn't? It wouldn't surprise me one way or the other."

"Did you turn up anything on a Hattie Black?"

"No, we ran the search but got no hits. Where did you get her name?"

"She's one of several women Dr. Broussard had an affair with over a decade ago. According to his journals he was at a seminar here in New Orleans. She was a graduate student. I sent letters to the various universities in the area but I haven't heard anything yet. And of course his journals didn't say which school she was attending."

"Is she important to the case?"

"I'm not sure but I don't think so. I'm just doing background checks trying to determine my client's veracity. Tell me, where does one go to experience a voodoo ceremony around here?"

Captain Bell raised his eyebrows. He had forgotten there was a potential voodoo aspect to the murder.

"Well, as a matter of fact, we've had to serve notices for abuse of animals in some of our voodoo districts. I can have one of my men take you around to some if you like."

"Yes, I'd like that very much. When I spoke with Father John Sabastian this morning he couldn't give me the name of anyone that practices voodoo here. He certainly wasn't very helpful."

"Naturally, our Father John wants everyone to be a good practicing Catholic."

"Naturally. And I just want people to answer my questions."

Captain Bell called Officer Orville Lutherford Butterfield to escort Detective Lincoln to their voodoo districts. Officer Butterfield informed Bill about his experiences with the locals who engaged in voodoo. He had never seen a ceremony or met any high priests, but had served notices to people who were violating animal protection laws. They pulled into the dirt driveway of Elden Robinson, a forty-five year-old man who looked twenty years older. Robinson had been convicted three times on animal code violations and was known to participate in voodoo rituals.

Officer Butterfield knocked on the door with his baton. After several seconds the door opened. The officer asked to come inside but walked in without waiting for an answer; Bill followed.

"Elden, this is Mr. Lincoln, a visiting religious researcher. He has just spent the last two days in our city talking with several Catholic priests and other religious folks. He asked if anyone knew anything about voodoo around here and that's why we're here. I'll wait in the car. I have some reports to finish. Why don't you tell him what you know."

Once again Officer Butterfield didn't wait for an answer and just headed for the car. Bill wanted to show the man some respect because you could always get more information by being friendly.

"Mr. Robinson, I'm trying to get some general knowledge regarding voodoo. I'm only a researcher. The person that I do the research for knows your Captain Bell who in turn called that policeman, Officer Butterfield, to drive me around. I have a ton of notes on the more conventional religions in your area and I thought I'd spend some time talking with people who may have insight on the more esoteric beliefs. Do you know anything about voodoo?"

Robinson viewed him suspiciously. This man had just strolled into his house behind Officer Butterfield. He had no idea who this person was. "I don't know anything about voodoo," he replied bluntly.

Bill quickly assessed the situation. He didn't want to strong-arm this man because then he'd never get the real low-down.

"I'm not here to make any trouble for you," Bill said coyly. "I could go elsewhere. Researchers do pay though," he said, reaching into his pocket to retrieve a crisp fifty. He turned, waived it, and started walking out still holding the fifty aloft.

"Wait. I may know a little bit about voodoo, just a little bit."

Hearing this, Bill stopped. "A little bit?"

"Yeah."

He went back into his pocket, and this time pulled out a twenty-dollar bill, and laid that on the table. "Why don't we find out just what 'a little bit' means."

Elden Robinson picked up the twenty and quickly stuffed it into his pocket. Bill sat down and pulled out his notebook, providing the obligatory 'researcher's' look. The Detective started by asking very general questions. After twenty minutes he laid a fifty on the table. Elden reached over and stuffed it in his pocket without missing a beat.

"Mr. Robinson, I'm from Oakland, California. My work there has brought me into contact with a certain voodooainne by the name of Marie 'Mama' Francois. I've attended her ceremonies where I saw her apparently receive the great voodoo god Damballa. She appeared possessed and took on snakelike movements. Her followers in Oakland believe she's the one true messenger of Damballa. Anyone else who claims so is said to be a fraud according to her. How do you feel about this?"

"Damballa is great indeed. He may possess many, so your Ms. Francois may be the fake. There are many charlatans who would do anything to promote themselves and some, Mr. Lincoln, are very good con artists."

"Have you ever heard of her?"

"I have not heard her name specifically. But, I have heard that a woman with extraordinary powers does live there."

"Now, Elden, through my research I have met another woman in LA named Jezebel Balboa. She also claims significant voodoo powers or a special knowledge. Have you ever heard of her?"

"Yes, I understand she is very knowledgeable indeed."

Bill was curious. The man knew the name of Ms. Balboa, but not Ms. Francois. Somehow he had expected the reverse.

"Do you know of voodoo priests who may have greater powers than Marie Francois?"

"But I don't know Marie Francois's abilities."

Bill sighed. He'd need to rephrase the question. "Do you know of voodoo priests here with 'extraordinary' powers?"

"I don't have any knowledge to compare with anyone."

"My findings suggest that Damballa only makes contact through women. Is this what you believe?"

"No, Damballa can communicate through anyone. Whoever told you that is a liar."

"Marie Francois told me that."

"Then she lied."

Bill picked up his note pad and wrote. He had learned more interesting insight from this conversation than any other since arriving in New Orleans.

"By chance, do you know a woman named Hattie Black?"

Robinson shook his head no.

"How can I arrange to observe a voodoo ceremony?"

"You can't. You must first be a true believer."

"I was invited to observe Ms. Francois's ceremony...entry to which required a donation of fifty dollars." He went into his pocket again and pulled out a couple more fifties, holding it in his hand. Elden watched closely.

"I think there could be a guest list. I'm not sure but I can check."

Bill slid the fifties back in his shirt pocket. "If I get invited to your ceremony that hundred is yours. You see, the guy I work for is writing a book of comparative religions."

He spent another twenty minutes with Robinson before standing to leave. He pulled one more fifty from his pocket, dropping it on the table. Robinson let it sit there, intending to pick it up after the Detective had left. He walked Detective Lincoln to Officer Butterfield's car. Bill gave Robinson his telephone number and asked when he might expect a call. Robinson said it would probably be a few days.

While riding Bill tried to figure out his next move. "Who's the local gossip down here? I want to ask some questions of people not related to the Broussard family. I'm tired of the goody-two-shoes stories."

Officer Butterfield glanced over, smiled and took the next exit off the highway. "Hungry, Detective?"

He said yes although he really wasn't. Shortly thereafter they stopped at a local diner. When they got out of the car Bill read the sign, Sally's BBQ and Flapjack Joint and underneath the bold letters, 'Ask for our Blackjack Special.' They walked inside and Officer Butterfield sat in his favorite spot.

"Sally, this is Detective Lincoln. He's down here collecting information on our illustrious Dr. Broussard. You do know they just busted him for that voodoo murder out in Oakland?"

"Yeah, you couldn't help but hear."

"Sally, Detective Lincoln is gathering background information on the Broussard family. He's talked with them but all he gets is warm fuzzy stories. Do you know anything that might be more, let's say, reality-based?"

Sally shifted in her seat pulling herself closer to the table. "The old man was a royal pain. He drank more whisky than a ship full of sailors. I felt sorry for his wife. When he died the world got better."

"What about Nathaniel?" Bill interjected.

"Actually, he and the girls were the only ones who didn't cause trouble. The other boys were destined to be like their daddy, but the local law enforcement put the fear of God into them boys early. They didn't have all that God-forsaken legal rights crap back then and the law had no problem putting your butt in line. The daddy spent a lot of time back in the bayou making and running bootleg whisky. Even the boys were in the fields trying to make a go of it. When the boys got caught, Sheriff took each aside and gave them the dickens! They straightened up after that. Their daddy never had any sense! There wasn't anything they could do with him. He was just plain crazy!"

Bill listened intently.

"What was Dr. Broussard like as a kid?" he asked.

Sally didn't miss a beat. "He was a good kid and he was quite a talker. He could sweet-talk a jar of honey out of a wild bear's paw. Let's just say he knew what to say to get what he wanted."

Bill's mind again reflected on Dr. Broussard. Was he conning everyone even now?

"Did he like girls?"

"Why, yes. He did. He especially liked the cheerleaders. He never had a chance of dating one because they went out with the athletes. Some people say he knocked up little Jenny McCray but I think it probably was his brother. Nathaniel had too much fear of those nuns in him to be messing around much with the girls. All he wanted to do was hold their hands and maybe steal a kiss. Why the nuns would've skinned him alive if he started acting like his brothers."

"Could Dr. Broussard have committed that murder?"

"Maybe, but I can't see it."

"Could he have an affair?"

"Sure, why not? He's human."

Bill had heard that one before. "Know anything about voodoo, Sally?"

"I don't mess with it or the people who do mess with it for that matter; I know that."

"Ever hear mention of the Broussard family associated with voodoo?"

"The daddy."

Bill's interest was peaked even further. "The father participated in voodoo?"

"Their daddy did everything. Ask that skirt-wearing Father Juan-ton."

"Father John?"

"Whatever. He knew their daddy well. If anyone knows anything that son-of-a-bitch knows something for sure. I know, because he spewed his guts out to that priest before he died. There were all types of rumors regarding the daddy. And that priest knows it all."

"What type of rumors?"

"I don't know and I really don't care! All I know is that there was something in that old man's past that, in his final days, drove him to that priest. He never had nothing to do with the church before, but when he was near death, he was following that priest around like a puppy dog follows his master."

There can be no doubt of our dependence upon forces beyond our control. Primitive man was so impotent in the face of these forces that, especially in an unfavorable natural environment, fear became a dominant attitude, and, as the old saying goes, fear created gods.

JOHN DEWEY

Chapter 35

With sirens blaring and lights flashing, three Oakland Police cars arrived at the hotel. Several officers approached the anxious proprietor in the parking lot. The owner pointed to the second floor, repeated his story...that the cleaning woman, entering the room, discovered a dead man on the floor! Horrified, she ran from the room and notified him. He had called 911.

The police secured the scene and brought in their evidence team and coroner. They checked the dead man's wallet. It identified the man as William Lee Taylor Sr. According to the note found nearby, his death was an apparent suicide. Orders issued from headquarters were quite explicit; secure the area, avoid touching the body and, leave everything to the investigative team!

—

"Please state your name for the commission, Sir?"

"Oliver Frenchie"

"Now, Mr. Frenchie, do you know a Mr. William Lincoln, former detective with the Oakland Police Department?"

250

"Ah…yes, Sir. I do."

"In what capacity?"

"Well, Mr. Lincoln used to place bets with me on sporting events."

"And, just what is it you do for a living, Sir?"

The witness hesitated, squirming in his chair. "Uh…I'm a bookie."

"I'm curious. Would you call that a legal profession?"

"Uh…no, Sir."

"And how long would you say that you have been engaged in this 'illegal activity'?"

"Umm…'bout ten years."

The District Attorney spent the next fifteen minutes asking questions that clearly showed the man had not lived an 'upstanding' life. He was letting the jury know up-front what the history and character of this witness was.

"Tell us, Mr. Frenchie, when did you first meet Detective William Lincoln?"

"I'd say it was about five years ago. Yeah, that's right, I remember now. He had walked into my office with Harvey Gooding… my good friend."

"And where is Harvey Gooding now?"

"Why, Harvey is dead! He was killed in the warehouse that day that Detective Lincoln went to investigate!"

"And, when you heard your friend had…died, what exactly did you think?"

"Nothing, at first. But when I discovered that Detective Lincoln was on the scene, I knew right away what happened. You see, Detective Lincoln had testified against my friend a few years back. And it was back then that Harvey had made the mistake of threatening him. Harvey said it was because of the false testimony Detective Lincoln had given. And everybody knew that as soon as Harvey got out of prison it would be only a matter of time, if you know what I mean."

The D.A. moved closer to the commissioners before asking the next question. "I'm afraid I don't 'know what you mean.' It would be only a matter of time before what?"

"Why, only a matter of time before Detective Lincoln found a way to eliminate Harvey of course. Threats made against a cop, I mean... police officer, are taken very seriously! Anyhow...Detective Lincoln kept pretty close tabs on Harvey. See, I know that because every so often he'd even ask me 'How's Harvey doing?' and 'When's your 'pal' getting out?' Believe you me, I knew what he was up to alright."

"So, you believe Detective Lincoln was somehow responsible for the death of Harvey Gooding?"

"Uh, sure I do. There's absolutely no doubt in my mind."

"Now, in what capacity would you say he was...let's say... 'responsible'?"

"He killed Harvey. He hunted him down and he killed him!"

The D.A. waited a few seconds before continuing. "What proof would you have?"

"Nothing, not in terms of the actual murder anyway. But, what I do have is evidence of the good Detective's gambling bets!"

Murmurs of conversation were heard from the commissioners, some were also writing notes.

"And, have you turned that information over to the District Attorney's office?"

"Yes, Sir. I have."

The D.A. picked up a manila envelope, opened it and placed the material in front of the witness. "Is this the information you spoke of?"

The witness examined the information and eventually nodded.

"Would you please state your answer for the record, Mr. Frenchie."

"Oh...yes, Sir."

"Now then, just how successful was Detective Lincoln at gambling?"

"Hmm...actually, he lost a lot of money."

"Do you think he could afford such losses on the salary he was making?"

"No way, at least... not in my humble opinion. No way."

"And were you aware that Detective Lincoln had taken an early retirement from the police department?"

"Why, no. Actually, I'm surprised, especially since he was in so deep with me."

The D.A. spent another twenty or so minutes asking questions before eventually allowing questions from the commissioners. The first questions came from Connie Chow.

"Okay. Mr. Frenchie, is Detective Lincoln's signature somewhere on those betting slips?"

"Yes, his name is there."

"So, you're saying he personally signed those bets?"

"Eh, no... I just wrote his name on them."

"So, his signature appears nowhere on any of the aforementioned slips?"

Frenchie looked hard at Ms. Chow, but acknowledged her point. "No."

"So, you could just as easily have written my name down on your 'slips' and handed them to the District Attorney?"

"What? What are you trying to say? I don't believe I understand your question."

Connie repeated her question.

"Well...yeah, I guess I could have. But, that's not what happened!"

"So, therefore, all we really have then is your indisputable word that Detective Lincoln committed this alleged activity."

"Well, yes. I guess so."

"And, do we have any real proof other than your indisputable word?"

"No."

"And you admittingly have willingly engaged in illegal activities."

"Well, yeah...I'm, I'm a bookie for heaven's sake."

"And would you say that that constitutes...'illegal activity' Mr. Frenchie?"

"Yes, I guess it would."

"And are you involved in any other 'illegal activities' at this time Mr. Frenchie? Please remember you are under oath here, Sir."

Mr. Frenchie did not answer. Instead, he looked over at the District Attorney. The D.A. stood up and addressed Ms. Chow, attempting to stem the negative perception Ms. Chow had painted. But Connie had made her point!

"Thanks for seeing me, Father."

"Sit down, Detective Lincoln. How may I help?"

"I'd like to know why Hendrik Broussard followed you around so before he died."

Father John was, once again, caught off guard by comments from Detective Lincoln.

"Who told you about that?"

"Several people. Now, are they wrong about this?"

"No. I don't think it's so unusual for a man to seek out a priest, especially if he believes he's dying."

"I agree. And, I suspect a man who perhaps may have lived an immoral life would want to repent his sins to someone. Wouldn't that be a fair guess, too?"

"Yes, very much so."

"I'll be direct. Do you have information that could be helpful to my investigation, Father?"

"Surely you're aware of the confidence between a priest and his parishioners?"

"Unfortunately, yes. So, is that what I'm dealing with here?"

"Yes, Detective."

Lincoln reached into his wallet and pulled out his card. "Well, if you ever feel the need to contact me, here's my number." Lincoln stood and shook the priest's hand. He looked deep into the priest's eyes. Father John held his gaze. This priest could not be intimidated; his grip was strong, his eyes clear and focused.

"What is it they say, Father, 'the truth shall set you free'."

Father John thought for a minute. "Yes, Detective, but who is to say what 'the truth' is? And remember, 'There were false prophets also among the people'."

Detective Lincoln, saying nothing more, turned and walked out.

Bill returned to Oakland in mid-afternoon. He stopped at Broussard's legal defense's office first to report the news of his New Orleans visit. Lead attorney Hank Buckston sat behind his desk smoking a huge cigar, his feet propped up on the desktop.

"Come on in, Bill, how was your trip?"

"Relatively uneventful."

"Anything interesting?"

He sat down.

"I heard how wonderful Dr. Broussard was growing up. But, I didn't hear anything useful towards his defense. Good stories from one's family and friends are to be expected."

"So, is that all?"

"No. Broussard's father was low-life scum who ruled his family with a heavy hand. His father was a known troublemaker. Curiously enough, before he died, he spent most of his time shadowing a local priest. They say he was like a dog following its master."

"What does the priest say about this?"

"He acknowledges the relationship but invoked his priest-client confidentiality privilege. He's not talking or offering any tidbits."

Buckston took a long drag and blew perfectly formed smoke rings. "Well, that's the daddy and not our Nathaniel."

Both men experienced a momentary silence.

"I spoke with a local down there who's into the voodoo scene."

Buckston's demeanor perked up. "And?"

"I found it interesting that he knows the name of Jezebel Balboa in Los Angeles but not that of Marie Francois from Oakland."

"I fail to see your point."

"I only said I found it interesting. There may be no relevance."

"Did he say anything significant?"

"Just your typical mumbo jumbo."

Buckston took another drag, blowing more smoke rings.

"By the way, Bill, Willie Taylor is dead."

"What?! How?"

"They say he committed suicide in his motel room."

"Suicide?" Bill shook his head.

"That's the initial conclusion."

"Well, if it turns out to be a suicide, then I'm the Easter Bunny!"

Buckston took another drag and the two men visited for another twenty-five minutes before Lincoln left. Later back at home, Bill called Connie Chow.

"Hello, Bill."

"I heard Willie's dead."

"Yes."

"How?"

"He was found dead in a motel room."

"Do you believe it was suicide?"

"The preliminary investigation confirmed it."

He listened closely to Connie's every word.

"What do you think?"

"I don't buy it, Bill."

"Why was he on the street in the first place?"

"Willie called me the day after he bolted. He said the day he took off the guard was nowhere in the apartment; plus he says he found the severed head of a chicken in his shower. So, that's why he ran."

"What about the guard? What's his story?"

"He claims his lieutenant called him early that morning, instructing him not to report to the apartment. He says he was reassigned for the day. He was told to report in at police headquarters at 7:00 A.M. That conversation was captured on his answering machine."

"Did his lieutenant leave such a message?"

"No. The voice analysis unit has identified it as being someone else impersonating his boss. Besides, as it turns out, the Lieutenant was in a seminar at the time the call was made."

Bill's mind was slowly putting the pieces together. Willie's enemies had devised a simple plan and had executed it brilliantly.

"I predict there was no bloody chicken head found by the authorities."

"That's correct."

"Did you tell them about Willie's call?"

"Yes."

"Did they believe you?"

"They noted it but they really don't know what to make of it. They tested for blood but found no traces."

"Connie, the police couldn't find a dead cow lying in the middle of the road! Did I miss anything else while I was out of town?"

"The Police Commission heard testimony from Mr. Oliver Frenchie."

He searched his memory cells for recognition. "Who's that?"

"He testified that he was a friend of Harvey Gooding, the man who died in the warehouse."

"Okay, so he was a friend, but what was his testimony about?"

"He said he was a bookie and that he handled your considerable gambling bets."

"My gambling bets! And what kind of evidence did he produce? I would guess that he had some sort of gambling slips with my name on them, but of course they were not signed by me."

"That's correct."

"And the District Attorney took the bait hook, line, and sinker. Like I told you Connie, you better draw a chalk line to the dead cow, because they'll never find it on their own! Anyway, what does the commission think?"

"I can't disclose that information."

"Well, let me get going then. Thanks, Connie."

"Bill."

He heard concern in her voice. "Yes."

"You know how the death of Willie affects you?"

"Do you mean that Willie was a thorn in Big Eddy's side and since that thorn has been removed, I'm most likely the next thorn in line. After all, I did arrest him on drug charges at Radcliffe's house."

"You can be sure that they'll be coming after you next, Bill. They have to."

"They're already doing that, Connie. I may need a good lawyer."

"There are plenty of them out there."

"Are you available if I need you?"

257

"If you ask and I accept, but I'll have to resign from the commission so as not to place myself in a conflict-of-interest situation. Still, if you want me, all you'll have to do is ask."

"Okay. Goodbye, Connie."

"Bill?"

"Yes."

"I just remembered there was one more thing."

He got a sinking sensation because of the tone in Connie's voice.

"I received an anonymous message on my machine that may give you cause for concern."

He waited; he was not about to ask.

"The 'voice' said, 'This is a casual observer. Tell your buddy, Detective Lincoln, that his girl Susan was seen out on the town with Radcliffe Dillard last night'."

He took a few seconds to contemplate the information.

"Well, it sure as heck doesn't sound like a casual observer. Goodbye, Connie."

He found his cigarettes, pulled one from the pack, and headed for his study. Bill picked up the phone and called Susan. She had promised to fix them dinner when he got back from New Orleans.

"Hello, Susan."

"Hi, Bill."

"I just got back from New Orleans."

"Welcome back. How was your trip?"

"Fairly uneventful. Just about what I expected, unfortunately."

"You didn't solve the murder then?"

"No such luck. We're not much further along than before I left."

"That's too bad. How was the weather?"

"Basically wet. We only had sunshine one day. As it turns out, it's their rainy season. What time is dinner?"

"Bill, can I have a rain check? Something's come up. I'll make dinner tomorrow night."

"Sure, what's up? Special work project?"

"No. Just something that I forgot that I need to take care of."

"Susan, call me when you're able to make dinner. It doesn't have to be tomorrow night. You sound busy. It's not that big a deal."

"Okay."

"I'll talk to you later. Goodbye."

He called a retired detective friend of his, Waverly Russell.

"Hello, Waverly?"

"Yes."

"Bill Lincoln."

"Hello, Bill, how are you?"

"I've got a little shadowing job for tonight. Are you available?"

"For you, sure."

"I want you to sit outside my girlfriend Susan's house starting at 6 P.M. Tell me who picks her up or if she goes anywhere. I received an anonymous tip alleging that she was out on the town last night with Radcliffe Dillard and tonight she broke a dinner date with me. I'm more than a little curious."

"I understand. What's her address?"

Bill gave him the information. He needed to know if the anonymous phone caller was providing accurate information. Susan, the one who had suggested dinner, was not the type to forget things. Bill retrieved Jacko's telephone number from his wallet. Jacko was laying low until he could figure out what to do. A woman answered the phone; he asked for Jacko. Bill, was told Jacko was there and was given the address.

Bill arrived twenty minutes later. Jacko, wearing the bandages from his beating, was limping. The sheer amount of dressing covering his face made him look like the clothed invisible man film character.

"So, how are you, Jacko?"

"I'm getting better every day but I still have a ways to go."

"Are they still looking for you?"

"Oh yeah. I may be a low priority, but if they happen to run into me they will finish the job."

"Do you have anything for me?"

"Hell no! I've stopped asking stupid questions. Look at me. Let's just say I've learned my lesson!"

"You should know…the only way I can help you get out of town is for you to give me something. I can't help you if you can't help me."

Jacko was peeking at Bill through his bandages. He had already decided the last thing he needed was to have the authorities get involved.

"I can get out on my own. Besides, if you start asking questions where I've asked, they'll know it was me that tipped you off. I'm not sticking my neck out any further."

"Jacko, don't you want the guys who did this to you caught?"

"You can't catch these people! Besides, the system takes too long. I'll be a cold corpse before the trial ever starts. Look what happened to Willie Taylor! Yeah!"

Bill acknowledged the point. Besides, Jacko knew the real score better than most. Bill couldn't play the high moral card with this guy.

"Jacko, I can get you far far away from here."

"Yeah. Just like Willie. He's far far away too."

"Willie was a fool. He was staying around to testify. That won't happen with you."

"No way. You cops are full of it. I can do better on my own. Yeah!"

"You're here because you started thinking for yourself, Jacko."

"That might be true, but it's because I was asking questions for you, Detective!"

Bill sat there contemplating an alternative. This was a no-win situation and he was wasting his time. "Jacko, I'm leaving now. Good luck."

"Goodbye, Detective."

He stopped by the law office of Hank Buckston before going home, finding all three lawyers there.

"What's up, Detective?" Buddy Miller asked.

"Nothing, so far. I just spoke with my former street informant. Unfortunately, he doesn't have anything. He's getting ready to leave the area. He's scared."

"What happened?"

"He was asking around trying to determine who Franklin Dillard Jr. has been sleeping with. There's a rumor Jr. is gay."

"Okay, you got me. Just how does that fit into the equation?" Dana Andrews asked.

"I don't know...yet. There're a lot of pieces to this puzzle and right now, I don't know where most of them fit. What are you working on now?"

"We're ready to concede it's Dr. Broussard's sperm in Hillary's body. We've had our own experts examine the evidence. Also, we now know there's no identical twin brother either."

"Whew! Boy am I relieved," Bill cracked sarcastically.

"Here's the telephone numbers for three of the women that Dr. Broussard had affairs with. We haven't found the fourth woman yet."

"Do you suspect that one of them may be the murderer?" Bill asked. "I'm asking because I need to know just how much time I should be spending working on this aspect of the case."

"We just need contact made in order to verify Dr. Broussard's statements. That's all."

After checking the time Bill grabbed the numbers and stepped into the next office to try to reach one of the women. He would try the others tomorrow since they each lived back east.

"Hello, is this Marsha Linsburgh?"

"Yes. This is Marsha Johnson, formerly Marsha Linsburgh."

"I am Detective Bill Lincoln. I'm investigating a murder case involving Dr. Nathaniel Broussard." He waited for a response but the quiet prevailed. "Do you remember Dr. Broussard?" he finally asked.

"Yes, I met him many years ago. I haven't talked with him in over five years. Why are you calling me?"

"Mrs. Johnson, could you please tell me how you came to know Dr. Broussard and just how well you know him?"

"I really don't care to get involved, Detective Lincoln."

"Look Mrs. Johnson, I'd really appreciate it if you would just tell me your story. I can almost guarantee you that if you're truthful, that this would more than likely be the last time you'd ever hear from me."

He heard a sigh and felt the gravity of her situation. She was a married woman with a decent life who certainly didn't want to be dragged into a murder investigation. She spent the next five minutes describing how she had come to know Dr. Broussard. She finished her story without ever mentioning the affair.

"Mrs. Johnson, did you have an affair with Dr. Broussard? Again, tell me the truth now, and you'll probably never hear from me again. But, if not, you may have a problem getting rid of me." There was a long pause.

"Yes, Detective."

"I'll need to know when and under what circumstances."

Mrs. Johnson now spent another six minutes describing details that complied with Dr. Broussard's journal. He bid her a goodnight, aware that she secretly hoped that this chapter of her life would be forever closed. So far, Dr. Broussard appeared to be telling the truth. He walked back to where the three lawyers were to report his findings.

"That's good news for us," Buckston said.

"Well, it's not bad news," Bill responded.

"In the law there are only two types of news, bad or good. And only the bad can hurt us!"

Bill spent another ten minutes talking before going home. A half-hour later he was sitting by the fire reviewing his notes for a morning meeting scheduled with Kasolkasky. He wanted to be prepared. At eleven forty-five the phone rang.

"Bill, this is Waverly."

Bill waited patiently to hear his report.

"Your lady friend was picked up by Radcliffe Dillard at her home around 7 P.M. I followed them to the Baxter Club in downtown Oakland. There was a celebration tonight at the club, a private affair. I disguised myself as a waiter and gained entry. It was a formal affair. Susan was Radcliffe's date for the evening. They sat two rows from the head table. The dinner ended at 10:15; a few people stayed for cocktails. Radcliffe and Susan had one drink afterwards before leaving. He dropped her off, but did not go in with her. That's my report."

"Thanks, Waverly. I'll send you a check tomorrow. Are your fees still the same?"

"Yup."

"Thanks."

Bill was wondering about how he'd handle this situation with Susan. He'd give her the opportunity to bring it up. But, he knew she never would unless pressed to. He decided to keep this one 'under his hat' until he needed it.

Chapter 36

While Detective Lincoln waited for Kasolkasky to arrive, he reviewed the report Brick had left him regarding Dr. Broussard's murder case. It left little doubt that Dr. Broussard would be charged and eventually convicted of murder. As he was finishing the report, Kasolkasky entered the room.

"Hello, Bill. It's been awhile."

"Yes, it has. You've got a tight report here. Do you think you've got your man?"

"Oh, yes. You don't?"

"Maybe, but he doesn't act the part. As a matter of fact, so far, almost everything he's told us has been confirmed."

"You should expect that he wouldn't act guilty, Bill."

"That's not what I mean. When you've done something wrong there is usually a flaw in your story. And if that's the case, when you tell your story over and over again, eventually something must break down. And that's my point, I haven't found that flaw yet."

"You will… just keep digging. Besides, it was your comments that led us to Dr. Broussard. The reason I called was to tell you that Radcliffe and Big Eddy want their day in court as quickly as possible. They're invoking their constitutional rights to a speedy trial. And since we're concentrating on the Broussard case now and we really don't care that much about Big Eddy or Radcliffe anymore, and Willie's dead, Big Eddy's case should be dismissed. Even if he were still alive, what sane jury would believe a two time loser like Willie Taylor?"

Bill could smell what was coming…like being downwind of a train hauling horse manure.

"And, I take it, I'm the only thing standing in the way."

"Yes."

"Well, Brick, what should I do?"

"It's up to you, Bill."

"Maybe what I should have asked you is…do you think that we should only prosecute the 'convenient' cases? Should we allow people to 'eliminate' the witnesses against them with impunity? If I remember correctly, I was given the full support of this administration in arresting Radcliffe Dillard, provided, of course, I had solid evidence against him."

Kasolkasky sat there listening showing absolutely no emotion. "Look, I hear speeches all day long, Bill. Are you running for office or something? For God's sake man, listen to yourself."

"No, Brick, you listen. These people broke the law, plain and simple. I was the witness and I have a job to do."

"They'll be going after you. Are you really ready for that?"

Bill glared at Kasolkasky. He didn't like what he was hearing. "I'm not about to be intimidated by any Gestapo tactics. You know, I wish we had a police force that didn't wear uniforms with a yellow streak running down their backs!"

"That's way out of line!"

"Oh, is that right?! So, you're saying the administration is going to back me up then? Tell me, Brick. Answer that question to my face, Goddamn it!"

Kasolkasky and Bill faced off; they were both livid. Kasolkasky's face was beet red and Bill's eyes glared. Kasolkasky turned away first and leaned against his chair. He knew that Bill was right.

"So this is Oakland's finest. Keep feeding the public that crap, Brick! You should be proud of holding such a high rank within such a 'fine' organization!"

Bill stormed out of the room. He was angry and needed to put as much distance between himself and the police station as possible. He drove to a local park and spent the next hour contemplating his next move. He had no faith in the police to protect him and he had too much integrity to walk away from doing what was right.

--

The morning newspaper carried another article by Franklin Dillard, Jr., blasting the Mayor's ability to run the city. Bill's telephone rang at 7:00 A.M.

"Hello?"

"I want information on that fag...and I want it NOW!" The line went dead.

Bill felt the irritation in the voice; the Mayor could become dangerous under this type of pressure. He called Tommie Cheng, the reporter, and scheduled lunch for that afternoon.

Bill met Tommie at a local pub on the fringe of Oakland. Bill arrived first, selecting a back-booth for privacy. Tommie arrived five minutes later.

They engaged in small talk until their drinks arrived.

"Tommie, I heard a rumor and want to know if you've heard it."

"What's the rumor?"

"Is Franklin Dillard, Jr. gay?"

Tommie's eyes lit up. He looked like a man who had just got the first four of five numbers of a lottery ticket and was waiting for the fifth.

"Now, that's quite a rumor! What's the basis?"

"I can't disclose that. Have you heard anything?"

"No, and I couldn't touch that unless I had major confirmations."

"I know. I just wanted to see if you did."

Bill sat back. His objective, to put a juicy tidbit out in the public domain, had essentially been met. Reporters lived for stories that could sell papers!

"How good is your source?"

"They've done good work for me in the past."

"Can you point me in a direction?"

"No, I just heard a rumor from two separate sources. No more than that."

Tommie looked up again. "Two sources?"

"Yeah."

"Both legit?"

"One is about as high up as an eagle can fly." Bill had thrown him a clue. "Have you read the paper this morning?"

"Yes."

"How's the wife and kids, Tommie?"

"They're doing fine. "

After finishing their lunch Tommie got in his car and reached for his paper. Bill drove to the lawyer's offices to complete his calls to the other two women who allegedly had had affairs with Dr. Broussard. Dana Andrews was there working; they chatted briefly. Forty-five minutes later Detective Lincoln returned to inform Dana that one of the women had confirmed the affair but the other had not.

"She denies it?"

"She admits to knowing him but nothing more. She maintains that if he insists on saying that they had an affair, that he was a liar."

"Oh, really?"

He nodded.

"And do you believe her?"

"I don't know. She sounded convincing, but then, so does Dr. Broussard."

"But we know that one of them has to be lying."

"Obviously. However, I'm inclined to believe Dr. Broussard."

"Why?"

"What reason would he have to lie about this? None. But a woman wanting to protect her marriage, now that's another matter all together. I'm not sure if this is relevant right now anyway."

"I agree. So...any word on the fourth woman?"

"No. I mentioned her name while in New Orleans but nobody had ever heard of her."

He headed out for lunch and pulled over to a corner deli to get a sandwich. As he opened the door, Macario walked out, lunch in hand.

"Hello, Macar."

"Detective Lincoln!"

"Is that lunch?" Bill asked, looking at his package.

"Yes. Exactly! I see now why you became a detective, Detective."

"I'm about to grab a bite to eat myself. Why don't you join me?"

Macario was about to flip him off but then thought better of it. He had nothing to lose. In fact, it might be interesting talking to Lincoln .

"Sure."

Macario walked back inside with Bill. They sat at a table in the rear. "How's it going, Macar?"

"I'm doing alright, Detective."

"Are you ready to go to trial?"

"Are you sure there's going to be one?"

He didn't care for Macario's answer or his tone…laced with cockiness. Macar had been talking with somebody and Bill had a good idea who that somebody was. "You have two trials. You were busted with drugs in your car and I busted you in Radcliffe's house for using drugs. How will you plead?"

"My lawyer is making a strong argument that the cops had no right to go through my car. Frankly speaking, I don't see the other trial ever happening. Something tells me that you'll come to your senses, Detective. Policemen need to spend more time solving real crimes."

When they finished lunch, Macario 'eased' into a brand new Benz. Bill knew he was not working at the gym anymore and could only guess how Macario obtained the car.

Three weeks passed before all hell broke loose. Bill woke up to read on the front page of the newspaper, completely out of the blue, 'RETIRED DETECTIVE MAY FACE INDICTMENT'!! Immediately he picked up the phone and began dialing frantically.

"Connie, what's going on?"

"Bill, what are you talking about?"

"Have you read the paper this morning?"

"No. What is it?"

"Read it, and then call me right back."

A few minutes later Connie returned his call. She also had no idea what was behind this latest attack. The story indicated that a Grand Jury was being convened for the purpose of hearing evidence against him. But when Connie attempted to confirm this, she discovered that the Police Commission had not voted to do anything! Powerful unseen forces were operating behind the scenes!

That evening he received a phone call from his emotionally distraught ex-wife. Someone had resumed calling their daughter Amanda, leaving obscene messages about her father. Betty begged Bill to stop whatever he was doing, and they both agreed that it would be prudent to bring Amanda back home from college immediately.

The trial of Radcliffe Dillard and Big Eddy was only six weeks away. Bill had already received one call from Police Chief Ron Ness asking him if he still wanted to press charges. Lincoln had confirmed he did.

Later that evening Bill noticed a car parked across the street from his home with someone sitting in it. The car had been parked there for over an hour, enjoying a perfect view of his house. After another hour of watching the car, Bill called a friend on the police force. Fifteen minutes later a policeman was tapping on the driver's window and asking to see some identification. The guy was clean. The man claimed he was just resting and after the policeman left, he too took off.

The following morning when Detective Lincoln walked outside, a box sat next to his paper. He observed it carefully but didn't touch it. He called the police bomb squad. Arriving within thirty minutes, two experts examined the box. A metal detector indicated a negative reading, but still they deployed the mechanical arm and shield in opening the container. The first inspector to observe its contents was perplexed to say the least.

"Damn, what the hell is this?"

The other expert walked over, peeked inside and looked over at Detective Lincoln, motioning him closer. The first explosives expert picked up the box and gave it to Bill who handled it gingerly before opening the top. He stared hauntingly at the severed head of a chicken…still oozing blood.

Sin has many tools, but a lie is the handle that fits them all.

OLIVER WENDELL HOLMES (SR.): THE
AUTOCRAT OF THE BREAKFAST TABLE.

Chapter 37

The next day Bill picked up Leonard 'Iron Hands' McDerch from the hospital. Lenny would live with him for the next few days. 'Iron Hands' had been Major Lincoln's point man in his old combat unit. He was a big strapping farm boy who had brought 'down home' values and extraordinary shooting acumen to the guerilla war of Vietnam. Quickly and easily he had made the transition from tracking animals to hunting down human beings. Thus becoming the most effective killing machine under Major Lincoln's command.

Lenny gave new meaning to deja vous. Lenny was caught in a 'time warp'. Bill explained to Lenny, as they were driving to Bill's home, that he had had an operation to save his life and that soon he'd get his memory back. Somehow Bill failed to mention that the operation had occurred over two decades ago! He told Lenny that some of their old enemies from Vietnam had tracked them back to the states and that he needed the Sergeant to watch his house. Detective Lincoln, still his commander, had Lenny's ultimate faith and respect. He would follow his orders unquestioningly.

The following morning Bill lay in bed thinking. He hadn't slept well. He was clock watching at 3:15 A.M., when suddenly a shadow fell over him. There was a full moon and someone else was in his room! He remained absolutely still, pretending to be asleep. He cursed himself, because his gun was out of reach. He then remembered…it was probably Lenny. The Sergeant wasn't sure where he was, so of course he was…patrolling! But, if Lenny perceived him as an enemy, Bill was a dead man!

"Sergeant McDerch," he commanded, "this is Major Lincoln! Why are you up?!"

Lenny recognized the voice, but not his surroundings.

"Excuse me, Sir. Patrolling, Sir."

"Go back to your bunk, soldier."

"Yes, Sir! Sir?"

"Yes, Sergeant."

"Where are we?"

"I'll explain in the morning. Goodnight, soldier."

"Goodnight, Sir."

In the morning Bill explained again to Lenny where he was and why he was there. He wrote the story down and placed it over the headboard of Lenny's bed. In Vietnam, this was how soldiers received their daily orders. Lenny's only instructions were to guard Bill's house. Bill directed him on how the security system worked… plus, he gave Lenny a gun and the code for disarming the security unit. Any intruders without the code were the enemy, plain and simple. He ordered Lenny not to sleep during the day. He knew that whenever Lenny went to sleep his short-term memory failed, forgetting everything that had been told to him earlier.

Bill drove to Buckston's office and found Hank there talking with Dana Andrews. Dana had informed Hank of Lincoln 's interview with the one woman who had denied having had the affair with Dr. Broussard. Buckston didn't appear at all concerned.

"Who do you believe?" Bill asked.

"I'll go with the good doctor," Buckston said, "And for the same reasons you yourself had given earlier."

"When do you expect to go to trial?" Bill asked.

"Well, as soon as possible it would seem. You see…Dr. Broussard wants a speedy trial. I'm trying to hold him off some but I'm not having much luck."

"What does the District Attorney think?"

"He's ready to go right now too. That's why I need you to continue to dig into things."

Bill headed into an empty office to phone Jezebel Balboa, the voodoo lady in Los Angeles. Finally, after three calls, he reached her at a volunteer community center.

"Hello...Ms. Balboa? This is Detective Bill Lincoln up in Oakland."

"Why hello, Detective."

"I just returned from New Orleans. By the way, I met someone who knows you. A gentleman named Elden Robinson."

"Oh yes. I remember Elden. He's a nice man. How did you meet?"

"Well, when I asked to meet some of the locals who knew the voodoo culture they brought me to Elden. We spoke for quite awhile and your name came up. He spoke highly of your 'talents'."

"That Elden, he's so sweet. Please, send him my regards."

Ah, good! Ms. Balboa acknowledges Elden. "Frankly, I forgot to ask him exactly how the two of you met."

"Simple. I used to live in New Orleans, that's where we met. I think he was born there but his parents are Haitian. Anyway, we use to socialize together, Detective."

"That reminds me, Elden is setting up an 'invite' for me so that I can observe an actual voodoo ceremony."

"Good for you! That should prove to be quite the experience!"

"Have you attended any ceremonies in New Orleans?"

"Certainly...many, but that was a long time ago."

"Do you still know any voodoo priests there?"

"No, I'm afraid not, not anymore."

He suspected she was being untruthful.

"Would you like to attend a ceremony with me? I could arrange to have another ticket sent."

"Thanks, but no thanks, Detective. I have far too many things to do right here."

Wow! She was actually turning down a free trip to New Orleans. Was this the same Ms. Balboa who was so 'hot-to-trot' for a free ticket to Oakland. Hmm...was she hiding something?

"Okay then. Is there anyone you want me to say hello to while I'm there, Ms. Balboa?"

"No, Detective; but thank you for asking."

Bill was about to hang up when for some reason he made one last comment. "Ms. Balboa, I almost forgot, one more person asked me to say hello."

"Oh?"

"Yes, Hattie Black. As a matter of fact, she said to give you a very special hello."

"Right...well, be sure to tell Hattie I said hello too. She's a nice girl. Yes, a nice girl."

"Pardon me, Ms. Balboa, my mind is slipping again. Hattie told me how she knows you, but I've forgotten. I guess, like you, I've just got too many things going on now."

"Maybe you need to slow down a little, Detective. You have to try to remember to pace yourself. It just so happens that Hattie is Elden's niece. Okay?"

"Of course! Thanks, I remember now. Good-bye for now, Ms. Balboa."

He wondered why Elden Robinson had lied to him about knowing Hattie Black. The fact that it was Elden's niece who had had an affair with Dr. Broussard was a most intriguing tidbit of information. Could be Elden was protecting her; after all, how many people would voluntarily offer a complete stranger information about their niece? His next move would be to a call a friend and ask to borrow his car. Before he could though, Bill's beeper went off. It was Monique.

"I'm upset. There's a question concerning my brother."

"Which one?"

There was a pause. "What do you mean?"

"Which brother? You do have two."

"Oh. I'm sorry, you're right. It's about Franklin."

"And what's your question?"

"Have you heard anything...well, peculiar concerning him?"

"Like what? What area are we talking about; politics, religion, sports, ethnicity?"

There was another pause. "Never mind." Monique faced a dilemma. If she mentioned the rumor and Bill hadn't heard anything, then she was only contributing to it. But she also knew Bill had reliable intelligence resources.

"Do you mean the allegations about his sexual preferences?"

"Yes, Bill. Who's spreading these rumors? Who told you about this?"

"I can't reveal my source. Who told you?"

"My brother told me someone was spreading these lies."

"Which brother?"

"Franklin."

"Who told him?"

"I didn't ask."

"Maybe you should ask him that same question."

There was another pause as Monique collected her thoughts. She found it disconcerting that Bill knew about the rumor. "Bill, I'd really like to know who told you?"

"Do you remember I asked you once why Franklin made those rather nasty remarks about the Mayor in the speech delivered on his veranda?"

"Yes."

"And what answer did I receive from you?"

Monique saw his point but still tried to argue hers. "I didn't know the answer. I'd have only been speculating."

"I understand. But what information did you offer me?"

"Would you still like to know why I think my brother said those things?"

"Yes, but if you tell me I'm still not going to reveal my sources."

"I'd like it if you'd stop by for a drink tonight, Bill."

He looked at his watch. "What time?"

"How's eight o'clock."

"I'll be there."

He hung up, walked to the offices up front and noticed Dr. Broussard was sitting there talking with Hank Buckston.

"Dr. Broussard, two women confirmed that they had an affair with you many years ago, a third denies it and I haven't found the fourth yet."

"Was it Mary who denied it?"

"Yes."

"Well, that doesn't surprise me."

"Why should we believe you?"

"Because it's true. Listen, I used to play a little game back in those days. The hotel room I'd rent would always be in my name, but...I would always tell the women that I rented it in the name of a fictitious couple. Our name would be Mr. and Mrs. Dubois Mary. I would use my middle name and the woman's first name. Women found that to be rather romantic. Now, you could probably bluff her into believing that those hotels retained all their records and that you have in your possession proof of our registration. Besides, why would I lie? I can only lose by jeopardizing my credibility. Right now, my word is all that I have left."

Bill agreed. He assured Dr. Broussard he'd try bluffing the lady. His pager went off. This time it was Betty.

"Our baby girl just received another menacing call. Bill, please! You've got to stop whatever you're doing. You've got to stop! She's upstairs crying. I've called the police but they're useless!"

Now he was livid. He would not tolerate anyone attacking his family. "I'll take care of it. Just don't let her answer the phone anymore."

Bill hung up and took off. He needed to clear his head. He drove to Jacko's house, took the steps two at a time and banged on the door. A woman's voice answered. He identified himself. There was a brief wait before the door opened. She led him to Jacko still wrapped in bandages.

"To what do I owe this visit, Detective?"

"How does Big Eddy operate? How did you get busted up?"

Jacko looked at him. He saw fire in Lincoln's eyes and he definitely didn't like Lincoln's demeanor.

"I don't want to discuss Big Eddy."

Lincoln closed the door then walked up to Jacko. He got right in his face! "Somebody is threatening my family and Big Eddy is the prime suspect. I want answers and I want them now! We can do it the easy way; it's entirely up to you, Jacko. But, I'd hate for you to need more bandages. My daughter was just threatened! Now, who besides Luka handles Big Eddy's dirty work?"

Jacko stared into his eyes; he knew Bill was not playing. In his present condition the last thing he needed was for anyone to get physical with him. Bill looked like the bull with a red cape being waved invitingly in his face.

"He likes to use Luka Brahn and Frantz Libor. They're both old school. Luka's the pugilist, a mugger in his youth. Frantz is the weapons guy, a sawed-off shotgun specialist. They're both big and powerful. The first punch is in the midsection to take the fight out of you before they hammer you to the ground."

"Where do they live?"

"Luka lives on Broadville and Frantz resides up in the Oakland Hills on Mountain Pike."

"I want their exact addresses."

Jacko got his telephone book and jotted down the information.

"And where do they hang out?"

"They spend a lot of time in that Italian bar over on Post. Luka likes that new billiards joint downtown. He's a real good player. And Frantz, believe it or not, bowls."

"Anything else?"

"No."

Bill started walking, but before he opened the door he stopped and turned around. "Who is Franklin Jr.'s lover?"

"I really don't know."

Bill left. He spent the next hour cruising the two neighborhoods of the addresses Jacko had given him. He also drove to the billiards place where Luka spent time in order to survey the surroundings. Next, he stopped at police headquarters where he asked to see the excess mug shot photos, the ones that were never used. There were thousands covering all categories. Within an hour he had found what he was after. He pocketed the pictures of three men, Luka Brhan, Frantz Libor and Big Eddy.

He headed back home to get ready for the visit to Monique's house. He showed Lenny pictures of the three men and declared that anyone who tried to break in, especially these three men, was the enemy. Bill handed him a silencer for the gun. Lenny quickly screwed the cold steel onto the barrel. Bill also gave him his pager number and Monique's telephone number.

He arrived at Monique's on time and was escorted into her living room. Monique was wearing a sexy little black leather skirt and white silk blouse.

"You look very nice, Monique."

"Thank you, Bill. Do you often flatter the ladies?"

"Rarely. But when it's deserved I do."

"I talked to Rad today."

"How's he doing?"

"Fine, but he said something strange."

"Oh, what's that?"

"He said he's been 'going out with' Susan."

"Susan who?"

"That's what I said. Apparently, your lady friend."

"I guess the rumor is true then. Somebody mentioned that to me the other day. I was going to call Susan, but I got busy."

"You don't seem too bothered by it."

"We're not married. Besides, she's an adult."

"How did this happen?"

"Your brother strolled by our table the other day at a local restaurant and took a liking to her. I have a feeling it's more because she's my girl in spite of her other obvious merits. I believe Rad wants to get 'under my skin' in light of his upcoming case, since I'm the sole witness against him."

"You're going to testify?"

"They broke the law."

"Laws are broken all the time. Shouldn't we focus on the more important criminals?"

"That's a good point. So, which laws should we ignore?"

They talked for another hour before Monique escorted Bill to her painting studio. She said she was exploring her creative talents. He complimented her. There were four completed pieces that she was interested in hearing his opinion on. He was one of the few people to see her work, because as she said, she was very shy about letting people view her creations.

"You're talented. I think you're still finding your style, but you're certainly a gifted artist."

"Thanks. I'm usually a fairly confident person, but when I paint I'm not as certain of my abilities."

"Just keep going. You'll find yourself eventually in your work. What's that one?" He pointed at a covered painting.

"Oh, that's a painting of Hillary, but it's unfinished. It's been very difficult for me to work on it. I become very emotional."

"May I?" he asked. She stood there, nodding gently. He lifted up the cover. It was only half-finished but it was beautiful. He saw Monique's difficulty. The power of warmth and innocence radiated from the yet completed portrait.

"From what everyone tells me about her I'd say that you've captured her essence."

Monique stared at the picture while leaning against Bill. She slowly started crying. He turned, holding her as they stood there for a few minutes, not saying anything. Monique was tense, gripping his arms tightly. After a few minutes her hold softened, but she continued leaning on him with her head buried in his chest.

"I miss her terribly!"

"I know. Everything everyone has said about her has been simply wonderful. She must've been a very special person."

"She was so loving you had to like her. I've never met anyone who embraced people like my little sister."

He remained silent. This was Monique's time to release her emotions. He wanted to be there for her.

"Why do some choose to kill the innocent, Bill?"

"Some do it for love, some for greed... some for spite; some do it for revenge or for just plain fun."

"Will we ever stop this senseless killing?"

"Probably not."

Monique continued to hold him. He was thinking it was time to sit down but they hadn't moved.

"You feel nice, Bill."

"So do you."

He was not sure why he had said that. It was true, but he wished he had said something else.

"I want you to hold me tonight, Bill."

He didn't say anything. He wasn't sure if he wanted further clarification of her request. He continued to hold her.

"Will you?" she whispered softly in his ear.

Bill was thinking, what type of question is that? What red-blooded man was going to say no? He was doing the honorable thing by being a friend, but now she had asked a question that had aroused him sexually. He was trying to think of an excuse to exorcize the invisible demons.

"I don't know where my relationship with Susan is going," he said weakly.

"This has nothing to do with Susan. I need you tonight," she whispered again.

As Bill held her he felt his beeper go off. He reached for it; the digits flashed his home number. "I have to return this call!"

"There's a phone over there," she said pointing to an unusual object sitting on the table. He dialed the number.

"Sergeant?"

"Sir. One male corpse is lying in your kitchen, Sir. What do you want me to do, Sir?"

"I'll be there in thirty minutes." He hung up and looked at Monique. "I have to go."

"Is it that important?"

"Yes."

"Can you come back tonight?"

"No, I'm afraid not. But I'll call to you later."

A minute later Bill was in his car heading home and within thirty minutes he was parked in his driveway. He knocked, used the code and opened the door. Lenny 'Iron Hands' McDerch stood in the kitchen doorway waiting. Bill walked past him and looked at a body wrapped in plastic. He pulled the plastic back revealing the man's face but didn't recognize him. Lenny stood by the body waiting for orders.

"Report, Sergeant."

"The intruder invaded the premises one hundred fifteen minutes ago. First, three telephone calls were made which I let ring through. The machine picked up each time but no messages were left. I believe the intruder was calling to determine if anyone was home, Sir.

Fifteen minutes later the enemy compromised the first alarm system with only limited difficulty. It took him just another fifteen minutes to defeat the second system. This man was a professional, Sir. When he entered through the window, I was observing the monitors; he appeared to be alone. I snapped his neck and quickly repositioned myself in case there were other potential intruders. After forty minutes I concluded he was alone. I secured the house and then made contact with you, Sir. I've taken the liberty of cleaning the area and wrapping the body in plastic."

"Let's dispose of the body, Sergeant. But first, let's take his fingerprints."

Bill called a buddy in another state, telling him to just put the phone down. He was establishing an electronic alibi. Bill and Lenny drove to a deserted area in a park, dug a hole, placed the body in it, put rocks and debris over the spot, then returned to base. They recorded the license plate numbers of all the cars in a two-block radius of his home, even though Bill actually believed the man probably parked his car somewhere within a one-block perimeter. He would have yet another buddy run the list of the plate numbers.

Bill started devising more extensive plans of where he was after he left Monique's, in case he needed an additional alibi.

He would wait a few days to run the license plate numbers and the fingerprints. He would wait to see if anyone filed a missing person report. He was confident this wouldn't happen but he'd go by the book so as to not draw any attention to himself.

The following morning Bill was up early fixing coffee before Sergeant McDerch got up to review his orders.

"Good morning, Sergeant."

"Good morning, Sir."

"How'd you sleep?"

"Just fine, Sir."

"Do you remember our day yesterday?"

"No, Sir. I don't remember a thing, Sir!"

Chapter 38

"Hello, this is Detective Bill Lincoln with the Oakland Police Department calling for Captain Bell."

"Captain Bell here. How are you, Detective?"

"Fine, Captain. By the way, you may recall you told me that you didn't know who Hattie Black was. Well, it was recently brought to my attention that she's the niece of the same fellow who Officer Butterfield took me to talk with about voodoo, Elden Robinson. I just thought you'd find that interesting. I certainly did."

"My, my, is that so? What an amazing coincidence."

Bill had heard that word again! There were starting to be far too many 'coincidences' in this case and he was determined to root out every last one of them.

"Look, I need her phone number and address. And, I'd like to avoid going through Elden. Is that possible?"

"We'll do what we can, Detective. I'll assign it to one of my men right away. I'm afraid Officer Butterfield does not have the, let us say, 'finesse' to obtain the information you desire, in the manner you've requested."

"You put that quite...diplomatically. Thank you in advance, Captain."

"Goodbye, Detective."

Bill put the phone down, walked into the guest room, and instructed Lenny to build a dog house in the back yard because he was going to buy a dog that very day. Lenny was elated; he loved animals! A few minutes later the phone rang...

"Hello."

"How are you, Detective?"

"Fine, and you, Crystal?" Bill reached and clicked the 'on' button of his little tape recorder.

"I'd like to talk with you. Can we have lunch?"

"Just lunch?"

"Yes, just lunch."

"Sure. When and where?"

"Can you meet me today?"

"Okay..." He was surprised not to have heard any outrageous flirting yet.

"I'll buy you lunch at our place. Let's say one o'clock. And, Bill, this is a rare occasion, because, you see, I never buy men anything."

"Uhh, I feel so...special. I'll see you there, Crystal."

Lincoln drove to the local animal shelter and found a large three-year-old male German Shepard. His name was Sparky and the shelter personnel acknowledged he was very smart. An hour later Sparky met Lenny and a new friendship began. Bill took off to the lawyer's office to talk with Hank Buckston.

Buckston and Buddy Miller were talking when Detective Lincoln entered. They both turned to greet him.

"Okay gentlemen, what do you want me to do about the woman who denies having had an affair with Dr. Broussard?" Bill asked.

"What do you think? Personally, I have some reservations."

"I want to know the truth. I say we should go after this woman!"

"Okay, if you've got the time then do it, but let's not consider it 'our' highest priority. I want to find Hattie Black, but first, we need you to scrutinize those police files again. Remember, you're working for 'us' now. So examine the records again, please, this time from 'our' perspective. We also need a thorough background check performed on Dr. Broussard. Those should be your top priorities right now. We don't need any 'surprises' come trial time."

Bill thought back to his New Orleans trip when he heard the word 'surprises'. He remembered that Sally, the owner of the 'BBQ and Flapjack Joint' had mentioned that some people thought young Nathan Broussard had 'knocked up' a teenage girl, but she thought it was the brother. Suppose it wasn't the brother? How would she know for sure? He would check his notes to find the girl's name. He left Buckston's office for police headquarters to review the files again before dining with Crystal.

At twelve fifty-five Bill entered the restaurant and was escorted to his table. Crystal joined him minutes later. Her hair was in a ponytail and she was wearing a short navy-blue skirt and white top. Half the men in the restaurant turned their heads to watch admiringly as she approached his table.

"Hello, Bill."

"Crystal, um…you look 'armed and dangerous' in that outfit!"

"Is that a compliment?"

"Unquestionably!"

"And so, does that mean you'd like to take me somewhere and 'pat' me down, Detective?"

Oh boy! He walked right into that one. "I thought we were here on business?"

"You've got to lighten up! All work and no play makes Jack a dull boy, Detective," she smiled boldly.

"How's Franklin?"

"That's why I invited you to lunch."

"Oh."

"Yes. You've asked me questions regarding my husband's sexual orientation. May I ask why?"

"I'm investigating the murder of your sister-in-law and I'm looking for a motive. I heard a rumor that your husband might be gay."

"What would that have to do with Hillie's murder?"

"I don't know, but I'm pursuing several different angles."

"I don't believe this line of questioning has anything to do with my sister-in-law's death."

"I'm not sure your beliefs will be helpful when I write my reports."

"My husband is running for high elective office and suddenly there's a very disturbing rumor going around concerning him. Bill, who told you about this rumor?"

"I can't disclose that. It's just like your legal code."

"This rumor can seriously hurt Franklin's chance of getting elected."

"I would imagine so, if true. Is it true?"

"Bill, you know that's irrelevant. We have to stop this vicious thing."

"Don't you think the first question is whether or not it's true?"

"Absolutely not! If the information is irrelevant then it shouldn't matter. Assume that he's gay, so what? Does that mean he's not the best man for the job? Of course not!"

He picked up his wine noticing that Crystal had yet to drink any.

"But if true, the rumor wouldn't be a rumor."

"A person's sexual orientation is completely irrelevant. We shouldn't be asking that question, ever. What does it matter?"

"I agree. But if the question is put to your husband, what will he say? People don't like politicians lying to them."

"I don't think he'd bother to answer. It's like asking, "Have you stopped beating your wife?" Some questions we shouldn't ever dignify."

"Some may find the question of value. I can think of several religious groups out there that may demand an answer."

"Bill, what's it going to take for me to get my answer? I'll do anything!" Crystal reached across and rubbed the back of his hand. She watched him closely.

"Crystal, would you violate an attorney-client privilege?"

Crystal could see where he was going and didn't answer the question.

"So, I've run into a man with principles. How very unsettling," she smiled.

"I wouldn't want to dishonor my profession, any more than you would yours. What are Franklin's chances?"

"Pretty good. But, it will certainly shift in the wrong direction if this rumor persists."

"How did you hear about it? Whom did you hear it from?"

"The people working on the campaign are making remarks. Not a lot, but enough."

Since Crystal appeared receptive, he tried to get more information. "Tell me, Crystal, how long was the Mayor 'seeing you'?"

"If you tell me what I want to know, I'll reciprocate."

"I'm afraid I don't like that deal."

"Then you'll have to suffer the consequences and not get an answer," she smiled sweetly.

Crystal didn't make anything easy.

"What's the Mayor like?"

"I think you've met him before."

"No freebies?"

"I'm certainly willing to trade."

"I'll pass."

"Bill, ninety-nine percent of the total male population would be putty in my hands at this point and here I am, stuck with you. Isn't this ironic?"

"It just goes to show that even you can't always get what you want!"

"Bill, let's go upstairs."

Crystal was looking directly into his eyes offering one of the most tempting packages he'd ever been offered. However, she was a married woman without any information that he needed.

"I'm not saying this is an easy decision, by any means, but…let's just sit here and have lunch."

"Bill, you're much too straight, but that's why I respect you. You have some semblance of principles, which I admire. So, we're really going to order lunch. Okay, I'd like to order first. Let's see…oh yes, I'll have the "Private Eye au jus"! It looks delish! That's the Detective upstairs sans suit…covered with a hot chick sitting on his lap, dressed only in her birthday suit, ready and willing to 'handle' whatever comes up…dish. Now then, ah…what will you be having, Detective?"

"Well… I'll stick with the broiled chicken," he smiled.

They had a lively conversation for the rest of their lunch before Bill returned home to research his notes. At home his notes revealed the name of the young lady who had allegedly become impregnated by one of the Broussard brothers. He made another call to New Orleans in an attempt to locate her... Jenny McCray

"Captain Bell, Detective Lincoln from Oakland again."

"Hello, Detective, and what can I do for you?"

"I was told one of the Broussard brothers may have 'knocked-up' a young lady named Jenny McCray. I'm trying to locate Ms. McCray. Do you know the story?"

"I'm sorry, Detective, but I don't."

"Can you do some research for me?"

"I can certainly try. Who might I contact? Any suggestions?"

"I'll leave that to you. I don't know your local players very well."

"What do you want specifically, Detective?"

"I want to know if she was really pregnant and, if so, who the father is."

"Anything else?"

"No. Not for now anyway."

"Give me a few days, I'll see what I can do. Goodbye, Detective."

He looked outside and saw Lenny and Sparky having a great time playing catch. Lenny had made considerable progress on the doghouse. Bill then noticed the blinking light on the telephone message unit. The phone message was from his ex-wife.

She had just received notice from their high school daughter saying someone had left a disturbing message about her father taped to her locker. He returned the phone call to calm his ex-wife down, but he was livid! They decided one of them would drive their daughter to and from school each day until they both knew this thing was finally over.

He returned to the window to watch Lenny and Sparky. Bill hoped that there would be many more fun-filled days of Lenny and Sparky playing together, but he wasn't sure of what the future would hold. He truly hoped that neither would get hurt knowing full well what he might ask could put both in harm's way.

At the end of the afternoon he walked over to Buckston's office to give an update on his findings, which wasn't much.

"The police have your standard file set-up. The DNA testing results is their smoking gun, plain and simple. Broussard had the opportunity since, according to witness accounts, he had left the affair early enough to have waited clandestinely in his car. His only alibi is his loving wife. His journals confirmed his affairs, but that's a double-edged sword. But at least if we decide to go down that route, we can show him to be honest and cooperative."

"Frankly, we need more. I don't like the way we're just bobbing around in the water. I also don't like the idea of this woman denying their affair."

When they had finished talking Bill retired to the back office. He placed a call to Sally's restaurant in New Orleans where he had first heard of the possibility of one of the Broussard brothers' possible indiscretions.

"Sally, who would know where Jenny McCray is today? And how do you know it wasn't Nathan Broussard who knocked her up?" Bill thought he would work this angle while the New Orleans Police Department did their research.

"Well, it's just gossip on my part. And I don't know where the McCray girl is today. I could call around for ya if you like."

"That would be great. Here's my number; leave me a message if I'm not in. And you do know there's a reward of twenty-five thousand dollars for any significant help leading to the arrest of the murderer of Hillary Dillard, right?"

"I didn't know that. I could sure use the money."

"We all could. Thanks, Sally."

He made two more phone calls before leaving the office. As he walked out of the building he saw two men sitting in a car across the street reading newspapers. One of the men looked like Luka Brahn! He drove off looking in his rear view mirror to see whether or not the car followed. It didn't. He turned the corner and pulled over to the side of the road.

He sat for a full five minutes but nothing happened. Bill took off again, somewhat relieved, but knew if they were professionals they wouldn't make such an obvious error anyway. He decided to circle the block and go back to see if the car was still there. He spotted it, but was unable to see the faces of the two men since the newspapers they were reading obstructed his view.

Bill arrived home to view a well-constructed doghouse and a message on his answering machine. It was from Sally in New Orleans! He would return her call within the hour. Dinner was served twenty minutes later complete with a full bowl of food for Sparky. Lenny recounted his day with his new friend. They were getting along marvelously, just as Bill had imagined. After dinner Bill retrieved his briefcase; he pulled out a picture of Big Eddy and handed it to Lenny.

"Sergeant, this is our enemy! He was an operative in Vietnam who was captured and found to work for the communists. We have conclusive proof of his compliance, and orders to eliminate him if the opportunity presents itself. Our government set me up in this house to be close to him. Your assignment, Sergeant, is to walk Sparky in the enemy's neighborhood for forty minutes and only if you get the opportunity, and I stress the word 'only', to apprehend him. If the opportunity does not present itself, then curtail the objective and return to base. There's no hurry, but there is critical concern not to get caught. I suggest you wear dark clothing and do not carry a weapon. Any questions?"

"He's not to be harmed or killed, Major?"

"If possible, I want him alive. But exercise caution, use whatever force you deem necessary."

"If I meet my immediate objective, Sir, what are my next orders?"

"Secure him and then page me immediately. And remember; do not go to sleep under any circumstances! If you do not hear from me and you start getting tired, then neutralize him and return to base. Our first task is to try to bring him in alive; but if you find that you can not, so be it."

"If I have to eliminate him, by what method?"

"It doesn't matter. But before you do, be sure to ask him who sent the man to break into my house and who is threatening my family. I want answers to those questions!"

"Yes, Sir!"

"Anything else, Sergeant?"

"What's his location, Sir?"

"I'll drive you and Sparky there and pick you up in exactly forty minutes. You'll spend fifteen minutes walking the dog in the neighborhood, then fifteen minutes sitting on a street bench a few hundred feet from his house. After that, you'll walk for ten minutes; I'll pick you up at a pre-designated spot. We leave in ten minutes."

Lenny went to his room to change into dark clothing. Bill called a friend on the police force in the next town and told him he needed to leave the phone line between them open for awhile to establish an electronic alibi. Bill put the dishes in the sink. When he finished, 'Iron Hands' McDerch was standing in the doorway dressed in black clothing. Sparky was standing by his side, tail wagging happily.

"We're ready, Major."

"Let's go."

Minutes later Bill stopped and pointed to the spot where he would extract Lenny. He drove further down the street to Big Eddy's house and dropped Lenny and Sparky off. He pointed to the bus seat where Lenny and Sparky would stop to rest. As he swung a u-turn, Bill stared at his rearview mirror and saw Lenny kneeling, putting a leash around Sparky's neck. Bill drove back home to call Sally in New Orleans.

"Hello, is Sally in?"

"Just a minute, please."

He waited almost thirty seconds before anyone answered.

"This is Sally, who's calling?"

"Sally, this is Detective Lincoln from Oakland, California. How are you?"

"Why hello, Detective! I'm fine, thank you, and I have information for you. Jenny McCray is a substitute teacher in New Orleans. She has one son; he attends a local junior college. I got the number from her uncle. I asked him who the father of her child was but he doesn't know. He said Jenny has always been hush-hush on that subject. He says she said the father had died, but she offers no details. The boy's last name is McCray though, if that helps."

"Sally, this is great. Thanks." Bill recorded the number and wondered if Jenny would talk to him. There was only one way to find out. He dialed the number.

"Hello?"

"Is this Jenny McCray?"

"Yes it is. Who's calling?"

"This is retired Detective Bill Lincoln from the Oakland Police Department. I have a few questions for you Ms. McCray."

"Why would you be calling me?"

"It's because while I was in New Orleans last week working a case, your name came up. Several people suggested they thought Dr. Nathan Broussard was the father of your child. Could this be true Ms. McCray?" He just tossed the question out there and crossed his fingers.

"I don't think that's anybody's business but mine, Detective Lincoln."

"Normally I'd agree, but our investigative team is trying to assess the character of Dr. Broussard. He's told us certain things. We're trying to determine their accuracy."

"So, did Nathan tell you he's the father of my child?"

"No, Ms. McCray, someone else did. We haven't even approached Dr. Broussard with that question yet."

"Don't you think you should start there, Detective?"

"Well, you're probably right, Ms. McCray." Bill wanted to keep her talking, but wasn't sure he could do it. "Tell me, when was the last time you talked with Dr. Broussard?"

"Why just a few months ago when he was in New Orleans."

"Do you socialize with his family in New Orleans?"

"I know them but I don't get to see them that often."

"Ms. McCray, in your opinion, do you think Nathan Broussard is capable of committing murder?" There was a slight pause before she responded. He listened closely.

"I've come to realize anyone is capable of anything. Nothing surprises me anymore."

"So, you believe he's capable?"

"I believe you're capable, Detective, and I've only met you over the phone."

"What was Nathan like as a kid?"

"He was like all the other kids. He played well with some kids and not so well with others."

Detective Lincoln wasn't making any progress and was unsure of where to go next. "Did you know Nathan's mother is very ill?"

"Yes. I was sorry to hear that, but she's lived a long life. I wish her well."

"Have you seen her recently?"

"Why yes, I saw her just last month."

"Does your son know the Broussard family well?"

"Please, let's not discuss my son! As far as I'm concerned this has nothing to do with him."

"I'm sorry, of course you're right. May I give you my number in case you think of anything else?"

"Sure, go ahead. But I don't see how I could be of any help to you."

He gave her the number, then hung up. He really wanted to know who her son's father was and so decided he would ask Dr. Broussard. If he didn't get an answer, he'd call Sally again.

--

'Iron Hands,' with Sparky on a leash, casually walked past Big Eddy's house for the second time. He checked his watch. It was time to go sit on the public bench. He hadn't seen anyone in the neighborhood during his walk other than a couple of cars driving through.

Bill had fifteen minutes before picking up Lenny. He grabbed the phone and called Monique since he hadn't spoken to her since leaving her house so abruptly.

"How's your brother Franklin doing in his bid to become a Congressman?"

There was a brief pause before she started speaking, almost as if she was caught off-guard. "It was going fine until that disturbing rumor started."

"Tell me, how's he handling it?"

"Right now, he's just ignoring it, but if it keeps growing he'll be forced to address it. Why are people so vicious?!"

"Normally, most people aren't; but your brother is running for high office where the battles are hard fought. Look, your brother said some pretty vicious things about the Mayor apparently without good cause. Wouldn't you agree?"

"You're right. It is a serious game, certainly not intended for those with weak stomachs."

"People who live in glass houses…"

"Are you saying Franklin deserves this?"

"No. I'm saying he has elected to play a game that attracts tough characters and rough rules. Your brother knows the game. So, is the rumor true?"

"Of course not!"

"You're positive?"

"I'm as sure as a sister can be. I don't live with Franklin and I'm not with him every hour of the day."

"Then you're not sure."

"Bill, this is getting us nowhere."

"I know, but I think you understand my point."

"Sure, I understand. New subject. When are you coming back so we can finish our visit?"

He had a fairly strong feeling about where this line of questioning was going. He vividly remembered their last time together. "Can't we visit over the phone?"

"I'd prefer us visiting over here so I can look deep into your eyes when you answer me."

"I'm not sure it's a good idea for me to be spending so much time with the sister of the man I'll be testifying against. There's such a thing as professional conduct."

"You were with me when you arrested my brother. I'm not sure what difference it would make now."

He conceded the point and looked over at his antique grandfather clock. "I have an appointment. I'll talk with you later, promise."

"Goodbye, Detective. Call me."

He got in his car and drove to the extraction spot. He waited five minutes before seeing Lenny and Sparky walking up the street.

"Report, Sergeant."

"We followed your orders, Major, but did not encounter any people. The only activity we observed were numerous vehicles driving through the neighborhood."

Bill dropped Lenny and Sparky back at his place before calling Dr. Broussard. He was at home and agreed to see Bill that evening. Bill could have asked him the question over the phone but, like Monique mentioned earlier, he wanted to see the good doctor's reaction when he answered. He arrived ten minutes later, pressed the doorbell and was met by Mrs. Broussard. She took him to Dr. Broussard's study.

"Will you be needing me, Detective?" Mrs. Broussard asked.

"No, Ma'am. I only need to ask your husband a few questions. Thank you." He knocked twice before opening the study door. Dr. Broussard was bent over writing at his desk.

"Hello, Detective, come in. How are you?"

"Fine. Dr. Broussard, this shouldn't take long. I just need to ask you a few questions."

"Certainly."

"Do you remember Jenny McCray from your hometown?"

"Yes, of course. I grew up with her."

"Does she have any children?"

"Yes, Jacob McCray. He's in college right now."

"Who's Jacob's father?"

Dr. Broussard looked right at Bill and without blinking an eye stated, "I don't know."

"You don't know?!"

"Why, no. Jenny became pregnant when she was about fourteen, and in those days everything was hushed up. She was spirited discretely out of town and we didn't see her again for about two years. I think she said she went to stay with an aunt. She never said why she left nor did she ever speak about it when she returned. Back then, things like that weren't discussed in polite company."

"I was told that some thought that one of your brothers was the father."

"That was purely conjecture, Detective. And if it were true, I'd certainly know. Remember, we're boys and we tell tall tales on everything, especially anything related to girls. If any of my brothers had even kissed Jenny, I'd know about it. None of them could hold a secret for more than two seconds!" he smiled.

Lincoln observed Dr. Broussard's demeanor closely and all appeared normal, but Broussard had said 'them' instead of 'us'. Had he meant that he could keep a secret better than his brothers?

"One rumor was that it was you who may have fathered the child."

"Me? I can assure you, Detective, that the first time I had sex was with my sweet bride."

The words flowed off Dr. Broussard's tongue so believably that he felt guilty for even asking the question. Nathan Broussard grew up under the nun's tutelage and his words seemed logical from a religious point of view, but how many people's first sexual experience occurred within the sanctity of marriage?

"Whom does Jacob look like to you? Does he favor any Broussard family member?"

"I've never looked at Jacob from that perspective. He has a lot of his mother in him."

"Why would there be a rumor that one of the Broussard brothers may have been the father?"

"I guess because we lived so close and played together so often."

"Who would know the father of Jenny's boy?"

"Why Jenny, of course. Besides her, I don't know. Jenny's parents are both deceased and her two brothers are much younger than she. Have you asked her?"

"Yes."

"And what did she say?"

"She wouldn't address the question and doesn't want anyone discussing her son."

"That sounds like Jenny." He chuckled.

"Well, thank you Dr. Broussard. That's it for now."

He walked back to his car bewildered because Dr. Broussard's responses were valid, but somehow intellectually Bill found it difficult that he couldn't offer any suggestions on who might know the identity of Jacob's father. Was he experiencing a master magician's slight of hand?!

Men make their own history, whatever its outcome may be, in that each person follows his own consciously desired end; and it is precisely the resultant of these many wills operating in different directions and of their manifold effects upon the outer world that constitutes history.

FRIEDRICH ENGELS: LUDWIG FEUERBACH AND THE OUTCOME OF GERMAN CLASSICAL PHILOSOPHY, 1886 QUOTED BY WILSOM, TO THE FINLAND STATION.

Chapter 39

Bill called Captain Bell requesting help with gathering intelligence on Jenny McCray's family. He wanted to know with whom she might've gone to live back when she had become pregnant.

"We know where she lives, Detective, but we have no news about the father of her child."

"I spoke with Jenny McCray yesterday. She won't say anything concerning her son. Can you find out who she might've stayed with when she was pregnant?"

"I believe I've got that, Detective. Dr. Broussard's sisters told my men where they thought Jenny was that summer when she left home. We got the address and telephone number of her aunt from the local authorities. I also have the telephone number at Jacob McCray's college dorm."

"I'm impressed, Captain. That was my next request."

"Thanks. Sometimes we actually know our business. Anything else I can do for you?"

"Yes. Arrange for a uniform to visit the aunt's house armed with a tape recorder. If a uniformed officer shows up on her doorstep it would give the appearance of an official investigation. They can simply tell her it's related to the Oakland Hills voodoo murders case. I'd like it to be done soon, before Jenny McCray starts getting calls saying people are asking around about her."

"I'll get on it right now. Anything else?"

"One more thing. What hospital did Jenny have the baby in so we might check the hospital records. I wouldn't have the officer ask the question directly of the aunt, but try somehow to get it indirectly from the conversation. That's what I need, Captain."

"Very well then, goodbye, Detective."

Bill knew he would need a story before he called Jacob McCray. It needed to be simple, yet to the point. Bill dialed the number. It only rang twice before being picked up.

"Hello?"

"I'm trying to reach Jacob McCray."

"This is Jacob."

"Hello, Jacob. This is Mr. Simmons from Admissions. We just had a slight accident in our office. A cup of coffee spilled into our filing cabinet damaging some of our files. Your file was affected. We're trying to restore them but could use some help frankly. It says here that your mother is 'J' McCray. We can't make out the rest of the writing. Jacob, what does the 'J' stand for?"

"Jennifer, J-E-N-N-I-F-E-R."

"We also can't make out the space for your father. It's completely obliterated; the whole category is illegible. What's your father's name, Jacob?"

"It was John. You'll have to ask my mother anything else. She filled out the paperwork. I didn't know my father and my mother never talks much about him. I've asked, but she always says, 'I'll tell you later'. She says my father died a long time ago and that the subject matter upsets her. You'll have to call her if you need more information about my dad."

"Yes, that's fine, Jacob. We'll do that. Have a nice day son and thank you for your help today." Lincoln's curiosity was piqued again. Just who was Jacob's father?

The doorbell rang. Two uniformed officers stood at his door requesting entry. Bill stepped back, allowing them to enter.

"I'm Officer Duffy and this is Officer Russ. Mr. Lincoln, do you know a Mr. Gerald Kincaid?"

"That's 'Detective' Lincoln, Officer. I'm retired from the force."

"I'm sorry…should have checked my notes."

"What can I do for you, Officer?"

"Again, do you know a Mr. Gerald Kincaid?"

"Sorry, no. Who is he?"

"He's a local man who's in the security business. And, he's missing."

"Sorry, I've never heard of him. Why?"

The two officers stared at him in disbelief. They knew something but so far weren't saying what. "Are you sure?" The officer took out a note pad and started recording the conversation.

"I don't know the man. Who is he and why would you think I might know him?"

"We got a tip that he was conducting surveillance of your house. Nobody has heard from him in a couple of days."

"Why would he be watching me? Who would've hired him and for what reason?"

"We don't know; it was an anonymous tip."

Bill put the pressure on them. "Officer, who provided the tip?"

"As I said, it was an anonymous tip."

"And did they say why this man would be watching me?"

"No."

"Officer, I'm on a special assignment for Mayor Efferton. If you'd like, we can call the Mayor right now so you can confirm that. Shall we do that?"

"Yes."

He grabbed the phone and dialed the Mayor's number. The Chief Executive's secretary answered. Although the Mayor was in a meeting, Bill knew his secretary had knowledge of Bill's employment through her boss's special funds payroll. "Linda, would you be so kind as to tell these officers that I'm employed by the Mayor's office?"

"Of course. Please put them on."

The officer talked with the secretary who confirmed what Bill had said. The officer's expression indicated it was not what he wanted to hear.

"Officers, I think you're wasting my valuable time and yours. Is there anything else?"

"May we search your house?"

"Sure, if you have a warrant. Anything else?"

"Yes, there is one other thing. Here's a request from the Grand Jury investigating the death of Harvey Gooding. You remember Mr. Gooding's death in that warehouse don't you, Detective? It seems Internal Affairs never closed the file and new evidence has turned up."

"This is a request, not a subpoena. So, I take it I'm not required to go before the jury."

"No. But it's advised that you do. Usually a subpoena follows an unanswered request. Do what you feel you have to do, Detective. I'm sure we'll see you in that courtroom one way or the other."

He stood there holding the Grand Jury request while the two officers tipped their hats in a mock display of respect before leaving. He didn't know whether he'd show up in the jury room and he was left wondering again who was behind all this. There was no evidence in the case supporting any wrongdoing, but yet they had never closed his file. Bill made a mental note to call Connie Chow to find out if she knew anything. He didn't feel he needed a lawyer, yet felt compelled to speak with one right now. He decided to drive downtown to check in with Buckston's office and discuss this situation.

Ten minutes later Bill pulled out of his driveway. Four blocks from his house, he glanced into his rear view mirror and noticed an old dilapidated truck. The truck looked strange because it had tinted windows! Usually, it was the newer, more expensive vehicles with that amenity. This truck was really beat up. He wondered who'd put any money into it. The truck maintained its proper distance for a couple of blocks before it signaled left to move into the passing lane.

The truck was about to pass when suddenly it slammed into Bill's car and pushed it over the embankment! Bill's car went cascading down the hill, traveling for approximately thirty yards before coming to a stop. Bill leaped from the car, instinctively grabbing his gun, taking cover behind a nearby tree!

He waited several minutes, wondering if the person driving the truck had stopped to come after him on foot. He waited patiently behind the tree, but saw nothing. Twelve minutes passed before Bill started walking briskly in the direction opposite from where the driver would come if he, indeed, had stopped. He wanted to get as far away as possible from that truck and it's driver. Bill wasn't hurt, but his car needed some work!

Three hours later he had rented a car and once again headed off to Buckston's office. Buckston was sitting behind his desk puffing on a cigar.

"I heard you were in an accident, Bill. Are you alright?"

"Yeah. Somebody forced me off the road and over a small embankment. It was an old truck with very dark tinted windows. Obviously, I couldn't see who the driver was."

"But why, Bill? Why?"

"It could be for any number of reasons. And recently, I discovered a severed chicken head on my doorstep; people are watching my house, threatening my kids and now this. Not to mention the fact that I also received a Grand Jury appearance request this morning!"

"A Grand Jury appearance request?"

"Yes."

"For what?"

Lincoln explained the circumstances and the allegation against him.

"You're not a popular man, Bill."

"Hank, should I honor the request."

"Do you have anything to hide?"

"Of course not."

"Would going before the jury help or hinder your position?"

"It certainly couldn't hurt! Which reminds me of a saying by Clarence Darrow, 'I have suffered from being misunderstood, but I would have suffered a hell of a lot more if I had been understood.'"

"I know that quote well. Anyhow, ultimately it's your decision," Buckston smiled grimly.

Bill sat down and crossed his legs. He would probably end up testifying since that might give the jury some help in making an informed decision.

"Have you talked with Dr. Broussard about the father of Jenny McCray's baby?" Bill asked.

"Yes. We talked, but he gave me the same story he gave you. Remember, Bill, he wasn't Dr. Broussard back then, but an adolescent. In that type of culture, religion and tradition are dominant. The truth rarely comes out. If her own uncle and son don't know the how or who, can we expect anyone else to know?"

"You know something, Hank, you lawyers try to make everything weird seem absolutely normal. Why, I wonder if you've ever met a guilty man! Have you?"

"'Guilt' is in the eyes of the beholder, Bill."

"So...I guess not. That was a simple question I asked. And, since I've arrested a lot of guilty people, I know there's no shortage of them."

"Broussard's answer doesn't bother me. It's logical and explainable."

"You've spent time with Dr. Broussard. Will you put him on the witness stand?"

"Absolutely. He's the most credible witness I've ever had. He doesn't rattle. Besides, without him we're toast anyway."

"Do you believe him?"

"I'm not in the believing business. I work for my client's benefit, providing them the best legal defense their money can buy."

Bill retired to the empty office to use the telephone. He called Mary Scott, the lady who had denied having an affair with Dr. Broussard.

"Hello?"

"Ms. Mary Scott?"

"Yes, who's calling?"

"This is Detective Lincoln with the Oakland Police Department. We spoke a few days ago."

There was silence on the other end.

"Ms. Scott, I'm about a week away from handing in my evidence report in this case, a copy of which will be going to the Grand Jury. Your name is in my report and to be perfectly candid, I expect the Grand Jury will be issuing a subpoena for your testimony. You have an excellent chance of fighting it since you live out of state, but I'm sure you know that in a high-profile case like this, you will attract media attention. I doubt that you want that. I believe we probably don't even need your testimony, but we have to check out all leads."

"Detective, I have a good family life and my husband could not take this type of exposure. Can't you just leave me alone?"

"Come now, Ms. Scott, a man is fighting for his life here. What do you think is more important?"

"Please, Detective...Please."

He could feel the intense emotion she was experiencing. He wanted to tell her to get on with her life, to hang up the phone, but he had a job to do. Detective Lincoln upped the pressure.

"For your information, we've secured the registration records for a couple named Mr. and Mrs. Dubois Mary." Bill heard the woman begin sobbing. He disliked this but his choices were limited.

"Detective, can this remain just between you and me? Please?!"

"I'll try. Ms Scott, this case most likely has nothing to do with you. We're simply trying to verify our client's story."

"We spent one night together, but we didn't engage in sex. Yes, we slept in the same bed and we kissed, but we didn't have intercourse. At the last moment I decided not to. That's my story and if he said anything different, he's lying!"

"Thank you, Ms. Scott, for your cooperation. I don't believe you'll be hearing from me again. Anyway, I certainly hope not. Goodbye."

He planned to discuss this with Broussard but it didn't matter what the doctor said. This lady admitted to being in the same room with him and that was good enough for him. Detective Lincoln updated Buckston with this new information and then headed for home. As he was leaving the building, Bill was especially observant of his surroundings. He checked out every nearby-parked car on the street and carefully examined the people walking along the sidewalks.

Later, at home, Bill instructed Lenny once again to walk the dog in Big Eddy's neighborhood. He dropped the Sergeant and Sparky off an hour later. Bill then drove over to Susan's house.

"How are you? It's been awhile."

"Yes it has, Bill. You're looking fit."

"I may look fit, but I'm getting tired. There are a lot of things taking place."

"How's the case going?"

"I'm not sure of the direction. Strange things are happening and I'm not sure if any has anything to do with the case. What have you been up to?" He was wondering if Susan would mention her new 'friendship' with Radcliffe.

"I've been very busy with work. There's no end to it."

"So, you've been bringing work home?"

"Always. I could work twenty-four hours a day at the job and still not get caught up."

"I guess I'll have to wait a little longer for that dinner you promised."

"Oh, Bill, I forgot! I'm going to have to start putting things down in my calendar."

Since she always wrote things down, he found her remarks deceptive.

—

Lenny 'Iron Hands' McDerch, with Sparky in tow, was walking back toward Eddy's house when they approached two men in front of the designated house smoking cigars. "Excuse me, Sir, but would you have the time?" Lenny asked one of the men.

"It's 8:45. Hey, that's a nice looking dog. What's his name?"

"Sparky. Stick your paw out Sparky."

One of the men kneeled and reached for Sparky's paw. The other man looked admiringly at the dog and Lenny stretched out his hand to stroke Sparky's ears. The man bending over started to pet Sparky; the man standing continued to observe everything.

"Nice house. Do you gentlemen live here?" Lenny asked nonchalantly trying to make conversation.

"I live there," said the man who was standing and pointing at the target house.

Lenny turned his head to follow the direction of the man's finger. "Do you have a dog, Sir?"

"No, I've thought about it, but my hours are too irregular. Where do you live? I haven't seen you around here before."

"A couple of streets over. I just started taking longer walks with Sparky. I need the exercise and walking him has been helpful."

"You look like you're in great shape."

"Thanks. I used to work out on a regular basis. I may look like I'm in shape, but I'm really not. My eating habits need to improve. By the way, my name's Gary Hinsaw."

"I'm Eddy Tevelle and that's Luka Brahn."

"The pleasure's mine."

Lenny was standing over Luka who was kneeling and petting Sparky. Sergeant McDerch observed that both were large men. He looked at the soft spot of Luka's neck and contemplated whether this was the right time. He could incapacitate the bodyguard with one vicious blow to the front neck section, but then Eddy would be fully on guard and cause Sparky to start barking and possibly cause neighbors to look out their windows. Lenny decided against taking any action.

"Well, I hope you gentlemen have a good evening. Sparky and I need to get going now."

Lenny and the dog started walking away from the two men and within a few minutes they had walked out of sight of Big Eddy and Luka Brahn.

—

Bill looked at his watch. It was time to pick up Lenny. He kissed Susan goodbye and took off. Ten minutes later he saw Lenny and swung over and picked him up.

"Report, Sergeant, please."

"I made contact with an Eddy Tevelle and Luka Brahn. They were standing outside the target house talking. The men noticed Sparky and asked about him. I engaged said parties in light conversation for a few minutes and determined the situation was not conducive to meeting our prime objective. After a few minutes, I disengaged and started walking to the designated extraction point."

"What did you learn, Sergeant?"

"A weapon would make the task much easier, but I'm not sure how the dog would react. He might start barking uncontrollably. There needs to be a vehicle nearby to pick up the body once I put him out of commission."

Bill thought about the situation and made mental notes. When they arrived back home, Bill's telephone answering machine flashed one message. Captain Bell was the caller.

"Hello, Captain."

"Detective...I have some information for you. The police in the neighboring town met with Jenny McCray's aunt and interviewed her. I have that tape. Would you like me to send it to you or play it right now?"

"Let's do both. Can you play the part that's most relevant right now? I don't need to hear the whole thing."

Bill heard the Captain setting up the machine. After a few minutes the Captain was back on the line telling him to listen.

"Mrs. Philips, I've told you the assignment our D.A. has assigned us. It's very important that we respond to the law enforcement authorities up north. A horrible crime has been committed and a man's life is on the line. We're required to simply gather the facts and not make any moral judgments. That's our only job. We know your niece had her baby here in this town, but we need to know who the father is. Can you provide his name?"

"I wish I could help you, Officer, but I'm not sure that I can. Jenny did have her baby here with me. I'm her aunt; her father is my brother. When she became pregnant my brother sent her to me. You know how it was in those days, Officer. The gossip would've ruined her life there."

"Yes, I can imagine. But you're sure you don't know the father?"

"No, Officer. I know that sounds hard to believe, but that's the truth."

"Mrs. Philips, besides your niece, who would know the father's name?"

"Why, Father Ryan would, but he died many years ago."

"Father Ryan?"

"Yes. He was the priest of the church that the family attended back in New Orleans. Why, he's the one who drove Jenny up here. He said not to ask the girl anything about the baby's father because it would only upset her. So, I never did. I just provided for her and her baby."

"So, Father Ryan knew."

"Yes. Jenny confided in him before ever thinking about telling her own family. The priest forbade her to tell anyone who the father was, not even her own parents. He felt it was in Jenny's best interests for her to remain quiet. It drove my brother batty. It kept eating away at his soul, but the priest was adamant!"

"I find it hard to believe that your brother didn't know, Mrs. Philips."

"My brother was hotheaded, but he would have never hurt his children. The priest knew that if my brother found out, he would most likely have killed the person who soiled his precious daughter. The priest put the fear of God in my brother in order to save another man's life."

Bill heard a click and the tape ended. A moment later Captain Bell's voice was in his ear.

"Hold on while I advance the tape."

Bill heard the 'whizz' of the tape recorder and then the 'click' and 'whizz' again, as Captain Bell tried to pinpoint the next spot on the tape. After a few moments, the Captain was back.

"Okay, I've got it. Here we go."

"Thank you very much, Mrs. Philips, for all your help. You've been most co-operative. By the way, did your niece give birth here in the house?"

"Oh no, Officer. She had the baby at St. Joseph's Hospital."

"Again, thank you. I'm sorry to have disturbed you. You've been very helpful."

The tape was shut off and Captain Bell was back on the line. "It appears you got what you need, Detective."

"Not quite, but we certainly do have a lot more information thanks to you. It's too bad Father Ryan is dead. I would have liked to talk with him."

"Sometimes we only get part of the puzzle. I'm sure you've faced this dilemma before."

"More times than I care to remember. I don't see Jenny McCray spilling her guts. If her own son doesn't know who his father is, I'm not sure we'll ever know."

"Do you think Dr. Broussard could be the one, Detective?"

"Who knows? The priest could've been protecting his own brother or anyone else. We can only speculate and I'm sure if the priest was involved, we're not going to find anything on the birth certificate regarding the birth father. Those priests are too clever to make a mistake like that."

"Well, the birth certificate says the father is John S. McCray. However, Jenny was never married. So, another mystery."

Detective Lincoln had run into yet another wall. "You'll send the tape to me?"

"Yes, right away.

"By the way, Captain, who succeeded Father Ryan?"

"Father Sebastian took over after Father Ryan's death. Father Sebastian was his right-hand holy man and his confidant, so it was only natural for him to take over. You've already met the priest."

Bill was staring into space. He had met Father Sebastian at the home of the dying Edwina Broussard, Dr. Broussard's mother. He'd bet his next paycheck that the priest knew whom the father of Jenny McCray's baby was, but judging from his brief meeting with Father Sebastian, there was no chance in hell the priest would ever disclose that information. Bill started thinking again…there were just too many coincidences.

"Damn!"

"What's up, Detective?"

"I spoke with Jenny's son Jacob after you gave me his telephone number."

"And?"

"I pretended that I worked in the school admissions office where someone had accidentally spilled coffee his records. I said we couldn't read his parent's information and asked for his help. He said his mother's name was Jennifer and his father's name was John."

"So. What are you saying, Detective?"

"I'm not saying anything, but what was that priest's name again?"

"Sorry, Detective, but it was Father Jim Ryan. You better get some rest. I think maybe you're working too hard."

"No, not that one."

"What are you talking about?"

"The priest who took over. What is Father Sebastian's first name?"

Now there was silence on the other end of the phone. "Well...his name is Father John Sebastian...Damn!"

"Learn What Is True In Order To Do What Is Right" Is The Summing Up Of The Whole Duty Of Man...

THOMAS H. HUXLEY:

Chapter 40

"Please state your name for the record, Sir."

"William Monroe Lincoln."

"Your occupation?"

"I'm a retired detective formerly with the Oakland Police Department, now in private practice."

"Have you ever been charged with a crime, Detective?"

"No, I've never been convicted of a crime."

The District Attorney stopped moving and looked at Bill. "I said have you ever been charged with a crime?!"

"No."

"Did Internal Affairs consider you the prime suspect in the investigation of the death of Mr. Harvey Gooding?"

"You'll have to ask Internal Affairs. I've never been charged with anything and I don't know whom they considered their prime suspect."

"Did they consider you a suspect?"

"I don't know. They asked me a lot of questions and I answered all of them. Again, I can't speak for Internal Affairs."

Detective Lincoln spent four hours answering questions from the Grand Jury and the District Attorney. By the end of the session he was tired and worn out. He had no idea what the Grand Jury thought after his performance that day but he refused to get angry, answering each question in a controlled manner. Only time would tell.

Afterward, Bill drove aimlessly in an effort to relax. After a few minutes of driving he glanced into his rear view mirror only to spot another car he believed to be following him. He pulled out his gun, laying it on the seat next to him. After another mile the suspicious car turned down another street and Bill breathed a sigh of relief. Needing a change of scenery, he drove out of town. He ended up spending an hour walking around a park in a neighboring community taking in the fresh air and fragrant flowers. He stopped for dinner, then headed back into town. While driving on the freeway he noticed the exit for Susan's house. He decided to drive there. He was in the mood to talk to someone, someone who was not a lawyer or a cop. Picking up his car phone he dialed her number as he drove toward her house. On the third ring she answered.

"Hello?"

"Hi, it's me, Bill."

"Bill, how are you?"

"Well, to tell the truth, I've had better days. I testified before the Grand Jury this afternoon." He turned onto her street.

"Oh, how did it go?"

"I'm not sure. The District Attorney was asking questions so outrageous you'd think I was a serial killer. I don't know what's going on. If that's any indication of what goes on in a Grand Jury room, the system's in trouble."

As he pulled up in front of her house, Bill noticed the shiny two-seater Mercedes Benz complete with the personalized license plates 'RAD' sitting in her driveway. While parking in front he saw someone standing at the window looking out. Seconds later the curtains moved; the image was gone, but he had a fairly good idea of who it was. His suspicions were confirmed moments later as he watched Rad casually walk out the front door toward his car. Bill was still on the phone with Susan.

"I thought I'd stop by, if you weren't busy, and talk about it."

"Oh, Bill, I'm kinda busy right now. Can we do it tomorrow?"

"Sure, it seems you've gotten very busy lately. What exactly are you working on?" Rad was only a few feet from Bill's car now.

"I'm just trying to nail down my stuff at the office. Its really been piling up."

"I'll talk with you tomorrow then. Goodbye, Susan." He put the phone back and rolled down the window. "Well, Rad, you do get around."

"Detective, it's so nice to see you. It appears our paths have crossed once again."

"What are you doing here, Rad?"

"Why, I'm just visiting my new friend, Detective. She's a charming young lady and as far as I can tell, very much available. So, I've decided to bring a little joy and class into her life."

"Well, I don't think she does drugs, Rad, so what would you have in common with her?"

"Well, for starters, she's a woman and I'm a man."

"That's a lot in common. I guess that settles everything."

"I don't imagine the lady has ever met a man like me before, Detective, the type that can show her how the privileged class lives."

"You mean she might actually get to see how high grade dope is processed and used?" Rad remained cordial, continuing to engage Bill in 'friendly' conversation.

"Speaking of which, how do you like the idea of prison food, Rad? Will you be bringing your own chef to prepare it?"

"Detective, I'm willing to bet you ten thousand dollars that you'll drop the charges before any trial takes place. But I realize you probably don't have that type of money. How about a thousand dollar bet? Or maybe a hundred dollars is more in your league?"

"I'll take that bet for a thousand, but I would prefer not to shake hands. You see… I'm allergic to cocaine residue."

"Have a nice day, Detective. Susan and I will be thinking about you tonight as we sip fine wine while dining at an elegant restaurant."

Rad turned and casually walked back toward the house, seemingly without a care in the world. Bill pulled off but was careful not to speed away; instead he drove slowly like nothing had happened. In truth, he was livid and vowed to make sure Radcliffe Dillard was brought to justice. While Bill was driving away another conversation related to the same subject matter was taking place in City Hall.

--

"I don't want this trial to take place. We need to get Lincoln to drop the charges. I want that to happen and you need to do it quickly. The trial date is almost here."

"Yes, Mayor. Right away, Mayor."

--

Detective Lincoln had retrieved Lenny and Sparky from their nightly recognizance in Big Eddy's neighborhood more than an hour earlier. Everyone was home when his pager went off. He didn't recognize the display and he wondered if it was a wrong number. Bill called and heard a familiar voice on the other end.

"Detective, I'm headed out of town for good this evening, but I need to talk to you."

"About what?"

"I want to give you my theory on why I got beat down."

"You know who Franklin's lover is?"

"I have a good guess."

"Who?"

"You know I don't like phones. Meet me at my old place in two hours. I have to take care of a few things first. I'll see you around midnight, and don't be late."

"Why are you doing this?"

"They beat me bad, real bad; and I want revenge! Maybe you can arrange something later?"

"Midnight it is then, Jacko. See ya then." Detective Lincoln had hoped to get to bed early, this of all nights, but he had to speak with Jacko before he left town. This might be the last time he'd ever have that chance. The phone rang five minutes later. Somehow he didn't think he'd get much rest this evening.

"Hello, Bill."

"Monique, how are you?"

"I'm fine, but how are you?"

"I didn't have the best of days."

"My father told me you testified before the Grand Jury this afternoon and my brother Radcliffe said he had an 'interesting' conversation with you outside your lady friend's house earlier this evening."

"The news travels both quickly and accurately along the Dillard grapevine."

"Do you want to talk?"

Bill was thinking that he wanted to talk, but mainly with Susan. He'd like to be able to talk the situation over with Monique, but he knew she also had other things in mind. Besides, he didn't think getting too social with the sister of the man he would be testifying against was very bright.

"I'd like to talk but I have an appointment this evening."

"Isn't it kind of late to be doing business?"

"In my world you conduct your affairs when it's possible. It's just the nature of my business."

"Is your business about our case?"

"I believe it could be."

"Can you tell me what it is?"

"No, not at this time. I'm not sure what the outcome will be. I'll find that out tonight."

"Well, when you want to talk, I'm here."

"Thanks, Monique."

"Goodbye, Bill."

At 11:30 P.M., Detective Lincoln left the house taking Sergeant McDerch and Sparky with him. They arrived in front of Jacko's place at 11:56 P.M. They all got out and headed up the stairs. Bill knocked but there was no answer. The place was dark, cemetery quiet. He tried the doorknob, but it was locked. Bill stood there perplexed wondering where Jacko was.

Lenny waited quietly. The only one who was active was Sparky. The dog was sniffing, wagging his tail back and forth at the door and staring at it. He smelled something. Bill decided it was time to go inside. Major Lincoln instructed Lenny to get the second gun and the police door jammer from the car. A few minutes later they were prying the lock off.

Detective Lincoln pulled his weapon, reached in and flicked on the light switch. Cautiously, they entered the room. Sparky, on leash, pulled Lenny toward a closed door. There were two sets of what appeared to be bloody footprints leading away from the door and out of the room. They tied Sparky to the table and slowly stepped toward the door where Sparky had been trying to lead them. Bill moved the door back with a broom while Lenny stood, weapon drawn, behind him. Bill flipped the broom over and started rubbing the nylon webbing against the wall trying to find the light switch, which he did. The light went on. Bill peered into the room and saw Jacko's dead body lying in a pool of blood complete with a severed chicken head protruding grotesquely from his mouth!

Chapter 41

The press conference was scheduled for 8 A.M. A third voodoo murder had occurred and the citizens were more than a little concerned about their safety. A crowd had formed in front of City Hall; they wanted action. The Mayor had been alerted at 12:30 A.M., soon after the body was first discovered. A full investigative team had been dispatched to the scene. Brick Kasolkasky even allowed Bill to call Marie Francois! Now, as Bill was watching the press conference, his thoughts drifted back a few hours earlier, to around 2 A.M., when the voodoo priestess and Ricardo first arrived on the scene.

The police forensics team and the coroner were collecting evidence while orchestrating the photographer's picture taking efforts. The long black sedan glided to rest, parking behind the last police car, which was still flashing its lights incessantly against the still night. Marie Francois and Ricardo, both draped in white, moved silently from the car to the base of the stairs. When a uniformed policeman saw the couple, he automatically waved them forward.

"Are you Ms. Francois and Mr. Bensway?"

"Yes."

"Please... follow me."

The policeman led them up the stairs to Detective Lincoln who was talking with Kasolkasky. Detective Lincoln greeted them, after which Kasolkasky cleared his men from the apartment. Madam Francois walked alone to the center of the living room...her eyes shut. Ricardo removed his jacket and motioned for the detectives to step back and remain quiet. The voodoo priestess unbuttoned her coat while Ricardo swiftly moved behind her, gently removing the garment. The voodooianne held both her hands together giving the appearance of meditation. She then turned slowly, walked toward the room where the body was, then stopped upon entering the room.

Ricardo stood behind her. Detective Lincoln and Brick moved forward to get a better view while maintaining their distance from Ricardo and Ms. Francois. Bill grabbed a video recorder. Ricardo was now totally focused on Marie Francois, his back toward Bill. Bill, quietly, began filming the scene.

Ms. Francois's head turned to the right. She held it in that position. Both her hands went up in front, as if she was suddenly blind and trying to feel for something in front of her. A long chilling moan broke the silence followed by the priestess speaking in tongues! Her hands reached out again, as if attempting to touch something, while she walked around the room seemingly oblivious of the bloody corpse.

Suddenly she cried out, "Damballa...Damballa Wedo...Oh Great One! If you are here, show yourself to your loyal servant. Damballa... Damballa...allow me to ride the great snake. I yield to your greatness. I bow in your honor. Take me...show me the way...take me to Legba! Damballa...Damballa...I am yours!"

Kasolkasky and Lincoln were staring, not knowing what was going to happen next. Ricardo stood at attention, observing the priestess, ready to react at a moment's notice to whatever might occur. She was now kneeling on the floor with her head in a prone position, her hands stretched on the floor out in front of her. Bill had seen Ms. Francois personify a snake before and he contemplated whether he'd again witness a similar transformation. The silence was deafening. All eyes focussed on the voodooianne. After several minutes of complete quiet, Madam Francois slowly moved, lifting her head. She appeared tired and worn but filled with the spirit.

She stood and walked directly to the corspe, to view it up close. Most people couldn't stomach such an awful sight, but the priestess observed the deceased like a pathologist.

She moved to within just inches of the victim's face. Again she reached out, this time as though trying to touch a force field surrounding the body. "Damballa Wedo...are you there?" Ms. Francois was sitting by the body with hands outreached at full extension, as though protecting it. She remained like this for several moments, and then rose to her feet and, with her long dress nearly touching the floor, she seemed to float away from the deceased. The voodooianne came to rest a few feet from the body before falling to her knees; her head slumped to her chest. She remained motionless. Her earlier movements had indeed reminded Bill of the voodoo ceremony he had witnessed before, where he first saw Mama take on those snake-like movements he'd never forget.

Several minutes passed but Madam Francois remained motionless, like a fallen statue in the center of the bloody scene. Suddenly, the booming voice of Ricardo rang out from within the room, startling the two detectives.

"Damballa...Father...are you here? We are ready to receive you Father. Show us the sign. Damballa...Damballa Wedo."

Ms. Francois remained in the prone position on the ground as Ricardo towered over her, his hands in a welcoming position for the great voodoo god to come enter the soul of his companion waiting at his feet. A full minute went by, but nothing happened; Lincoln stopped recording and pulled his sports jacket off, placing it over the camera to conceal it. Another thirty seconds went by before Ms. Francois lifted her head up from the floor, still kneeling. She looked into the eyes of Ricardo and shook her head. Apparently, the voodoo god would not come.

Ms. Francois raised her left hand. Ricardo grabbed it, helping her to her feet. They said a few words to each other, then turned and walked to where Detective Lincoln and Kasolkasky were standing.

"Damballa is not here. This is not voodoo, but rather someone trying to make it look like it is."

"How do you know?" Brick asked.

"I'm a voodooianne. I know. I called out to Damballa. If he were close he would have come. He's not near us. He was never here."

—-

That was the image Bill envisioned as he contemplated the murder scene. His thoughts shifted back now to the press conference at hand.

"Mr. Mayor, is our city safe?"

"Very much. The last two murders appear to be connected."

"In what way, Sir?"

"As you might expect, I'm not at liberty to disclose that information. Naturally, it's confidential."

A sea of hands was raised, each beckoning for his attention.

"If you know something, Mr. Mayor, why aren't you advising the citizens on how to protect themselves? Who is most at risk in this city?"

"I can assure you that just about every citizen is safe from these horrific crimes."

"If you know who it is, why don't you arrest him?"

"We don't know who yet. Still, we've reason to believe that the vast majority of the citizens of this city are very safe."

The press conference continued for another forty-five minutes with very little concrete information being gleaned by the media. Detective Lincoln sat in the conference room at the police station watching the spectacle on closed circuit television. Kasolkasky and the Chief were at one end of the stage waiting for questions; questions that the Chief Executive couldn't answer. The Mayor raised his hand, indicating that the session was over. Bill got up and walked in the direction of Jim Efferton's office. A meeting was scheduled for right after the press conference.

"Please... sit down gentlemen," the Mayor, while standing behind his desk, commanded. "I want to hear exactly what happened. We're facing a nightmare here! I need to understand everything that's happening out there. Bill, I understand you found the body?"

"Yes. I received a call from Jacko Barnaby, one of my informants, at about 10 P.M. last night. He was leaving town for good, so he called me to arrange one last meeting. He said he wanted revenge."

"Revenge?"

"Yes, Mayor, because he was beaten-up a few weeks ago and almost died from his injuries. He was seeking an answer for me and also trying to make a little money."

"What do you mean, Bill?"

"Jacko had been trying to find out for me who Franklin Dillard, Jr's lover was. He was beat up pretty bad for asking too many questions. He had decided to leave town for good. Before he left he was going to share with me his theory. Jacko didn't trust phones so he asked that I meet him at his old place, around midnight. When I got there I knew something had gone terribly wrong. I broke in only to discover him murdered. I called Kasolkasky and notified the police. Now, you know as much as I do."

"Who do you think killed him, Bill?"

"I don't know. It would seem that Franklin Dillard's lover might know the answer to that question."

Everybody secretly glanced at everyone else while pondering the thought. The Mayor had reflected on that revelation too and already the wheels were turning in his mind.

"Anybody have any idea who Franklin, Jr's lover is?" the Mayor asked.

No one offered an answer.

"Where was Dr. Broussard last night?"

"He was home."

"Does he have an alibi?"

"Only his wife."

"There's some more evidence in Dr. Broussard's favor," Kasolkasky observed. "Bill suggested that we send two officers over to his house. They went to Dr. Broussard's garage and felt the engines of his two cars. They were both cold."

"Bill, you went to Jacko's apartment, but no one was there. Was the door open?"

"No. I brought my dog with me. He was acting very strange. He smelled something inside. I broke the lock and entered. The rest is history. I called Brick a few minutes later."

"This may not sit well, a member of law enforcement breaking into a house," the Chief said.

"Officially, I'm not a member of the law enforcement team. I'm a private citizen, Chief. Please arrest me if you're that concerned with what I did."

"I'm supposed to uphold the law, Bill."

"I know that, Chief. Maybe that's why you should arrest me."

"Let's get back to business, gentlemen," the Mayor interjected. "So, what did the voodoo lady have to say?"

"Only that voodoo wasn't involved. She said somebody was faking it."

The Mayor put his hand under his chin to reflect on that. He didn't know what to think about these voodoo people. They appeared just as confused as the police. "Okay, what's our next step, gentlemen?"

"We're awaiting the lab reports," the Chief responded.

"Chief," said the Mayor with some restraint, "I'm not sure we need to wait for a lab report to tell us our next move. Frankly speaking, I don't expect the lab results to tell us anything new. Do you?"

"We can't be sure, Mayor."

"Bill, what are your thoughts?"

"I don't work for the police anymore, Mayor. You fired me. Remember?"

"Thank you for reminding me." The Mayor noticed that Detective Lincoln hadn't answered the question. "Also, the trial date is getting very close for Radcliffe Dillard and Big Eddy. Are you still bringing charges after all? You've got other cases that require more attention; yes?"

Everyone waited for Bill's answer.

"So I'll ask you, Bill, what's it going to take to get you to drop the charges?" the Mayor asked.

"Change the law. I believe it's still a crime to use illegal drugs in this country. I was a law enforcement agent at the time I busted those people for using illegal drugs."

"Alright then, the trial will happen. Anything else?"

The meeting ended. The Mayor asked Chief Ness to remain for a few minutes. They huddled together speaking quietly.

"You told me a neighbor saw two men and a dog outside Jacko's door trying to gain entry. The car was the same type that Detective Lincoln drives."

"Yes, Mayor."

"But Bill told you he was alone with his dog?"

"That's what he said, Mayor. You heard him yourself."

"And there were two sets of bloody footsteps leading away from that room?"

"That's right, Mayor."

Meanwhile, Bill drove to the police photo lab and had a video copy made of the scene he had filmed last night. He sent a copy to Ms. Jezebel Balboa. He wanted her opinion of the performance by Ricardo and Marie Francois.

Bill's pager went off. It was his home number so it had to be Lenny. Lenny alerted him that he had just received a call from Elden Robinson of New Orleans, inviting him to a voodoo ceremony that coming weekend. The cost would be two hundred dollars. This was a special ceremony by the voodoo priest but if he preferred to wait for another month, the price would drop to a hundred dollars. Bill thought he was being conned, but that was okay. He called Marie Francois and left a message asking her to please call him back. He then dialed Elden Robinson's number.

"Hello, Mr. Robinson?"

"Yes."

"This is Bill Lincoln from Oakland. I just got your message about the upcoming voodoo ceremony."

"Are you still interested, Mr. Lincoln?"

"Most definitely. I just left a message with my employer. He wasn't there but I can assure you we're interested.

"Good. I can assume you'll be attending then?"

"Yes. Besides, I'd like to make this trip a vacation, not just business. With that in mind, I'm thinking of bringing my wife along. How much more would it cost to take her to the ceremony?"

"How does a hundred dollars sound?"

"What about fifty? We're not rich, Mr. Robinson."

"Okay then, two fifty total."

"I can do that. My employer will pay the two hundred. I'll pay the fifty. I'll see you on Saturday."

"Goodbye, Mr. Lincoln."

He got back on the phone to try to find Jacko's girlfriend. Her name was Carmen-Maria and she was Mexican-American. He put out the word that there was five hundred dollars for anyone who could get him to her. At four o'clock, Marie Francois returned Detective Lincoln's call.

"Hello, Ms. Francois, thanks for coming out last night."

"I'm sorry we weren't much help."

"Quite the contrary, you confirmed that voodoo was not involved. That's a positive negative."

"Then I was glad to have been of some service."

"Frankly, Mama, I could use your help again right now."

"How so, Detective?"

"Well, I just got an invite to a voodoo ceremony to be held in New Orleans this coming weekend. I want you to accompany me as my wife. I need a voodoo expert with me."

"That offer is hard to refuse, Detective."

"Then you'll accept."

"Yes."

"Great! I'll get back to you with the details."

He drove to Buckston's office to get a status report. He parked his car then took several minutes surveying the area. Seeing nothing unusual, he walked inside.

"Hello, Hank?"

"Oh hi, Bill. I understand we had another of those voodoo killings! Will they charge our client with that one too?"

"It's doubtful. Two uniformed officers were dispatched to Dr. Broussard's house soon after the murder. Both of Broussard's car engines were cold. That's certainly in his favor.

Like before, his only alibi is his wife."

"I'm told it was you who discovered the body, Bill."

"Yeah. I was supposed to meet the victim at midnight. He wanted to share an epiphany with me... the identity of Franklin

Dillard's lover. In other words, the deceased was an informant of mine who knew Franklin Jr. to be gay."

"Interesting. The Dillard family gets more intriguing by the minute. Is it your belief that there's a link between Hillary's untimely death and Franklin Jr.'s questionable lifestyle?!"

"That's one of the angles I'm playing. It's just tough to get any information. Nobody, and I mean nobody, is talking!"

"Are you sure Dr. Broussard is not the father of Jenny McCray's child?"

Hank sat in his chair and blew a trademark smoke ring into the air.

"What does that have to do with the murder of Hillary Dillard?"

"Maybe nothing, but it would say something about our client's truthfulness. By the way, I'm heading back out to New Orleans this weekend. I received a call from Elden Robinson inviting me to attend a voodoo ceremony. It will cost two hundred fifty dollars…two hundred for me and fifty for my 'wife'."

"And who's your wife?"

"How about…Marie Francois!"

"So, what's the connection with Robinson?"

"I met him the last time I was in New Orleans. The police took me to him to learn about the voodoo culture there. It was Ms. Balboa who said she knew Elden and his niece, Hattie Black. Hattie is one of the women Dr. Broussard 'knew' years ago."

"Another one of those coincidences?"

"To say the least."

"Go for it then. The more information we get our hands on the better for our client."

"And of course you've never defended a client who was guilty?!"

"Remember, that's not my job, Bill. Again, that's for a jury to decide."

Bill went home. He had rented a van shortly after the first night Lenny had walked Sparky in Big Eddy's neighborhood. Bill would drive his car with Lenny and Sparky following in the 'new' vehicle. Detective Lincoln had attached a bogus license plate to the van. The license plate was registered to a car used in the witness protection program. He was trying to protect himself and Lenny as best he could. The grandfather clock chimed, reminding him it was again time to escort them to Big Eddy's neighborhood.

"Remember, Lenny, you've met Eddy once before just a few days ago. You don't remember because of your slight memory problem, but your memory will come back one day. It just takes a little time. Again, your alias is Gary Hinsaw. That's the name you gave Big Eddy the last time." Bill pulled out his eight-inch hunting knife, handing it to Lenny.

"You might need this, Sergeant. Now, carry on."

Lenny took the knife, strapping it to his lower back for quick access. He reached into the back seat to retrieve the dog leash. Fifteen minutes later, he and Sparky were strolling down Big Eddy's street. Bill got back in his car and drove home.

He decided to call Susan. He hadn't heard from her since their last conversation over his cell phone outside her house.

"Hello, Susan."

"Hello, Bill."

"Any reason you haven't called?"

There was a moment of silence. He waited. She was the one on the spot and if the roles were reversed, he knew she'd wait patiently for him to respond. The silence was rapidly approaching the awkward stage.

"I'm embarrassed. I didn't have the energy or the nerve to pick up the phone. I don't know what's happening to me."

"What do you think is happening to you?"

"You sound like a therapist."

"Well, you're acting like you need a shrink."

"Oh, Bill, I guess I'm living in my Cinderella dreams. A prince in a two-seater Mercedes has showed up on my doorstep with not one but two glass slippers. I know there's a bunch of other women who have tried on those slippers, and yet, I'm still unable to resist the temptation."

"If you were the therapist and your patient told you that story, what would you advise your client to do?"

"I know what you're saying and you're right. But, I can't seem to take my own advice. He's so sweet-talking it's sinful."

"Susan, why do you think he's suddenly interested in you?"

"Bill, I know why. But I want to believe that he finds me so irresistible that he just can't live without me. He says these things to me and, as he's talking, I know he's only mouthing the words. I also know that I want to hear them. I think maybe we both need counseling."

"No. Only you. Rad knows exactly what he's doing."

"Will you be patient with me, Bill?"

"You know I can't stand weak minded women."

Again, silence passed between them.

"You didn't answer my question."

"Look, I'll talk to you later, maybe."

He hung up the phone, poured himself a drink, and then walked back to his study. He felt the strong urge for a smoke after that call. He was very disappointed. She knew that she was being used and that bothered him. He was halfway through his drink when the phone rang.

"Bill, it's Monique."

"How are you?"

"Fine. I heard you were the one who discovered the third voodoo murder victim."

"Yes."

"Was that where you were going when we talked last night?"

"Yes."

"Why were you going there?"

"It's related to your brother."

"Radcliffe?"

"No."

"What does this have to do with Franklin?"

"It had to do with his sex life." He heard silence and waited for Monique to talk.

"I don't understand. What are you saying?"

"The person who died was an informant of mine. He was leaving town permanently. He was almost killed last month for asking questions related to your brother. He was going to share his suspicions with me last night."

"Bill, this is a little unbelievable."

"What part is unbelievable?"

"The whole thing!"

"Do you think your brother has a normal marriage?" Again, he heard silence. He waited patiently.

"What's a normal marriage, Bill?"

"Look, I'm not interested in playing word games, Monique."

"But I'm not. Marriages are different for everyone."

"Don't you get it? I'm trying to find the person who murdered your sister."

"I know, and I'm trying to salvage the family that's still living."

"I can admire you for that, but that's not my responsibility. I want answers to some downright perplexing questions. I want to know why my informant was killed and by whom. I think his family may want to know too."

"I can totally understand that. Especially knowing how horrifically he died."

Bill was silent now. Her point was well made. Everyone's perspective was different in this case.

"I'm sorry if I offended you. I know your sister was brutally taken from you."

"I just don't want to lose anyone else…I'll talk to you later."

"Goodnight, Monique."

As he was putting the phone down, Lenny McDerch and Sparky came walking into the room. Lenny shook his head, signaling that nothing had happened that evening.

Man with the burning soul has but an hour of breath,
To build a ship of truth on which his soul may sail
Sail on the sea of death, For death takes toll
Of beauty, courage, youth, Of all but truth.

John Masefield: Truth.
Philip the King and Other Poems, Heinemann, 1914

Chapter 42

At 2:30 P.M., Detective Lincoln accepted a collect phone call from Ms. Jezebel Balboa. She had received his overnight mail delivery.

"Hello, Ms. Balboa."

"Good afternoon, Detective. I believe this evidence proves my point."

"In what way, Ms. Balboa?"

"Those two voodoo frauds. It is obvious from the film that Damballa was there that night. Did you see the misery on the victim's face? Did you see how the furniture was turned and how the body was laying? Did you see how the victim's eyes remained open? I could feel the touch of Damballa on that man. Mark my words, Detective, there was voodoo performed in that room that night!"

Bill was flabbergasted! Yet again, Ms. Balboa was saying the exact opposite of what Marie Francois had said. One was obviously lying, but which one? He had his suspicions.

—

Three days later Bill and Marie Francois flew to New Orleans. The voodoo ceremony was scheduled for Saturday evening. He left Ms. Francois at the hotel to rest while he drove into town to meet with Captain Bell and Father John Sebastian. The police visit was merely a courtesy call. Captain Bell still had not contacted Hattie Black, Elden Robinson's niece, without Robinson's knowledge. Every source they had also knew Robinson. He was a very influential force in his community. Also, no new information had surfaced concerning the identity of the father of Jenny McCray's son. Bill felt that Father Sebastian could provide that answer, but he didn't presently have the key to open that lock. He thanked Captain Bell then drove to the church to meet the priest.

He knocked on Father Sebastian's door. The priest answered and welcomed Detective Lincoln.

"I was surprised to hear you were back in town, Detective. And even more bewildered that you wanted to talk to me again. I'm flattered, but I'm not sure if you're spending your time wisely."

"Thank you for seeing me, Father. How's Mrs. Broussard doing?"

"Not very well. She's very sick; I don't know how much longer she'll be with us. She's in God's hands now."

Bill nodded. "Father John, I think you can help me in another area."

"Oh, what area is that, my son?"

"I'm trying to determine the identity of Jacob McCray's father. I believe that information will help in our defense of Dr. Broussard."

The priest raised his eyebrows and placed his arms across his chest. He then shifted in his chair. It was obvious by his body language that the question had stirred his interest.

"I don't see the connection, Detective. Perhaps you could explain to me why that's important."

"Naturally, it's important that we believe in our client. As we do our research we find certain things that need confirmation from, let's say, independent sources. Now, there's compelling evidence that Dr. Broussard committed this murder. However, he's maintained that he's completely innocent. He's told us many things that are true, which are supported by both evidence and the many who believe in him. Still, there are also quite a few people who think he's the killer. The last time I was here I uncovered a few unflattering things about our Dr. Broussard. One rumor has it that he might actually be the father of Jenny McCray's son. Dr. Broussard maintains he isn't, but we need corroboration and, quite frankly, I think you can help us."

"Why would you think that? I barely knew Dr. Broussard when he was a teenager."

"You took over for the priest who served the Broussard family. Not only do I believe he knew who the father was but I also believe he told you."

Father John said nothing. Bill was confident he was on the right path… Father John knew!

"Look, I don't have any proof, Detective, but would it help if I said that I'm fairly confident Dr. Broussard is not the father of Jenny's son?"

"And if I ask why you believe that, would you tell me, since you have no proof?"

"You must have faith, Detective."

"Yes, well…Father John, do you happen to know the name of Jacob's father on the birth certificate?"

"Our meeting is over, Detective. Thank you again for coming!" With that, the priest stood, walked to the door and opened it.

In response Bill stood, gathering himself; then he queried, "Would you be willing to voluntarily submit to a DNA test for us, Father?"

The priest stood by the door waiting for Bill to leave and would not acknowledge the detective's question. Lincoln looked long and hard at the priest, and then left. He drove until he saw a pay phone, stopped, and dialed Jenny McCray's number. He didn't actually think he'd get anywhere but at least he could try.

"Hello, Ms. McCray?"

"Yes, who's calling?"

"This is Detective Lincoln, from Oakland. I'm here in New Orleans on business. I just finished my meeting with Father Sebastian. Would you mind terribly if I dropped by for a short talk?"

"What about, Detective?"

"I'd like to ask you some questions concerning your relationship with Dr. Broussard."

"I see. Well, you'd better ask your questions right now, over the phone! I have no interest in meeting with the likes of you!"

He asked some meaningless questions, she gave superficial answers. For his last question he asked, "Ms. McCray, Jacob's birth certificate said his father's name was John S. McCray. Is that right?"

"Goodbye, Detective!" The line went dead. Bill drove back to the hotel to rest before the evening's voodoo activities started. At eight-fifteen there was a knock on his door. Elden Robinson was standing there with a small thin man standing next to him. He had only been expecting Elden. The smaller man had on a hat and wore a dark wool suit and bowtie. He was medium-complexioned with a thin moustache. He looked Caribbean.

Detective Lincoln invited the two men inside. Marie Francois was sitting in the room by the bed. Bill had called her from her room over a half-hour earlier. And since he had told Elden that he was bringing his wife, Ms. Francois had placed personal items all around the room.

"I'm sorry, Mr. Lincoln, but I came to refund your money. There isn't going to be any ceremony tonight. Unfortunately it's been canceled," Elden muttered.

"What happened?"

"Our priest is sick. He's unable to bring the message."

"I'm sorry to hear that. When will the next ceremony be held?"

"I'll call you when it's time. Here's your money." Elden reached into his pocket. Bill could feel how tough it was for Elden to return that money and he knew instinctively that the only reason he was doing it was because of the small man standing there beside him. The short guy was calling the shots!

"My name is Bill Lincoln, Sir, and this is my wife, Marie. What is your name, Sir?" Bill asked the small man.

"My name is Bowman. Willis Bowman."

"Nice to meet you, Mr. Bowman. What, may I ask, do you do for a living?"

"I'm a mortician, Sir, plus an elder in the church. You said you're from Oakland, California?"

"Yes, Sir."

"And just what type of religious research do you do?"

"I work for a renowned religious researcher. I go on the road for him as he's far too busy writing to do any traveling himself these days."

"And, you do this full-time?"

"Oh no. I'm retired and only work part-time."

"So, what type of work did you retire from, Mr. Lincoln?"

"Well, I was a policeman for twenty years."

The small man burned a look at Elden for a brief instant. He then turned and addressed Ms. Francois. "How long have you been married, Mrs. Lincoln?"

"For fifteen years."

"Have you ever been to New Orleans before? You look familiar."

"No. This is my first visit. And, I must say, it's beautiful."

"How many children do you and Mr. Lincoln have?"

"Why, we have three wonderful boys."

"How old?"

"Ten, eleven and thirteen."

"I'd like to send them a gift from our church. Why don't you write down your home address so I can send them a token gift from our lovely city." Willis Bowman stepped forward to Marie Francois and handed her paper and pen, whereupon, she wrote down her own address. "Do you know anything about voodoo, Mrs. Lincoln?"

"Just a little. I'd like to learn more. I was very much looking forward to the ceremony."

"Perhaps another time. Well, Elden and I must be going. It was a pleasure meeting you. Goodnight."

"Goodnight."

Bill looked at Ms. Francois knowing full well that the evil little man had played them like a fiddle. "Have you ever seen Bowman before?"

"No, but I've seen his kind…and he's a dangerous one."

"Do you think Elden will call?"

"Not in this lifetime."

Bill and Ms. Francois talked for a while before going to dinner. The rest of the night was uneventful. In the morning, they flew back to California. Bill was driving Ms. Francois home when he decided that he wanted her to meet Dr. Broussard. Bill called the Broussard residence and spoke with Mrs. Broussard. She said her husband was in the backyard and would enjoy some company. He had no idea what to expect but Ms. Francois was willing and besides, he had nothing to lose.

Twenty-five minutes later Mrs. Broussard was leading them to the backyard where her husband was working in his garden.

Dr. Broussard enjoyed tilling the soil, tending to his flowers and vegetables. He had done too little of it as a child since the nuns sheltered him from physical labor, but it now provided him relaxation.

"Good afternoon, Dr. Broussard."

"Hello, Bill."

"This is Marie Francois"

"How do you do, Ms. Francois?"

"It's my pleasure."

"Dr. Broussard, Ms. Francois is a voodooianne."

"You are?! Why, I've never met one before. Well, actually that's not true. I've met a few when I was a little boy back in New Orleans. But that was a long time ago."

"Have you ever attended a ceremony?"

"Yes, but again, it was during my youth. My father took me to one once when he couldn't find a suitable babysitter. I went to two others when I was in junior high school; we kids were looking for something exciting to do. It was quite the experience. Certainly that was the last time I attended a ceremony. Do you worship Damballa?"

"Yes! He is my light!"

"How were you chosen, Ms. Francois? Was your mother before you also a voodooianne?"

"No. But she was sensitive. Also her sister, my aunt, was a healer. I inherited the gift from them. I knew things when I was a little girl that no one else knew."

"I would like to attend one of your ceremonies some day."

"I'll make sure you receive an invitation."

Bill was amazed at how comfortably they conversed on the subject matter. It appeared Dr. Broussard had a wide range of knowledge in many different fields. They talked for another thirty minutes before he drove Marie Francois home. On the way, Bill asked her a few questions.

"What did you think of Dr. Broussard?"

"He's very knowledgeable and quite astute. He seems like a very nice man."

"Do you have an opinion as to whether he could be the murderer?"

"His outward appearance is most congenial, but it's the heart that we must come to know. I do not know the heart of this man, but my feeling is… he's not the murderer."

While driving back to his house he received a frantic call from Betty. Someone had dropped a package off on her front steps gift-wrapped complete with ribbon and bow. It was addressed to "Mrs. William Lincoln". When she opened it, she found three severed chicken heads drenched in blood. Betty had screamed and then ran into the house to call the police. She was nearly hysterical now. Bill dropped his foot and sped toward her house.

He stayed at Betty's until he had contacted his police and security buddies. They set up a schedule so that someone would always be there. Both his daughters were home now. He decided he would not allow his oldest to return to college until this mess was all over. The death of Jacko had shaken him! He wondered for the first time if this was really worth it. He soon dismissed that thought. Allowing someone to intimidate him was untenable. The thought of allowing any murderer to get away with his crime by boldly using scare tactics, including brute force, was not an option!

At home that evening Bill conducted exercises, along with Lenny, to see how Sparky would react around violence. Bill disguised himself and sat outside in a chair. Lenny walked Sparky on a leash from inside the house to the backyard where Bill sat waiting. Upon dropping the leash, Lenny immediately attacked Bill, wrestling him to the ground. Sparky got excited, started prancing and barking! Lenny ordered Sparky to be quiet. Sparky, still excited, stopped barking. They repeated this exercise several times until Sparky learned not to bark. He growled, but that was about it. Sparky had learned fast.

At 7:10 P.M. Bill received a call from Connie Chow. "Bill, our commission is scheduled to hear another witness against you in that warehouse shooting matter."

"What? Why this is getting to be quite the little frame up. Who is it this time?"

"Bill, it's another mystery guest."

"I should've known that. What does the commission think about all this nonsense?!"

"I can't disclose that information. However, the hearing is in the public domain. Afterward, I can tell you more."

"When do you meet?"

"End of this week. I'll talk with you then."

"Goodbye, Connie. Thanks again." He found his telephone directory and looked up the number for Captain Bell. He tried the home number first. "Is Captain Bell there?"

"Yes. May I ask who's calling?"

"Detective Lincoln, Oakland P.D."

"Just a minute please."

Just about a minute passed before Captain Bell picked up. "Hello, Detective, to what do I owe this unexpected pleasure?"

"I'm calling to ask if you have had any luck locating Hattie Black?"

"I'm sorry, no. Her uncle is so omnipresent in her family that it's been impossible to find out her whereabouts without him knowing."

"Do me a favor then, send Officer Butterfield over with the assignment. Robinson is on to me anyway so it really doesn't matter. I need to start tying up some loose ends. I have a feeling Butterfield can do the job quickly."

"No doubt he can, but I hope Elden is not a close friend of yours."

"He's not. Besides, I'm feeling the heat up here and it's time to get things moving one way or another."

"Sounds like you're taking off the gloves."

"Oh yeah, they're definitely off."

"Just so you know, I'll be sure to tell Officer Butterfield that I expect him to abide by the law."

"Thank you, Captain. Please tell him that I'd also like to know the name of the voodoo priest who Robinson serves. I was supposed to attend a ceremony yesterday, but Robinson claimed they had to cancel due to the voodoo priest's mysterious illness. Obviously, I don't buy that. Now, you know I can't pay Officer Butterfield directly, that would be unethical, but tell him I'll make a three hundred dollar donation to the charity of his choice in exchange for this information."

"I'll be sure to let Butterfield know. Anything else?"

"If he can get the name of the person who impregnated Jenny McCray out of Father Sebastian, I'd be inclined to dramatically increase that reward. Somehow I don't think that's going to be possible though."

"Then I won't even mention it to Butterfield. That type of temptation would only get him in trouble I fear!"

"Goodnight, Captain Bell."

"Goodnight, Detective."

The trial of Radcliffe Dillard and Big Eddy was fast approaching. Radcliffe had callously wagered that the trial would never even happen. Big Eddy could ill afford to put himself at risk, not with his record. Two people had been mercilessly slaughtered! And now he and his family were also being threatened! Bill ordered Lenny to dress in dark clothing, then handed the sergeant a gun complete with silencer. The stakes had risen sharply!

They drove towards his ex-wife's house. Lenny dropped Bill off a block away before driving into the back alley. Bill talked with several of the neighbors who were outdoors. He wanted people to see him. Why, he even asked them for the time before he left each of them.

He greeted his children and chatted with his friend, there to guard the house. Lincoln told his security friend to keep everyone out of the room he'd be using. Bill then called an old Army buddy out of state, another electronic alibi.

Bill left the house by quietly opening the window in the room and sneaking out. Lenny picked him up behind the house and they hurried off to Luka Brahn's favorite pool joint!

Luka played pocket billiards on Monday evenings and Bill was certain he'd find him there. Ten minutes later they pulled up in front of the pool parlor. Bill told Lenny the guy inside, Luka, was one of the Vietnam operatives who had sold his own soldiers out and was now part of the Mafia. He also said that he had received direct orders from the CIA to eliminate this man. Lenny would follow Major Lincoln's orders.

Bill retrieved the cell phone he borrowed from another close friend and dialed the pool hall. There would be no trace of this call on any of his phones! The 'Cleaner' was called to the phone.

"Luka, this is Detective Lincoln. I'm standing outside the poolroom by your car. I need to talk to you right now. Do you think you can spare a few minutes? I promise, this won't take long."

Sure enough, when Luka looked out the window, he saw Bill talking on a cell phone right next to his car.

"What's this about, Lincoln?"

"Actually, I want to talk with both you and your boss. I've got an offer for Big Eddy regarding the upcoming trial. I might not testify if he agrees to certain conditions. The only problem is I've got to know tonight!"

"Alright then, I'll be right there."

Luka came walking out. Bill bent over pretending that he had dropped his phone. "Let's get in the van where it's private. By the way, unfortunately my phone's not working now. Do you happen to have one I could use?"

"Yeah. I'll get it." Luka walked to his car to retrieve his cell phone. Bill got in the van. 'Iron Hands' Lenny was lying down on the floor with a blanket covering him.

"Remember Sergeant, when I say, 'Luka, when I was in Vietnam we had beautiful starlit nights just like this,' I want you to uncover yourself, put a gun to Luka's head and keep it there! If he makes even one false move, drop him!" The Major and the Sergeant had used codes like this before in Vietnam.

"Yes, Sir." Lenny took his gun out; moments later Luka got in the van, cell phone in hand.

"Did you tell anyone inside you were talking to me?"

"No, why?"

"Just curious that's all. Are you expected back inside? Do you have a friend waiting for you?"

"No, why? Just curious again?"

"I know your boss is behind this campaign to scare my family. I want you to know that my family is too important to me to play this little game. I want you to call Big Eddy and tell him I want to meet right now, outside his house, so we can straighten this whole thing out."

"I don't know what you're talking about, but I'll call him. You say somebody is scaring your family, Detective?" Luka asked with the most innocent face a hit man could muster. He started to dial. Moments later, Luka was chatting with Big Eddy. Bill started the van and drove in the direction of Eddy's house.

"Yeah. I'm sitting here in Detective Lincoln's van right now. The Detective wants to cut some sort of deal with ya. It would appear that someone is bothering his little family and he thinks you might be able to help him put an end to it. He's even talking about dropping the charges against you. You want to talk to him? We're about to drive over and park outside your place. The Detective apparently needs to have his answer quickly." Luka had the phone wedged in between his shoulder and his head. He was listening quietly.

"Let me talk to him," Bill said, still driving.

Luka spoke into the phone, a few seconds later he handed the phone to Bill.

"Eddy, is there anyone there with you?"

"Just me, Detective."

"I want to make this fast. We'll be over in a few minutes."

"I'll be waiting."

Bill wanted to keep Eddy talking. That way he couldn't call anyone. Bill felt safer knowing they were not using his phone. He glanced over at Luka. Luka was watching him carefully.

"Eddie, I think you're behind the recent unpleasant incidents involving my family."

"Do you have any proof of that, Detective?"

"I'm also convinced that you killed Willie Taylor!"

"Any proof, Detective?"

"And, I know you killed Jacko, too!"

"Detective, you're really on a roll here!"

"I'd like for each of us to sign agreements and leave them with a lawyer that we can both trust."

"And what exactly would these agreements say, Detective?"

Bill was making this up as he drove along. Again, all he wanted to do was keep Big Eddy talking. "I'm the detective who wants to solve this case and actually, I'd like nothing better than to see you confess."

"Really now, you must stop drinking on the job, Detective," Eddy chuckled.

"I'll sign an agreement that I won't bring charges against you from the night of Radcliffe's party. You see, you're still facing those charges and I'm still the only witness! These charges are for real Eddy. Besides that, if my family gets hurt, I'll come after you. I'm not Willie Taylor!"

"And you know what, I'm not Willie Taylor either."

"You go to trial in two weeks. The case against you is airtight. You've already got two strikes against you. And frankly, I don't think you'll find a sympathetic jury anywhere. People are tired of drugs and thugs."

The van rolled up in front of Big Eddy's house. Bill put the car in park, leaving the motor running. "We're in front of your house, Eddy."

"Put Luka on the phone."

"Luka, have you been following the conversation?"

"Yeah, but I think the Detective is blowing hot air."

"He does make some interesting points though."

"I agree, Boss. Our Detective is a most intriguing guy." After several moments, Luka handed the phone back to Detective Lincoln.

"Detective, why don't we talk inside my house."

"I would, but I need to drop two books off so my daughter can finish studying for her exam tomorrow. I believe we can finish our business during a leisurely drive over there and back, if that's alright with you?"

"Sure, why not. I'll be out in two minutes. Just let me secure me casa first."

Bill put down the phone and turned to Luka. "Eddy will be out in a few minutes."

"Okay then. Do you mind if I smoke?"

"Go right ahead. By the way Luka, isn't it beautiful out tonight? When I was in Vietnam, we had beautiful starlit nights, just like this….ya know."

Luka was rummaging in his breast pocket for his cigarettes when suddenly he felt the cold familiar touch of precision machined steel against the back of his neck! Luka froze, allowing Bill to slowly reach over and retrieve the gun from Luka's shoulder holster. Bill reached under his seat and pulled out a set of handcuffs. He slapped them on Luka while Lenny held the gun to his head. He then stuck black adhesive tape across Luka's mouth to completely silence him.

"Luka, don't do anything stupid. My associate here will kill you if you do. I need to talk seriously with your boss. I don't have time for any foolish conversation like the one we just had. As soon as he signs the contract it's over. I'll have my assurance. It's that simple, so just sit there and be a good little boy. Do you understand? Nod your head if you do."

Luka nodded. He didn't have a choice. Lenny lowered himself so Big Eddy couldn't see him as he approached the van. He dropped the barrel of the gun in Luka's lap, pointing it menacingly at the 'family jewels'. Bill had pulled out his own gun and was now nuzzling the barrel into Luka's midsection.

Big Eddy came walking out his front door a minute later, heading directly to the van. Bill opened his door and stepped out as soon as Big Eddy was upon them. He opened the back door and then swung the gun around, pointing it directly at the massive Italian. Eddy noticed the silencer.

"Lay down on the ground, Eddy, face forward." Eddy did as he was told.

"Now, place your hands behind your back."

Big Eddy obeyed. Bill handcuffed Eddy, took his gun and then put him in the back seat. Lenny quickly put leg irons on him. Bill got back in and then drove to a deserted spot in the park, the same place where Lenny and Bill had previously disposed of the intruder's body. They dragged both men out as Bill spoke to them.

"I'm going to separate the two of you and then ask you questions. I expect your answers to coincide. If they don't, then I'm not gonna be very happy. But first, we're going to dig a hole to make sure you both understand that I'm not joking."

He handed a shovel to Luka and told him to start digging. Lenny watched Luka dig while Bill took Big Eddy aside.

"Eddy, who killed Willie Taylor?"

Big Eddy looked at him but was silent. Bill pointed the gun at Eddy's kneecap and Eddy spoke reluctantly.

"I had him killed."

"Tell me why."

"I had to send a strong message, ya see. You don't rat out Big Eddy. You know how the game is played, Detective."

"Who put the chicken head in Willie's shower?"

"I know a guy on the force who needs cash every now and then."

"I want a name, Eddy."

"Harry Thompson."

"Why would Harry do it?"

"Harry owes me nearly twenty-five 'thou' in gambling debts. He's an awful gambler."

Bill knew this to be true. Harry worked in the witness protection program. Harry, for some unknown reason, pictured himself as a gambler and a ladies' man. And, although he was neither, you couldn't convince Harry of that.

"Now, who killed Jacko?"

"I did, of course."

"Why?"

"He was asking questions he should not have been asking. That's why. He was given a very clear warning and he chose to ignore it. I can't have people ignoring me. It's very bad for business, Detective."

"Who sent the guy to break into my house?"

"I don't know. I didn't."

Lincoln studied him closely. He didn't know if Big Eddy was telling the truth or not. "What's your relationship with Radcliffe?"

"Rad and I are partners. We work on projects together from time to time. Rad only does large projects. That's because dealing with the small stuff is far too risky for the small amounts of money that would be involved."

"How were you going to stop me from testifying, Eddy? Remember, I'm the only eyewitness against you."

"Rad told me he'd handle it."

"You're facing a third strike and you put this in the hands of Rad?"

"Yeah. He made a convincing argument."

"Tell me what it was."

"It was never about his plan, just about his reputation. He told me in no uncertain terms that he'd handle it. Do you think I'd put my faith in him if I didn't think he could get the job done? I'm facing a third strike here, Detective. Rad told me he had connections. We've been in some tight situations before and Rad has always come through."

"Who actually killed Willie Taylor and Jacko?"

"Luka and his henchman."

Bill looked over his shoulder, taking a quick glance at Luka who was still digging under the watchful eye of Lenny. "Who is Franklin Jr.'s lover?"

"That I don't know."

"Is he gay?"

"I would assume so. I don't know for sure, but that would be my guess."

"You've never asked Rad?"

"Yeah, I asked once, but he just ignored me. No big deal."

"Tell me about Crystal."

"What do you want to hear?"

"What's her claim to fame? Was she seeing the Mayor?"

Big Eddy, still looking directly into Lincoln 's eyes, was trying desperately to read him. He had no idea what Bill was thinking of or what he was capable of. Detective Lincoln was emotionless. Eddy had been surprised by the last question. He wondered how Bill got that information.

"Yeah, that's what I heard. Crystal likes to have a good time and there ain't too many men that I know who can say no to her."

"And so how many times have you been with her?"

"Oh, I've been there once."

"Does Franklin Sr. know about Rad's secret life?"

"You kidding me? I believe Franklin Sr. knows more about what's going on in Oakland than you and me combined."

"What about Rad's mother?"

"I don't know. My guess is no, but I don't know."

"Who threatened Connie Chow's daughter?"

"I did. I had to let people know that this is for real. Willie Taylor was not ever going to testify against me. My reputation wouldn't be worth 'nothin' if that happened."

"Would you have hurt her?"

"No. It was just a scare tactic. Connie Chow couldn't hurt me. She was only his lawyer."

Because it had a ring of truth to it Bill could accept that answer. "Who's threatening my family, Eddy? Who put chicken heads in front of my wife and children's door?" This was the question that he needed answered. He knew the answers to most of the other questions, but not this one.

"Now that, I really don't know. I assume it was Rad, or perhaps the police. Now, if it weren't happening already, I'd be the one doing it. I'm the one who's at greatest risk here. Rad may get a smudge on his record, but I could go away for life! But no, it wasn't me, Detective."

Bill believed Eddy was telling the truth. "Would you harm my family, Eddy?"

Eddy was silent. He didn't like this question or the gun in Bill's hand.

"I asked you a question and I expect an answer."

"I'd hurt anybody in this situation, Detective."

"Thank you, Eddy, I believe you're telling the truth. Who killed Hillary Dillard?"

"I don't know. If I did, that person would be dead right now."

"Who do you think did it?"

"I would assume Dr. Broussard."

"Why?"

"Because of the evidence. After all, they've got his sperm."

Bill thought about Big Eddy's last answer. Again, it rang of truth. "Have you heard anything about him in the streets?"

"No. But that doesn't mean anything. Give me some time and I can find out just about anything for you."

"How long would you need?"

"Give me three days and I'll have a file on him the police would envy." Eddy was now negotiating for his life.

"Eddy, you've been in Oakland for years. Have you ever heard anything regarding Dr. Broussard that has raised your eyebrows?"

"We just don't travel in the same circles, Detective. Rad once told me the guy has had several affairs. If he's capable of lying to his wife, he's capable of lying to anyone."

Bill looked over at Luka and Lenny again. "Don't move, Eddy. I'll be right back." He walked over to where Luka was digging to survey the large hole. Bill turned and saw Eddy still standing in the same spot. Eddy was wearing cuffs and leg irons so he couldn't get far, even if he decided to try.

"Luka, who killed Willie Taylor and Jacko?"

Luka remained silent while looking in the direction of his boss.

"I'm only going to ask one more time. Who killed Willie Taylor and Jacko?"

"I don't know. I wasn't part of that."

Lincoln turned and waved for Big Eddy to come over to the group. Bill gave the key to Luka and told him to unshackle the leg irons on Eddy. Luka did it and handed the key back to Detective Lincoln.

"Eddy admitted to the killings saying that you were the one who actually carried out his orders Luka. Is that true?"

Luka looked at his boss but didn't say anything. Being from the old school, he could feel his time was at hand.

"Sergeant McDerch, would you please send Luka to his maker."

A fraction of a second later, Lenny, who was standing behind Luka, slipped a garrote around the throat of Luka and pulled it tight. Luka was still handcuffed and couldn't fight Lenny off. Just under two minutes later, Lenny loosened his grip and Luka Brahn's inert body lay on the ground before them.

"Please take his handcuffs off, Eddy," Bill said while pointing at Luka and giving the key to Eddy. Eddy hobbled over and removed the handcuffs from the dead man.

"Now please drag Luka's body into that hole."

Bill went to his bag, pulled out several postcards and a contract. He handed them to Eddy along with a pen and a book to write on. Bill instructed Lenny to take Eddy's handcuffs off.

"I haven't decided what I'm going to do with you yet, but first I want you to sign the contract we talked about. Just sign on the dotted line. Don't even bother reading it."

Eddy obediently signed.

"Now, I want you to sign these three postcards and write these words. On the first write, 'I'm having fun, Detective, are you?' On the second write, 'Wish you were here'. And on the third write, 'Don't hold your breath waiting, Detective. Have fun!'"

Detective Lincoln retrieved the postcards and the contract from a noticeably shaken Big Eddy. "You're in a bad position, Eddy. You're facing real prison time and I'm the only one who can testify against you with credibility. And, you admittedly have the capacity to hurt my family."

"I promise, Detective, to leave you and your family alone."

Bill looked hard at the gangster and then went into his pocket and pulled out his cigarettes.

"Would you like a smoke, Eddy?" he asked solemnly.

"Yeah."

"They smoked in almost complete silence as the cigarettes burned to the halfway point. The surrounding area was very quiet as if all the animals were secretly watching the human activities. Lincoln never took his eyes off Big Eddy and the gangster had his eyes riveted on both Lenny and Bill. The gun remained steadfast in Lincoln's hand.

Reflections of his past flashed across Big Eddy's mind. Ironically, he thought, he had been in this situation so many times before but the roles had been reversed. If you had asked him yesterday if the Detective was capable of this type of violence he would've had to think about his answer. However, the dead body of Luka was in close proximity, completely answering the question.

"Even if I believed your promise, which I don't simply because you can't afford to keep it, there's still the death of Willie Taylor and Jacko. Those two may not have been society's best but...and then there's also the threat to Connie. You had your goons scare her by approaching and threatening to hurt her daughter. That just wasn't very nice, Eddy."

Eddy said nothing.

"Goodbye, Eddy."

Lincoln squeezed the trigger, sending a soft lead bullet cruising through the brain of Big Eddy Tevelle.

Chapter 43

Lincoln received an urgent call from Kasolkasky the following afternoon. "Bill, something strange is going on. Luka Brahn's family called the police station this morning looking for him. They're concerned because their father didn't come home last night. They've been calling everywhere but to no avail. His car was found still parked outside his favorite pool hall."

Lincoln, standing in his study, pulled a cigarette from his pocket and lit up.

"Was he at the pool hall last night?"

"Yeah. Apparently he received a phone call and then left almost immediately. It's been reported that he said he'd be right back, but he never returned."

"Who was the phone call from?"

"No one seems to know. Luka didn't disclose that."

"Have they called his boss, you know, Big Eddy?"

"Yeah, but so far, no one is answering at Eddy's house either."

"Hey, maybe they're out of town doing a 'business' deal together."

"If you hear anything let me know."

"Sure Brick, but I gotta warn you, I'm not in the business of playing nursemaid to thugs."

Two hours later Bill got a phone call from New Orleans. It was Officer Butterfield.

"Hello, Detective, I hear you're willing to make a donation to my favorite charity!"

"If you've got some relevant information one of my sponsors will gladly pay the fee."

"Well, I have some information and, by the way, my favorite charity is me!"

He was not at all surprised by Butterfield's revelation. After all, charity begins at home!

"If your information is solid, I'll instruct my sponsor to cut you a bank check. You can forward the money to the charity of your choice. So now, what do you have?"

"I'm calling you from the residence of Elden Robinson. He's been gracious enough to give me what you needed. Unfortunately, he seems to have sustained a few minor cuts and bruises...oh my. I told the man that he needs to watch where he's walking," he laughed. "I'll put Elden on now so that he can give you the good news himself! Also, I thought you might like to call Hattie Black while I'm here. That way you can be sure Elden doesn't call her first to...let's say, unduly influence her."

"Thanks, Butterfield."

"Hello again, Elden. I remember you told me that you didn't know a Hattie Black, but now I find out she's your niece! What gives?!"

"Why did you lie to me about your profession?"

"Elden, let's be very clear here, I'm not here to answer your questions! You're here to answer mine! I want an answer now or do I have to speak to Officer Butterfield again?" Elden knew exactly what that meant.

"Look...I wanted to protect my niece. You've got to understand!"

"Protect her from what, Elden?"

"From you. I don't know you, and here you're asking me questions about my niece who I love dearly."

"Well, now you know I'm a detective, don't you?! So, where is she?"

Elden was hesitant but what else could he do? He turned and glanced at Butterfield who, while looking at him, was rolling his baton across the palm of his hand. "She lives in Miami, Florida. Her address is 2444 Walnut Place, Apartment 3C. Now, please tell me why you need to talk to my niece?"

"That's my business, Elden. But, if it will ease your mind any, it's nothing too big. I just need her to answer a few little questions. She's not in any real trouble. By the way, when did she first move to Florida?"

"She moved there about five years ago. She went to live with her aunt, my sister, who helped find her a job."

"Had she attended college?"

"Yes. She went to New Orleans' Longs Junior College and she also attended seminary school for two semesters."

"Is she married?"

"She was, but she's divorced now."

"Any kids?"

"No."

"What's her current home telephone number?" Elden gave up the number. "Now...who's your voodoo priest, Elden?"

At first, Elden was silent. While reluctant, he seemed much more willing to give information about his family than to discuss his precious voodoo relationships. "Why do you need that information?"

"Elden, I won't tell you again, this is not about you asking me questions. Have you got that?! It's only about you answering mine! Now spill!"

Elden fell quiet again. He glanced over his shoulder again at Butterfield and company standing there glaring at him. Butterfield was still rubbing that fat nightstick and grinning evilly! "Dr. Juwan Gumble."

"He's a doctor?"

"Yes, he has a doctorate in religion."

"Does he know the voodooianne in Oakland, Marie Francois?"

"No, I don't think so."

"Does he know Jezebel Balboa in Los Angeles?"

"Yes. Ms. Balboa used to live here. They know each other well."

"Does Hattie know Dr. Gumble?"

"Yes, for a time she used to live in New Orleans."

"So now, when do I meet him?"

Elden went silent yet again. "I tried to arrange that. Remember? But he got sick."

"Right, I remember. But my question was, 'When do I meet him?'"

"I'll set something up."

"Listen, I want a specific date, Elden. Call me within forty-eight hours with an appointment. By the way, what else does he do for a living?"

"What do you mean what else?"

"What I mean is what type of job does he go to every morning? How does he support himself?"

"I don't know. He's my spiritual leader. That's all I know."

"So, how do you contact him?"

"By phone."

"And what's his number?"

"I can't give that out. It's private...it's, it's confidential."

"What's his number, Elden? Listen, don't make me have Butterfield get that number from you! I'm getting really tired of people trying to stand in my way."

Elden took a deep breath then gave him that number too.

"Now, put Butterfield back on the line."

A few seconds later, Bill heard the officer's voice.

"Butterfield here."

"Thanks. I'm going to call Hattie Black right now. I'll call you right back when I'm finished. I'm also going to call this voodoo priest that Elden follows. He was a bit too tight lipped about giving me his number."

"Go ahead. I'll just sit here and wait for your call. I'm sure Elden doesn't mind."

He dialed Hattie Black's number. It rang twice before being answered.

"Hello?"

"Yes, I'd like to speak with Hattie, please."

"Just a minute. Who's calling please?"

"Bill Lincoln...an associate of Elden Robinson."

"You know Elden? This is Hattie's aunt. She lives with me."

"How are you? I was just on the phone with your brother. He says hello."

"How is my brother?"

"He's fine. He sends his regards."

"I'll get Hattie for you."

He waited for almost two minutes before Hattie picked up the line.

"H-H-Hello, this is Hattie."

"Hello, Hattie, my name is Bill Lincoln. I was just on the phone with your loving Uncle Elden. He gave me your number. Hattie, I'm a retired policeman recruited to work on a very important case. Let me start by saying that you're not in any kind of trouble, but I believe you might just be able to help me catch a murderer."

"Of course. What can I do for you?"

"I'm told you went to college in New Orleans about ten to twelve years ago?"

"Yes, that's right."

"Do you recall meeting a Dr. Nathan Broussard while there?"

There was silence for a moment before she responded, "Who?"

"Dr. Nathan Broussard?"

"No. I've never heard of him. Sorry."

"Are you sure, Hattie?"

"Yes."

"Hattie, Dr. Broussard has already told us about his affair with you. We also have collaborating evidence that you shared a hotel room with him. You haven't done anything wrong, not yet anyway. We're just trying to confirm his story. In case you didn't know, he's currently under investigation for murder." There was silence again. Bill waited it out.

"What does this have to do with me?"

"Nothing. We just need to check out his story. Right now one of you is definitely lying. Again, he's got evidence that says you were there with him. So, who's lying here Ms. Black?"

"Okay, I slept with him; but just one time! I swear! I was young. I didn't know what I was doing! It happened just once. Please, you can't tell anyone!"

Once again, he could feel the anguish over the line. No one could have ever dreamed that their encounters with Dr. Broussard a decade earlier would ever resurface to haunt them years later. "Why did you lie to me, Hattie?"

"Because I was ashamed of what I did. I had only just met him you know."

"But why did you lie to me? I still don't understand that."

"At first I really forgot his name. It's been a long time. I'd forgotten all about it."

"So, you have one-time affairs often?"

"No, of course not!"

"Then why would you say you forgot his name?"

"I'm so sorry. I'm just so embarrassed."

"That's all I needed, Hattie. I shouldn't be bothering you any more. Thanks."

Dr. Broussard appeared to be telling the truth once again. Of course this both helped him and hurt him. Why was he having affairs? Bill called the voodoo priest.

"Hello?"

"I'd like to speak with Dr. Juwan Gumble."

"Who's calling?"

"Detective Bill Lincoln from the Oakland Police Department."

"One moment please, let me see if he's in."

A minute later the same person was back on the line. "I'm sorry, but Dr. Gumble is teaching a class right now. Could you please leave your name and number? He'll call you back."

"Dr. Gumble is not sick?"

"Sick?! Why, he's as sturdy as a horse. Who told you he was sick?"

"I was told he canceled a 'service' recently due to personal illness."

"No, the ceremony took place. I'm not sure why someone would tell you that."

"Maybe I misunderstood. If you don't mind my asking, what does Dr. Gumble do for a living?"

"Certainly not. Dr. Gumble administers to the needy on a full-time basis."

"But, I was under the impression that he's a full-time voodoo priest?"

"Yes, that's true. For those who don't know, that's part of what a voodoo priest does. He's very popular with his followers. Detective, just why are you calling?"

"I'm working on a case and would like his advice. You've heard of the Oakland Hills voodoo murders?"

"Oh yes. In fact the accused man is from our area."

"Yes, Dr. Broussard was raised there. I wanted to talk to Dr. Gumble about the case because of his extensive experience with voodoo. By the way, where did he get his doctorate?"

"Right here at State University."

"Do you happen to know when he received it?"

"Oh yes. It was twenty years ago. I know because we had an informal celebration just last month, complete with cake and candles."

"Thanks. I'm very much looking forward to talking with him about voodoo."

"As you should. Dr. Gumble is very knowledgeable and I'm certain he'll be more than willing to help you. I'll gladly give him your information. Goodbye, Detective Lincoln."

Bill dialed Elden Robinson's number to talk with Officer Butterfield. Butterfield could now vacate Elden Robinson's home. Later that evening Detective Lincoln drove over to Betty's house to see his daughters. He was still concerned about the threats against his family. And since he actually believed Big Eddy's story, that only served notice that somebody else was still out there!

The following day an official search began for Luka Brahn and 'Big Eddy' Tevelle. Twenty-four hours had passed and still there had been no sign of either man. Radcliffe Dillard had become quite nervous because, for the first time, he was dealing with a truly unknown factor. Could he be next? He had tried to reach Big Eddy, but even his sources couldn't help.

Radcliffe's trial was scheduled to start in less than two weeks. His lawyers had already managed to separate his case from Big Eddy's. Originally, Eddy's trial was to start a few days earlier than Rad's. Right now, however, Eddy Tevelle's case would have to be delayed if they couldn't locate him. Still, Radcliffe's trial would begin as scheduled and this had Radcliffe very concerned, very concerned indeed!

Detective Lincoln received a phone call from Susan around 6:30 P.M. that evening. "Bill, I want to apologize to you for what happened the other day."

"And what day are we talking about?"

"When you wanted to talk and I said I was busy working on business things. But in truth, Radcliffe was at my house. I didn't have the nerve to tell you that, not until Radcliffe told me that he had been outside talking with you. He finally got around to asking me the other day if I had any dirt on you. I realize now that that was the only reason he was interested in me. I want to apologize. I've been so very foolish."

"Yeah, okay. Apology accepted."

"So, when do you think we can get together and talk?"

"Uh, look I'll call you. Right now, I'm too busy. My family is being threatened and there's just a whole lot going on."

"I'm sorry. Please let me know if I can do anything."

"I need to go, I'll call you when I'm able to. Goodbye, Susan."

"Goodbye, Bill."

Moving decisively into action, Bill called Captain Bell at his home.

"To what do I owe this unexpected pleasure, Detective?"

"I need your help again."

"Well then, just what do you need?"

"I need one of your men to go to your State University and dig up everything they can find on Dr. Juwan Gumble. I'm told he received his doctorate in religion there exactly twenty years ago. And here's something you might find interesting. It seems the man now practices voodoo full-time."

"Huh, is that so?"

"You have an interesting community, Captain Bell."

"No more interesting than yours, Detective Lincoln."

"That's probably true. Thanks in advance for your help. Good evening."

The following morning the indictment was served to Detective William Monroe Lincoln for the death of and civil rights violation of one Mr. Harvey Gooding. All together there were some twelve charges. Bill read the first three then called the firm of Berkland Law. He asked to speak to either of the two partners, Bennie Pews or Matt Silverstein. Bennie took his call.

"Hello, Detective. And what can I do for you today?"

"I've just been indicted for the wrongful death of a man named Harvey Gooding. I need an attorney. I want the original 'Zebra Boys'."

The term brought back a lot of memories for Pews. When they started their law firm back in the sixties, people had dubbed them the 'Zebra Boys'. This was because the animal was both black and white, reflecting the racial makeup of the two founding partners. Back then the two flamboyant lawyers constantly challenged the system. Bill had Bennie's full attention. Somebody was rattling Detective Lincoln's cage and he was not going to sit idly by and take it!

"Bill, why don't you come down here tomorrow so we can talk?"

"What time?"

"Let's see... how does 1 P.M. sound?"

"I'll be there."

He hung up the phone. A few minutes later, he received yet another call. This time the caller was Captain Bell.

"Hello, Detective."

"You have something for me already?!"

"Yes, in fact, two things. An hour ago, Mrs. Broussard, Dr. Broussard's mother, passed away. I'm sure you know that she had been ill for some time?"

"Yes. I'm sorry to hear that."

"The second bit of news I've got is an interesting development concerning our Dr. Juwan Gumble."

"Great! What did you find out?"

"Well, he did receive his doctorate exactly twenty years ago like you said. But the most noteworthy thing I found was a picture of him from his yearbook."

"How's that, Captain?"

"Dr. Juwan Gumble looks as white as I do!"

"What?!"

"You heard me right. You're looking for a white voodoo priest!"

Chapter 44

"Bill, tell me about this indictment," Bennie Pews said. "The whole thing is a pack of lies. I've been indicted because the police department and the Mayor want me to drop the charges against Radcliffe Dillard. They've got these bogus witnesses to come forward and now they're pressuring me directly."

"Why would they want to do that?"

"Because the Mayor believes that he can only stay in office by the grace of one Franklin Dillard Sr."

"Bill, what about these charges?"

"The hell with the charges! Listen to me, I've got tapes of the Mayor and police officials instructing me to go after Radcliffe."

"You've got them on tape?!" Silverstein and Pews looked at one another. Feelings from the days gone by were resurging once again; it felt good! In the world of high-profile politics, facts were irrelevant. High profile inuendo and conversations caught on tapes were much more effective in shaping public opinion. Both lawyers knew that if the police took years to look into a case, but never uncovered anything, it was highly unlikely they'd have anything now. They now clearly saw Bill's perspective. The 'Zebra Boys' knew how to put on a road show, and their eyes gleamed at the thought.

"I've got a few samples in my briefcase. Here are my notes telling of the day, the circumstances, and also who's talking on the tapes."

He played several tapes for the two attorneys and over the next hour had them completely transfixed. Bill had dynamite. This type of publicity would get national exposure!

"Anyone who takes my case has to understand one thing. This is 'Pro Bono'! The publicity will be their payment. Now, if you gentlemen don't want to handle it my way, then I'll just find another law firm."

Bennie and Matt looked at each other; they both knew they'd take the case. The potential upside was obviously too great to even consider declining such an offer.

"I'm going home, folks; you've got twenty-four hours to make your decision."

Detective Lincoln packed up his materials, leaving the two men sitting there. He decided to stop by Buckston's office to find out if there'd been any new developments. All three lawyers were there. They informed Bill that Dr. Broussard had been allowed to travel out of state to attend the funeral of his mother.

"Do you think he'll come back?" Bill asked.

"Well, if he doesn't, then he's probably the killer."

"Why did the police let him go?"

"He posted the additional bond."

"I didn't know Broussard had that type of money."

"He doesn't. Franklin Dillard Sr. put up the cash."

"Hey, I've got another interesting little tidbit," Bill announced.

The three lawyers were about to disband but definitely remained seated.

"The voodoo priest that was supposed to preside over the ceremony I was to attend is white!"

"Gee, I'd say that's pretty unusual! I never would've expected that one! Who is he?!"

Bill then gave them all the information that he had on Dr. Juwan Gumble.

"So, does it mean anything?" Buckston asked.

"I have no idea if it has any relevance yet."

"Look, keep at it, Bill. Something has to give. I'm sure."

With that last exchange the group broke up. Bill found an empty office from which to call Jezebel Balboa. He was curious what she knew about the good Dr. Gumble.

"Hello, Ms. Balboa."

"Hello, Detective.

"I was wondering, do you still know any voodoo priests in New Orleans?"

"Actually, it's been so long I can't remember any of them anymore."

"Oh, that's right. You have been away for some time now."

"Yes. It's amazing how quickly time passes."

He was presenting her with the opportunity to lie. "Somebody in the police clerk's office just handed me a short list of voodoo priests currently practicing in New Orleans. I have no idea if any of these names are accurate or not, but at least, I thought I'd run them by you."

"That's fine, Detective. Go right ahead."

He made up the first few names.

"Harold Chapman?"

"No. Sorry."

"Wardell Brown?"

"No. Never heard the name before."

"Othello Wadsworth?"

"No. No recollection."

"Juwan Gumble."

There was a slight hesitation from Ms. Balboa. "No. I don't think so. Sorry."

"Well, I thought I'd at least give it a try. Thanks, Ms. Balboa."

"No problem, call me anytime, Detective."

"By the way, there's a note here indicating that one of these people is white. I think it might be the first guy on the list, Harold Chapman. I must confess to you I never thought a voodoo priest could ever be white. Is that even possible?"

"Detective, you're beginning to sound like a racist. Voodoo is open to all."

"What?...me, a racist? That's highly unlikely. But Ms. Balboa, are you implying that you know white people who are voodoo priests and priestesses? I can envision whites attending the ceremonies, but I never imagined there were any who were actually priests!"

"You must not be so close-minded, Detective."

"Now, Ms. Balboa, in your long involvement with voodoo, are you telling me that you've actually met a white voodoo priest?"

"I've heard of them."

"You have? Where?"

"In my general talks with people in the field."

"Oh, I see. Well, I've never in my wildest imaginings considered white voodoo priests before. So, it was very interesting for me to read that note. I suspect that if you ever met one, you'd remember. I just think the whole concept is fascinating."

"Well, Detective, maybe one day you'll meet one."

He was taping the whole conversation. "Well, thank you, Ms. Balboa. I guess I can toss this list now."

"Goodbye, Detective."

Bill was curious. Why were so many people lying to him? He wanted to talk to other people who he was certain had lied to him and Jacque Vestable's name came to mind.

Jacque worked at Skyline University and was from the Haitian culture. He had told the police that he didn't know where voodoo ceremonies were held in Oakland, which, of course, was a bald-faced lie. Bill called the school and was told that Jacque and his co-workers were playing softball over on Backer Field at the annual academic staff versus employees game. He decided to drive over to ask Jacque a few questions.

When he was halfway there he pulled over and stopped to use a pay phone. He pulled a handkerchief from his pocket to disguise his voice. He dialed Radcliffe Dillard's number. Rad picked up the line on the second ring. Usually, Rad would not be in, but ever since the disappearance of Big Eddy he'd been spending much more time at home, his doors locked and an armed security guard posted outside.

"Hello?"

Rad heard the shrill voice of someone who sounded half-mad!

"Hee hee hee...Hee hee hee.....I got your Big Eddie, Raddie-poo,... For now... I'll bide my time, but soon... I'm coming for you!"...Hee hee

hee...Hee hee hee!!!" Click, the phone line went dead. Rad stared at the phone. An uneasy sensation came over him. Detective Lincoln put more coins in the telephone and called Monique at work. After two minutes of being transferred to several different people, he heard Monique's sweet voice.

"Monique, this is, Bill."

"Hello, how are you?"

"Fine. I don't have much time before I have to meet somebody, but I need an answer from you."

"On what?"

"Let's say, on a scale from one to ten, what would you say is the possibility of your brother being gay?"

"What are you asking me?"

"I'm asking for your opinion."

"Bill, why are you asking this question?!"

"Monique, I'd really like an answer. Can you venture a guess?"

"Bill, you know I can't answer a question like that."

"Well, gotta go. I can't be late. Goodbye."

Bill was rattling some cages. As he started to walk to his car his pager went off. It was police headquarters.

"Hello, Brick, Bill here."

"Just wanted you to know a bit of information we just got."

"What's up?"

"We checked the DMV car registration of the Broussard family. It seems Dr. Broussard has three cars registered."

"Damn." Bill felt a sinking sensation. "Where's the third car?"

"We don't know yet. Remember, Broussard was allowed to leave the state!"

"Well, check it out. Thanks, Brick."

Suddenly, he felt relieved again, realizing how a small piece of information could easily lead one astray in this bizarre case. Bill had momentarily forgotten that Big Eddy had committed the second and third voodoo murders, but Kasolkasky didn't know that. He continued driving to the softball field. As he approached he encountered such a large crowd of people that he almost turned around.

Bill took a seat in the stands and watched for Jacque. After about ten minutes, Bill saw Jacque stroll up to the plate. They were playing slow-pitch softball. Jacque batted southpaw stance, waiting patiently for a few pitches. On the third pitch he swung, hitting the ball deep into center field. The outfielder ran all the way back to the fence. He caught the ball on the warning track, retiring the side. Jacque appeared to be quite the softball batter.

Jacque's team now took the field. Jacque ran out to second base and the players started throwing the ball back and forth. Bill noticed the somewhat unorthodox movement of Jacque and finally realized it was because again he was left-handed. Most second basemen were right-handed. But, because Jacque was a southpaw, he had to take an extra step to throw the ball to first base. Bill looked at his watch and left. He would contact Jacque later.

There was a message on his car phone from the owner of a downtown bar.

"Is Joe there?"

"Yeah, Joe here, who's this?"

"Bill Lincoln. You just left me a message?"

"Yeah, that's right. Why don't you slide by sometime soon so we can conversate." This was one of the places where Jacko used to hang out.

"Sure, Joe. What's a good time?"

"Whatever. I'm here from twelve-to-twelve everyday."

"You know what, I'll be right over."

He didn't know what the guy wanted to 'conversate' about, but Joe knew Jacko, which was reason enough for him to 'slide' over there right now! Bill, after accelerating his car, saw the flashing lights of a patrol car following him. He pulled over holding onto his Mayor's office identification card. He rolled down his window when he saw the officer in his rear-view mirror finally approaching his car some three minutes later. Bill was pretty sure that the officer had radioed in his license plates by now too.

"May I see some identification, sir?"

Bill handed him the card.

"May I see your driver's license please?"

When the officer ignored the card Detective Lincoln knew it was not your ordinary stop. He pretended to search for his license in his sports jacket's inside pocket while secretly turning his small tape recorder on. He then retreived his driver's license for the officer. The officer was wearing wrap-around reflective shades. Bill couldn't see his eyes.

"Is there a problem, officer?"

The policeman didn't answer. He took Bill's license and returned to his patrol car. Bill observed the officer talking on his radio. He took the tape recorder out of his pocket, putting it between the seat and the console, out of view. Only a couple of minutes had passed before another police car pulled up behind the first. Lincoln smelled trouble!

The two officers talked, then the first one got back on his radio. After a few more minutes, both officers approached Bill's car and ordered him to "Step out of the vehicle, sir!" He did exactly as they asked.

"Is this your car, Mr. Lincoln?"

"Yes. And it's Detective Lincoln. I'm a retired police officer."

"Mr. Lincoln, what's in that bag partially hidden under your seat?"

"Whatever you put there, officer. You're the only one who'd know that."

"Hey, Fred, what do you think it is?"

"Oh, I'd say it's about two-point-five grams of cocaine."

"How'd you figure that one, officer? You're standing over twelve feet away."

"Well, it's my many years of experience in law enforcement. I've reached the point where I can just look at a guy and know if he's dirty. And you're dirty, Detective Lincoln!"

Bill remained still so as not to antagonize the two policemen. He engaged them in conversation for the benefit of his 'little friend.'

"Who wants me off the street, officer?"

"You need to get your priorities straight, Lincoln. You need to start listening to good advice when you hear it."

"I get a lot of advice, officer. Just whose advice are we talking about?"

"Oh, you know who."

Detective Lincoln was arrested and booked at the city jail on drug possession charges. He called Lenny McDerch at his first opportunity and had Lenny call Berkland Law, immediately, to tell them what happened. He also ordered Lenny to drive himself to the hospital. Bill could not leave 'Iron Hands' alone, unsupervised. A few hours later Bill met with Bennie Pews, directing him to contact Tommie Cheng, the reporter. Bill and his lawyer talked for nearly an hour.

The following morning the headlines in the newspaper read, **'VOODOO MURDER INVESTIGATOR BUSTED FOR DRUGS'**. The story also mentioned that Detective Lincoln, who himself had recently brought drug charges against Radcliffe Dillard, was currently being indicted on murder charges! This was a nasty article, very unfavorable toward Detective Lincoln , to say the least.

Bill had spent the night in jail awaiting his arraignment. It was the next afternoon when Kasolkasky stopped by, informing Detective Lincoln that Dr. Broussard had missed his return flight to Oakland, and so far, nobody had been able to contact him. The news completely surprised Bill. The newspapers were already set to print their headlines concerning Dr. Broussard's mysterious disappearance.

"Listen, you've got at least two bad cops on the force."

"I've had their files pulled. I'm already looking into their backgrounds."

"I left a tape recorder that I had switched on squeezed between my seat and the console. It should still be there unless somebody discovered it."

"Okay, I'll look for it."

"Do you believe any of these charges being brought against me, Brick?"

Brick didn't answer. He got up, gesturing to the jailer to let him out. Forty-five minutes later, Bill instructed Bennie Pews to go to his house to gather the collection of audio tapes.

During visiting hours Susan spent a little more than an hour with Bill. She was very concerned, both about his situation and about the powerful people who he appeared to be up against. Bill hoped not to have to use the tapes. He'd try first to use the law. But, if it got too rough and it became necessary, he'd start playing hardball! He knew, once he brought out the tapes, this game would get downright ugly.

He spent another day in jail waiting to be arraigned. While frustrating, it also came as no surprise. Dr. Broussard was still missing; the media was having a field day with that. There were literally thousands of places for Broussard to hide in New Orleans, that is if he was still there. Bill had another visitor, Joe, the bartender Bill had talked to just before his untimely arrest.

"Gee, I was wondering what happened to you the other night, then I heard you'd been arrested."

"Just what did you want to see me about, Joe?"

"I understand you're looking for Jacko's lady friend?"

"Yes. Do you know where she is?"

"No. But, I know how to get in touch with her."

"Great! I'd like to talk to her."

"I understand there's a reward?"

"Yes, you'll get it if you can put me in contact with her."

"So, when do you want to see her?"

Bill wished he wasn't in jail. And he knew his release was not about to happen until, at best, the following day. The police would delay it as long as they legally could.

"As soon as possible."

"Done. I'll see if she'll agree to come tomorrow."

"Well, as you can see, I'm not going anywhere."

The following day Bill expected to be released. Legally he would have to be either charged or released. If he was charged he'd simply post bail. In the morning after breakfast, Dr. Broussard's wife visited him. She felt compelled to tell Detective Lincoln that her husband was innocent and that her husband had decided that he could no longer trust the authorities.

"How could his sperm end up in the body of a dead woman?" Then she pointed out that Bill himself was now in jail. "I've spoken with you on several occasions, Detective Lincoln, and I know those policemen are not telling the truth!"

Bill felt it was highly unlikely that Dr. Broussard was the murderer, but even he could not be one hundred percent sure. A couple of hours later, Joe escorted Jacko's girlfriend, Carmen-Maria, to Bill's jail cell. Bill vaguely remembered her. He only had a few questions for her.

"Do you have any idea who might have killed Jacko?"

"No. I was waiting for him at my mother's house. My baby never showed up," she quivered.

"Did Jacko ever tell you who he thought Franklin's lover was?"

"Well, I once overheard him mention the name Chad in connection with Mr. Franklin. But, that's all I know. I really don't want to know anything else." She looked down at the floor fighting back the tears.

"If you ever want to know who killed your boyfriend, call me."

She gazed tearfully into his eyes, part of her wanting to know, but now she was resigned to the fact that her Jacko was dead. A strong inner feeling told her that the less she knew the better off she'd be.

After Joe and Carmen-Maria left, nothing else eventful happened until Bill was finally brought before the court. While they were discussing the charges before the judge, a strange thing happened. The District Attorney stepped forward and asked the judge to withhold setting bail because new evidence of more criminal activity had been uncovered against William Monroe Lincoln. The judge asked to know what and, with that, the District Attorney handed her some papers. A sidebar was held. A lengthy discussion followed and finally Detective Lincoln was charged with drug possession and denied bail due to other pending charges. Bill was returned to his cell, his attorneys informing him that potential evidence might exist linking him to the mysterious disappearance of one Gerald Kincaid, the man who Lenny 'Iron Hands' McDerch had neutralized in Bill's house.

Bill sat staring at the cold gray walls, walls that perfectly reflected his mood. This latest twist had thrown him for a loop. He knew he could beat the other charges, but this newest unexpected development, totally beyond his control, had unnerved him. And, he was worried! At the first opportunity he called Tommie Cheng, leaving a message inviting Tommie to come back. Bill was about to start playing hardball!

The police issued an 'All-Points-Bulletin' to pick up Dr. Nathan Broussard. The case now had gained wide public interest so naturally the New Orleans' police were anxious to make the collar. The Broussard family was not assisting the authorities in any way. It was strongly believed that the family had helped their kin throughout this entire episode and, if so, would probably continue to do so.

Detective Lincoln made Tommie Cheng an offer that was impossible to resist. He wanted Tommie to set up an anonymous newspaper column and print information from the tapes. Tommie readily agreed and anxiously waited for Bill's permission to start. However, Bill would talk with the Mayor first to demand an end to his legal problems.

Bill directed Bennie Pews to invite the Mayor to his cell. Detective Lincoln wanted to make sure it was an invitation the Mayor wouldn't be likely to refuse. Bill had retrieved the home number of Chadwick Beamont Wellington Jr., the high-society son of the old banking money Wellington family. The son was often seen at the ritziest functions and always accompanied by the daughter of some equally well-known family. Chad was considered one of the most eligible bachelors in town. But now the man was also in his late forties and the likelihood of him getting married seemed more and more remote. Bill dialed the number, disguising his voice in an effort to sound like Franklin, Jr.

"Hello, Wellington residence, who may I ask is calling?"

"Franklin Jr."

"Is Mr. Wellington expecting your call, sir?"

"No."

"Just a moment, sir."

Half a minute passed before the phone was again picked up.

"Frank?"

"I think someone's on to us!"

"Why do you say that?"

"Crystal recently received an anonymous call with some very disturbing inuendos."

"Like what? Tell me!"

"Not now. I'll discuss that with you later. I've got to go for now."

Bill hung up. He was only allowed fifteen minutes each day for telephone privileges and he needed to make a few more calls. His next call was to the Oakland Police Department where he left a message for Detective Clarence Jones. His final call was to Hank

Buckston, Dr. Broussard's attorney. Buckston updated him on the on-going efforts of the authorities in New Orleans. It appeared they had dramatically escalated their efforts to track Dr. Broussard down.

At six o'clock that evening Bennie Pews and Matt Silverstein arrived. They, Detective Lincoln and the other two men, would be escorted to the Mayor's office around 6:30 P.M. The lawyers brought one of the tapes; all of the tapes had been copied and were stored safely away in several locations throughout the city. Bill was still hoping not to be forced to play his hand, but he'd do whatever was needed to get those trumped-up charges dropped. The security car was parked underneath the City Hall building. Bill was handcuffed, as was standard procedure.

The Mayor was sitting smugly behind his desk. The city's chief bureaucrat looked up, then stood and invited everyone else to sit down. Nobody shook hands. Nobody exchanged pleasantries. The Mayor spoke first. "Gentlemen, you called this meeting today to share with me information of a sensitive nature. Well, I'm listening."

Bennie Pews spoke next. "Mayor, we have reason to believe that our client has been falsely incarcerated. As such, we believe that all charges brought against our client should be dismissed summarily. Furthermore, let it be known that we have in our possession compelling evidence that several high-level government officials instructed our client to pursue certain high-profile individuals, which I might add, was both professionally and successfully accomplished. We also have reason to believe that these very same high-level officials are now actively participating in spreading rumor and innuendo against Detective Lincoln. And that this malicious and wrongful activity is the only reason for our client's wrongful incarceration. Thus, it is our obligation as his attorneys to represent our client to the best of our considerable ability, by using any and all means at our disposal."

"And just what does that mean, Mr. Pews?"

"It means that we intend to raise the public's awareness on how business is routinely done here in our fair city. A vicious crime occurred. Even you called several press conferences to keep citizens updated. And in this same spirit when injustice occurs in high places, it is the people who must be kept apprised. We intend to do just that."

"And what method would you choose to accomplish this?"

"Naturally, we'll use the media to let the people know how one of their own is being exploited. We have several audio tapes in our possession that will raise many serious questions. We trust you will have the necessary answers required to address those 'concerns'."

The Mayor's ears perked right up when he heard the word 'tapes'. Besides, he didn't like the self assured cockiness of these lawyers. They had too much confidence and that smacked of trouble. Detective Lincoln was not the type to roll over for anyone, which is one reason why the Mayor had employed him in the first place.

"What's on these tapes, gentlemen?"

"Mayor, you can read about them just like everyone else will in tomorrow's newspapers. Our client would not want to show any favoritism."

This was an election year. Everyone in the room was fully cognizant of that fact.

"I need to know more about what I'm dealing with here."

"As I told you, taped conversations involving people in high places. And I can assure you that the major newspapers are very interested! Our client only wants a few simple things...first and foremost is his freedom. We believe you can help us, Mayor. You command great influence and respect. People will listen to you."

"Gentlemen, I'm only one man and besides, the law is the law. I don't influence judges or grand juries."

"Now that you mention it, we also believe you may have great influence with certain people, people responsible for bringing evidence to grand juries. As of now this meeting is over. Our client has made arrangements to send the first set of tapes to the newspapers tomorrow. Expect the first article to appear the following day, that is, if there is no appreciable change in our client's legal status. Good day, Mayor."

The lawyers and Detective Lincoln left. Bill had instructed them to make the meeting short, to be the ones to end the meeting. This took the feeling of control out of the Mayor's hands. Bill was immediately escorted back to his jail cell.

The following afternoon Detective Lincoln learned the drug charges against him had been dropped, a partial victory! The two police officers, who had arrested him, had been suspended based on the evidence found on the tape Bill had left in his car. Bill called Crystal Dillard next. He wanted everyone aware that as long as he was in jail, no one was safe. No one!

"Hello, Crystal, this is Bill Lincoln."

"Good afternoon, Bill. Where are you?"

"Why, I'm still in jail, of course. Certain charges have been dropped, but a few still remain."

"I can't believe it. You must have made some serious enemies."

"It appears so. But enough about me, I called you because I just heard a rumor that you may be interested in."

"What's that?"

"It's about 'Chad'."

There was a brief moment of quiet before Crystal quickly responded, "Chad who?"

"That was my reaction too! Listen, I've got to go. They don't give you much time to talk on the phone here and I've got to make several more calls. Sorry. I'll get back with you soon. Promise." Click!

He placed a call to Ms. Jezebel Balboa next. A female friend of Ms. Balboa answered the phone. She was friendly enough, saying that Jezebel had just stepped outside to get something from her car. She asked who was calling. "Jacque Vestable" he said. Bill had spoken with Jacque twice and felt he could mimic Jacque's voice well enough over the phone for a short conversation. A few minutes later the lady said her friend had just walked into the room. Bill could hear her say, "A Mr. Vestable is calling."

"Hello, Jacque?"

"Yeah look, I'm scared. The police are watching me."

"Just stay calm. Don't panic."

"Have you heard anything?"

"No. Just be patient."

"I think I need to take a vacation."

"Look, just stay put! You need to stay right where you are until you're told otherwise. You hear?"

"Yeah. I hear."

He now knew that Jezebel Balboa and Jacque Vestable were acquaintances. He had a feeling that if he asked either whether they knew one another they'd lie. The only person who seemed to be telling the truth was Dr. Broussard, but the evidence still pointed squarely at him. This was now compounded because he had failed to return to Oakland.

At six o'clock that evening, Detective Lincoln received a most unlikely visitor, Radcliffe Dillard. Rad appeared wearing an expensive suit, Italian shoes and silk tie with quite a unique pattern. When Rad stepped in, suddenly Bill recognized the enormity of his situation. Only police officials and people with real clout were allowed to visit prisoners in their cells! All others were required to wait in the visitor's waiting room for the prisoner to be brought to them.

"Have a seat, Rad. Pick your spot. To what do I owe this unexpected pleasure?"

Rad sat on the only stool in the cell taking a good look at his surroundings. His distaste for the environment was etched on his face.

"Detective, you seem adversely affected by the force of gravity. I'm not sure how much further down you can go," he smiled broadly.

Bill ignored his comments. "Why are you here, Rad?"

"Why, I came to settle our bet, of course."

"I'll accept a check."

"I expect mine in cash. I've never liked checks."

"Your trial is only a few days away."

"That's right, Detective. That's why I'm here. What's it going to take for you to drop those charges?"

Bill stared at him, wondering what made this guy tick. "Rad, why are you so different from your other brother and sisters? Franklin Jr. is an attorney who's running for political office. Your sister is a design engineer, personable and with the potential to be a talented artist. What happened to you?"

Rad was curious about Bill's latter statement. "What type of artist is my sister, Detective?"

"Haven't you seen her paintings? She has real talent."

"That's what I like about you, Detective, you're so easily duped! You imagine your woman only has eyes for you and you imagine my sister to be a talented painter. Perhaps then there's a chance I could also sell you the 'Brooklyn Bridge'?"

"I'll grant you that Susan was easily swayed by your opulent lifestyle. Money, even illegal money, will turn heads."

"So, that's the type of women you attract, Detective?"

Bill let that one go. Rad scored a half-point there. "But your sister has real potential. I've seen some of her work."

"Detective, I only happened to have grown up with my sister so, I don't possess the 'in-depth' knowledge that you have," Rad said sarcastically. "I assure you that my sister can draw straight lines given a ruler. But hey, I'm only her brother, so what would I know?"

Detective Lincoln felt another sinking sensation. He wanted to challenge Rad, but on what grounds? Was he going to say that Rad didn't know what he was talking about? Bill was starting to feel like he'd been played, again.

"Detective, the reason for my visit today is to inform you that there exists a video tape of you and an unnamed accomplice, carrying what appears to be a dead body out of your house. Interestingly enough, the date happens to coincide with the disappearance of a certain Mr. Gerald Kincaid. Now, let's act like two intelligent people. If you bring charges against me I'll be forced to give this tape to the authorities. If you drop the charges then this tape will disappear. We can both go on with our lives. Oh, by the way, you should know that I rather fancy those new big headed 'C' notes."

He looked hard at Rad because if what Rad said was true, Bill would be paying him that thousand dollars. Bill knew he could beat the charges that the D.A. had tried to bring against him and the drug charges had already been dropped. But this latest charge, with a potential tape existing, was a real threat to him. He examined Rad's story closely. Rad didn't say that he possessed the tape, only that one existed. Someone was feeding Rad this information and Bill didn't like it one bit.

"I want to see this tape first."

"Sorry, not going to happen. You'll have to take my word for it, chump, I mean, Detective."

Bill stared at him. "I'm still in jail, Rad. How does accepting your deal change that?"

"Detective, you're in jail for other alleged crimes. That's your problem. All I'm allowing you to do is not have to deal with this potentially major problem."

"I need time to think about it."

"Detective, you've got until tomorrow afternoon. I'm going to meet a dinner date now. Let me know by 3 P.M. tomorrow. I'll call you since that will be easier. If you say no, I'll have the tape delivered to the D.A. before 5 P.M. My charge is only a misdemeanor, but you'll be dealing with a felony. Think about it, Detective. And by the way, I'll accept a check from you. I don't normally do that, but I trust you. Goodbye, Detective."

Radcliffe signaled for the jailer to let him out. Bill remained seated, contemplating his next move. He didn't see any way out. Rad might be bluffing, but did he want to take that chance? The thing that bothered Bill was that Rad had said that he and another person were caught on tape. That other person could only be 'Lenny'. That knowledge made Rad's threat believable. But, who made the tape? Could the police be setting him up? Bill remembered the two policemen who came to his house asking about a Gerald Kincaid. But why would the police give this information to Rad? Detective Lincoln was once again, bewildered.

The core of the difficulty is that there is hardly a question of any real difficulty before the Court that does not entail more than one so-called principle. Anybody can decide a question if only a single principle is in controversy.

Felix Frankfurter:
Address; N.Y. Times
Magazine, November 28, 1954

Chapter 45

Detective Lincoln woke up weary in his cell after a restless night's sleep. Last night he felt certain he wouldn't press charges against Rad, but the thought of compromising his principles kept gnawing at his soul. He knew intuitively that he was about to commit political and social suicide. But, as things stood, Rad would not walk. He was going to force Rad's hand to produce the tape.

Detectives Clarence Jones and Dick White were his first visitors of the day. He convinced them to tape-interview Jacque Vestable. Bill was determined to pin Jacque down about his knowing both Dr. Gumble and Ms. Balboa. Bill also asked about Dr. Broussard.

Jones then spoke, "Two of Dr. Broussard's relatives have already been beaten up, or should I say, interviewed by the police. The New Orleans police department don't like the idea of a murderer hiding out in their city."

After the two detectives took off, Bill continued to try to figure out this most perplexing puzzle. You could usually tell who the good guys were, but now everyone was changing places from black hat to white, all the time. Bill mulled over the details until 3:15 P.M. when he received a call from Radcliffe. Dillard.

"Well, Detective, what's it going to be? I feel like I'm dialing for dollars!"

"I'll see you in court, Rad, unless I see that tape first. If I don't see that tape, you're going to stand trial."

There was silence. This was not the answer Rad was expecting.

"Detective Lincoln, you're making a tremendous mistake. I assumed you were more intelligent than this. Might I ask why?"

"Sure. But, you could never understand, Rad. It's about principles. I don't think you know the meaning of the word."

"Do you understand the meaning of power, Detective?!" Rad said with bold bravado.

"I know it can be abused. I hope the Dillard name doesn't get too sullied in the trial."

"You're making the worst mistake of your miserable life, Detective!"

"Show me the tape, Rad."

"We'll see. Oh by the way, your lady friend kisses quite well!" Click...the line went dead.

Lincoln hoped there was no tape, but if there was, he hoped to see it before it was passed on to the authorities. Rad's trial was only three days away now, which meant something was going to happen soon. Tomorrow would be the first day for a series of newspaper articles based on the tape collection of Detective Lincoln. He had until 5:00 P.M. today to say 'yes' or 'no' to publishing the articles. Lincoln was waiting for the Mayor to call or make contact with his lawyers before he authorized the publication.

Detective White stopped by in the evening bringing the taped conversation the detectives had earlier with Jacque Vestable. They listened to it together and as Bill suspected, Jacque denied knowing Jezebel Balboa or Dr. Gumble.

"What does this mean?" White asked.

"I don't know, but it's another piece of the puzzle."

"I'll put the tape in your file at headquarters. See you around." Detective White left.

A half hour later Bill received a visit from Monique Dillard.

Monique looked around the cell, amazed at its small size. They talked casually for twenty minutes. Suddenly she grabbed Bill's hand, holding it with both of hers.

"Let it go, Bill. Whatever is keeping you in here, let it go. You're not thinking straight now."

Monique talked in a very hypnotic voice like a psychiatrist. She was completely focused so all he had to do was allow her to guide him. He felt almost totally disarmed.

"Everything's going to be alright. Just stop being so stubborn. You can learn to bend, Bill, without breaking. It's no sin to bend a little."

He took his other hand, placing it on top of Monique's. They were soft and warm…he felt very comfortable with her so close.

"Bill, you could walk out of here right now. All you have to do is say the word."

"They have charges against me. It's not that simple."

"Bill, you're fighting for no reason. The drug charges have already been dropped. The charges against my brother are so minor compared to those you would face. It just isn't worth it."

"It does seem rather trivial."

"Look at your cell. You could be home. I could be nestled in your arms. You've got to think this through, Bill."

He listened while holding her hands. If he were Catholic he'd confess his sins, right then and there.

"I feel so tired. Everything is becoming such a struggle."

"That's because you're fighting everyone. Let it go, Bill."

"You make it seem so simple."

He looked into her large beautiful hazel eyes. Her eyes kept sending hope to his obvious despair.

"Bill, remember that warehouse many years ago? You killed that man, didn't you?"

He looked away not saying anything.

"And you killed that man who broke into your house."

He continued not to look at her. She squeezed his hand, then stopped and softly rubbed it. Her touch was so gentle. He was a man in trouble; she was his siren.

"You could walk out of here, you have the power. You could make this all go away. Just do it, Bill, don't play this game. You have much too much to lose."

He allowed her words to soak through to his clouded brain. Did he want to fight and win a battle, only to lose the war?

He rehearsed his many thoughts. When he was a boy, when he didn't know what to do, his gut would always lead him in the direction. He felt this same feeling right now.

"Monique, would you do a portrait of my two daughters?" he said softly while continuing to caress her hand. There was a long moment of silence. He stared at her hands.

"I've stopped painting, Bill."

He kept focusing on her hands, not looking up.

"Bill, you can walk out of here. Think about that."

Monique stood up to leave. He looked up, but remained seated. Monique put her right hand on the back of his neck, then gave him a deep, lingering kiss. "I'll be home waiting for you, Detective."

Monique left Bill staring at the clock. It was 4:45 P.M. He had only fifteen minutes to decide whether or not to call the newspaper to stop the story. He was certain his gut would make the right decision. He continued to sit there listening to his body while watching the minutes slip away. The clock reached 5:00 P.M.; his decision made. Tomorrow's headlines would cause quite a stir. He also knew the pressure on him would intensify.

Where force is necessary, there it must be applied boldly, decisively and completely.

Leon Trotsky:
What Next? 1932

Chapter 46

Detective Lincoln woke up to a commotion among the prison personnel! Turning over on his side, he saw five guards huddled in the hallway reading one paper.

"Hey, Lincoln, have you seen today's paper?!" a prison guard yelled down the hallway.

Bill ignored him, rolling back over. He knew what was on those tapes and the Mayor, the Chief and Kasolkasky, would have to deal with it!

"Hey, Lincoln, are you up?"

"No!" he yelled back down the hallway.

The guard approached his cell, paper in hand. "Have you read the paper this morning, Lincoln?"

"I know what's on those tapes."

"What tapes?"

"Can't you read, officer, or didn't you graduate from public high school?"

The guard glanced at him again but ignored the comment. "Looks like you're one of the voodoo murder suspects."

The officer showed him the front page. Bill couldn't believe his eyes! In bold letters the front page read, 'AUTHORITIES SUSPECT VOODOO DETECTIVE OF FOUL PLAY IN 3RD MURDER.'

"The article is all about you, Detective, and why you're a suspect. What tapes are you talking about?"

Bill took the paper from the security guard. The story read that Jacko's neighbor had heard someone knocking next door. He got up, looked outside, and saw two men with a dog standing in front of Jacko's door. There were two sets of bloody footprints leaving the room where the body was found. Bill had never mentioned to anyone who was with him that evening other than the dog. One of the shoe prints matched Bill's own shoe size close enough for the police to have developed suspicions. He was the first one on the scene and it was he who had reported the murder to the police.

At first glance the headline was incredulous, but as Bill continued reading, he could see how the authorities might suspect him. He had no alibi and Lenny couldn't remember anything from one day to the next! On the same front page was Bill's article, but nobody had even bothered to read it yet. He read his own article and it seemed, even to him, no one would care what he had to say about city officials if everyone suspected him of being a murderer? With these new suspicions about Detective Lincoln, his own article made him look manipulative and untrustworthy. Bill's tapes were not worth much now.

At noon he received a visit from Kasolkasky. Brick wanted to go over Bill's testimony in the upcoming trial of Radcliffe Dillard. Bill remained the sole witness against Rad. The two other people who were going to testify that they did drugs with Rad had not only reneged, but had moved out of state!

"Let me show you this, Bill."

A guard rolled a VCR unit in. Bill saw Radcliffe talking to a reporter, "When Detective Lincoln came into the room, he saw me standing over Eddy Tevelle with drugs in my hand. As luck would have it he came in at the wrong time. I had just walked in myself and saw what was taking place. I took the drugs out of Mr. Tevelle's hands and told him sternly that this type of behavior would not be tolerated in my house. Mr. Tevelle was brought up there by a lady selling drugs who had come to my party uninvited."

The tape went on, like watching a movie about someone else. Bill was in that room, but if you believed Radcliffe, Bill had accidentally mixed things up. Bill heard Radcliffe answer another question.

"If you check the results of my blood test from that night you'll see that I was drug free."

Bill wondered how much money it had cost to 'lose' Radcliffe's chemical analysis and substitute another.

"Well, Bill, what is your testimony?"

"I guess it's what Rad said. I guess I was wrong."

Kasolkasky and Bill just looked at each other before Brick stood and left. Detective Lincoln's confidence had been shaken to the core. He looked and felt like an empty shell. He called the newspaper to stop the publication of any more articles from his tapes. His lawyers agreed.

--

After three weeks Detective Lincoln was still strategizing on how to get out of jail. He was frustrated. He knew how the police system worked, but even so, he was still annoyed. He had to deal with the confinement. Rad's trial had been postponed a few weeks due to Big Eddy's disappearance.

One Monday afternoon Bill received a visit from Father John Sebastian. He was the last person on earth Detective Lincoln expected. Bill was brought to the visitor's station. He picked up his phone, as did Father John.

"Hello, Detective."

"Father."

"I've come to seek your guidance."

Perplexed, Bill responded, "You've come to a strange place for guidance."

"Yes, I have. I tried to talk with the authorities in New Orleans, but they seem more inclined to hunt Dr. Broussard down than to listen to me."

"I don't see how I can help you, Father...not from in here anyway."

Father John glanced at their surroundings, acknowledging the statement. He then refocused on Bill. "You've collected many fragments of the whole. This information might provide the 'glue' you need to put it all together."

"Before we go any further I'd like for you to answer one question," Bill interrupted.

"Which one is that?"

"Do you have any connection with Jenny McCray's baby? The birth certificate names the father as John S. McCray."

The priest locked eyes with Bill.

"Why do you need to know? I fail to see the relevance."

"It's one of the pieces of that puzzle, a 'fragment of the whole'."

The priest remained silent as he continued to ponder the question. After nearly twenty seconds, he broke his silence.

"Yes."

Bill sat motionless, staring at the priest.

"Detective, you don't think too highly of me right now, but please allow me to continue. I said I'm associated with, but I assure you, I'm not Jacob's biological father. I learned who the father was from my predecessor, Father Ryan. Jenny was pregnant when we first met. Father Ryan asked if I would lend my first and middle name to the birth certificate in the event the hospital needed the father's name. Father Ryan filled me in and I agreed. If you like, I'll submit to a paternity test."

Bill sat back. Once again, his initial thoughts had been wrong. Getting a handle on some of the evidence in this case had been like grabbing for a cloud.

"Who is Jacob's father?"

"That would be Dr. Broussard's father."

Now, he could now see why the priests did what they did. If Jenny's father had found out who had 'knocked-up' his baby girl, someone would've died...especially since both men were so volatile.

"Father Ryan kept everything quiet. If he hadn't, there surely would have been deadly consequences. He made Jenny swear before God that she wouldn't tell anyone that Hendrik Broussard had raped her. Hendrik was a brutal man with evil ways. He lied, cheated and whored around. To put it bluntly, he was Edwina's nightmare. In spite of all this, or perhaps because of it, Edwina remained a good Catholic. After she married him and discovered what he was really like, she only stayed with him because of her vows. But it wore her down. She protected her children the best way she could and had the priests and nuns fight for Nathan, the brightest of all her children. Hendrik hated the priests, but also feared them, that is, when he wasn't drunk.

"Hendrik had lived a very hard life and in the process destroyed most anything that he touched. When he discovered that he was dying…he changed. He started hanging around the church and began following me around. It was strange, at first, and as he became sicker he started confessing his sins. Surprisingly, it's these confessions that I now disclose.

"Hendrik simply did not want his wife to be embarrassed by him anymore. And while she was alive, he made me promise that I would never say anything about his many indiscretions. I've kept my vow all these years."

"Edwina knew of his evil ways and she also swore me to secrecy. It was also she who said that if I ever needed to say anything to help her family, that I would be free to do so. I tried talking to the New Orleans Police Department, but they appeared to be disinterested. Of course I'm not sure what they could do anyway."

"What are you talking about, Father?"

"I'm talking about yet another of the despicable deeds of one Hendrik Broussard."

"What exactly are you talking about, Father?"

"Hendrik, as you can well imagine, consorted with many women. He has several bastard children that Edwina would never acknowledge. She especially swore me to secrecy on that. She never wanted her own children to know they had several half-brothers and sisters. She hated her husband for desecrating the sanctity of their marriage. She was a good Catholic girl after all."

Lincoln listened mesmerized. He knew the priest was trying to tell him something he very much needed to hear.

"Hendrik did anything and everything that you could imagine. Why, he told me he had even slept with a voodoo woman! He said he had had a child with this voodoo woman and that the woman refused to allow him to see it. Since he was drunk most of the time, he didn't much care. But I remembered his story and thought that maybe you'd want to hear it. In addition, I've done some research over the years and I've uncovered that child's identity."

"Would it be Gumble, Father?"

"Why, yes! I'm impressed!" The priest looked at Detective Lincoln in amazement. Bill, indeed, had done his homework.

"Well...it's a small world, Father. Have you ever met Dr. Gumble?"

"No. But I have made several inquiries over the years. He appears to be a particularly vengeful individual. I thought you should have that information too!"

Father John and Lincoln talked for another hour before the priest finally left to go back home. Bill had sworn the holy man to secrecy. And if Bill was to help Dr. Broussard he knew he must first find a way to help himself. In order to get out of jail and to make sure he was safe from any additional charges, Bill needed the priest to remain absolutely quiet...for now anyway.

Late that same morning he called the newspaper requesting a meeting that afternoon with Tommie Cheng. Next, Bill contacted his lawyers. He wanted assurance that no longer could anyone use that 'dead body in a warehouse' case, as a weapon to control him. There had been far too many behind-the-scene manipulators pulling his strings! Making officials accountable in the public eye was about the only guarantee there was in Oakland politics.

Later that afternoon, he was escorted back to the visitor's area to meet Tommie Cheng.

"Bill... it's been awhile." Tommie's smile was infectious.

"Yes it has, Tommie. Thanks for coming."

"What can I do for you?"

"I want you to resume printing those series of articles that we suspended."

Tommie's eyes opened wide for a split-second. No one in their right mind would continue to print those articles unless they knew them to be absolutely true and could prove it.

"I can do it. You know this is front-page stuff," Tommie announced, wearing an ear-to-ear grin. "You also know that you're asking for more trouble!"

Bill returned Tommie's smile but didn't feel the need to respond... that was all too obvious.

"When will you run the next article?"

"Tomorrow."

Tommie and Bill shook hands before the reporter left.

—

Bill's article stirred a veritable storm of telephone conversations throughout the city the following day. The law firm of Berkland Law was representing Bill. They didn't want any publicity since their client was under investigation for the third voodoo murder. Now their client had instructed them to go public with the fight once again!

Detective Lincoln had told his attorneys that he had a good idea who the Dillard girl's murderer might be. Bill wanted his attorneys to be aggressive! Confident that Bill was innocent, they would be so.

Bill's main problem was his lack of funds. Because Dr. Broussard had skipped bail, the court was in no mood to have that happen again...not in any other high-profile case, let alone the same case. His bail was set at three million dollars! Bill didn't have that kind of money but he knew one person who did. He now had to devise a plan to make that person cough up the money!

During the same time, at City Hall, the Mayor met with Chief Ness and Brick Kasolkasky. They were obviously irritated over the article published so prominently in that day's newspaper.

"Why is he releasing these articles again?" the Mayor asked.

"He's frustrated. Incarceration may be getting to him."

There was a moment of silence while everyone contemplated the Chief's answer.

"Lincoln's a seasoned professional. I don't think he'd crack after only a few weeks in jail. Look, the man is a combat seasoned Vietnam veteran," the Mayor responded.

"It's revenge!" Kasolkasky offered. "He's dropped so low that he figures he can't go any lower!"

"Bill's always had a weakness for the truth," the Mayor reflected.

"If that's the case then what's next?" the Chief asked. "How do we get him to stop?"

"We don't appear to have anything else to threaten him with. If he's not afraid of the charges he's facing now, I'm not sure what we can do," the Mayor contemplated.

"How will this whole thing play out with the public?" the Chief asked.

The Mayor he had been thinking about just this question for some time and not liking the answer. He couldn't understand Bill's motivation. But then again, he knew if he were in jail for four weeks, he'd be mad as hell too...madder than a possum thrown into a coon's nest!

"Gentlemen, I think we need to find out all we can about our dear friend," the Mayor said. "I have a feeling these articles are going to continue, so we need whatever's knowable at our disposal in order to abort them. Do you understand?"

Both men nodded 'yes' before leaving the room.

--

Two days later the next article appeared, again on the front page. A press conference was held. The original 'Zebra Boys' were back and the rhetoric was flying hot and heavy. They gave an opening speech that lasted a full ten minutes before accepting questions.

"Mr. Pews, why is your client still in jail?"

"Good question. Our client has been assessed an excessive bail figure due to the outrageous and intolerable discrimination practiced by the judicial machine in this city."

"I don't understand, Mr. Pews. The judge is a person of color, an Asian-American. How can you cry discrimination?!"

Bennie Pews, looking at the reporter, paused for a few moments before answering the question. "Sir, I said nothing about racial discrimination. I was referring to occupational discrimination. Our client is a retired police officer, and we all know that when the authorities believe that one of their own has gone bad that they need to make an extreme example of them."

The reporters frantically recorded his remarks. The racial angle wasn't going to play well, not in this case, but an alternative strategy had been found.

"Mr. Pews, Sir, it doesn't appear that your client's background is unblemished. Presently, he's being investigated for the death of a man in a warehouse several years ago, a recent missing person case, and he may even be implicated in the latest voodoo murder! How do you explain this?!"

Matt Silverstein, quickly responded. "These are very weak allegations indeed, Sir. In the first case, the police have no evidence of any wrong doing by our client. Detective Lincoln routinely answered a police call for help. The man who died was a convicted felon who passed while committing a crime. In the second case, all we know is that a person is missing. I repeat, that's all we know. There's a rumor about a videotape but has anyone seen it? No. And the third instance of alleged criminal behavior can easily be explained away. When you hear the explanation you will understand why our client has chosen his current course of action."

"What else is on those audiotapes? Do you have proof that this administration is corrupt?" a Hispanic reporter queried.

Matt Silverstein remained at the mike in response. "If not corrupt, then at least unfairly manipulative. They've become lazy and they simply don't want to do the work or be accountable for their actions. Our client was hired because the police had not made any substantial inroads in the Hillary Dillard murder investigation. It was our client who got things rolling! He also busted a prominent individual for drug possession. And, since that incident, many strange things have happened to him. One such strange occurrence was the false arrest of our client on drug possession charges! As it turns out the two officers involved planted those drugs in an effort to discredit our client.

385

It should also be noted that those same officers have since been dismissed from the force. Now, what does that suggest to you?"

The press conference continued for another fifteen minutes before the attorneys ended it. Pews and Silverstein had raised many questions, which would ultimately require answers from city officials.

Bill watched the press conference from the lock-up's communal television set. After the press conference ended, Bill called Monique's number and left a message. He requested a visit from her that very night. Bill also called the police department to talk with Dick White. He asked Detective White to find out when Jacque Vestable's next softball game would be played and further requested that he videotape the game. White agreed to Bill's requests.

Tommie Cheng waited in the visitor's area for Bill wanting to know which tape Detective Lincoln wanted released next. Bill suggested the one that had captured the transaction giving him the green light to arrested Radcliffe Dillard. Tommie knew this was going to be big!

––

That evening, Monique arrived promptly at his cell. Once more he was reminded of the Dillard's clout. Monique squeezed his hand while sitting down next to him. It had been awhile since her last visit. Bill still remembered the conversation vividly. She had encouraged him to just roll over and play dead.

"Bill, I know you're putting those articles in the paper. I've read the last two."

"And here I thought those articles were anonymous! I read them, too. Quite interesting stuff."

Monique wasn't sure what game he was playing. In her mind, there was no doubt that Bill was behind the articles.

"Are you the author?"

"I'll plead the fifth. I'd rather discuss other more relevant things. The information in the articles is what's relevant."

Bill was being elusive now when Monique wanted some answers. Of course, when he wanted answers, she had acted evasively.

"Okay then, why did you call me, Bill?"

He looked at her while crossing his legs. He knew he had her full attention, not to mention a lot of other people who were reading the articles.

"Well, I want two things from you." Bill waited for her to say something before going on.

"And what are they?"

"The first request is for you to paint a portrait of me. And the second is for you to raise the money to get me out of jail."

Monique was unable to immediately respond. Bill had caught her unprepared. "I told you before that I've stopped painting."

"Yes, I remember."

"And considering the articles in the newspapers, I think you're asking the wrong person to help you. Some of those stories directly and adversely affect my family."

"Yes...I know."

They both sat there looking at each other. Monique found the whole conversation disturbing and stood to leave. She wasn't sure if she should've come. Now she almost wished that she hadn't.

"I have to go now. I don't think I'll be able to help you, Bill. Good luck." Monique motioned the guard to unlock the door. Bill remained seated and watched her. She turned to face him one more time. The guard closed the door and walked a few steps down the hall to wait for her. "I'm sorry." She turned and started walking away.

"Monique."

She stopped briefly, but didn't say anything. He looked at her sternly, then stood and walked to the end of his cell. He put both hands up, grabbing the bars and leaning forward. "For your information," he said softly, "I believe I know who killed your sister."

She hurried back. "Who?" Her eyes were wide as silver dollars. She was now standing only a few inches away. "Bill, who killed Hillary?!" she asked again in an impassioned voice.

He stood there for a moment, not moving. He continued to look at her for several silent seconds then waved for the guard to come back. "Sir, this visitor is leaving," he said calmly. "And I'm not seeing anymore visitors this evening. Goodbye, Monique. Remember...I want two things."

He turned around and laid down on his bed while Monique continued staring pleadingly at him. The guard stood waiting to escort her out, but she was not ready to go...not yet...not now!

Chapter 47

Tommie's next article was plastered all over the front page of the newspaper! Telephone lines were jumping off the hooks throughout the city! The 'mystery' author portrayed Detective Bill Lincoln as being setup by high-ranking city officials. Members of the media wanted to interview the Mayor, the police chief and other involved personnel. If Lincoln was wrongfully accused in this case, what was the likelihood he was being falsely accused in the warehouse murder case?!

Several squadrons of reporters were camped out on the sidewalk at both City Hall and police headquarters. Lined up with them were dozens of political activists as well as representatives from the offices of Berkland Law, each with their bullhorns and their signs. The crowd didn't have a protest rally permit, but the police were not about to arrest anyone either. They had already gathered too much momentum; it would only fuel the flames. The Mayor stayed holed up in his office in a desperate effort to avoid the media.

Bill received an urgent phone call from Monique later that morning. "Bill, I really need to know who killed my sister!"

"Monique, I have a theory. But, it's not conclusive."

"I want to hear it."

"Nobody is gonna hear anything until I'm out of jail and I'm free of these allegations."

"When did you develop this theory?"

"Look, I'm not saying anything, not until I'm out." Bill listened to her silence as intensely as he had her spoken word.

"Bill, I'm very serious. I hope you're not toying with me."

"Are you serious! I'm the guy who's been in jail for weeks on trumped-up charges and behind-the-scenes manipulations that I believe had your family's blessings. I'm the one who's been toyed with here!" he said raising his voice an octave with contrived emotional anguish.

"I haven't done anything to you, Bill."

"You 'need' to be in your studio painting that portrait for me."

"I've stopped painting I told you!"

"And I've stopped being a detective. I suggest you put your faith in the police. Let them tell you who murdered your sister." Silence… He knew Monique was quickly processing information.

"Just how sure are you?"

"I'm tired of talking. I've asked you for two things, my portrait and my bail! Goodbye, Monique!" Click! He hung up, not giving her a chance to respond. He was tightening the screws!

Chief Ness stopped by the jail to see Detective Lincoln early that afternoon. The Chief was visiting another prisoner trying to get evidence and decided if there were time, he'd visit Lincoln.

"How's it going, Bill?"

"Well, as you can plainly see, I'm having a splendid time, Chief. Why, things couldn't get much better. Why would I ever want to go home when I can live like this?" Bill responded sarcastically, lifting both arms wide like a preacher welcoming his congregation.

The Chief, caught off-guard, was not sure what to say. "What will it take to get this thing straightened out, Bill?"

"Get me out of here! Now!"

"There are charges."

"Drop the charges!"

"It's not as easy as that."

"Oh, yes it is! Radcliffe Dillard's lab results …'misplaced'! That just goes to show ya how easily evidence can disappear. And I know it's nobody but you behind the D.A., dragging up all those bogus witnesses, in a case so old that nobody can remember jack about it! Sure, the police have no witnesses for years! And now, suddenly, witnesses are coming out of the woodwork like roaches! Oh, and I allegedly killed some 'missing person'. So, who do you suppose tipped off the police? And where's the mysterious videotape? Has anyone seen it? And, let's not forget, I'm supposed to have killed my own informant too. And oh, by the way, this after I talked with Monique Dillard beforehand. Can you imagine a killer who would actually tell someone that he's got a late-night appointment with someone he plans to kill? Come on, Chief...get real!"

The Chief decided to let Bill blow off some steam by not responding immediately. Detective Lincoln was obviously hot.

"But now, Bill, you've got to know that these newspaper articles are not helping your situation any."

"Oh, is that right? They brought you up here didn't they? They damn sure seem to have energized the media! I believe a lot of people are interested in the way the law is conducted in this city. You know what, I think I'm getting a raw deal. What do you think, Chief?"

"Look, Lincoln, what can we do to put a stop to these articles?"

"Chief, get me the hell out of here!"

"We've already had one high-profile suspect leave the state. That's why your bail was set so high."

"Well...you had the wrong man, Ron. Dr. Broussard is innocent!"

The Chief watched Lincoln closely. He could hear the commitment in Bill's voice. It wasn't so much what Bill said, but how he said it. "Why do you say that?"

"Because I have good reason to believe that I know who the real murderer is!"

"Who?"

Bill picked up his cigarettes...he needed to calm down!

"Before I share my theory with anyone, I expect to be out of this place. And I want every conceivable charge against me dropped, forever. You got that? I'm not going through any of this crap again!"

"Is Dr. Broussard involved?"

"Listen, just get me out of here," Bill said once again then sat on his bed. "I've already told you you've got the wrong man!" Bill stared him down.

The Chief waited a few moments, then left Bill's cell. Now, he was even more concerned! He had the news media going ballistic trying to get answers, and he was being told by a very reliable source that Dr. Broussard was not their man. He and his police department were not in an enviable position. An eerie feeling crept over him. He called the Mayor's office to make an appointment.

One-hour later, Detective Lincoln was visited by Franklin Dillard Jr., who was brought directly to Bill's cell.

"May I come in?" Franklin asked. Lincoln was sitting on his bed.

"Of course. And were you just out for a leisurely stroll?"

"I spoke with my sister. She told me you have a theory about who killed Hillie. So, is that true?"

"Why, yes...it is."

"I assume then it's not Dr. Broussard."

"You can assume all you want. I'm not talking to anyone else until I'm out of this place and every one of the bogus charges brought against me is dropped!"

"All I'm asking is whether or not you believe Dr. Broussard is responsible. There are over six billion people on earth. All you'd be doing is eliminating one from that pool."

Bill knew he was in control now. All the 'high-brows' were showing up on his doorstep!

"You know what...it appears that everybody around here has a hearing problem! I must be in the wrong business. Maybe I should have been an ear doctor!"

Franklin Jr. couldn't fault Bill for the stance he was taking. Still, he did see some opportunity in the situation. He was sure Detective Lincoln thought someone else had murdered his sister. The fact that Bill had been wrongfully incarcerated for so long could even work politically for Franklin Jr. He could take some hard-hitting shots at the Mayor and his administration for jailing the one person who could prove the police department had fingered the wrong person as the murder suspect!

"My sister says you asked her to raise the bail money. If she does that will you share your theory?"

"I've requested your sister do two things. In addition, least I forget, I also expect all charges against me be dismissed…forever. You getting all this?!"

"Bill, I'd like to help you and I'd also like for you to be part of my election campaign. Will you not consider that?"

"First things first. I want out of jail, now! Matter of fact, just so you know, after you leave here I plan to call your opponent to ask him if he'd be interested in getting me out. The only thing I'm willing to talk about right now with anybody is getting out of here! Do you understand me?"

Franklin was making no progress. Bill was unreceptive, had no interest in politics, was pissed and in an excellent position to make demands.

"How do we know that you're for real?"

"My word is my bond. But, as I told your sister, you can always put your faith in the police department to find your sister's murderer. Hey Franklin, here's one for you. Why did you say those mean-spirited things about the Mayor at your house during your speech?"

Franklin wondered why he had asked that question. He wasn't about to give him an honest answer.

"I told the truth. I think that's what the people expect in their leaders."

"Well, I think you had a different motive, Franklin."

"And what would that be?"

"When I get out, I just might tell you. Right now, everybody needs to be working on my behalf. Anything else would amount to an irrelevant side issue. Remember this, if I die in here I doubt if you'll ever know who killed your sister."

Franklin thought about that revelation and, unfortunately, had to agree with it. But, he did have other concerns. "What about my brother, Radcliffe? How will he be affected?"

"Listen, first I want every charge against me dropped, period. As far as your brother is concerned, he's guilty of drug possession. Now, I expect my word to be taken seriously. How can you believe my theory if you don't believe me when I say that your brother was using? You can't have one without the other."

"Suppose we don't help you?"

"No problem. You're not the only game in town. Who knows, I might ask some other wealthy family to help me, like the Wellingtons or the Scarsdales. They're both pretty charitable."

Franklin flashed the 'if looks could kill' look at Detective Lincoln when he heard the Wellington name. He now understood how dangerous Bill could be. He had a newfound appreciation for the detective's intelligence gathering ability. Franklin knew, now more than ever, that he definitely had to hear Bill's theory.

"Do you know the Wellingtons or the Scarsdales?" Franklin asked.

"Not very well. I've run into 'Chad' and his father from time to time," he sighed, matter-of-factly. "I'm sure some affluent person might be interested in my plight."

Franklin felt played! Very few people knew of his friendship with Chad, and out of the blue, Bill had tossed his name out there. Was this a coincidence?!

"I'll be in contact with you, Bill. I have to go now."

"Goodbye, 'Frank'! You hang in there now!"

Franklin nodded his head and left. Bill's parting shot still stung, even as he walked away.

During Bill's next phone session, he called Detectives White and Jones and asked them to contact the Miami-Dade, Florida Police Department. He wanted to begin the process of getting information on Hattie Black. He'd do this in an effort to pressure her into cooperating with the police. Hattie had had an affair with Dr. Broussard, but initially lied to Bill about it. Now since their superiors had instructed them to do anything within reason that Detective Lincoln asked, the detectives again agreed to his request.

Bill's first visitor the following morning was Monique Dillard. Bill stood when he saw her and then sat back down on his bed after she entered his cell. Monique put her briefcase down and sat on the bed next to him.

"You didn't bring your paint brushes?"

"Bill, if I raise the money, what do I get specifically? I need to know. We need to be very clear with each other."

"I've asked you for two things. I haven't said what I'll do yet. By the way, the next major thing I'll need is for my name to be cleared.

All the bogus charges against me have to disappear completely. That responsibility is in the police's and your father's arena. Everybody has their part."

"How did my father get into this?"

He glanced at her then turned away. He was getting tired of playing games. Of course there was the possibility that Monique hadn't figured it out yet. But according to Bill's analysis, that simply was impossible.

"Monique, you had two things to do. Which ones have you completed?"

"I need to know what I get for raising the money."

"You get the satisfaction of knowing that an innocent man is free."

"That's not good enough."

"Well, that means I'll be forced to call your brother's political opponent and the Wellingtons. I have a list of potential funding sources. My lawyers will be announcing the start of a public fund as well. Quite a few people have taken an interest in my situation. The local paper has already pledged fifty thousand to the 'get me the hell out of jail' fund. They just happen to think I have an interesting story to tell."

Monique carefully considered his threats. If Franklin Jr.'s political opponent supported Bill financially, and Bill found her sister's murderer, that would not bode well for her brother's political future. She didn't know why Bill mentioned the Wellingtons, but she sensed her brother's concerns there too.

"What will happen to my brother Rad?"

"I don't know, nor do I care to know."

She desperately wanted to hear his theory, but he was playing rough. She couldn't blame him any either.

"Monique, I need to start making my phone calls so I'll have to ask you to leave...now."

Bill knew she would come up with something. She didn't want him to start calling around the city.

"I can get the money, Bill."

"Great! Now, when are you going to start painting my portrait?"

395

"Bill, you can't be serious."

"If you can't do both, then I must start my calling. It's all up to you, Monique."

"You're going to make me say it aren't you?"

"Make you say what, Monique?"

Monique turned her face away from him, breathing deeply. She wanted to dislike Bill, but she couldn't. She disliked herself at this point for her deceptions.

"I don't paint," she whispered.

"So, why did you concoct that story in the first place?"

"I thought it might give you extra incentive in finding the murderer of my sister."

He heard the hollowness of her words and he continued. "So, it was your idea?"

"Bill, I admitted I don't paint. You made me say it. I'd like for it to end there. I can get the money. Besides, my father would like to talk to you. After all, he'll be the ultimate source of your bail money."

"Tell the Mayor, the police chief and your father, for that matter, that I want all the charges against me dropped...immediately! And I want a public statement made to that effect. I want it made perfectly clear that every one of the accusations was false and that I'm totally exonerated. I also want that old warehouse case closed permanently."

"You must know I don't have any influence over the Mayor or the Chief."

"Monique, guards escort you to my cell. I have to meet most everyone else in the visitor's area. Somehow I believe you carry some influence."

Monique listened closely, then waited a few minutes before speaking.

"I'll see what I can do."

"Have them work with my lawyers."

"Who are your attorneys?"

"Why, the 'Zebra Boys', of course."

Monique got up and left.

Later, when Bill was allowed telephone privileges, he called Franklin Jr.'s political opponent and the Wellington family for funds. Both were interested in helping him.

Chapter 48

Detectives Clarence Jones and Dick White flew into Miami-Dade to interview Hattie Black the next day. The Oakland detectives interviewed her for nearly two hours at police headquarters.

Detective Lincoln's lawyers had announced the establishment of a fund to obtain bail financing. The first telephone call Bill received after that announcement was from Monique.

"Bill, I thought I told you I'd get the money! What is this news about still establishing a fund?"

"I'm still in jail facing bogus charges...that's all I know. I'm talking with anyone who can get the job done!"

"Those charges just can't disappear overnight."

"Sure they can. Why not? This is Oakland."

"Bill, I'm doing the best I can!"

"Hey, that's great. So am I. I'll talk to you later."

His first call was to the Mayor's office. He was relatively sure that if Jim Efferton were there, he'd take the call.

"Mayor's office."

"Linda, this is Bill Lincoln. Is the Mayor in?"

"He's in a meeting, but let me see if he can be interrupted."

A few moments later Lincoln heard that distinguished voice.

"Hello, Bill."

"Good morning, Mayor."

"To what do I owe this call?"

"I just wanted you to know that I heard what the next article in the paper will be."

He waited for the Mayor's response, knowing the Mayor was very interested, but not wanting to appear so.

"I'm not sure what to say, Bill."

"Well, if you're interested, tell me so and I'll tell you what it is. If not, I'll hang up and stop bothering you."

Bill put it right in the Mayor's face. Hardball was fun when your 'stuff' was working. Lincoln was throwing one hundred plus mile an hour screwballs and all he saw after his release was the fine gray dust coming off the catcher's mitt….Strrrike!

"I'm interested, Bill," the Mayor said, very dignified.

"I thought so. Listen, I was told by an anonymous source that the next article would be about the discovery of the bodies of four drug dealers that were slain over a year ago. I understand there is a quote by you regarding the importance of that case compared to the Hillary Dillard case. That's what I was told."

"I don't suppose this article could be stopped from being printed?"

"Maybe, but you'll have to act fast! That's only my opinion. I heard that if you get in touch with Berkland Law with the right information, they would have the authority to stop the presses. Oh, yeah, for your information, that article will be printed the day after tomorrow. Goodbye, Mayor." Click!

He had wanted to hang up on the Mayor ever since he'd been placed in this situation. There was now immense pressure on everyone.

Late that afternoon, Bill received a visit from Matt Silverstein informing him that he should soon be out of jail. The attorney had been having conversations with some very high-level people.

Matt said, "The Mayor wants you to cancel that next article."

"The answer is no! Let them do what they're supposed to do first. I don't need any more time sitting in this cell."

"I'll relay that message. Personally, I think you're making the right decision."

The next day, Bill Lincoln was released from jail with all charges dropped. Detective Lincoln's attorneys called a press conference. The Mayor and the Chief of Police were on the podium along with

Bill's lawyers answering questions. Reporters jockeyed for position as a flood of hands waved for attention.

"Why was Detective Lincoln released on all charges, Chief Ness?"

"The evidence showed that all the accusations turned out to be false."

"Didn't you know this before you arrested him?"

"No, certainly not. We followed procedures. We went through all of them, but needed time to determine what was legitimate. The charges were of such a nature that we had to arrest him. As you know, gentlemen, murder is a serious crime."

"Why did you suspect him in the third voodoo murder?"

"Detective Lincoln was first at the crime scene and there were two sets of bloody footprints coming out of the room. Bill originally told us he was there alone with his dog. A neighbor told police there were two men trying to gain entry. He described the automobile; it was similar to Detective Lincoln's car. He also said there was a dog. Those are the reasons that Lincoln became a suspect."

"Who was the other man, Chief?"

"Detective Lincoln has finally told us. It was a man who used to be a soldier in Detective Lincoln's Vietnam platoon. That man is mentally disabled and Detective Lincoln was trying to protect him from the media. We've checked the hospital's records, which showed the man was staying with Detective Lincoln during that time for a few days. The doctors have indicated that spending time with Detective Lincoln is a good thing for him. Everything checks out."

Another reporter, Tommie Cheng, stood up and asked a question that Detective Lincoln had given him.

"Would anyone care to comment on the previous case regarding Detective Lincoln in that warehouse situation?"

Bennie Pews stepped forward to answer that question. "Detective Lincoln has been completely exonerated of those charges. The alleged witnesses proved totally unreliable. As a result, the police department has signed an agreement with Detective Lincoln affirming that the case is closed permanently! This is how confident the department now feels about Detective Lincoln's innocence in this matter."

Tommie asked another direct question of Chief Ness. "Chief, what about the charges brought by Detective Lincoln against Radcliffe Dillard? What has happened to them? I read where the original lab blood report was misplaced. What's the story there?"

"We're still investigating that case. We should know something soon. That's all I can say at this time."

The press conference ended twenty minutes later. Detective Lincoln once again was a free man. Bill and his attorneys walked across the street to a restaurant to celebrate. Bill finally felt vindicated and the lawyers were ecstatic over the publicity. While sitting there talking Bill received a phone call from Monique Dillard asking to join them. Fifteen minutes later, Monique was sitting at their table enjoying the festivities.

"Bill, I'd like to congratulate you and your lawyers on that press conference. You are now the poster boy for the poor and downtrodden here in Oakland. You have confirmed their belief, once again, that the system is naturally geared against them."

"Thank you. But, I must say, I don't relish the memory of my time in jail. It was not a pleasant experience."

"But you are to be compensated most handsomely for your stay I understand."

"That's because my attorneys did a most admirable job for me."

"And we must say that our client has a most remarkable way of putting just the right type of pressure on those who reside at the center of power in this city," Bennie Pews replied.

"Bill, I wouldn't want to intrude too far, but if you're not doing anything this evening my father would like to meet with you."

"Sorry, I'm busy. But tell him thanks for the invitation."

This was not what Monique wanted to hear so she made another attempt. "Would you be available tomorrow night?"

"I'll let you know when I have an opening on my calendar," he smiled slightly. He was not ready to give up his position of control. He had sat in jail while others toyed with his life. He wanted to let others feel what open-ended waiting felt like.

"I'm spending time with my daughters. I haven't been able to see very much of them in the last few weeks." He looked over at them, sitting across from him, beaming. They were lovely young ladies.

"Yes, I can understand. It appears they adore their father," Monique said while looking at them. This was the first time she'd met Bill's offspring.

"Where's Susan, Bill?" Monique asked.

"She's out of town at a conference. She'll be back in a couple of days. She called earlier."

The festivities went on for another hour before people began to leave, and finally, two-and-a-half hours later, there were only two people left, Bill and Monique.

"What are you doing the rest of the evening, Detective?"

"Well, I'm as free as a bird!"

Half an hour later they were in his den, Monique opening a bottle of choice Merlot. Bill sat leisurely on the couch. Monique offered him a glass of wine and then sat down next to him.

"A penny for your thoughts," she said.

"I was just thinking about how nice it is to be home again."

"I can only imagine. By the way, your daughters are lovely. It's obvious they've been well-raised."

"Thank you. Now only if I can just keep my youngest one focussed. She's very bright, but is getting a little boy-crazy! Her older sister really helps out in that area. She respects her older sister's opinion."

"That brings back precious memories of me and Hillary. She used to ask me all types of questions about everything! We used to make girl talk for hours. I hope your daughters will always have each other, Bill."

He didn't say anything, just nodded. He remembered her terrible tragedy as a brief twinge of guilt swept over him. He also recalled vividly where he had been for the last five weeks. He knew that Monique had played only a small part and had been manipulated, but he was still not about to reveal what he knew just yet. He wanted to talk with Franklin Dillard Sr., but he'd do it when he was good and ready, not at Dillard's whim.

"How are your parents doing?"

"As well as can be expected. They still don't go out. Hillary's death still weighs heavily on them. They've accepted their loss, but they still can't understand why it happened. You've met my mother. Have you ever spoken with her for any length of time, Bill?"

"Yes, your mother can move people. When I spoke with her she looked me straight in the eye and made me promise to help."

"Mother can be totally consuming. She exudes great passion and if you're not careful, she can suck you into her projects. Why, I can remember a time when she used to try to save the world. Eventually she came to realize, it's just too big and there's just too much to do."

"Now, I can only imagine."

"Will you help her, Bill? Can you?"

"I said I would."

Monique wanted him to say when. However, she knew she couldn't move him any faster than he wanted to go. She willed herself to let it go, to let him do what he had to do.

They talked for another couple of hours about subjects other than Hillary's murder. Monique got up again to fill her glass. When she returned she changed the topic once again.

"Bill, you remember that night at my house when I showed you my alleged paintings? Do you remember what I wanted from you?"

He remembered quite vividly, holding her and wondering when she was going to step back. She never did. He remembered she had wanted him to stay the evening. He had hinted about Susan, but she had said that this wasn't about Susan.

"Yes, I remember."

"That...was for real, Bill."

"Reality is a state of mind."

"Well, my mind was on you that night."

"That was an interesting evening."

"Tell me, when was the last time you were with a woman, Detective?"

He looked at her and slowly smiled. "Well, it's safe to say it's been at least a few weeks."

"And, do you still find me attractive?"

"You don't bring a starving man to a quality restaurant and ask him if he'd like to try something on the menu. The answer is rather obvious."

Monique put her glass down, then took his and set it aside. "Would you please put on some music, Detective?"

Bill thought a moment, then walked over to his stereo. He selected a soft jazz station on the tuner. He returned to the couch, but before he could sit back down, Monique stood up and asked ever so sweetly, "May I have this dance, sailor?" She held her hand out, he took it and gently, together they walked to the middle of the floor. Bill put one hand around her waist and held her other hand in his. They danced for only a few minutes before Monique whispered softly in his ear.

"You must know by now that I find you very attractive, Detective."

"I believe we've been here before."

"You feel so nice."

"You're very forward, Ms. Dillard."

"Is that bad?"

"I didn't say that."

"Then I'll take that as a compliment."

"I meant it as such."

When the song ended they stopped, but remained standing together. Another song began and Monique continued to hold onto him, pulling him even closer!

"Bill."

"Yes?"

"I was just going to kiss you, but I think it's better if I ask permission first."

"Oh, I see," he said this smiling broadly, his eyes slightly intensifying in their very focused survey of Monique's.

Entranced, Monique now took her hands and locked them behind his neck. Bill's mind flashed back to Radcliffe's party when she had done the same thing. He was feeling very 'good' back then and those same feelings had returned.

"Do you want me to ask?"

"You are free to choose, Monique."

"But what do you want me to do, ask or just do it? Which would you prefer?"

"I think it's always proper to ask."

"Well, is that so? You are such the gentleman, Bill." She continued to hold him and then the phone rang. He used it as an opportunity to release her. He walked to the phone and picked up the receiver. A moment later, Monique was by his side giving him a shoulder massage. It felt very sensuous and very relaxing.

"Hello."

"Bill?"

"Yes."

"Brick. Sorry to disturb you, but we're at Jacque Vestable's apartment. He's dead. It looks like an attempted robbery, but we're not so sure. There are several suspicious things."

"What's your location?"

He wrote down the address and told Kasolkasky, "I'll be right over!"

"I have to go."

"What's happened?"

"Jacque Vestable has been murdered."

"Who's that?"

"He's part of the mystery surrounding your sister's death."

--

Lincoln stepped through the door of Jacque Vestable's apartment and found Kasolkasky talking with the coroner. The body was covered. Bill walked over to it and lifted the sheet up. Jacque's throat had been slashed and there were several punctures tightly grouped in the heart area. The killer had made sure his victim was dead... dead...dead! Minutes later, Brick led him through the evidence.

"The victim's wallet is missing and the place appears ransacked. But, there are many valuable things still here. I think the killer wants us to think it was a robbery or maybe he was looking for something very specific."

"Any signs of voodoo, Brick?"

"No."

"We need to get a copy of his phone records."

"So, what do you think, Bill?"

"I don't like the convenient timing of his death. Is it just a coincidence that I get out of jail and Jacque Vestable is killed? Especially since I had your men contact the Miami Police Department."

"I know what you mean. I sent Jones and White to interview Hattie Black."

Bill observed Kasolkasky closely before asking, "What did you just say?"

"I said...I sent Jones and White to Miami to interview Hattie Black."

Bill now understood why Jacque was killed. "Listen, Brick, call the Miami Police Department and have Hattie Black placed in protective custody. I've got something I need to take care of."

"What's going on, Bill? And why protective custody?"

"Don't ask. I'll tell you later. But if you ever want this case solved you'd better do it."

He rushed out the door. He used his car phone to call his own number hoping that Monique would still be there. It rang, the answering machine picked up. He asked Monique to pick up the line if she was there.

"I'm here, Bill."

"What's your father's number?"

She held her breath for a moment then gave him the number.

"Is he home right now?"

"Yes."

"Stay right there, someone will call you right back."

He called Franklin Dillard's number and after two rings, his manservant answered.

"Dillard residence."

"This is Detective Bill Lincoln, I'd like to speak with Franklin Dillard Sr. Tell him this is important."

"Very good, Sir. Right away, Sir."

Twenty seconds later, Franklin Sr. was on the line. "Detective Lincoln?"

"Yes, Sir. I heard you were interested in having a meeting with me."

"Yes."

"Presently, I'm standing at the scene of a murder. A murder, which I believe is linked to your daughter's death. If you want to talk to me, I suggest we do it tonight, at my house. We should speak in private. Monique is there now waiting for me. I suggest you call her and ask her to go home. I think we need to talk right away, but if you'd prefer to do it tomorrow, we can do that."

"I prefer to do it right now."

Chapter 49

Around 10 PM the doorbell rang; Detective Lincoln turned on his hidden tape recorder. He then opened the door for Franklin Dillard Sr. Lincoln led him to his living room.

"Before we discuss my theory I have some questions for you, Mr. Dillard"

"I understand, that's fine. Ask your questions."

"Your daughter showed me a painting of Hillary one night when I was at her house. The painting was only half-finished, but it was beautiful. At the time she claimed to be the artist. I was moved by it. She admitted to me recently that she doesn't paint. Now, I'd like to know whose idea that was."

"It was mine." Dillard didn't say anything else, but instead just sat there waiting.

"Another thing happened to me the very next morning after that eventful evening. I received an unexpected visit from two uniformed officers who believed a Mr. Kincaid had been in my home. I also thought it curious that the night I was called away to your daughter's place my house became vulnerable to burglary, even though my home happens to have a very sophisticated security system. Do you know anything about Mr. Kincaid or the burglary?"

Dillard noticed the phrasing of Bill's questions and he concluded, correctly, that something was definitely up.

"Detective Lincoln, are you taping our conversation?"

"Yes," he responded without hesitation.

Dillard nodded. "I'm responsible for Mr. Kincaid. What else?"

"I'd like to know why."

"Since you were making more progress than the police department, I wanted to know if you were hiding anything."

"Who was Kincaid?"

"He was a former CIA operative who had taken early retirement. He was a man who quite literally couldn't be traced."

"You have a tape of me and my friend moving a package that night."

"Yes."

"I'd like that tape."

Dillard reached into his sports coat pocket pulling out a brown bag. He tossed it to Bill.

"This is the tape?"

"Yes."

"How many more copies are there?"

"That's the only one."

"How do I know that?"

"I give you my word."

Bill observed Dillard closely. The older man's eyes were totally focused on him. Dillard was regal in both appearance and aura. If he were not telling the truth then Bill would have to leave the investigations business. Dillard reminded him of Dr. Broussard. The man's body language and eye contact exuded honesty and integrity.

"I spent weeks in jail on bogus charges."

"They weren't all exactly bogus."

Once again Bill stared hard at Dillard, maintaining eye contact with him.

"I was in jail."

"You were also going after my son."

"Your son broke the law."

"So did you, Detective Lincoln."

He continued studying Dillard. The man was tough. But Detective Lincoln wasn't about to roll over or play the lap dog. He felt justified in his actions.

"Mr. Dillard, I don't think my situation and your son's are anywhere near the same."

"I never said they were. All I said was… you too broke the law. I didn't make a moral judgment…merely an observation."

Dillard was right. That's all he had said. Bill was the one now feeling a moral defense of his own actions.

"And what would you have done, Mr. Dillard?"

"I'm not sure. I suspect my actions might have been similar to yours, I'm sorry to say."

Again, he studied Dillard. The elder man was being honest. Bill respected that.

"And, Mr. Lincoln, what would you have done in my position?"

Bill pondered that question, admitting to himself that he also would most likely have acted similar to Dillard. Bill's silence was his answer leaving only one conclusion to be drawn.

"I'm sorry you spent that time in jail. I didn't want to do it, but you're a different type of man, Detective. Most would not have chosen the path you took. Why would I want to put you in jail when you were doing more to find the person who murdered my daughter than anyone else? You just wouldn't fold when the pressure was applied. I was protecting my son. As I told you before, you were working for me. Here's your salary for those five weeks…tripled."

With that, Dillard reached into his pocket and pulled out a check already made out to Detective Lincoln. Dillard stood, took the check over to where Bill had been sitting, laying it down.

Lincoln scanned the check. Dillard was a generous man and with the money Bill would soon receive from the City, he'd have a tidy nest egg. Lincoln put the check down but continued standing.

"What about Radcliffe, Mr. Dillard? I still have a problem there."

"What's your problem?"

"I don't like the fact that the police lost the lab report on your son. I have a real problem with that."

"You'll have to talk to my son about that. I was not involved. I'm sure Rad let people know that money was available to anybody who could do the job."

"I want the name of the person who 'lost' that report."

Dillard saw the seriousness in Bill's eyes and also heard it in his voice. He stood, walked to the telephone and dialed a number.

"Rad, this is your father. I'm standing in Detective Bill Lincoln's study at the moment. I want you to drive over here immediately!"

Dillard hung up and went back to his chair. He was a man who handled his responsibilities well.

"Who put the severed chicken heads on my doorstep and at my ex-wife's house?"

"I didn't. But I don't think that one is too hard to figure out. It had to be either Eddy Tevelle or my son Radcliffe. Personally, I suspect my son, Rad."

"Tell me, what does your son do for a living, Mr. Dillard?"

"Why I believe you already know the answer to that question, Detective."

He waited for Dillard to say more, but the man was silent. "How did it happen?!"

Dillard folded his arms across his chest and stared at the wall. For a moment, Bill wasn't sure if Dillard was still with him, Dillard appeared so aloof.

"I don't know what happened. Rad has a completely different set of values. I think we gave him too much. My son has a 'peculiar' mindset. He never appreciated what it took to 'earn' the life of affluence he desires. I think this may have been the single greatest failing of my life. I failed Rad as a father."

"I'm not so sure that's true, Mr. Dillard. I think maybe Rad failed you as a son."

"I don't know, but I do know his chosen life style has brought me great disappointment. And yet the greatest tragedy of all was losing my beautiful Hillary. That day and every day since has been a nightmare. I have felt such rage, that at times I could not speak. I could've killed that day! A man like myself, with the utmost respect for the law, had lost that reverence! And with each passing day, with us getting no closer to finding out who had done this terrible thing, it felt like a slow torture. I still have such rage, Detective! You should know now that I'm not leaving here until I hear your story."

"I know...just like you should know that no one is going to hear anything until I get my questions answered."

Twenty minutes later, the doorbell rang. Bill walked to the door, opened it and stared into the face of a somewhat distraught Radcliffe

Dillard. Rad had the demeanor of a man who really didn't want to be there, but was under firm orders to comply. Apparently, he had left his arrogance at home.

"Come in. Your father's in the living room." Bill escorted Rad to Franklin Sr.

"Detective Lincoln, could you please leave us alone for a few minutes? I need to explain the gravity of the situation to my son. I'll call for you when we're ready."

Dillard was looking directly at his son the whole time he was speaking.

"Sure. I'll be in the kitchen."

Fifteen minutes had passed before Bill was called back into the living room. Rad had confessed that it was he who hired someone to put the severed fowl's heads on Bill's doorstep and his ex-wife's.

"Who lost the lab report, Rad?"

Rad glanced over at his father who now stood there stone faced. This was time for the truth. The consequences for being less than honest were much too high to contemplate.

"Officer Milstone."

"How much did it cost?"

"Ten thousand dollars."

"I'll want you to testify against Milstone. We can't afford to have his type on the force. Don't you agree, Rad?"

Rad glanced at his father again, briefly, and nodded his head.

"I want your word, Mr. Dillard, that you'll help me remove Officer Milstone from the police force."

"I'll help you," Dillard replied.

Bill turned to face the son. "You need to stop selling dope, Rad. But that's between you and your conscience. I want you to write and sign a statement describing what you did regarding Officer Milstone. I want it tonight before you leave here. Your father will be a witness. And there's one more little matter. You and I had a little bet on whether or not I'd bring charges against you. With your statement tonight, I believe I've won that bet. Wouldn't you agree, Rad?"

Rad stood there but didn't say anything. His posture showed defeat. Whatever his father had said to him had changed him, at least for the moment.

"Rad, I asked you a question."

"Yes! It's your show, Detective."

"Then you owe me one thousand dollars; I'd like that issue resolved tonight. I'm not going to do anything right now about those drug charges. I'll decide that later. I just might give you a break, but that all depends on you, Rad. I don't want the thousand. Instead, what I want you to do is volunteer three hundred hours of your time to a community service program in place of the money. Your father can select the program. Is that agreeable to you?"

Rad was not about to provoke either Bill or his father at this point. Detective Lincoln had implied he would not necessarily pursue the drug charges if he saw some significant change in Rad's life.

"Yes. I'll agree to that."

"Good. Now I'd like for you to get started on writing that statement."

Twenty-five minutes later, Rad had finished. Lincoln and Franklin Sr. each witnessed it. Bill folded the document and put it in his pocket.

"Rad, our business is done. I'll have to ask you to leave now. Your father and I still have other confidential matters to discuss."

He escorted Rad to the door then returned to the living room. Dillard was sitting, ready for Lincoln's next set of questions, if there were any. He would have liked to talk to Dillard about life in general, but that wasn't going to happen tonight.

"Are you ready to hear my theory?"

"I'm ready."

"I'm sure you realize this is just my theory, that I don't have the evidence yet to arrest anyone."

"I understand."

"I believe your friend, Dr. Broussard, was intentionally targeted for destruction. He was targeted by a half brother that he never knew existed. You see...Dr. Broussard's father was Hendrik Broussard. Hendrik, as it turns out, was a real piece of work. He was a dysfunctional who drank, womanized, gambled and pretty much mistreated everyone...even his own family. He also fathered several children out of wedlock. One of those offspring's mother was, it just so happens, a voodooianne."

"What's a voodooianne?"

"Indeed. See, that's a woman who has attained high priestess status in the voodoo religion. She is rumored to have 'great powers' according to the faithful. Hendrik bedded this voodooianne and a child was produced. The child had his father's complexion and features. So naturally, he looks white. I have a picture of him, if you're interested, in my file. While growing up this child, raised by his mother, never knew his father. It should come as no surprise that he became a voodoo priest himself."

He observed Dillard who was sitting there, engaged. Dillard's eyes never left Bill.

"When he was a teenager he learned who his father was and went to see him. He knocked at the door of the Broussard house only to meet his father's legal wife, Edwina Broussard. When he identified himself, she became incensed. She cursed him, telling him never to return. He never did. The die was cast on that dreadful day. That was the day, I'm convinced, that the young man began to plot his revenge."

Dillard was leaning forward in his chair listening closely.

"Years later, in the remaining few months of his miserable life, Hendrik Broussard spent a great deal of time with a priest by the name of Father John Sabastian. He confessed his sins to him and that's how I came by certain information. Father Sabastian came to visit me after Edwina Broussard died and Dr. Broussard went into hiding. Both Hendrik and Edwina Broussard had individually sworn the priest to secrecy at the end of their lives. But Edwina had told the priest that if ever any of her 'confessions' would help someone in her family, he could and should disclose what he knew."

Bill focussed on Dillard. The man was watching him intensely. There was nothing to do but finish the story. The intense attention of Franklin Dillard Sr. now controlled the atmosphere in the room, despite his silence. Bill continued...

"By the way, Father John is willing to testify. Our voodoo priest's name is Dr. Juwan Gumble. He still lives in New Orleans, and, interestingly enough, he knows Jezabel Balboa and the late Jacque Vestable. As you know, Jezabel Balboa is the psychic who called us from Los Angeles saying she could help the police solve the case.

She told us there was a voodoo mark on the victim, which turned out to be true. I now believe she knew this because Jacque Vestable had told her. I believe Jacque Vestable was the man who killed your daughter and made it look like some voodoo ritual, by order of Dr. Juwan Gamble! Your daughter just happened to be…an innocent…in the wrong place at the wrong time."

Dillard was still totally focused on Detective Lincoln, but Bill could tell that from the look on his face it had all come together for him. Dillard was experiencing an epiphany!

"As I mentioned when I called you earlier this evening, Jacque Vestable was killed today. Police at the scene say it looked like a robbery, but I don't think it was. I have a tape recording of a call to Ms. Balboa. I had disguised my voice pretending to be Jacque. You can hear why I'm sure she knew Jacque. Our interviews with Jacque indicate that he knew the culture of voodoo, but quite naturally, he lied repeatedly to us about his level of involvement. The police didn't view him as a suspect. Besides, they thought he was right-handed. But as it turns out, he's ambidextrous! I have a tape of him playing softball. He hits and throws left-handed! As you know, its believed that Hillary's killer was left handed."

"About a decade ago, Dr. Broussard stopped being a faithful husband and had several affairs while on the road. One of those affairs took place in New Orleans, with Hattie Black. Hattie was either a student or was pretending to be a student at the time. Hattie's uncle, Elden Robinson, is a voodoo worshipper and follower of Dr. Gumble. I believe Dr. Gumble instructed Hattie Black to obtain Dr. Broussard's sperm during his time of impropriety and vulnerability. Our Dr. Gumble is a very cunning man indeed. He will not be easily apprehended."

Bill stopped to allow Dillard to ask questions. But, Dillard knew the facts of the case as well as anyone. There just wasn't any question. He could see the picture as clearly as Detective Lincoln…now.

"Good work, Detective! You've more than earned your money."

They both sat there without talking. Dillard was thinking. Bill knew that Dillard had two roads to choose from, the legal and the illegal, but he had no idea which path Dillard would choose.

415

Dillard stood and shook Bill's hand. "I need to be alone. I've got a lot of thinking to do. The one thing I know is that I want you to remain on my payroll. I want your services to continue."

Bill looked Dillard in the eye and saw the strong will of the man. "You should know that I'm not a contract killer, Mr. Dillard. I believe in the law. I'd only go outside the law if I were forced to. When people don't do their job and it results in my life or my family's life being placed in jeopardy, then I'll do what I have to do. But I won't kill on the orders of others."

"I know, Detective."

Bill started to walk Dillard out, but then he stopped and went over to the cabinet where the hidden tape machine was, and opened it. He took the tape out and destroyed it in front of Dillard. He then took Radcliffe's confession out of his pocket, handing it to Dillard.

"You handle your son any way you see fit, but I want that officer off the force."

A grateful Dillard agreed, slipping the confession into his pocket as he thanked Detective Lincoln one more time. There was an obvious sign of respect that Dillard had for the detective. Bill opened the door and Dillard walked out into the darkness. After taking a few steps, he turned and stopped.

"When will you be available?"

"I'm spending a week with my daughters."

Dillard nodded, then turned away into the coolness of the night.

Going To New Orleans

Chapter 50

When Detective Lincoln returned from spending the week with his daughters, there was a message from Kasolkasky waiting for him. Brick notified him that the police had uncovered a potential piece of evidence regarding the murder of Jacque Vestable. The security system where Jacque Vestable lived was set up to take snapshots of the entrance area whenever the doorbell was engaged, any time between 8 P.M. and 6 A.M. As a result, they had recovered the image of a small mustached man, slight of build, wearing a hat. His picture had been shown to all the residents, but none could identify him.

Bill looked at the picture. "That's Willis Bowman!"

"Who's that?"

"He's that guy from New Orleans I met when I went there to attend a voodoo ceremony; the service, supposedly, which never took place. My contact person was Elden Robinson, but this other guy, Bowman, showed up at my hotel accompanying Robinson. Robinson gave me back my money because the voodoo priest was 'ill'. I later discovered that was a lie. Bowman, from the beginning, seemed like a dangerous person. I'm certain that he killed Jacque Vestable."

"Why?"

"Sit down, Brick. Let me tell you who I think killed Hillary Dillard."

Bill spent the next twenty minutes reviewing the case with Kasolkasky. Before this, Kasolkasky had been absolutely sure that Dr. Broussard was the killer, but now because of Detective Lincoln's new theory, he was just as convinced of Dr. Broussard's innocence.

"So, what's the next step, Bill? How do we nail this guy?"

"That's going to be difficult. The death of Jacque Vestable eliminates a direct and immediate link. First, we have to get Hattie Black out of harm's way before we go after Bowman. Unfortunately, Bowman is not going to make that easy. We'll need a warrant for his arrest."

"I'll start the wheels in motion. I think this photograph along with the information you just gave me should be enough 'to get the ball rollin'."

By the end of the day, Kasolkasky had a warrant for the arrest of Willis Bowman and Lincoln had re-activated his license as bounty hunter! The license gave him the right to cross state lines in pursuit of people wanted by the courts. Bill also called Captain Bell, in New Orleans, with an update. The Captain immediately called off the manhunt for Dr. Broussard.

Two days later, Detective Lincoln and his associates landed in New Orleans. They drove out to a completely furnished rented house with two domestic servants, paid for by Franklin Dillard Sr. In the house with Detective Lincoln were Detectives Clarence Jones and Dick White, Marie 'Mama' Francois, Lenny 'Iron Hands' McDerch and Sparky. Bill called a meeting shortly after their arrival.

"We'll spend the day today driving around the city. That way, everyone can start getting familiar with the terrain. Captain Bell has provided two officers to help us. We're going to bring Elden Robinson in and tell him what we know. And unless he cooperates, we'll threaten to put the word out that it was he who fingered Willis Bowman. Besides, his niece, Hattie Black, also needs protection. She's another important link and if Jacque Vestable was killed because of his involvement and knowledge, she faces a similar fate. Elden will deal with us because that's the only way he can save his own miserable life as well as his niece's. Any questions?"

"How do we get our hands on Bowman?" Clarence asked.

"Simple, we'll attend the next voodoo ceremony. Captain Bell's sources say that there'll be a ceremony at the end of this week."

The meeting lasted an hour. Everyone was made aware of Lenny's handicap. Marie Francois was there to help with any questions regarding voodoo and, although she was not required to attend the voodoo ceremony, she had every intention of doing so. She wanted to experience first-hand, this man who allegedly possessed special powers conveyed on him by the great voodoo god. She wanted to see this outrageous 'fraud' with her own two eyes!

Two days later, Officer Butterfield drove out to Elden Robinson's house and delivered him to police headquarters. Detective Lincoln and Captain Bell entered the interrogation room and waited. A few minutes later, Elden Robinson was ushered in. Butterfield was right behind him, nightstick in hand! Robinson was visibly shaken. Although there were no obvious bruises on Robinson, Bill had a feeling that if Robinson was asked to strip, Officer Butterfield might have some explaining to do.

"Here he is, gentlemen. Let me know when you're finished with him," Butterfield said menacingly. He liked this part of his job.

"Thank you, officer," Captain Bell responded. "Sit down, Mr. Robinson."

Elden sat in the only chair available, relieved to be away from Butterfield. It was only ten thirty in the morning, but Elden had perspiration stains on his shirt due to the heavy humidity and from 'interaction' with Officer Butterfield.

"I'm Captain Bell. You've already met Detective Lincoln."

Elden watched the two men, but said nothing.

"We've brought you here on official business. Do you know Willis Bowman?"

"I didn't do anything wrong!"

"You're not being accused of anything, Mr. Robinson. We just want you to answer a few questions."

Elden, looking at Captain Bell, realized he had said something stupid. Unfortunately, this only made him look like he had something to hide.

"Yes, I know Willis Bowman. Why?"

"Where can we find him?"

"I don't know. I don't know where he lives."

"Well, rumor has it that you know him very well."

"Sure, I know him, but I've never once been to his house. I don't know where he lives."

"What's his telephone number then?"

"I don't know that either. Willis just shows up on my doorstep from time to time, or I'll see him at worship."

"Do you know Jacque Vestable?"

"Who?"

Elden's various facial expressions and his evasively darting eyes told Bill that he was lying.

"He's dead, Elden," Bill said for his first words to Elden.

Elden was speechless; He was also visibly shaken!

"I think your niece, Hattie, is next, and therefore is in grave danger!"

"What are you talking about?!"

"Your buddy, Bowman, killed Jacque Vestable."

"How do you know that?"

"Oh, we know. Look, we even have the papers for his arrest." Bill pulled the warrant out of his jacket pocket, handing it to Elden. Noticeably trembling, Robinson read the document, then handed it back.

"You should know that your niece will almost certainly be killed next."

"What are you talking about?"

"Your voodoo priest, Dr. Gumble, caused Hillary Dillard's untimely death in order to frame his half-brother for murder! Your spiritual leader instructed Jacque Vestable to murder someone, anyone, and then plant the semen that your niece Hattie had clandestinely procured during an affair with Dr. Broussard. But you knew all this, didn't you, Elden? You've already figured it out."

"I really don't know what you're talking about," he said weakly. "Please, you've got to believe me!"

Bill ignored his mutterings and continued talking.

"We also have an arrest warrant for you too, as an accessory to murder! But we're willing to give you one chance, Elden...one chance only! You get the opportunity to redeem yourself and go back to living what you'd call a normal life. Otherwise, you'll spend the rest of your natural life behind bars! Do I have your attention?!"

Elden sat there contemplating his options. He'd seen the warrant for Bowman. He knew Bill had definitely put it all together. He himself had figured it out when he heard that Dr. Broussard had been arrested, and later, when he found out that Hattie's name had been mentioned in connection with an affair with Dr. Broussard. It had all come together. Many years ago, Dr. Gumble had asked him to get Hattie to do something very special for him. Elden was now justifiably concerned about his and his niece's shaky situation.

"Alright then. What do you want me to do?"

"We need your help in order to apprehend Bowman. First, where does he live?!"

"Honestly, I really don't know. He has my number and address, but I don't have his. He's a man who likes his privacy."

"We know the next voodoo ceremony is scheduled in two days. We're going as your guests. We know that Bowman is always there. All we need is a way to get in without causing undue suspicion. You'll put us on the list. I'll give you the names to use. When do you normally turn in your guest list for the ceremony?"

"Tomorrow afternoon."

"Good. You'll have it before then. There will be five of us. I understand that you have whites who also attend your ceremonies?"

"Yes. That's true. Dr. Gumble has quite a diverse following."

Bill was tempted to ask if that was because Gumble himself looked white, but he didn't. "What time do people usually arrive?"

"About 10 PM."

"What time does the ceremony actually begin?"

"Around 11 PM."

"We'll be carrying weapons."

"You can't do that! They check everybody at the door. It's mandatory."

Bill looked at Captain Bell, then back again at Elden. "Alright, we'll leave the weapons in the car. Where will we find Bowman?"

"He's usually walking around. He doesn't have a designated spot."

"Where's your niece, Hattie? The authorities in Florida have been unable to locate her."

"I don't know. Have you talked with my sister, her aunt?"

"We can't find her, either."

"Then, I don't know. They might be visiting another relative."

They talked for another thirty minutes before Officer Butterfield escorted Elden back home. Detective Lincoln felt uneasy about not being able to carry a weapon inside. Captain Bell responded by saying he'd have men posted outside and that Bill could wear a wire. Bill agreed.

Back at the house, Detective Lincoln held another meeting to discuss their plans and update his team. Bill alerted everyone that Bowman was extremely dangerous. Once inside, they would be on Bowman's turf and that could make things quite difficult. Bill looked out the window and saw his friend and Sparky playing. He was not totally sure that he should be bringing Lenny into the project. His parents were told that their son was on a pleasure trip. Bill wished Lenny could stay there and play with Sparky for as long as he liked, but Bill was also pragmatic. If the team was going to attend the ceremony without weapons, then he wanted the sergeant with him. 'Iron Hands' McDerch was the most efficient killing machine Lincoln had ever met. If anything went wrong, Bill had more confidence in having Lenny by his side than anyone else on the planet.

To survive it is often necessary to fight, and to fight you have to dirty yourself.

George Orwell (1903-1950)

Chapter 51

Two days had passed and the team was busy putting on disguises. Since Bill and Marie Francois had already met the shadowy Willis Bowman in the New Orleans hotel room only months before, Bill and the voodooianne faced the greatest exposure. Bowman had accompanied Elden that evening and had spoken briefly with both Bill and Marie. It had become painfully obvious that night that Bowman had his suspicions about both of them.

Marie Francois chose to wear a long Caribbean styled dress, leather sandals and an earth brown turban wrapped around her head. She also had horned-rim glasses and a darker make-up, so, unless you knew her very well, she was 'incognito'. Detective Lincoln sported a fake beard, mustache and tinted glasses. He was relatively certain that Willis Bowman would not recognize him.

Elden Robinson was instructed to pick up Detective Lincoln's team at 9:30 PM. Detective Clarence Jones rode shotgun with Elden. Everyone else piled into the other two unmarked police vehicles. They drove for some forty miles to a rural area then turned onto a hard-packed dirt road called Dugan Street. It was another good half-mile before they reached their destination, a large stately house, sitting by itself on several acres of land. The ample unpaved parking area was at least three-quarters full. They parked their vehicles and walked up to the front door. Each person was methodically searched for weapons. Fifteen minutes later, two more unmarked police cars pulled into the parking area, parked and waited. One of those held Officer Butterfield. He had volunteered for the assignment.

The living room and dining room areas were already filled with people. They were busy conversing about the many blessings they had received through the priest. Most were people of color, but a good twenty percent or so were as white as the driven snow. This was especially fortuitous, given the racial mix of Detective Lincoln's team. He particularly didn't want Dick White and Lenny to draw any unwanted attention. Detective Lincoln's team began mingling throughout the crowd searching for Willis Bowman.

At 10:45 PM the entire crowd drifted to the backyard where several roaring fires blazed. There were no other sources of light. Detective Lincoln had instructed his men to find things that could be effectively used as a weapon, 'just in case'. As such, each man had secreted a knife from the kitchen before walking toward the back with the rest of the faithful.

At precisely 11:02 PM, Officer Orville Lutherford Butterfield, feeling the familiar twinge of boredom from his physical inertia, got out of his car to stretch his legs. Even though he wore plain clothes, there was nothing anyone could do about the innate swagger in his walk or his overall police-like demeanor. Somehow, he just looked like a cop. Butterfield spotted two women talking near several trees about thirty yards from the parking lot. He walked over to see what they were doing. Seeing him, they turned back toward each other to await his arrival. He stood in front of them now and asked...

"How are you ladies doing today?"

"Just fine, officer."

Well, his first reaction was bewilderment. After all, he was in plain clothes. How did they know he was a policeman?! Before he could ask his next question, a ten-inch razor-sharp serrated edged blade ripped through his throat! Blood jetted through the air landing on the garments of the two women. Officer Butterfield sank to the ground as the cold terrible steel was being twisted and pulled through his soft tissue and landed against the hard vertebrae defining his spinal cord! Three more hard swift stokes were made through his back seeking the heart region. The body's nerve centers were still firing; the body twitched violently as the two women quickly dragged the corpse behind a nearby tree. Willis Bowman watched cautiously as the women carried out his deadly orders!

The backyard crowd was huge. Bill stood next to Marie Francois in order to hear her take on things should anything unusual happen during the ceremony. So far, there was nothing that required the voodooianne's expertise. Bill kept scanning for Willis Bowman. He was surprised that none of the team had sighted him yet.

"When do you think the ceremony will start, Mama?"

"Not yet. People are still getting settled. Nothing will happen for probably another fifteen or twenty minutes."

"Good, I'll be right back. I'm going to look around."

Bill nudged Lenny and they both started slowly walking back inside. The house was almost empty with only a few people left in the kitchen. Bill and Lenny sat down in the living room and talked until the people in the kitchen left. They then got up and walked down the hallway. If anyone were to ask them what they were doing, Detective Lincoln had instructed Lenny to say that they were 'looking for the restroom'.

They knocked lightly on the first door. No answer. Bill turned the doorknob, poking his head inside. He observed a room with several overstuffed chairs, a bookcase lined with books, also, what appeared to be ancient Egyptian artifacts, and a medium-sized television set. They walked in, opened the closet door, but found nothing unusual. Bill took one more look around before leaving. They walked to the next room across the hallway and repeated the procedure, again they found nothing unusual. They closed the door and while moving to the third door they heard a voice behind them.

"Can I help you, gentlemen?" a man inquired as Bill and Lenny turned around to innocently face him.

"Why yes, Mon. Could you please tell us where the restroom is?" Bill asked, slipping into his Jamaican accent.

"Of course. It's the last door down the end of the hallway facing you," the man said courteously.

"Thank you so very much," Bill replied. The man turned and went about his business. Bill and Lenny glanced at each other, but said nothing. They waited a moment before again moving on to the next door.

Outside in the parking lot, two small groups of darkly attired masked men quietly approached the two unmarked police cars. Pointing guns at the undercover officers, they removed the policemen from their vehicles, gagged and handcuffed each of them and then proceeded to lock them in the trunks of their own cars! The men then walked off cautiously in the direction of the ceremony. A sinisterly smiling Willis Bowman again watched from a safe distance.

There were two doors left in the hallway. One door was the restroom and the other was locked. Bill wanted the locked door opened. He walked to the head of the hallway to watch for intruders while Lenny took skeleton keys, courtesy of the New Orleans Police Department, from his pocket. Detective Lincoln also had another set of keys in his pocket, which he would try should Lenny's set fail to work. Several minutes passed before Lenny defeated the lock.

They immediately stepped through the door into the darkness and found themselves on the landing to a stairwell leading downstairs. A light switch jutted out, but they didn't turn it on. Off in the distance a flickering light was burning. The determined pair started moving slowly down the stairs holding the rail as their eyes adjusted to the darkness. A strong, pungent odor that neither could identify permeated the air. This caused the intrinsic mystique of the situation to be even greater, and even more suspicious. Both firmly held their knives, their only weapons.

They continued creeping down the stairs, eventually hitting bottom where, once again, they stopped and listened. They heard nothing, but that strange smell was now certainly getting much stronger! It was intense and quite exotic in nature. Wavering images danced on the walls. Bill and Lenny were still quite a few yards from the light source as an eerie feeling began to engulf them. They were in the basement of this old home with its stoned walls. The masonry reflected an ancient architecture. It felt 'old-worldly'. A cold shiver ran down Bill's spine. Suddenly, Detective Lincoln had a desire to be anywhere but where he was. He felt bad vibrations; Lenny, too, was on edge.

"Are we going forward, Major?"

He wanted to say no, but he couldn't. His intellect, once again, overrode his feelings and he responded...

"Yes, Sergeant. Let's go, but slowly."

They inched forward like turtles parading through sand. Suddenly for Lincoln, flares and fires were exploding everywhere like popcorn on a hot burner! Bill was experiencing a Vietnam flashback, harkening back to when they were out in the bush, engaging enemy fire at night. As Major Lincoln viewed the combat scene, it had a strobe light effect, similar to the inside of a 1970's disco club. Reality and absurdity became intertwined.

Lenny was at point, just like back in 'Nam'. That heady smell captivated them. What was it?! The odor alone compelled them to move forward, drawing them, like two thirsty men envisioning the image of an oasis in the desert.

There were many hiding places, forcing Detective Lincoln to be ever so vigilant. Lenny peered cautiously, watchfully...straight ahead. His job, once again, was to search out any enemy presence ahead. Bill, like in 'Nam', protected their sides and their rear. They were a lethal team. Unbeknown to the other, each had images of the war racing violently through their brains.

The spot from where the light emanated was yet another room. As they approached it they stopped just outside to listen, but heard nothing. Both glanced briefly at each other before moving to the edge of the open door. Lenny quickly peeked inside the room; Bill kept his eyes focused on the area behind them. Then Lenny disappeared inside, a few seconds later, Bill followed.

A strange, ghastly sight greeted them...stopping them cold! The room was full of lighted candles placed on the floor, side by side, only inches apart. On the walls, a horde of mounted candles burned brightly, with still another thirty or so candles placed around a fixture that had Detective Lincoln completely transfixed. A woman's dead body was spread out before him in the manner of a crucifixion! She was nailed to a wooden cross and had strange markings carved into her body. A mask of terror and torture had been captured on her face. The woman had obviously died an unspeakable horrible death!

Detective Lincoln knew they were in terrible danger. He grabbed his radio, sending out the alarm to his outside men! He waited, and when he heard nothing he assumed it was because they were underground and the signal was being masked. Bill tapped Lenny's shoulder and they started to slowly retrace their steps. He needed to warn his team, but first he needed to take every precaution for himself and Sergeant McDerch.

Before going any further, Detective Lincoln suddenly grabbed Lenny's shoulder and stopped him. Bill turned around, scurrying back to the room to look once more at the dead woman. Lenny, patient as always, waited and watched. When Bill rejoined his friend, it was with even more concern in his eyes. Lenny knew the Major well and wondered what could have shaken his commander so.

"I know who that woman is! That's Hattie Black! Let's go, Sergeant, we're in grave danger here!"

The fire starters had the torch flames reaching for the sky. The crowd, quite large, was settling down awaiting the ceremony. Detectives Jones and White stood by Marie Francois. They had surveyed the crowd searching endlessly for Willis Bowman, but so far, nobody had spotted him. Suddenly, the conga drums started! The beat was rhythmic, hard driving, primal! People started swaying to the hypnotic tempo. Clarence was subconsciously transported back in time, reliving the voodoo ceremony he had attended in Oakland several months earlier.

Detective Lincoln's team stood there and watched as a small, petite woman dressed all in white, slowly walked on stage into the middle of the presentation area. The crowd was quiet now, but the drums continued their pounding methodical beat. The woman remained still, watching the crowd until the drums submitted gracefully to her presence.

She walked slowly back and forth across the stage studying her audience. It was obvious she had been there before. Her demeanor signaled that she was in control. She walked to the edge of the platform, a mere arm's length away from the crowd. As she reached out, people touched her hand while falling to their knees. The people reached to touch her and she allowed it, although there were bodyguards between her and the crowd.

"Hattie Black is dead!" Bill exclaimed as he and Lenny rejoined the group.

"What?! What are you talking about?!" Clarence asked looking at Bill, startled, with eyes bulging. He was wondering fiercely and stated, "What is Hattie doing here?!"

"Hattie is down in the basement of that house nailed to a cross!"

Bill pulled out his radio and pushed the 'on' button. He needed to contact the men outside. Again, he heard only blistering static, causing him to be even more concerned.

"We're in serious trouble."

"What do you mean?" Detective White asked in a heightened voice.

"Think it through. We haven't seen Bowman, Hattie Black is inside the house, dead, nailed up like she was crucified and now I can't make contact with our backup outside. We've been set up!"

The group listened intently to Bill's remarks. They were worried and it showed in their emphatic facial expressions.

"So, what do we do?"

"I'm not sure. But I do know one thing, we need weapons!" Bill's hands, without thinking, automatically went for his cigarettes and moments later he was deeply inhaling smoke as he listened closely for any ideas from his team.

Initially, they all stared at one another but seconds later, while they strategized, they heard the booming voice of the lady in white. She had to be wearing a mike.

"My brothers and sisters! Welcome! All praise to Damballa!" she cried out as a charge of energy surged from the crowd. "All glory be to the Great One!" she continued as the crowd   responded.

"First, we need to get closer to the house. Let's get away from this crowd," Detective Lincoln instructed.

"You don't think we need to stay in the crowd?" Clarence responded.

"I don't know, Clarence. Does anybody have any other ideas?"

Nobody said anything. The situation was unnerving. They felt trapped and vulnerable.

"At least let's get on the fringe. I don't like where we're standing."

Everyone agreed and slowly, one by one, they moved toward the back of the crowd. The lady in white began speaking again...

"My brothers and sisters, we are gathered here to worship our Lord! And we have been blessed to receive his disciple! He brings us the word and the power! Our God blesses us with his love and he sends us his words through his devoted apostle, the most-wise one, the honorable and blessed Dr. Juwan Gumble! Let us praise him for he bears witness! Embrace him now, so that he may bestow upon us the blessings of Damballa!"

As if by magic, Dr. Gumble materialized from seemingly nowhere. He was wearing, of all things, a wolf's head mask!

"How did he do that, Mama?" Clarence asked.

"He was wearing a black cape that was completely wrapped around him. In this type of light it would make him invisible. He stood up, allowing the cape to quickly fall off him and, as you can see, he's wearing very bright colors...so, voila! In other words...it's an illusion...a trick!"

Gumble stood erect now receiving love and praise from the audience. He finally raised his hands to settle the crowd. This, obviously, was a great man to them. They believed he was chosen by their great god to speak to them.

"My dear brothers and sisters. It is so good to be with you again... so very good. It fills my heart with gladness to be standing here before you. All praises be to Damballa!" he said to the crowd.

"All praises be to Damballa!" the crowd responded back.

"Glory to he who protects and gives grace to those who believe!" Gumble bellowed to the crowd.

"Glory to he who protects and gives grace to those who believe!" the crowd again repeated.

Gumble continued to control the crowd at will. He stood about six feet tall. He was lean with an athletic look. His father had been Creole and his mother was a voodooianne of undetermined origin. The rumors were he was mixed, but in his pictures he looked white…and he was the consummate showman! It was the way he stood, his timing, an alpha male who understood the psychology of leadership, especially within such a controlled setting.

Detective Lincoln's group was now standing on the outskirts not too far from the house. Everyone focused on Dr. Gumble, except Bill, who was constantly scanning the crowd. He had instructed Lenny to do the same. He wanted to know if anyone was observing them.

"Brothers and sisters, you came here for worship and I must regrettably fail you this evening. I came to bring you the words of our Spirit, the Great One from whom all blessings flow. But my faithful friends, that is not to be this evening."

The crowd began to murmur.

"We have evil among us tonight!" he shouted.

The crowd gasped!

"Yes, I could hardly believe it myself, but there are those who have come here this evening with the most evil intentions. They came bringing the sins and decadence of their world right here into our very midst!"

Dr. Gumble had the crowd's complete attention. Detective Lincoln and his team began looking around at each other. There was little doubt in their minds; they knew what Dr. Gumble was about to do. Bill also knew that they were only safe for the next few minutes. For once one of Gumble's henchmen identified them, the crowd would surely set upon them.

The fact that there was no contact from Captain Bell's outside men could only mean something bad had happened to them. That suspicion made Bill leery of trying to escape to the parking area. Were they waiting for them outside?

"Look my friends, look at the horrible deed they hath wrought tonight!"

Gumble turned as if playing a part in the theater, holding up his right hand as a cue, while two men carried a stretcher with a sheet covering what appeared to be a limp body. They brought it right up to Dr. Gumble and set it down. Dr. Gumble stood there surveying his audience. The congregation was anxious. The people wanted to know what was on the stretcher, even as the voodoo priest milked the situation for all it was worth

"My dear brothers and sisters, the horrible evidence of evil doing is here beside me. I have not told anyone before tonight, but there is a sinister group of people who have been threatening me! They say the Great One that you and I worship is not! They say that I am wrong for getting down on my knees and praying to the Great Spirit, Damballa!" he boomed into the mike.

"That's blasphemy! Who would dare threaten Damballa's faithful servant?" a voice cried out. The crowd was in an uproar. They were anxious to know who was attacking their religion.

"Who are these Devils?!" another voice cried out. "Tell us, most worthy one, tell us who speaks these untruths!"

Bill looked around. He knew what was coming, like predicting the sunrise the next morning. The only person who knew what they looked like tonight was Elden Robinson. Sometime, very soon, Elden would take his cue from Gumble and point the finger at Detective Lincoln's group.

"These infidels have served notice tonight. It is a strong message...one that leaves no doubt to their intentions. Look...see now what they have done!"

Dr. Gumble reached over and quickly snatched the cover off the lifeless form on the stretcher, allowing the crowd to view the mutilated corpse of...Officer Butterfield! His face was all but unrecognizable! The crowd was aghast. The angry people began shouting. They wanted to do something.

Bill was watching everything, desperately trying to come up with a plan. He removed his disguise. He whispered to the others to do the same. He was going to make it as hard as possible to be recognized and thus identified. They were on the fringe of the crowd now. Then, as before, everyone's attention was focused on Dr. Gumble. Lincoln whispered something in Lenny's ear and then told the others to stay put. Bill and Lenny separated, moving forward toward the stage.

"This humble servant was murdered, slaughtered like an animal! I prayed with this man on many occasions. He was a loyal follower of our God, the great and mighty Damballa. Let me read you the letter they attached to his lifeless body. Bear with me now...my dear friends."

Dr. Gumble waited for one of his men to bring him the letter, allegedly written by the killers. A young security guard, dressed in a dark double-breasted suit and bow tie, approached the unmasked Dr. Gumble, handing him an envelope. The priest glanced up to find a sea of faces waiting anxiously, wanting desperately to know what the note said.

"My good people, allow me to read this letter to you."

His hands had gone to his side as he took his reading glasses from his pocket. Removing his headgear to accommodate his eyewear, he slowly adjusted the glasses onto his face. Gumble was taking his sweet time before the distressed crowd. He had finally stopped looking at them to focus on the letter. His first words were emphasized.

"We warned you! Damballa is not all-powerful. He is not the Almighty One. In the name of the one true God we curse you for your wicked ways!"

Dr. Gumble ripped off his glasses and faced the crowd. Here stood their leader, proclaiming there was an evil group among them that evening, challenging their belief in Damballa.

"It is signed, 'The Holy Five'. There are five unholy people here tonight who have infiltrated our beloved union intending to wreck havoc and sow their seeds of evil in our midst. Who has the audacity to challenge the authority of Damballa?! Who would speak such untruths other than the sons and daughters of Satan himself!"

The crowd was hanging on Gumble's every word. They were putty in his hands, waiting to be molded according to the voodoo priest's desire. Detective Lincoln was close to his ultimate destination. Both he and Lenny had made their way to the back of the platform area. The crowd of people was maddeningly thick up front. It was like being at a concert and going around the crowd to come through the back of the stage area. There was so much focus on Dr. Gumble up on the platform that even the guards were not at their stations in back, but were now in the crowd, listening. Bill was coming in from the right side and Lenny from the left. One guard who had stayed at his post, challenged Lenny.

"I'm sorry, Sir, but this area is off-limits to the general public."

"I was sent here to deliver a message to the security officer in charge. Where is he?"

"Who sent you, Sir?"

"Willis Bowman."

"Come with me, Sir."

As soon as the man turned around, 'Iron Hands' threw a chokehold on him, and in one smooth movement, with an instantaneous surge of strength, 'twisted' his neck! Lenny then dragged the man's dead body out of sight, took the man's strapped-on knife and put the security guard's hat on. He continued forward with his assignment from the Major.

"My good friends and true believers in the Almighty One, the Great Damballa, who else among us knows of the Satanists and can identify these murdering infidels?!"

Gumble was standing there, both outstretched hands up, as if pleading to anyone who could help to come forward. He stood there looking from one person to another, both arms still fully extended.

"I know who they are!" a man yelled.

Everyone turned to see who was talking.

"Who said that?!" Dr. Gumble shouted in the direction of the voice. There were so many obstructing his view.

"It's me, Dr. Gumble, Elden Robinson! These heathens who cursed the name of Damballa approached me! They tried to recruit me, but I said I despised them! 'I won't have anything to do with you,' I said! They then threatened me too!"

"Who are these enemies of Damballa?"

"I was shocked when I saw them here tonight. I saw them talking with that man who died earlier. I recognized the clothes that he was wearing. They are pure evil!"

"Brother Robinson, can you identify these people?"

"Yes."

"Show us, so we might cleanse ourselves of their evil ways! Where is our head of security?"

"He is here next to me, Dr. Gumble. I was telling him my story just before you started   speaking." Next to Elden Robinson stood Willis Bowman.

"Where are they, Brother Robinson?"

"I spotted them over there!"

Elden was pointing in the direction of Detective Lincoln's team. The crowd followed the direction of Elden's finger and, as they did so, Bill and Lenny walked on stage behind Dr. Gumble. Lenny slapped an ironclad chokehold on Gumble and then…all hell broke lose!

People jumped up on stage making threatening gestures, but Dr. Gumble instinctively whimpered through his microphone for them to stay back. Bill was standing next to Gumble with a knife at his throat. Dr. Gumble had been taken hostage right before their eyes!

Detective Lincoln yelled into Gumble's mike to get his message to the audience.

"Listen to me! Follow my instructions and Dr. Gumble won't get hurt! My friend here can and will kill him instantly if I give the order! He's a professional. Don't make me have to do it! Listen to me now!"

Lincoln ordered Gumble to reason with them. Bill knew intuitively that Gumble would do anything to save his own life.

"Get back, please! Do as he says! Move back! Listen to him! Please, get back!"

The people on stage started moving back. They were angry, wanting to attack, but they realized Dr. Gumble would be killed if they took that course of action. It was blatantly obvious that the man with his arms wrapped around their leader's neck could crush it easily. This man, after all, was massive!

"Everyone move back, we're coming through!" Bill ordered. "Clear a path for us! We're going to the house! Get back! Don't make us have to kill him!"

The crowd reluctantly parted allowing Bill and Lenny to slowly walk through them to the house. Angry people were shouting obscenities and continued making threatening gestures, but Bill and Lenny slowly made their way forward. Clarence, Dick and Marie Francois had started making their way to the house when Bill announced his intentions from the stage. It took several very tense minutes, but they were now inside the house, the place completely surrounded by the mob.

"Call the police! Get help over here now!" Detective Lincoln barked out his first order upon entering the house.

Clarence picked up the phone. As he was dialing the line went dead. He slammed the phone down. Nobody bothered to ask him why; the answer was obvious.

"Listen! Stay out of any room with a window!"

They moved into the hallway where Lenny tied Dr. Gumble's hands securely behind his back.

"Open the door to the basement. We might have to retreat down there quickly. Our time is at best limited. Bowman is not about to just let us walk out of here. That's not to his advantage."

Bill turned abruptly to address Dr. Gumble.

"You must have a weapon here. Where is it?!"

"No, we don't use that type of thing here. This is a place of worship!"

Detective Lincoln abruptly grabbed him tightly looking dead into his eyes. This was a life and death situation. His cold stare sent a chilling message.

"Where's the weapon?!"

Gumble didn't answer.

"Sergeant, start breaking his fingers one by one until he tells us."

Lenny was standing behind Gumble. He grabbed the doctor's forearm with one hand, and his small-finger with the other, and bent it all the way back. Snap! Gumble cried out in pain, but Lenny continued to hold onto him.

"Break another one, Sergeant."

"No more! Please, no more...I'll tell you!" Gumble shrieked. "There's a gun in my room. It's upstairs. I'll show you." Pain and sweat now showed on Dr. Gumble's face.

"Take him upstairs, Sergeant. Get the gun. There's probably more than one. If you don't have the gun in thirty seconds, break another finger! One of you go with him," he said to the two detectives. Clarence volunteered to go.

"Hurry-up!"

They were back within two minutes with three loaded weapons. Detective Lincoln took one, gave one to Lenny and then asked the other two detectives which one was the better shot. Dick White acknowledged he was, Clarence concurred. The gun went to

Detective White. Bill was feeling better now that he was armed, but there were still far too many anguished people out there for him to think they were safe. If they lost Gumble as a hostage they would be in for a really rough time.

Bill knew that Willis Bowman was the most dangerous among the men outside and would be formidable to deal with. Bowman, a cold-blooded killer, was not about to let any of them get out of there alive. Bill was sure Bowman would sacrifice Dr. Gumble, if necessary. Lincoln wanted to engage the crowd immediately, before Bowman was given much more time with them to shape their thinking. Unfortunately, they were a mob now, so he might be thinking wishfully.

However, he had to try. Bill grabbed Gumble by the collar, and using him as a shield, walked to the window. He pressed the gun against the back of Gumble's head.

"Listen to me, we're police officers! Let us call headquarters and we'll prove to you that we are who we say we are! This whole thing can end quietly and peacefully!"

"Let Dr. Gumble go first and we'll do that!"

"No, call the police right now and talk to the Captain! He'll tell you who we are!"

"First, let Dr. Gumble go! We can talk after that!"

Bill heard the unmistakable voice of Willis Bowman. As long as he was talking to Bowman, nothing good could happen. He obviously needed to talk to someone else.

"Give me a few minutes. I want to talk this over with my team. I'll be right back."

Bill walked the voodoo priest back to the others.

"Gumble, if you value your life, you better put someone else in charge other than Willis Bowman! You've got one opportunity to live and that's by going to trial and taking your chances. But you're going to die here for sure if you don't do something soon. As a matter of fact, I'll kill you myself if that mob breaks in here, because that's exactly what Bowman intends to do. He knows we have a warrant for his arrest. Why, he's just dumb enough to believe that if he kills us, that the warrant goes away. That's crazy! He also probably figures that if he kills me, since I'm the one who figured the whole thing out, he's got a good chance of getting away. Bowman is going to get you killed, Gumble!"

Dr. Gumble thought about Detective Lincoln's remarks while holding his broken finger. He knew that he was in a most precarious situation. Lincoln's people would kill him if they thought they were about to be killed. And Bowman, not only was a dangerous man, but a desperate one, too. Fortunately, Dr. Gumble concurred with Bill's assessment of their predicament. Their fates were bonded.

"I agree with you, Detective. Listen…there might be another way if I can't convince Bowman. There's a secret entrance out of the basement. However, you must realize that the tunnel hasn't been used for years and it may take some time to get the door open. That door is very old. But, it's certainly worth a try."

"Is that the door in the room where Hattie Black's corpse is?" Bill asked.

Gumble looked at him, wondering how he knew about Hattie. But the game was over now. Everyone in the hallway was fighting to stay alive.

"Yes, the door is behind Hattie," he said remorsefully.

Bill turned to his team, instructing everyone to follow the sergeant. "Lenny knows where Hattie Black is. There's a door behind her, a potential escape route that requires opening. Get going! And give me that other gun just in case. I'm staying here with Gumble. We're going to try to convince somebody to call the cops!"

The others took off following Lenny. Bill turned back to Gumble.

"What makes Bowman tick? How can you get someone else to lead those people out there?"

"That's going to be difficult. Bowman is unique. I don't know of anyone out there who can stand up to him. He can be totally ruthless. That's why I chose him in the first place."

Crash! Suddenly, without warning, the two kitchen windows were smashed and all the windows in the living room were busted out… glass was flying everywhere! Bill spoke into Gumble's mike again telling everyone to stay outside. Dr. Gumble was alive and well. He let Gumble speak to prove his point.

"My brothers and sisters, I'm alright! However, do not come in and I will be fine! We've made a grave mistake... these people are policemen! They are not the Satanists!"

"We want Dr. Gumble... We want Dr. Gumble..." the crowd began to chant. There were only a few saying it at first, but it quickly built to a crescendo.

"We want Dr. Gumble! We want Dr. Gumble! We want Dr. Gumble!" the mob was in a complete frenzy and Detective Lincoln was sure he knew who was driving them. Next, they   started pounding on the sides of the house. Bill turned around just in time to see Clarence come racing back.

"What in God's name is going on here?!" he asked frantically.

"Bowman is getting them all worked up. They want to see Dr. Gumble. How's it going downstairs? Were you able to get the door open?"

"No. Not yet. We're still working on it. It's an old door like he said, but Lenny is doing his best. Actually, we're taking turns. Do you think you can you hold them off? We need more time."

"I don't know. It's getting crazy."

Clarence was trying to listen to Bill, but the pounding on the sides of the house was deafening! Detective Jones couldn't take his eyes off the walls; they seemed ready to come down.

"You should also know that Ms. Francois is acting strangely."

"How so?"

"She's just staring at Hattie Black. Man, that scared the living hell out of me. These people are sick!"

"She's just staring?"

"Yeah. She hasn't moved since she walked in that room. She just started staring at the   corpse that's nailed to that board. It's an eerie sight."

"While you're standing there, hold onto one of these just in case. You never know what might happen next."

Bill handed Clarence one of his guns.

"We want Dr. Gumble! We want Dr. Gumble! We want Dr. Gumble!"

The chorus continued unabated. Pictures slid off the walls while old dried paint fell from the ceiling. Detective Lincoln wondered how long the house could withstand this type of beating. Then, everything was quiet, no more shouting…no more pounding. The silence was frightening! Bill didn't know what was going on outside. The seconds turned into minutes and then the booming voice of a man talking through a bullhorn, just outside the window, exploded inside the room. The sound bounced wildly off the walls.

"People inside, listen to me! We want Dr. Gumble! What have you done to him?! We want to see him for ourselves! If not, we're coming inside! We don't trust the sons and daughters of Satan! We want to see him, do you hear me?!"

Bill talked into Gumble's microphone.

"Don't come in! I'll shoot him if you do! He's all right! I'm going to let him talk to you again!"

Bill motioned to Gumble that he should speak once more.

"Brothers and sisters, do as he says! I'm all right, but you've got to stay outside! Please, do not attempt to come in! If you do, my life will be in danger!"

"We want to see our leader! And, we want to see him now! Do you hear us?!"

Again, the 'unmistakable' voice boomed into the room making Bill want to hold his ears.

"Listen, I'm going to let Dr. Gumble stand up and walk to the middle of the room! I have a gun on him and I won't hesitate to shoot him if he tries to run! Give me a few minutes and I'll let him stand up! Do you hear me?!" Detective Lincoln yelled into the mike.

"We're waiting!" the voice responded.

Bill took off his belt and fastened it loosely around Dr. Gumble's feet. His arms were already tied. Bill wanted to make sure that he'd only be able to shuffle his feet. While they were in the hallway, he instructed Gumble to go no more than eight feet into the living room. There, his followers would be able to see him, and he'd still be in close range of Detective Lincoln. Bill didn't want to do this but the crowd was getting too emotional and, unfortunately, a madman was controlling them. Bill turned to face Dr. Gumble. He needed to say something before the priest stepped away from him.

"Listen closely, Gumble. We are close to escaping. Don't even try doing something funny. Believe me when I tell you I'll kill you if you try to escape. I won't leave you here alive so that you can tell them that we're escaping out the secret tunnel. Do you understand?"

Dr. Gumble had visions of stepping into the middle of the room and then escaping. However, Bill had quickly changed his mind on that plan. Bill was also holding Gumble's own gun and the priest knew all too well that it held soft lead bullets…cartridges designed for maximum internal damage. Surely he didn't want one of those projectiles exploding in his body!

Bill looked at his watch. Detective Lincoln needed to stall as long as possible. He was not going to do anything until he heard noise from the outside. Two more minutes dragged by before Bill again heard the now all too familiar refrain.

"We want Dr. Gumble! We want Dr. Gumble! We want Dr. Gumble!"

Bill waited patiently to hear the voice on the bullhorn. That would allow him a few more moments. After almost another minute the bullhorn was blasting again.

"We want to see our leader now! Right now! You've got sixty seconds to comply or we're coming inside! Do you understand?!"

He waited a few more seconds before responding.

"I hear you! All right, in sixty seconds we're going to let Dr. Gumble walk out into the middle of the room. You'll all be able to see him. Mind you, I have a gun trained on him. I'll kill him if anybody tries to come inside! I give you my word that I'll do that! This situation can be resolved peacefully. I want you to call the police. If I weren't telling the truth, would I ask for the police to be called!?"

"You own the police! We want to see our leader and we want to see him now!"

"All right, here he comes!"

Detective Lincoln looked at Gumble as he put the gun squarely in his face. The cold silver gray gun looked enormous to Gumble with the barrel pointing between his eyes. Click! Bill had switched off the safety button producing a very distinct sound, a sound that sent a chill down Gumble's spine. Bill had the voodoo priest's full and undivided attention.

"Okay. You know what to do. Just take a few steps out there so they can see you and then return. My gun will be aimed at your spinal cord the whole time. Any questions?"

Gumble shook his head, no. He turned, waiting for Lincoln's signal.

"Listen, Dr. Gumble is coming out. Do you hear me?!"

"We're waiting!" the man with the bullhorn responded.

Detective Lincoln nodded to Gumble and he slowly started to hobble out. A half-minute later, he was standing approximately eight feet away with his back fully exposed to Clarence and Bill. When he appeared before the crowd the chant was started again.

"We want Dr. Gumble! We want Dr. Gumble!" and it got louder and stronger.

The pounding abruptly started again; Bill wondered how long this would continue. He kept his eyes focused on Gumble and stayed clear of the windows. He didn't want to be a target. Dr. Gumble raised his undamaged hand to wave to his followers. The noise was almost unbearable. Nobody was able to hear anything over than the incessant hammering on the walls.

Suddenly, as if he were viewing a television show, Bill watched as the head of Dr. Gumble exploded in front of his eyes! Flesh and blood was splattered on the wall as the body abruptly dropped to the floor. Detective Lincoln knew Gumble was dead before the body even touched the rug. It was a direct hit. The shouting and the wall beating stopped abruptly too, as if someone had hit a switch. And then Bill heard the man with the bullhorn.

"They killed him! They killed Dr. Gumble! Do you hear me? They killed our leader. Let's go!"

Clarence raised his gun, but Bill grabbed him saying...

"No, save your bullets. We can hold them off longer from the bottom of the stairs. Let's get out of here! Move!"

As they turned to run, a hail of bullets streamed through the windows. Bill took a hit in the fleshy part of his side and fell. Clarence reached over to help him up and together they ran to the stairway. They closed the door and hurried down the stairs. At the bottom, Clarence reached up to knock out the light causing particles of glass to rain down on them. Detective Lincoln instructed Clarence to wait there and to fire on anyone attempting to follow. That would, hopefully, discourage them for a while. Bill, holding his side, gave his gun to Clarence and then started walking to the back room to check on the status of the escape door. Bill heard two shots fired. Seconds later, he heard another hail of gun discharges.

He turned the corner only to witness Marie Francois on her knees before Hattie Black. He stopped for an instant, but went past her to where Lenny and Dick were trying to pry open the old weathered door. They just simply didn't have the proper tools.

"How much longer?"

"I don't know, Major. It should've given by now, but it hasn't."

"Damn! Keep trying, Sergeant! We don't have much time! Give me your gun, Dick. I'm going back to help Clarence. They just killed Gumble."

"What?!"

"Yeah, Gumble's dead and we've got a mob on our hands. Hurry up or else we'll all end up dead! They're coming. Clarence is trying to hold them off!"

Detective Lincoln raced back to rejoin Clarence while continuing to hold his injured side. It was very dark now. The only light was coming from the candles burning in the back room. Bill could see flashes of light every time a gun went off. He called for Clarence and Jones answered...

"Here Lincoln!" Bill worked his way toward him. "How's your ammo, Clarence?"

"Low...I'm only shooting when I think I have a clear shot. I got three of them. I think there are five more that got down the stairs though. It's so dark, nobody can see very well."

"Let's start falling back slowly, Clarence." Bill directed.

Before their enemies' eyes fully adjusted to the darkness, Detective Lincoln wanted to put as much distance between them as possible. Bill and Clarence started their retreat.

Seconds later they were back in the room of burning candles. They each had only one bullet left in each of two guns. The third gun was empty. Lenny and Dick were drenched in sweat and still they hadn't broken through! Ms. Francois remained on her knees apparently in a trance. Bill didn't know what to make of her. Bill and Clarence were standing in the back with Lenny and Dick, leaving only Marie Francois in the middle of the room when they heard the unmistakable sounds of other people approaching the area.

"Detective Lincoln, come out here!"

Again Bill heard the voice of Willis Bowman. He wondered if this was to be the end of the line. With only one bullet left, he contemplated whether to try to get Bowman, or to use it on himself. He didn't want to think about what a man like Bowman would do to him.

"Lincoln, I'm talking to you!"

Bill took one step out to face his adversary. Bowman was standing behind two of his four henchmen. They all had guns. Bill didn't know how many bullets they had left, but he suspected that they had more than he did!

"I'm here, Bowman. You don't have to shout!"

"You killed our leader. Why did you do that?"

"I'm sure the autopsy report will reach a different conclusion."

"So, you think you'll get out of here alive, Detective?"

He ignored the question.

"The authorities know you killed Jacque Vestable. They have the evidence. That's why we have a warrant for your arrest!"

Willis Bowman was thinking now. He was wondering how much of this, if any, was true. Of course, Elden Robinson had told him that he had read the warrant, so some of this story was definitely true. But he couldn't believe Detective Lincoln was telling the whole truth.

"The police seem to have a problem catching people. Would you not agree, Detective?"

"It all depends."

"I guess I should be shaking in my boots, huh, Detective? They seem to be having trouble catching Dr. Broussard in his own backyard."

"Yes, and just like him you'll always be looking over your shoulder."

Bowman was doing the talking, but he was careful to stay safely behind his henchman. He was not about to let Bill have a clear shot at him. Lincoln heard the creaking of a door being opened. Lenny had finally broken through! But now there wasn't enough time for

Bill to make his getaway. No one knew what was on the other side of that door, but there were at least five men, all apparently with loaded guns, standing on the opposite side of the room. Even if they made a break for it, the hail of bullets into the tunnel would probably get most of them. Bill was thinking the end might be very near.

"What is that noise I hear, Detective? What are your friends doing back there?"

"They're making a bomb, Bowman! We're all going to die right here!"

Bowman smiled wickedly. He liked Detective Lincoln's creative retorts. His ominous smile showcased a gold-capped front tooth.

"You're holding your side, Detective. Were you hit? Is that blood I see?"

"Just a scratch. Nothing for you to concern yourself over, my friend."

"Would you like a band aid?" Bowman grinned mischievously.

At last, the door was open. Bill hoped the others would go through it to safety. However, his team, sans Ms. Francois, was still standing in the corner listening. Bill could feel the time slipping away from them. This game was just about over.

"Tell your buddies to come out so I can see them, Detective. Let's conclude our business. I'm getting tired of this cat and mouse game. So, please, tell your friends to do as I say. Don't make me mad, Detective!"

Bill stood briefly staring in Bowman's direction, before saying anything. He was about to order his team to move out; he'd guard the door as long as he could. Then suddenly, Marie Francois rose to her feet, turned, and faced Bowman and his men. She was not the same person anymore in her walk, or manner. An unusual aura surrounded her!

Her voice was even different! It was deep, strong, and commanding. The tone was like a man's husky voice; it was as though she were speaking through a microphone! The sound came booming out of her!

"Infidels! Unholy vermin who dare play with the Almighty One. You have used his name in vain to exploit and corrupt! How dare you! How dare you commit such a fraud, you dare to desecrate his holy name! Ye shall not trample on his righteousness, on his saintliness and expect not pay the ultimate price. Prostrate yourselves before His Holiness! Kneel before the Great One! I command you in his holy name, to kneel before him!"

A glowing Marie Francois stood there majestically, pointing at the five evil men before her. Bowman's gang was hesitant and understandably confused. Who was this woman?! The four men looked at their boss. He too, was at a loss for words. Her voice threw them all. It was so heavy, so demanding of attention and absolute obedience. Was something using her as a vessel, projecting its voice through her? Uneasiness pervaded the room. Bill's mind jumped to the scene in 'The Exorcist' where the demon occupied the child's body. Something supernatural was likewise happening right before his very eyes.

"I say unto you, that the unholy shall prostrate themselves before the Lord, to ask for forgiveness for their wretched despicable behavior! Look at this deed of intolerable vexation, thus perpetrated upon the innocent in his holy name!"

Madam Francois turned, facing Hattie Black's corpse . She walked to it, then caressed the face of the dead woman in her hands and stared at the sight. She then whirled back around and again pointed at the five 'devils'.

"Sinners, heathens, immoral imposters! You dare to exploit his name. You manipulate and defy for power and profit! You bring dishonor to that which is most honorable, disgrace to the beautiful and untruthfulness to the glory and righteousness that is His name. Prostrate yourselves before the divine! In the name of Damballa, Damballa Wedo, the All-Knowing One, the one from whom all blessings flow, I command you! I command you in the name of the greatest god of all! Submit to Him, now! I command you, in the name of the Father!"

As Marie Francois stepped forward, Bowman's henchmen slowly recoiled. They were understandably frightened. They had guns in their hands, but were afraid to use them. They glanced at each other, and then at Bowman. Bowman just stood there even as his men kept moving backward. The priestess kept inching forward until magically the voodoo practitioner was standing before Willis

Bowman; his men were several steps behind him. Bowman gripped his gun tighter, but was still unsteady and unsure. Who, in their right mind, would face him like this?! He had talked with this woman once before, but this, this just was not the same person. Madam Francois unnerved him! He was losing bodily control now!

She seemed possessed, but by what? Bowman knew Dr. Gumble was a fraud along with all the others he'd ever met. That's why he had always gotten what he wanted because he could see through their game. But he had never seen anything like this! He actually took a step backward, then another and another...Finally, he stepped back into a corner. He was trapped! His men were standing to the side watching him, not knowing what to do.

The high priestess stood only inches away, but he still had his gun. He didn't know what was stopping him from pulling the trigger. This woman was certainly mad. Crazy! After all, who had the audacity, the unmitigated gall to confront Willis Bowman complete with gun, gripped ever so tightly in his hand?!

He watched, as though hypnotized; she slowly raised her hand as if moving in slow motion, pointing her finger straight at him. Her amplified voice pounded his ears rocking him to his core!

"Thou art evil and wicked! Thou shalt be departed from me in the name of Damballa, the wise one, the merciful one, the one who knows and gives all! Thou shalt kneel now and beg for forgiveness. For evil must not beget evil; for unrighteousness must be made right. For I say unto you, thou shalt not use his name in vain, thou shalt not perpetuate wickedness and destruction for he and he alone shall give mercy. Prostrate yourself, now...I command you...now!"

The voice was throbbing with righteousness and conviction. She had raised her clenched right hand above her and her eyes were wide open, drilling a hole into the mind of Willis Bowman.

Then, without warning, Bowman pulled the trigger, pumping soft-hot lead into the body of Marie Francois, but it appeared to have...no effect! For precious few seconds, which seemed like an eternity, there was raw silence...then, momentously, Madam's hand came sweeping down, like Zeus hurling a thunderbolt, grabbing Bowman by the throat! She ripped it apart in one swift stroke!

A strong breeze quickly moved through the room extinguishing most of the candles. The four henchmen reactively started firing into the voodooianne's torso. Seconds later, complete darkness blanketed the room. Detective Lincoln then heard the shrill high-pitched screams of men. Bill turned, grabbed his team, and scurried down the passageway. The shooting had stopped, but the yelling and screaming only intensified... and then silence, 'dead' silence. Detective Lincoln and his men kept moving forward, never once looking back.

Freedom in general may be defined as the absence of obstacles to the realization of desires.

Bertrand Russell: Freedom, edited by
Ruth Nanda Anshen, Harcourt Brace, 1940

Epilogue

Bill was hospitalized for two days due to complications from his gunshot wound. It was not serious, but the doctors wanted to make sure his wound had healed sufficiently, before releasing him. He picked up the newspaper. The headlines read that the incumbent had beaten Franklin Dillard Jr. by a few thousand votes and retained his congressional seat. A large picture of the winner donned the front page while a smaller one of Franklin Jr. and Crystal graced the second page of the article.

Mayor Jim Efferton had retained his seat. The Mayor had run a low-keyed campaign, winning by a comfortable margin.

Detectives Jones and White came by to visit and to show Bill their report. He read some of it and smiled.

"I've been laid up in this hospital for two days now. So, tell me, what did those New Orleans' investigators find out? "

"Not much. The whole house burned down, like someone had poured gasoline inside and torched it," Detective White said.

"Any trace of Marie Francois?"

"Nothing! Man, there's no trace of anything! The fire was bad. Really bad."

"Bill, what happened in there? How did we ever get out alive? None of us are quite sure."

Bill looked at the detectives and put his hands up. "You wouldn't believe it if I told you. Mama was not Mama...I mean I saw her take a lot of bullets! But I swear, it was as if she was invulnerable or something! And Bowman... I watched her rip his throat open with her bare hands! It never fazed her that Bowman and his thugs were firing a hail of bullets at her! She was simply...magnificent! After that, I high-tailed it out of there. I wasn't far behind the rest of you. That's my report, fellas. And, I'm sticking by it! So now, go write that one up! You're on your own guys!"

"Who's going to believe this stuff?" Clarence said.

"That's not my problem. I don't have to report it. I'm retired, remember?"

"What about that first psychic lady, Jezebel Balboa? Do you think we can charge her with anything, Bill?"

"Probably not. Just don't use her anymore. She's got fraud written all over her."

"Like I was saying, the Dugan St. residence in New Orleans is burnt to a crisp. There isn't much in the way of evidence there. We've got 666 Natas Lane roped off but there isn't much there in terms of hard evidence either."

"Well, you can always speculate in your write-up," Bill said.

"What do you mean?"

"Spell Natas backward and then look at the numerical address. Let your mind wander. Put some flavor in that report!"

"Thanks, Bill, but the Chief might not bend that far. Hey, again, good luck and thanks. As far as we're concerned, you saved our lives."

"Don't mention it. Just don't be so quick to jump to judgment next time."

The two detectives stayed for another ten minutes or so before taking off. About an hour later, Bill received a visit from six people... four of the Dillard clan, Franklin Sr. and his wife Heather, Franklin Jr. and his wife Crystal, and Dr. and Mrs. Broussard. They had come to pay their respects.

"I want to sincerely thank you for finding the murderer of my daughter, Detective Lincoln. My family owes you a great debt of gratitude," Franklin Dillard Sr. said. "I read the preliminary police report. I realize now how much danger you and your team faced. The report credited you as the primary reason that the others are alive today."

Bill was listening to Dillard and the others, and even though he really wanted to get some rest, he sincerely appreciated the accolades. Too many times before his achievements had gone unacknowledged. He would relish this moment.

"We had an interesting situation down there. I certainly would not want to repeat the experience, that's for sure!"

"We can't bring back my Hillary, Detective Lincoln," Mrs. Dillard said, "but the burden of not knowing has been lifted. I knew, when I first met you, that you were special. I just knew it! I could see it in your eyes! You said then that you would do your best, that you would help us. I truly thank you from the bottom of my heart."

"And, of course, we thank you, too," Professor Broussard remarked. "If it wasn't for you I'd still be on the run, in jail, or maybe even dead. You gave me back my life! Thank you for believing in me in spite of the so called 'evidence'."

"Well, originally I actually believed in your guilt. So, don't give me too much credit."

Franklin Jr. and Crystal also thanked him. Bill was feeling on top of the world, but there were just too many compliments. He appreciated it, but there's a point where it gets a bit overwhelming. Finally, after nearly forty-five minutes, the six of them said their good-byes and left. They walked to the elevator, pushed the button, and then Crystal 'remembered' that she had forgotten her book.

"Hold the elevator, I'll be right back," she said and quickly walked off.

She returned to Bill's room, picked up the book she had intentionally left on the table and walked directly to the bed and kissed him deeply and passionately.

"I don't know why but I just had to do that. Bye, Bill." She turned and two seconds later she was gone.

At three that afternoon, the McDerch family arrived. The McDerches had brought their son, Lenny, with them. He was back at the institution now, which was, after all, his home. When Lenny's parents heard that Bill was in the hospital, they decided to visit him. They wanted to thank Bill again for spending time with their son. Although their son had just spent days with Major Lincoln, they knew that Lenny had no recollection of it. They also wanted to thank Bill for getting that dog, Sparky, for Lenny. The hospital had a pet center and Sparky now stayed there with Lenny.

At five, Monique stopped by to pay her respects. She was wearing a white with blue polka-dot dress and large hoop earrings. As usual, she looked great! She walked to his side and kissed him on the cheek before sitting down.

"How are you?"

"Getting worn down from all my visitors I'm afraid."

"But, you're our hero. You have to expect that."

"I was just doing my job."

"That's not what I heard. You're a most interesting fella, Detective."

"Should I take that as a compliment?"

"By all means. There's something else about you that I like. You can't be bought."

"Try me," he said and smiled.

"Okay, I'll give you five dollars, no, make that twenty, to sleep with me your first night out of the hospital."

"I didn't know my market value was so low!" Bill smiled again.

"Well, I think the money stream traditionally flows in the opposite direction, Detective, from the man to the woman. So, you might consider this the highest compliment a woman can 'pay' a man."

"I see. I guess I was looking at it the wrong way."

"Of course you were."

"I'm going to have to sharpen my analytical skills. I seem to be a little slow on the uptake with you."

"All the more reason you should probably spend more time with me."

"Oh, I see."

Bill heard the door open. He looked up and saw that he had another visitor. Susan had just entered the room. "Hello, Susan. Allow me to introduce you to Monique Dillard," Bill said.

Susan hesitated for a moment before walking over to shake Monique's hand. "Hello, Monique."

"Good evening, Susan. Detective Lincoln has mentioned you on several occasions."

"I hope I'm not interrupting anything. Is this a bad time, Bill?"

"Detective Lincoln and I were just finishing our visit. My family was here earlier, but I couldn't come when they came."

"How's Radcliffe?" Bill said. "Is he doing his community work?"

"He's started. And from what I hear, he's actually enjoying it! We'll see. Time will tell. Goodbye, Detective Lincoln. Get well, soon. I mean that! And it was very nice meeting you, Susan."

"Same here, Monique."

Monique stood and started walking out, then turned around and said, "Oh, Detective, I almost forgot, here's that twenty dollars that I owe you." She went back and put twenty dollars on the table by his bed and then walked out.

"How are you, Bill?"

"I'm fine, and getting better."

"And how are your girls?"

"Fine. Amanda was just here an hour ago with her girlfriend that's having some problems. She's soliciting advice for her friend."

"You did a great job. Everybody is talking about it."

"Yeah, they're wearing me out talking about it."

"Have you thought any about us?"

"I'm thinking."

About the Author

This is a first novel. The author is an analyst with a California Central Valley city where a real life murder had recently rocked the national headlines and where several years earlier yet another high profile case had consumed the national airwaves linking a US congressman with an intern. The author has an undergraduate degree in mathematics and a MBA. Mr. Carrington is on several boards in his community, an avid tennis player, golfer, wine maker, chess player, and a general conversationalist. Born and raised in Peekskill, NY, the author has been living in California since 1981.

An avid editorial reader, the novel started as an intellectual exercise after reading the backcover of a now famous author. That author also had no formal history in writing. Another story about Detective Lincoln is almost finished and will be published soon.

Printed in the United States
43325LVS00003B/67-204